He placed a hand on the small of her back.

It was nothing more than a light touch, a small gesture from one friend to another, yet she still held her breath until they reached the curb on the other side of the street.

He threaded his fingers through hers as they approached the steps that led to the inn's front porch.

"In case we have an audience," he whispered when she stared down at their interlaced hands.

"Right," she said, heat coursing through her veins. "Good move."

But what would his next move be? Would there *be* a next move? How should she react if there was? Then she spotted Pearl through the window in the door and decided someone had to make a move soon or risk blowing their cover.

"Gran!" she whisper-shouted, nodding her head in the same direction. "She's right inside. We should play this whole good-bye part up, you know? For her sake." *And maybe for mine.*

Ben raised a brow. "Are you suggesting a kiss good night, Doc?"

She bit her lip, then smiled nervously. "Would... you... be open to such a thing?"

"Actually," he said, "if this *had* been a real date, I'd have had the good night kiss all planned out. Would you like to hear how it would have gone?"

PRAISE FOR A.J. PINE

"A sweet...love story."
—*Publishers Weekly* on *My One and Only Cowboy*

"*My One and Only Cowboy* was an entertaining romance that was woven with wit and warmth."
—GuiltyPleasuresBookReviews.com

"*Cowboy to the Rescue* delivers the goods!"
—ReadAlltheRomance.com

"A steamy cowboy romance novel that is sure to warm your heart!"
—LovelyLoveday.com on *Hard Loving Cowboy*

"*Hard Loving Cowboy* was a delightfully sexy read that made me want to go in search of a cowboy of my own."
—KimberlyFayeReads.com

"Sweet and engrossing."
—*Publishers Weekly* on *Tough Luck Cowboy*

"Light and witty."
—*Library Journal* on *Saved by the Cowboy*

"A fabulous storyteller who will keep you turning pages and wishing for just one more chapter at the end."
—Carolyn Brown, *New York Times* bestselling author,
on *Second Chance Cowboy*

ALSO BY A.J. PINE

Meadow Valley

Cowboy to the Rescue (novella)

My One and Only Cowboy

Crossroads Ranch

Second Chance Cowboy

Saved by the Cowboy (novella)

Tough Luck Cowboy

Hard Loving Cowboy

MAKE MINE A
COWBOY

A Meadow Valley Novel

A.J. PINE

FOREVER
NEW YORK BOSTON

Copyright © 2020 by A.J. Pine
Hometown Cowboy copyright © 2017 by Sara Richardson

Cover design by Elizabeth Turner Stokes
Cover copyright © 2020 by Hachette Book Group, Inc.

Forever
Hachette Book Group
1290 Avenue of the Americas, New York, NY 10104
read-forever.com
twitter.com/readforeverpub

First Edition: August 2020

Forever is an imprint of Grand Central Publishing. The Forever name and logo are trademarks of Hachette Book Group, Inc.

The publisher is not responsible for websites (or their content) that are not owned by the publisher.

The Hachette Speakers Bureau provides a wide range of authors for speaking events. To find out more, go to www.hachettespeakersbureau.com or call (866) 376-6591.

ISBNs: 978-1-5387-4981-4 (mass market), 978-1-5387-4982-1 (ebook)

Printed in the United States of America

OPM

10 9 8 7 6 5 4 3 2 1

*To the magic of books—bridging the
distance that keeps us apart.*

ACKNOWLEDGMENTS

This is a strange time, folks. Right now, I'm sitting on my couch while my kids play a card game on the floor, one of our cats naps in our pet stroller (which has yet to see the outdoors because it's still snowing), and I contemplate the fact that we haven't left the house in days because we are in the middle of a pandemic. I don't know what the state of the world will be when this book lands in your hands, but I do know that I am beyond grateful to my amazing readers for choosing Ben and Charlotte as your means of escape, comfort, or just pure enjoyment in what I hope will be a happier, safer time for all of us. Thank you.

Thank you, Emily Sylvan Kim, for always having my back not just as an agent but also a friend. I hope we get to see each other in real life in the not-too-distant future.

To Madeleine, my editor extraordinaire, thank you for championing my California cowboys, for helping me keep my timelines straight (I still want to write a book that takes place in just one day), and for always making my stories the best they can possibly be.

Jen, Chanel, Lia, Megan, and Natalie, I'm so grateful for you each and every day. I couldn't do any of this without you and your support. Love you!

S and C, I love you three thousand times infinity.

MAKE MINE A COWBOY

CHAPTER ONE

Ben glanced around the well-appointed doctor's office. A couple hours ago, he was in bed dreaming of a beautiful woman with whom he'd recently spent an equally beautiful, worry-free couple of weeks, pretending this day didn't exist. That was how Ben spent most of his time, ignoring the more serious side of life. He'd gotten pretty good at living for the day and not worrying about the future. His *own* future, at least. But today was different. Today wasn't about Ben. It was about his brother Sam. Sam was as good as they came, and because of that, he deserved good news. So Ben silently begged whatever higher power would listen that Sam was as healthy as he looked.

Everything from the embossed medical books on the shelves to the framed certificates and accolades on the walls said that Dr. Kegan knew his stuff. And the high-backed upholstered leather chair behind the desk and matching love seats—one on which Ben sat wedged between his newly reconciled mother and father while Sam and his girlfriend, Delaney, sat on the other—said the good doctor knew his stuff *well*. Which was a good thing, because he was about to spell out the rest of Sam's future.

Six months ago, Dr. Kegan had drawn Ben's blood for the exact same reason—to determine whether he carried the gene markers for early-onset Alzheimer's. Ben hadn't made a production of it, hadn't sat face-to-face with the doc and been told that sometime in the next twenty to thirty years, his brain would start to deteriorate just like his father's had. No, Ben had opted for a phone call to the lab followed by several pints at Midtown Tavern. Then it was home to an empty bed at the ranch he ran with his brother and friend. There was no one there to comfort him or help him ease into the news, but that had been his choice. He didn't want to burden Sam and Colt with a future he couldn't avoid. He didn't want to burden anyone with what he knew he couldn't change. No attachments meant no mess, no broken hearts, no pain. *Work hard and play harder*, right? Wasn't that the saying? Ben respected the motto—at least the second half of it.

"They always leave you waiting," he said, shaking his head. He pushed himself up from the couch and began pacing. "Doctors. They know what they're about to tell you could change your whole life, and then they schedule you a half hour before they even *think* about entering the room. I swear, bedside manner goes out the window as soon as they get the cushy office and all the awards and—"

"Hey there, little brother," Sam interrupted. "I appreciate you getting all wound up on my behalf, but I'm in no rush. But if you need to be somewhere . . .".

Ben raked his fingers through his hair and stopped pacing.

"Sorry," he said. "I'm just anxious—for you."

The office door clicked open a crack, and they could hear the doctor before they saw him.

"Lori, please tell Mrs. Dunlap I'll call her later this afternoon. She took the news a bit hard. Wait, you know what? Tell her I'll stop by after we close up shop here. We can talk about options for Mr. Dunlap's care, and she can show me pictures of the grandkids."

Delaney laughed. "You're right, Ben. His bedside manner is the worst."

Ben scowled and leaned on the arm of his brother's couch rather than sitting all the way down again.

"Good morning, Mr. Calla—" Dr. Kegan caught himself when he realized Sam had come with a full entourage. "Good morning, *everyone*, I suppose."

Sam stood and shook the doctor's hand.

The two men were roughly the same height and of similar lean build.

Ben narrowed his eyes. The two men looked nearly the same age as well. Had Dr. Kegan been that young six months ago?

"Hope you don't mind," Sam said, interrupting Ben's thoughts. "Brought the whole family."

The doctor waved Sam off. "Of course not. I love giving good news to a packed house."

Delaney sprang to her feet and grabbed Sam's hand. "Good news?" she asked excitedly.

A weight lifted immediately from Ben's shoulders. His brother was okay. *He* wasn't, but Sam was. He thought he might be angry or resentful, but all he felt was complete and utter relief.

The doctor smiled and clapped Sam on the shoulder. "I was going to wait until I was sitting at my desk all professional-like, but what the heck? Congratulations, Mr. Callahan. Just like your brother, you are in the clear. Keep in mind that your genetic code means you're both safe from early-onset Alzheimer's but normal risk factors still exist for anyone to develop the disease later in life. Medicine is making strides, though, so who knows—"

"What did you just say?" Ben interrupted. He was standing now. They all were, Ben's parents included.

Dr. Kegan crossed his arms. "I said normal risk factors still—"

"*Before* that," Ben said, taking a step closer. "The part about *both* of us being in the clear. Because I spoke to someone at the lab six months ago who told me otherwise. I've spent half a year thinking that life as I know it is on a ticking clock."

The doctor stared at Ben for several long seconds before he spoke. "The lab told you your results were... *positive*?"

Ben let out a bitter laugh. "Are you telling me they were wrong?"

Dr. Kegan rounded his desk, picked up the phone, and dialed a four-digit extension. After a few beats, he said, "Hi. This is Davis Kegan over in neurology. I need to verify results for a Benjamin Callahan."

Ben winced at the use of his full name. He felt like a kid in trouble. But this might actually be worse since he was about to be told *again* that by the time he was his father's age, he'd likely be living in an assisted living facility as well.

Dr. Kegan cleared his throat. "No. *Not* Benjamin Wallace Callahan. Benjamin *Phillip* Callahan."

Ben glanced toward his father, who was holding hands with his mother. His illness had torn their family apart—

and then brought them back together. His parents had something rare, something he didn't believe existed in the real world, but he was damn happy it existed for them.

He held his breath as he waited for the doctor to hang up the phone, and it felt like everyone else was holding theirs too. He wasn't sure if he should be hopeful or angry or both. So he figured not breathing was the logical course of action.

"Uh-huh," Dr. Kegan said. "I see. Yes, this will have to be reported. Thank you."

He hung up the phone, and the room was so silent Ben swore he could hear his own pulse.

Dr. Kegan cleared his throat. "So it turns out the lab has another Benjamin Callahan on record—a sixty-two-year-old man from Bucks Lake. *He* tested positive for early onset. *You* did not. I am so sorry for the mix-up, and it will be dealt with. But, Sam *and* Ben, you are both in the clear."

His mother gasped, and Ben saw his father swipe away a tear. He expected his brother to kiss Delaney before anything else, but instead Sam pulled Ben into a firm embrace.

"Everything is different," he said when Sam stepped back.

It felt like a haze had cleared. He got that nothing in life was certain. He could walk out of the hospital and get run over by an ambulance. He could choke on a cherry pit after sneaking a taste from Anna's produce delivery to the ranch—and he almost had once. Thank goodness Luis, their chef, knew the Heimlich.

"No one dies in my kitchen," Luis had said. "And stop stealing my fruit!"

Technically, it was *Ben's* fruit since he was co-owner

of the ranch, but he wasn't going to argue after Luis saved his life.

And now it had just been saved again.

"I need to go," he said absently. He wasn't sure where, but he needed to get out of this office.

"Ben, wait," his mother said, but he shook his head.

"I'm okay," he insisted. "Really. I just need to think."

About how he'd been living his life—all fun and no connections. About whether or not he could change after living that way since he learned his future might look a lot like his father's.

He'd counted on Sam and Colt for backup at the ranch, often shirking his duties because in the long run, it didn't feel like it mattered. Maybe this was a start. For once he could do something for his brother that mattered, even if it was simply doing his job.

"Take the night off," he said to Sam. "You and Delaney should celebrate. Colt's got lunch and dinner, and I can cover the evening activities or make sure one of the part-timers can."

Sam's eyes widened. "I'm going to take you up on that before you change your mind. Thanks, Ben. Are you sure you're—"

"I'm good," he insisted.

He backed out of the office door and into the hospital corridor.

Just like that, a switch had flipped. He suddenly wanted to make something of his life, like taking his career seriously, to start. And maybe it was time he stopped living in the ranch's guest quarters and built himself a home, started establishing some permanence in his life.

On one side of the ranch, there was a piece of land owned by the bank. Ben had had his eye on it since he moved to Meadow Valley just over two years ago, not that he'd have done anything with it. It was his *What if?* It was how he busied his mind when there wasn't someone to leave the bar with on any given night. The bank was willing to unload it for a steal since the previous owner had already poured the foundation for a house and small stable—and then had lost their financing and let the property fall into foreclosure. No one wanted to dig it up and start from scratch, so Ben looked at it as a secret challenge. He designed a home to fit the layout, a home he'd never build. But now? If he bought the land, that would prove he could commit to something that really mattered, that it wasn't too late to turn his life around after letting it unravel.

He followed the detour signs to bypass some indoor construction and somehow found himself at the ambulance entrance of the emergency room. He was about to pivot and retrace his steps when he saw Lieutenant Carter Bowen wheeling a gurney into the ER. And sitting on the gurney, with one arm immobilized and eyes narrowed, was Carter's great-aunt and owner of the Meadow Valley Inn, Pearl Sweeney. Ben scanned the area, half expecting to see Pearl's granddaughter Charlotte North there as well—the woman who'd been the subject of his R-rated dream this morning—then reminded himself she lived in New York and had returned home a week ago after what they'd both deemed a very enjoyable fling.

"What happened?" Ben asked, rushing to Pearl's side as Carter called out things like *minor laceration* and *possible dual fractures* to the admissions woman behind the front desk.

Pearl waved Ben off. "Oh, I'm fine. I was on the ladder clipping dead branches from the tree in front of the inn—curb appeal is everything, you know—and I lost my balance. It's nothing."

Carter turned around, his eyes full of worry as he glanced from his aunt to Ben. "She most likely broke her right ankle and wrist. Her elbow needs sutures, and—" He blew out a calming breath. "You could have killed yourself, Aunt Pearl. Don't you have someone on staff who can take care of stuff like that for you? Hell, call me over anytime. That's what family is for."

Pearl's jaw tightened. "Are you telling me I'm too old to take care of my own inn?"

"No," Carter insisted. "I'm not stupid enough to suggest something like that. But you are the heart and soul of that place—of this *town*, even. If something happens to you, it's not just the inn that suffers."

"The inn!" Pearl cried, her anger morphing to something more like fear. "If you're right about my injuries, then I can't walk or cook or—"

It looked like reality was finally setting in.

"I'm right," Carter said. "I'm sorry, Pearl, but once they fix you up, it's going to be a long road to recovery. You're going to need live-in help. And you'll need to increase everyone's hours at the inn so you can take care of yourself. I'll do whatever I can when I'm not on shift, but it's not going to be enough. We can put the call out on the *Meadow Valley Courier* webpage. Maybe people can sign up for shifts."

Pearl sniffled, all of her bravado dissipating. Ben hated seeing her like this.

"I can't ask my employees to take on twenty-four-hour shifts," she said. "That's all me. They have their own responsibilities and families to go home to." She patted Carter on the cheek with her good hand. "You're so good to me. I know you'll help when you can, but you have your own life to worry about. Everyone in town does. I'll have to see what's in my budget, but if I'm going to need overnight support as well as someone to help me get around the place, that means dipping into my savings, and—"

Ben rested a hand lightly on the older woman's shoulder. "We'll figure this out. You've got a whole town behind you, Pearl."

He got it. He ran a ranch. She ran an inn. It was more than a job. It was a lifestyle, and she'd need someone to fill in every hour of the day she couldn't work, which right now looked like it was all of them.

She held her head high and nodded. "Maybe you weren't the right man for my Charlotte, but you have a good heart, Ben Callahan."

Did he? Pearl had been none too happy about her granddaughter's fling. *She needs someone with staying power. Someone that will convince* her *to stay in Meadow Valley where she truly belongs.* Those had been Pearl's words to him only a week or so ago. Was it possible it was this easy for him to convince her otherwise? Maybe he wasn't the best at showing it to his brother, his parents, or the few others he let past his own wall of bravado. But his heart was there, beating behind his rib cage. It might be a little rusty, but it still worked, didn't it?

"What about the chief?" Ben asked. Chief Burnett and Pearl had been dating for quite some time. "Can he help?"

She shook her head. "I can't ask him to do that," Pearl said. "He has an entire fire station to run. Adding more hours to his load isn't safe for him—or for you, for that matter," she said, eyes back on Carter. "You both do forty-eight-hour shifts as it is."

Carter nudged the gurney forward, and Ben moved out of the way.

"We need to finish this discussion later," he said. "We need to get you evaluated by a doctor and sent to radiology and verify the fractures, make sure they can be set without surgery. Ben, do you think you could swing by the inn and make sure everything is okay, let them know Pearl's out for the rest of the day? Also, I hate to ask, but I'm on shift until this time tomorrow. Could you maybe give Pearl a lift home if I'm not available?"

Ben nodded. "I'm on it. I'll head back to town and see what I can do about getting some extra help at the inn. I'm sure your staff will be more than happy to step up until you get released, and we'll worry about more permanent help after that," he said, hoping to reassure Pearl. "How long do you think X-rays and all that will be?" he asked, directing his attention back to Carter.

"A couple of hours at least."

Ben nodded once. "Then I'll be back in a couple of hours."

Pearl grabbed his hand. "I don't know what I'd do without you, Ben Callahan."

"I owe you, Callahan," Carter added, then turned his attention back to his aunt. "Okay, Aunt Pearl. Let's see what kind of damage you did and get you all fixed up."

Then Carter wheeled Pearl away, leaving Ben standing there with a gift—not that Pearl's injuries were any sort of boon. But he'd been gifted a second chance at life and now with his first shot at showing he could be something more than the selfish ass he'd been for months. He wasn't going to mess this up.

Ben had not only checked in on Pearl's staff but he'd also stayed at the inn for the entire two hours helping check guests in and cleaning breakfast dishes while the kitchen staff prepped for lunch. By the time he'd made it back to the hospital, he found out Pearl was being prepped for surgery.

Things were more serious than we thought, Carter texted when Ben arrived back in the waiting room. If you want to head home, I can let you know when she's released. IF she's released today. It all depends on when the orthopedic surgeon on call has a break in their schedule.

But Ben felt the urge to stay, to see this thing through and be there for Pearl like he'd said he would.

Already cleared my calendar for the rest of the day and can move things around tonight if needed, he replied. If it's okay with you, I'll hang out until you have news.

Carter responded immediately. Remind me to buy you a beer next time our paths cross at Midtown.

Ben laughed. I'll hold you to it, he texted back. Are you staying with Pearl until then? Can I come check in on her? How about I head down to the cafeteria and grab us both some coffee and something to eat?

Ben was restless and wanted to do something to help.

Sure, Carter said. That would be great. I'm sure Pearl would love the company. It'll give me a chance to check in with the station and make sure everything's okay over there.

So Ben made his way to the cafeteria and did as he'd promised. He also stopped at the gift shop and picked up a few Get Well balloons to hopefully brighten up the otherwise sterile room.

It turned out to be another few hours before the surgery actually took place, and by then, Ben was all in.

"I'm not leaving until it's done," he'd said as Pearl was wheeled out the door, Carter following her to the operating room. "Want to make sure all went well. And who knows? You might still need a ride home." He winked at Pearl, knowing that she was likely spending the night at this point.

And then he'd headed back to the waiting room, made himself as comfortable as he could in one of the waiting room chairs, and... waited.

Apparently that waiting turned into him nodding off. What could he say? Doing stuff for others—the whole *not* being selfish thing—was draining, physically and emotionally. Even if Pearl didn't put *him* on a pedestal, she was like a grandmother to him. For a guy who had put said emotions on hold for not only the past six months but also since his father received his own diagnosis, this whole putting-his-energy-into-caring-about-others thing was going to take some getting used to. What better way to do so than with a nice, long nap?

CHAPTER TWO

Charlotte North stood in line at her favorite New York City bodega, grateful she was on time enough that said line wasn't yet out the door. She waited in the narrow space between the magazines and newspapers and the wall-to-wall selection of candy in front of the check-out counter. She could *smell* the coffee, but what she really needed was to taste it. Or have someone inject it into her veins. But the coffee in her insulated thermos, which she'd just filled to the brim, was still too hot to drink. By the time she found a seat on the subway, it would be ready for the perfect first sip, but oh how she needed that perfect first sip now—or ten minutes ago.

She'd been home from Meadow Valley for a week already, but somehow it still felt like she was on California time. Or maybe, despite her best judgment, she still longed for lazy mornings and a warm body she could wake up next to.

She shook her head and quietly scoffed at herself.

Sharing her bed was *not* something Charlotte did

regularly. Not for lack of enjoying such activities but because such activities did not fit into her routine. And she certainly relied on routine.

Today, she told herself. *Today my life will get back in sync.*

And she'd stop thinking about how good it felt to forget about the real world for a while.

Or how good it felt when a certain cowboy did certain things to her that made the real world so easy to forget.

"It's dark when I wake up in the morning and dark when I get home from work. Why is daylight saving time a thing?" a woman asked from behind her. "Also, I already finished my scone. Do you think they'll still charge me?"

It was the same opening to almost every morning conversation.

Charlotte looked over her shoulder and smiled at Vicki, a woman who lived in the same neighborhood and ran on a similar schedule. They rode the same train to work, but Vicki got off two stops earlier.

"How were the boys this morning?" Charlotte asked, inquiring about Vicki's twin sons. She knew about her bodega buddy's family life *not* because she'd asked but because Vicki was the kind of person who told you everything whether you wanted her to or not. Charlotte— not great at small talk—was always grateful for someone who could carry the entire conversation. All it took was one question, and Vicki took care of the rest.

"Still sleeping when I left, thank goodness," she said. "One of these days, I'm going to talk my clients into afternoon instead of morning appointments, but that'll have to wait until Bill can change *his* schedule so he can pick the boys up after school." She sighed, then tucked her mermaid-colored hair—a mixture of varied shades of blue and purple—behind her ear. "Don't do the whole married-with-kids thing, Char. You won't know which way is up." Then she held up her index finger and shook her head. "Scratch that. *Do* it. Do it all because it's the best ever, but make sure you have a Bill—not *my* Bill, of course—to *remind* you which way is up when you forget. Or where your missing phone is when it's already in your hand. That's why I almost had to skip the coffee and scone and head right to the station. Glad I'm not the only one in a rush." She laughed, then tapped Charlotte—who'd completely turned around to face her—on the shoulder. "You're up!"

Charlotte blew out a breath and spun to face Antonio, the older man who owned the corner shop and made the best pot of coffee this side of Manhattan. Maybe in the entire city.

"Miss Charlotte!" the man exclaimed. He called every woman *Miss*. "You're running late again this morning."

She winced and inserted her debit card into the chip reader like she'd done every morning for the past few years.

"Thanks for noticing," she said. "Again."

Antonio laughed. "Hard not to notice when it's so unlike you. You're just so dependable. I can set my watch by your arrival. How do I know what time it is if you're three to five minutes late?" he teased.

She narrowed her eyes at his smartwatch. "The internet makes sure you don't forget."

But Antonio wasn't entirely off base. Charlotte was never late. At least, she hadn't been up until this transitional week. Not for years. She hadn't taken time off since medical school, which was fine by her, because time off meant time away from routine, and time away from routine just got her out of sync. Like now. But part of her contract with Children's Pediatrics and Dentistry was that practitioners were required to take their four weeks of paid vacation, plus a generous helping of personal days, though preferably not all at once.

"A burned out doctor is *not* what our patients need," Dr. Nowak—one of the two managing partners of the practice—explained upon asking Charlotte to sign on the dotted line, which she'd done happily. Squeezing in those four weeks before the end of the year wasn't easy. Even knowing she'd lose the days if she didn't use them, Charlotte had yet to be successful. But when your boss finally says, "Take some time off before I change the lock on the office door," you book a last-minute trip to see your favorite person in the whole world—your gran. And you meet a man you never intended to meet who *maybe* let you forget about routine for a while but who *never* made you a cup of coffee as good as Antonio's—or at *all*.

But Ben Callahan did make her wonder what it would be like to wake up on the regular with a warm body pressed to hers rather than rolling over onto cold sheets. Not *his* warm body, of course. Ben Callahan didn't do *on the regular*.

Then again, neither did she.

"Miss Charlotte?" Antonio asked, snapping her back to the present.

"What? Sorry. Still on vacation time. I won't be late again!"

He waved her off. "It's good to have you back, Miss Charlotte. See you tomorrow morning?" he asked, his thick salt and pepper brows raised.

"And the morning after that," she said. "And the morning after that."

* * *

Charlotte's phone buzzed as she unlocked the office—she was the first one in as usual. She liked the fifteen to twenty minutes she got to herself to get her bearings before the phone started ringing off the hook with the latest child ailments of the day.

Mom: Look at this view! The bride and groom are going to look AMAZING with this in the background.

Attached to the message was a photo of a castle on a cliff overlooking the sea.

Amazing, Charlotte texted back.

Mom: One of these days you'll take a vacation and come with us on location! You don't know what you're missing!

It's Dunnottar Castle. We're doing photos here first and then heading over to Stonehaven. Wish you were here. Dad says hi. Mwah!

And then the texts stopped.

This was pretty much how she communicated with her parents these days, via text across international date lines. They were free spirits, wedding photographers who traveled the globe to capture clients' destination weddings. Their daughter? Not so much.

What was wrong with a little structure, with always knowing what came next?

"Nothing," Charlotte mumbled to her phone as she made her way behind the front desk and into her small office.

She took off her winter jacket and exchanged it for the white coat she wore to see patients. Then she pulled her planner out of her bag and opened it to the pocket where she'd tucked away the picture she printed the night before, the one of her and Gran that she'd taken at the Meadow Valley Inn the morning before she left. She taped it onto the wall next to the one of both her grandparents, when Gramps was still alive, and sighed as her throat tightened.

And then she flat-out *laughed*.

Belly laughed.

Because while she and her grandmother stood in front of the inn, arms around each other's waists as Chief Burnett snapped the photo with Charlotte's phone, there was Ben Callahan sitting on the porch swing, one cowboy boot crossed over the other and his Cattleman tilted up. He was staring straight at her, a devilish grin spread across his face.

"Photobomber!" she said, still laughing, the tightness in her throat dissipating.

Ben Callahan might not be any more than a fond memory of the one time Charlotte let go of the real world and the stresses that went along with it, but he was a memory that made her smile, even when she wanted to cry.

The office phone rang, and she blew out a breath. She heard someone answer it up front, which meant the day had officially begun.

"Dr. North?" she heard a few moments later on her office phone's intercom.

"I'm here, Patti," she responded to their office assistant.

"Kyle Scanlan is on his way in. Mom thinks it's another ear infection. I'll grab his chart and put it on the door of exam room one."

"Thanks, Patti," she said.

Ear infection. Good. Well, not *good* for poor Kyle Scanlan. But good to start the day with something easy, routine, and fixable.

* * *

By lunch—and it was a late one today—Charlotte finally felt like her week was back on track. She collapsed into one of the chairs in the breakroom and waited for her frozen meal to do its thing in the microwave.

"Dr. North?" Patti's voice came through on the intercom, and Charlotte picked up the phone that was on the wall.

"Hi, Patti," she said.

"Sorry to interrupt your lunch. But there's a call for you on line one. Someone named Carter Bowen."

Charlotte's heart sank. She'd just seen her cousin in Meadow Valley. And while she loved him dearly, they weren't the chat-on-the-phone type of cousins. Charlotte wasn't the chat-on-the-phone type of person. Period.

So why was he calling her now, especially on her office line?

She took a steadying breath, trying not to remember the time years ago when an unexpected call from Meadow Valley had carried with it the worst kind of news.

"Thanks, Patti," she said, a lump already forming in her throat.

Receiver pressed to her ear, Charlotte pressed the blinking button for line one.

"Carter!" she said with forced cheer. "Miss me already?"

"Your cell is on Do Not Disturb, isn't it?" he asked.

"Um . . . yes. I'm at work. Hi to you too?"

"It's Pearl," he said without any further explanation. No smile in his voice. Just the two words she dreaded the most.

"What?" she asked, her voice breaking on that one word.

"She's okay," he added. "Sorry. I should have led with that. Or maybe hello. I'm just outside her room while she talks to the doctor, and I don't want her to hear me . . ."

Charlotte let out an exasperated groan.

"*Jesus*, Lieutenant. You're a *paramedic*. You're supposed to have better bedside manner than that!"

Her cousin laughed, which meant whatever happened to Gran wasn't so bad that Carter couldn't laugh.

"She told me not to call you," he said. "And when Pearl tells you *not* to do something and you still do it, there's usually hell to pay."

"Carter? Carter, get back in here and tell them I'm not spending the night in the hospital when I have a perfectly good bed—a much more *comfortable* bed—at the inn."

Charlotte breathed a sigh of relief at the sound of her grandmother's voice.

"See?" he said. "It's like she can see through the damned wall."

"*Carter*," Charlotte said. "Tell me what happened."

"Right," he said, his voice barely above a whisper now. "She was on a ladder trimming branches in that overgrown tree in front of the inn, and she fell. Broken wrist, ankle, and a few lacerations. But she's going to be fine."

Charlotte swallowed and reminded herself that she was a doctor. When it came to stuff like this, so much could be fixed. That was why she'd gotten into medicine in the first place.

"I'll come back," she blurted. "To Meadow Valley. The practice won't love it, but I still have a little more vacation time I need to get rid of. They'll understand. I'll come back, make sure she gets home okay, and spend a few days helping her adjust."

Carter was quiet for several long seconds.

"The ankle break is too severe to be set without surgery," he finally said. "They're prepping her now." Another pause. "Char... The wrist alone would have been bad enough. But the ankle? A bone break like that on a woman her age? She'll be in a wheelchair for at least six weeks, possibly two months."

Two months. The words hung in the air while neither of them spoke.

"If you tell her I told you, I'll deny it," Carter said with a soft laugh. "But this is big, and I didn't want to keep it from you. Of course, I'll keep you posted on how everything goes, and we'll figure out getting her help at the inn even though she claims she'll be back at it this time tomorrow. We've got it under control."

Charlotte shook her head and let out a small laugh. Gran *was* stubbornly independent. Charlotte should know. She took after the woman.

"I'm coming back," she said again. "For however long it takes. I'll figure it out on my end and get on the first flight out of New York I can find."

"Whoa," Carter said. "That is *not* why I called. If she gets out of surgery and finds you here—"

"She'll be *relieved*," Charlotte said. "She'd never admit it, but she needs more help than anyone there can give her part-time. Again, the practice won't love it, but I have a couple weeks left. The other five or six weeks, I don't know. I'll take it unpaid, extend my contract, whatever I need to do. But I'm coming back to take care of Gran and the inn, and there's nothing you can say to change that."

Charlotte wasn't able to do a thing to save her grandfather from the heart attack that took his life, but she could make sure that Pearl didn't put herself at risk again.

Carter laughed. "You're worse than she is, aren't you?" he asked.

Charlotte smiled. "I learned from the best."

CHAPTER THREE

"Oh my God. Where is she?"

Ben heard the woman's voice, but it didn't register that she might be talking to him. So he readjusted his hat over his eyes and went back to sleeping off his feelings.

"Hey!"

He heard the voice again, and this time it came with a kick to the toe of his boot. He took his time straightening and pushing the brim of his hat up so he could see who his assailant was.

"Doc?" he said, calling Dr. Charlotte North by the nickname he'd given her when they'd enjoyed a no-strings-attached fling—his favorite kind—before she'd gone back to New York and he'd gone back to life as he knew it.

His vision registered the disheveled auburn ponytail and the wildness in her green eyes. He'd spent weeks being the cause of such wildness, but this was different. Especially since he was pretty sure he'd been in the hospital waiting room this whole time and *not* in bed with Pearl Sweeney's granddaughter.

Then it clicked. "Oh, damn. Pearl. I'm sorry. I just—"

"Fell *asleep* while my gran was in surgery?"

Ben sat bolt upright. "I was just going to shut my eyes for five minutes. Twenty tops." He chuckled. "Guess the day took a lot more out of me than I thought."

Waking up to her though...He'd done it before, but seeing her now felt...*he* felt...

Charlotte crossed her arms. "My grandmother broke bones that needed to be surgically set, and you're *laughing*?"

He stood. "No. Shoot. Doc, that's not what I meant." He reached for the hand that gripped her rolling suitcase with white knuckles, but she snatched it away.

Okay. He deserved that. He could see how things might look, but he was here, at the hospital, waiting to make sure her grandmother was okay. If he could just explain...

He opened his mouth to do that, but she didn't give him the chance.

"Carter said she's in recovery." She lifted her chin and smoothed out nonexistent wrinkles in her clothes. "I just need to read her chart and verify what he relayed to me, and then everything will be fine."

"Doc," he said softly. He had this sudden urge to make sure she was okay, but she shook her head.

"Call me Charlotte, please. I need to go see her and make sure she knows there's nothing to worry about. I cleared it with my practice. I'm taking a two-month leave of absence until she's back on her feet."

And she spun on her heel and left, abandoning their conversation *and* her suitcase.

He grabbed the handle and wheeled it after her, but before he could catch up, she was already hightailing it into the nearest elevator.

That went well.

He glanced out the waiting room window and saw that it was pitch dark outside, so he pulled out his phone and finally checked the time.

"Eleven-*thirty*?" he said aloud and then laughed. "She's pissed that I was sleeping thirty minutes before midnight?"

He shook his head at no one in particular. She was out of sorts. He got that. And he guessed he wasn't the first person she expected to see upon arrival.

It wasn't like he was prepared to see Charlotte North again so soon either. Or under such circumstances. And was it bad that while she'd yelled at him he thought about the last time he'd heard her—uh—*speak* with a raised voice? It had been her last night in town. And maybe a time or two the morning after. He wasn't going to send her back to New York without a reminder of the best part of her stay in Meadow Valley.

Maybe after things with Pearl were settled, he could show her a good time again.

He shrugged and turned toward the exit door, pausing before he left to glance at his buzzing phone. It was Carter.

Are you still here? My cousin said she saw you. They're obviously keeping her overnight for observation. Sorry I forgot to tell you when surgery was done. Just one of those days, you know? Will keep you posted about a ride home after she's released tomorrow if you're still up for it.

No problem, **Ben texted back.** And tell your cousin when she's ready, I'll drop by the inn with her suitcase. She left it in the ER waiting room. And before you say you'll come grab it, I'd like to be the one to deliver it straight to the owner. I'm wide awake now, so I'll be up for a while.

He strolled through the door and out into the brisk, dark night.

It had only been a week since she'd left Meadow Valley, but seeing Charlotte again—*today*—it felt a little like a sign.

Their time together had been great. No, scratch that. It had been damned near spectacular. Head clearing and distracting but...the thing was, the thrill of seeing her unexpectedly should have only awakened feelings a bit below the belt. But it hadn't. Okay it *had*, but there was something else.

He paused when he got to his truck and blew out a steadying breath. Then he shook his head and laughed.

Slow your roll, Callahan.

This *something else* was nothing more than the culmination of his medical news on top of Doc—*Charlotte*—arriving here after receiving the news about Pearl. Coincidence. *Not* a sign. He threw the suitcase into the bed of his truck and absently whistled a tune.

A two-month leave of absence, huh? He guessed the good doctor would be looking for another distraction, and who better for the job than a man who was newly in the service of doing for others?

Because oh the things he could do to—er, *for*—her.

CHAPTER FOUR

Charlotte sat in the chair of her grandmother's hospital room and stared at the sleeping woman. Gran was okay, but it was going to be a long road to recovery.

Maybe she shouldn't have lashed out at Ben like that, but she needed to be angry at *someone*. She couldn't be angry at her mother for being MIA because she'd followed up her gig photographing a wedding in Scotland with a thirtieth anniversary vow renewal in Salzburg. Her mother and grandmother hadn't seen eye to eye since Charlotte's father had lured her mother away from Meadow Valley, first to L.A. and then to the farthest reaches of the world—as long as the happy couple was equally happy to pay their fee. And when her mother couldn't make it back to the States in time after Gramps died, the rift between the two had only grown wider.

Charlotte had played the middle ever since, trying to coax her mom back to Meadow Valley for at least a short visit while also trying to coax Gran to text or call her daughter to let her know she still thought of her.

"A relationship can survive physical distance," Pearl would say, "but not emotional absence. And your mother's been gone longer than she's been overseas."

Yet that was how Charlotte had survived since they'd all lost Gramps. Emotional distance. Solving the problems she could—with science and medicine and clear-cut answers.

What would Charlotte say when Gran woke up? "Mom sends her love from Austria. Sorry she can't be here after you almost killed yourself."

She exhaled and closed her eyes. Her neighbor back in New York, Megan, tried talking Charlotte into joining her meditation class, but Charlotte always found an excuse to decline. Mostly it was due to time, and mostly that was the truth. But the other truth was that it was simply easier to do her own thing, to read her medical research journals and stay connected to a world that made sense. A world that had hypotheses and experiments. Conclusions and answers. Plus, as far as meditation was concerned, there was an app for that—several, actually. And each one she'd tried using—which she hated to admit was probably a few *more* than several—had failed. Miserably. It was like she thrived on stress. *Not* that she wanted to. She simply didn't know how to relax. But she could really use some de-stressing right now.

She opened one of her many meditation apps and followed the first direction, which was simply to focus on her breathing as she attempted to tune out the hustle and bustle of the medical staff outside the door.

Inhale...exhale...inhale...exhale...

Still inhaling and exhaling, she heard her alarm on her phone go off—not here in Gran's hospital room but in her memory.

Wait. It was working? It never worked. This had to be some sort of fluke, but it was a fluke she needed, so she followed the thread.

She was in a bed, rationalizing that if she didn't open her eyes, then it wouldn't really be morning. And if it wasn't morning, it meant her vacation wasn't over, that she wasn't heading from Meadow Valley all the way back to New York City. Not that she didn't love New York. She did. She missed her bodega with the best coffee, the cacophony of horns honking, morning commuters shouting into their wireless earpieces, and the ridiculously handsome stranger in the three-piece suit who always got on at the stop after hers and somehow ended up in her train car. They never spoke and likely never would, but the routine of it—the familiarity of her entire morning commute—comforted her.

The alarm sounded again. Or maybe she'd set a second one so she wouldn't miss her flight. But—ugh—just a few more minutes before dealing with the real world. She threw a pillow over her face to block out the morning light.

She felt the covers pull away from her side, and warm lips pressed a kiss to her naked hip. It was the kind of kiss that definitely melted a girl's worries away—or turned them into something steamy.

She hummed with delight, then fumbled for her phone on the nightstand, silencing it for good.

Kisses trailed up her side, dangerously close to her now-exposed breast, and a strong hand gently uncovered her face so those same warm lips could find hers.

"I'm gonna be late," she said, her voice half pout and half purr.

But Charlotte North didn't do anything by accident,

which meant she'd worked in enough time for a little of this when she'd set her alarms last night.

She finally opened her eyes, squinting against the morning sun sneaking in through the shuttered windows. And there he was—Ben Callahan—her cowboy. Well, her vacation cowboy. She didn't have time for much else, and lucky for her, her cowboy was on a permanent vacation from anything resembling a relationship. It had made for a perfect escape from reality, and after today there'd be a whole country between them.

"Do you want to be late?" Ben asked, his dark hair sticking up at all angles, his jaw covered in scruff.

She propped herself up on her elbow and tousled his already tousled locks.

Looking at him, at those mischievous blue eyes, she wanted to be all kinds of late. She wanted to miss her plane. She wanted to prolong the fantasy as long as she could.

"I could be late," she said. "As long as I'm not keeping you from anything."

He glanced at his naked wrist and then grinned that devilish grin that had gotten her into this same situation— the day they'd met.

"Nothing important on the docket today other than making sure I put a smile on your face that lasts the whole flight home."

He pulled her on top of him, and she yelped with laughter.

"Just like that, Doc," he said.

She rolled her eyes and pretended the nickname annoyed her. And it would have if anyone else had said it, but Ben somehow made it sound sweet, sincere, and almost real.

It might have been the closest thing to a relationship she'd ever had. But it wasn't *real.*

He kissed her, and she forgot what she was thinking.

Kisses were good like that.

Charlotte hummed softly.

Someone cleared their throat, the sound most definitely coming from *outside* her meditation-induced memory.

Oh God. Had she hummed out loud? Did it sound like—

"You awake there, cuz?" a voice whisper-shouted.

Her eyes flew open to find her cousin Carter standing in Pearl's doorway.

"Yes!" she whispered back, then stood and tiptoed to the door, grateful she hadn't woken her grandmother with her hum. Moan? WHAT DID CARTER HEAR?

"Must have been a good dream," he said with a grin.

She backhanded him on the shoulder. "Cut me some slack. I just flew across the country worried out of my head. And it's"—she glanced at her watch—"almost *midnight*. Which means for me it's about three a.m."

Carter held his hands up in a peace offering. "I will say nothing else about whatever—or *who*ever—you were dreaming about." He laughed and then mimed zipping his lips. "And you? Worried? That's a first."

Thank the stars for his discretion—and for a familiar face when everything else felt like chaos.

"I'm *not* worried. Not anymore now that I know Gran is in the best possible hands. The surgeons did a great job. And she's resting comfortably. While I wish circumstances were otherwise, all is right with the world—or will be in a couple of months."

Carter laughed. "Do you read your patients' charts to wind down at the end of the night? Or do you just snuggle up with the *New England Journal of Medicine* and call it a day?"

Charlotte glanced down at the chair in which she'd been *meditating*—at the medical journal that had been splayed on her chest. "If you must know, it's *Pediatric Allergy and Immunology* these days. The office is going to start doing allergy testing after the first of the year, so I want to make sure I—"

"Know everything about everything?" Carter teased. "You're still you."

Charlotte rolled her eyes, but she actually enjoyed her cousin's teasing and the familiarity of being in a place where people got her.

Before coming out for the fall festival, Charlotte had only seen Carter a handful of times since they were kids, their paths crossing when they'd both visit Meadow Valley in the summer—him traveling all the way from Houston and her from L.A. Somehow Meadow Valley had reeled him in though. Or maybe it was his fiancée, Ivy Serrano, who had done that. She guessed it was a combination of the two. For Charlotte, this had only ever been a place to visit. Now she had to find a way to make it home for the next six to eight weeks.

Carter grabbed Pearl's chart from the door and nodded toward Charlotte.

"You already read it, I assume?" he asked.

She shook her head. "Didn't have to. Dr. Alvarez and her nurses filled me in as soon as I got up here. Dual fractures in the ankle, both pinned in place during surgery." Her foot was wrapped in a soft splint and bandage to manage the post-surgery swelling. "She told me I have to bring Gran back in a week for the plaster cast. The wrist, luckily, was set without surgery, but it was still a bad break. They want her in a sling so she doesn't get over-confident and start using her hand before she should."

Carter smiled. "Sounds like Doc knows who she's dealing with."

Charlotte's eyes widened at her cousin's use of *Doc* and hoped he didn't notice. She'd been so cold to Ben in the ER, but in her defense, he was sleeping when he should have been...what? It made sense now. He'd been there waiting for Pearl, which meant he'd been there to help. She just hadn't been mentally prepared for him to be the first person she saw. Not that there was any way to prepare for seeing your vacation fling asleep in an emergency waiting room because he was worried about your grandmother too.

"Hello? Charlotte? Did you hear anything I just said?"

She blinked and saw Carter's hand waving in front of her face.

"What? No. Sorry. Guess I got caught up in thinking about what could have happened. She's really lucky, you know?"

Carter nodded. "She is, but she's not going to feel so lucky being confined to a wheelchair. That's what I was saying when you zoned out. There's no way she can use crutches or even a cane without her right hand. She can't do any of the cooking for the inn let alone run the place. Are you sure you know what you're in for?"

Charlotte forced a smile and nodded. "The inn's kitchen has a microwave, right?" She let out a nervous laugh. When Carter called her earlier today, he'd assured her Gran's injuries weren't life-threatening, but he'd also made it clear that Pearl was in no shape for her day-to-day duties at the inn and that she wouldn't be for quite some time.

Pearl was it for Charlotte—the one constant in her life that wasn't work or routine. Even if Gran was 3,000 miles away, she was the closest relationship in Charlotte's life. Gran was her *person*, and Charlotte hadn't thought twice about dropping everything to help her—which meant she really hadn't thought this through. Leaving her job and her stable life to run an inn? What the hell was she thinking? She couldn't cook, and she certainly didn't know how to fold a fitted sheet or . . . or even register guests.

Seriously. What had she done?

Carter winced. "Pearl has a small cooking staff. I'm sure it'll be fine. Just in case, though, I'll see if Casey from Midtown Tavern can stop by tomorrow and give you a few pointers. Just try not to let Pearl know if you start serving pub fare. She'll flip."

Charlotte laughed, for real this time. "If it's between that and my favorite Trader Joe's meal for one, I'm guessing she'd prefer the pub fare. You think Pearl will be relieved or even more worried when she finds out *I'm* her temporary replacement?"

Carter laughed too. "You'll be fine," he insisted. "Also, the nearest Trader Joe's is close to two hours away, so you're probably going to have to make some changes to your diet staples." Carter glanced at his watch and then back at Charlotte. "Okay. You've been up for almost twenty-four hours. We need to get you to the inn."

"Oh my God," Charlotte said. "What time does breakfast start? What do I need to do? Who do I need to call?"

Carter placed a hand on her shoulder and gave her a reassuring squeeze. "It's okay," he said. "We've got tomorrow covered. Let me take you home so you can get settled and sleep. You don't need to worry about anything other than getting some rest."

Instinctively, Charlotte reached for her suitcase. Suddenly, she realized it hadn't been there since she'd made it to Pearl's room.

"Oh my God," she said.

"What?" Carter's brow furrowed.

"My suitcase. *All* my things. I wheeled it into the ER, and I have no idea what happened after that."

Carter grinned.

"Ben Callahan texted me. Said he grabbed it when you left it behind and that he'll swing by the inn and bring it to you whenever you get there."

She cleared her throat. "Well...text him and tell him he can drop it off now...before I get there."

Carter shook his head. "No can do. He said he wouldn't feel right handing it over to anyone but the owner. But I'll call him and tell him you're on your way." He raised a brow. "I'm guessing the guy wants to see you. Hey, that's not who you were— I mean, when you were dreaming just before..."

"Of course not!" she lied.

Her throat tightened. She sure did enjoy seeing *him* in her mind's eye, but that was all she had time for. No distractions this time around. No leaving reality at the door. She was here to play caretaker for her grandmother and for all the patrons and employees at the Meadow Valley Inn.

She swallowed. "Oh my God, Carter. What did I sign up for?"

He wrapped an arm around her shoulder and gave her a reassuring squeeze. "You signed up to do a really good thing for someone who needs you. And don't worry. You've got an entire town to support you. Take it from someone who less than two years ago was an outsider too.

Now this place is more of a home to me than Houston ever was."

She nodded. "So everyone welcomed you with open arms as soon as you got here?"

He shook his head. "Oh hell no! A probie in my company tried to run me out of town. Took getting trapped under a burning ceiling beam in Mrs. Davis's old house to set things right, but it's been smooth sailing ever since."

A burning ceiling beam? How had she not heard about this?

"Have you ever given a pep talk before?" Charlotte asked. "Because that one sucked."

Carter laughed. Pearl stirred in her bed, but she didn't wake.

Charlotte shushed him, and they moved farther down the hall from her grandmother's doorway.

Carter brought up Ben Callahan's number on his phone's screen and initiated the call. He put it on speaker, and Charlotte held her breath. Why? She had no idea. But she was well aware that she was neither inhaling nor exhaling as she listened along with her cousin.

Ring. Ring. Ring. Ring. Ring. Ring. Ring.

"Hey. It's Ben. You know what to do."

Beep.

Carter groaned. "Thought you said you'd still be up, Callahan. I'm taking Charlotte to the inn. I'll make sure she has what she needs for the night, but if you could swing by with her suitcase in the morning..." He glanced at his cousin and winced. "You know what? Make that early afternoon. Thanks, Ben."

Charlotte scoffed. "Early afternoon? What am I supposed to do without my stuff until early afternoon?"

Carter shrugged. "*Sleep*. Pearl has toiletry type stuff for purchase, right? We'll grab you a toothbrush and some toothpaste. Maybe even a Meadow Valley Inn T-shirt for you to wear to bed. You're set until tomorrow. Maybe next time think twice about storming off without your suitcase."

Her mouth dropped open. "How do you know I *stormed*?" she asked, incredulous.

Carter raised a brow.

"Okay. Maybe I stormed. I was— And *he* was—" But there was no use in arguing. Her cousin was right. The inn had what she needed to make it through the night, and chances were she *would* sleep past noon, if her body even remembered how to do such a thing.

She blew out a long breath. "Fine. Let's go. But if he calls you back before we get there, we're going to the ranch for my stuff. Okay?"

Carter crossed his heart. "Scout's honor."

She laughed. "You were never a Boy Scout."

"Fire lieutenant's honor, then. That's gotta hold some weight."

He put his arm over her shoulders and pulled her close. "It's good to have you back, cuz," he said and kissed the top of her head. Then he gave her a warm smile, and the weight of the day lifted, if only slightly. His dark auburn hair matched hers, a reminder that while they hadn't been close growing up, they were family. The next two months were *not* going to be easy. But she had support. She could do this.

They paused outside Pearl's door, and Carter nodded toward his sleeping aunt. "She didn't want to ask too much of her employees, but they rallied as soon as they all learned how bad the fall was. They've got your back. And so do I."

Charlotte pressed her lips together and tried to smile back. She could swab a reluctant child's tonsils like nobody's business, diagnose an ear infection in seconds, and administering vaccinations? Please. She could do it without her patient shedding one tear.

But running an inn? No clue. And she only had one afternoon and evening to figure out how to do it. By the time Gran came home tomorrow, Charlotte wanted her to see the Meadow Valley Inn as the same well-oiled machine she'd left it the day before.

"Okay. Let's go," she said. "Time to sleep off this day and then give myself a crash course in the art of hospitality."

"In that case," Carter said, "your chariot awaits."

Charlotte startled awake and for a moment didn't know where she was. Then the familiar layout of the room—the bed facing the bathroom, her clothes from yesterday balled up on the dresser—sunk in, and she let out a breath.

She grabbed her phone from the night table and looked at the screen.

1:10 p.m.

But she'd set an alarm for eight—and had likely shut it off in her sleep-deprived state. She knew she wasn't expected to get to work this morning, but sleeping the day away was unacceptable. She could be learning. She could be getting to know the staff. She could be...

She sprang out of bed and realized she was wearing nothing but a Meadow Valley Inn T-shirt and her underwear.

A knock sounded on the door, and she gasped, promptly forgetting her attire as she ran to open it.

A knot tightened in her stomach.

There stood Ben Callahan—cowboy hat on his head and devil-may-care grin spread across his face.

"Mornin', Doc. Or should I say, good *afternoon*?" he asked, tipping the brim of his hat up with a flick of his finger. "Fancy seeing you here. Love the outfit, by the way."

She crossed her arms over her chest, but her shirt rode up. Then she crossed them over her knees but realized that hid nothing. So she promptly slammed the door shut, raced over to the dresser, and grabbed her wrinkled pants. Then she ran her fingers through her hair, pulled it into a ponytail, and groaned.

He's seen you first thing in the morning before, she reminded herself. It was just usually post-orgasm that she looked so disheveled, which meant he was happy no matter what her appearance. Now though? And after she yelled at him last night?

She groaned, ran into the bathroom so she could splash some water on her face and brush her teeth, and was back at the door in—she guessed—less than two minutes after having slammed it.

There he stood, still grinning, and he had the audacity to wink at her.

"Take two?" he asked.

She tried to ignore how sexy he looked standing there with her luggage no worse for wear beside him—or how it was sort of nice of him to have taken care of her suitcase in the first place. It also didn't help that her attempt at meditation turned into a replay of their last morning in bed together. The time they spent together was a fantasy—a really fun fantasy both of them always knew was going to end. She wasn't on vacation anymore. She didn't have time for fantasies or fun or...cowboys.

"Thanks for bringing my suitcase," she said coolly, reaching for the handle.

Ben slapped a palm down over said handle at the same time so that she grabbed his hand rather than the case.

She sucked in a sharp breath and pulled her hand away.

"Come on, Doc. Aren't you going to invite me inside?" He tilted his head down just a notch to meet her eyes. Charlotte was tall at five foot eight, but Ben still had at least half a foot on her. He was a strong physical presence, but she was strong too. She could resist his charm, his use of that silly nickname she'd never admit she liked. But nicknames were personal. They evoked connection, and although their bodies had connected on more than one occasion, those *occasions* were behind them. In the past. They would not be *connecting* again.

"Please," she said, trying not to sound cold. "Call me Charlotte. We're not— I mean, we don't…you know… anymore."

He grinned. "Is the good doctor tongue-tied?"

She groaned. "No, it's just that yesterday was a long day, and I'm still catching up. I don't have it in me to argue with you right now."

"Are we arguing? I wasn't aware. I thought we were having fun. You remember fun, right? And I didn't mean to sound like an insensitive jackass. Couldn't forget about your grandmother if I tried. I'd have asked how she was doing, but Carter filled me in."

At this she smiled, her shoulders relaxing. "Why, Ben Callahan, are you getting all sincere on me?"

He laughed. "I see your talent to banter has returned."

"Look," she said, then motioned between them. "This was fun, but we both agreed it had an expiration date. I need to focus on the inn, on taking care of my grandmother. That's the only reason I'm here. As soon as she's up and about again, I need to get back to my life. I don't have time for anything else. We need to keep the past in the past."

Ben held up his hands. "Doc..." He cleared his throat. "I mean...*Charlotte*. While I do enjoy that you always think I'm hitting on you, I wasn't going to offer anything other than taking your suitcase inside. Maybe show you how to use Pearl's registration software and where she keeps the longnecks in the cooler. It's 5:00 somewhere, right? It's the same system we use at the ranch, so I know it well. But, hey, if you've got everything under control, I'll get out of your hair. Just wanted to do my part—for Pearl, of course."

He started to back away from the door.

"Wait," she called after him. Charlotte swallowed the knot in her throat. She wanted to prove to herself that she could do this, to prove that she was as self-sufficient behind the welcome desk of a small-town inn as she was wearing a white coat in an exam room. But she'd assumed people called for a reservation and she just wrote it down in a fancy ledger or something. She was sure they had something similar at the pediatric practice where she worked, but *she* didn't make patient appointments. That was Patty and Patti, the two front desk receptionists.

Ugh. She needed help and from the very person she didn't want to find helpful or caring or concerned because *past in the past* and all that.

"Registration software?" she finally said.

Ben winked. "Customer calls, books a room, and *you* enter it into the system. Keeps you from double-booking. You wouldn't want a couple of honeymooners showing up and asking them to share the suite with the couple who hasn't left yet, would you? Can't say that would go over well on Yelp. Do people still Yelp, by the way? I should see what they're saying about the ranch if they do."

Charlotte's palms grew damp and her pulse quickened. Where was her routine? Her certainty? Without those things, she was at a loss. "Um...right," she said. She was already in over her head.

He crossed his arms. "I'm thinking that you might be in need of my...expertise."

He was either teasing or flirting or both. But Charlotte's head was spinning so much that she couldn't tell, and she wasn't sure she wanted to know. She cleared her throat. "Okay. Yes. I need to learn how to do that. Like, right away." And even though she'd just woken up, a cold beverage sounded *really* good after the night she'd had. When was the last time she had a drink in the middle of the day? Better yet, when would she be able to do this again? After Ben showed her the ropes, she'd be off and rolling—on duty pretty much twenty-four-seven.

Ben grabbed the suitcase by the handle, not bothering to extend the rolling arm.

"That thing weighs at least fifty pounds," she said. "You can just roll it on in if you want."

Then she realized that her whole life fit into one large suitcase. Suddenly fifty pounds seemed lacking.

He shrugged. "This is quicker. Besides, aren't you impressed by my brute strength?"

She let out a nervous laugh. "Showing off doesn't impress me."

And that was the problem. She *was* impressed. She'd initially found the idea of Ben Callahan attractive. A strong, sexy cowboy who literally made people swoon. This was no exaggeration. She saw it firsthand at the fall festival—how he drew looks from basically anyone with a pulse, how strangers flirted with him, how all the locals, especially women, knew his name. It hadn't bothered her. It *still* didn't. Ben was a story to tell her friends—well, as much as her colleagues and neighbors were her friends—back home. She had no circle of girlfriends she brunched with on Sundays or anything like that. There was hardly time in her life for that. But if she did, she'd tell them about the man ripped from the page of an L.L.Bean catalog. She'd talk about how he was a *really* good fantasy—who was now going to teach her one of the most important aspects of running the inn, which didn't feel very fantasy-like at all.

"Well," Ben said, lifting the case with ease and depositing it on the luggage rack beneath the window on the opposite wall. "If upper body strength doesn't do anything for you, there's always my brain."

He raised his brows.

She wiped her damp palms on her pants.

"I'm good with just learning the computer system," she said. "That's all I need."

The last thing she needed was to find Ben Callahan's brain attractive too—or to move into the highly unfamiliar territory of what she might actually *want*.

"As you wish, Do—*Charlotte*," he said with a grin. "Happy to be of service."

CHAPTER FIVE

Ben left Charlotte to start unpacking—since she clearly wasn't going to be staying in his bed this time around—and headed back toward the lobby. *Not* that he expected any sort of interaction like they'd had before. It was just that the last time he saw her, she was naked. In his bed. Okay, fine. She *did* get dressed before heading to the airport, but that was nothing more than a technicality.

He rummaged through Pearl's cooler and found the shelf with ice-cold bottles of beer. The inn wasn't exactly a beer-serving establishment. That was why they had Midtown Tavern. But Pearl liked to kick back on the porch swing with a longneck every now and then. If Ben happened to be in the area, she shared one with him too.

He paused before leaving the kitchen. He needed to figure out a game plan. He and Charlotte had had a good thing going during the fall festival, but he'd never looked past that. For a guy who thought he'd had an expiration date of his own—or at least a time when life would get a lot harder for him and anyone he let get close—he never counted on more than having his fun until he couldn't any longer.

Now he had his life back. A healthy future. And suddenly Dr. Charlotte North looked...different.

Her auburn hair, her freckles, and her full pink lips—not to mention that she could ride bareback like no one's business—all of it still drove him mad. But what would it be like to let himself *feel* something for someone like her—someone who, from the moment they met, saw right through him? Where would he even start? Maybe it wasn't the wisest choice to start with the first woman to cross his path since getting the news about his false diagnosis, but he couldn't get the idea of *What if?* out of his head.

"Except she's still leaving, idiot," he mumbled to himself. "Just not today."

Besides, he didn't have the first clue how to do *different* or more or anything of that sort. It didn't stop him from thinking he might want to try it out, especially with someone where the chemistry was undeniable—even if it was purely physical right now.

"You're still an idiot," he said under his breath again. "But maybe you're just the idiot she needs."

When he made it back to the lobby with two perspiring beer bottles in his hands, Tyler—the front desk assistant—was just hanging up the phone.

"Room seven-A just called—Pearl's granddaughter?" Tyler said. "She wanted to know if I had a detailed breakdown of the daily schedule, from sunup to sundown and everything in between. She even asked if I had a spreadsheet that laid out which hours had the highest surges in reservation calls. She seemed a little...intense."

Ben laughed. That wasn't how he would have described the woman with whom he'd spent a fun-filled, no-strings-attached fling, but then again, that woman wasn't the whole Charlotte North, was she? He raised a brow. "Hey, you think I could borrow that laptop?" he asked. "You can forward any telephone bookings to Charlotte's room and we'll take care of it. The sooner she learns the ropes, the less overwhelmed—and *intense*—she's going to be."

Tyler nodded. It was early afternoon on a Monday in October. There probably wouldn't be many calls for them to field.

"What time do you punch out?" Ben asked.

Tyler checked his watch. "In about forty-five minutes."

Ben grinned. "We'll be out in fifteen and you can call it a day. Paid early leave." He cleared his throat. "As long as your interim boss agrees, of course."

That would give him plenty of time to show her the ropes. Then she'd be steering the ship, and Ben could stay until Tyler's shift ended to make sure she was comfortable in her new role. And to see if—maybe, *perhaps*— the energy between them wasn't as one-sided as Charlotte made it seem.

Tyler handed Ben the laptop from the front desk, a shock of sandy waves falling over his eyes. "Thanks, Mr. Callahan. I might actually have time to eat before class later this afternoon."

Ben winced. He was turning thirty in nine weeks, on New Year's Day, in fact. He didn't think that was so old. But Tyler's *Mr. Callahan* made him feel otherwise. He'd gotten all the way to the point where kids barely out of high school saw him as a mature adult, yet he didn't feel like he'd earned the label.

He switched the two bottles to one hand and grabbed the laptop with the other.

"Fifteen minutes," he said again, and Tyler nodded.

Ben crossed behind the desk and past the stairs that led to the second floor, to the hallway that housed the first-floor rooms.

The door to room 7A was open a crack, so he nudged it farther with the toe of his boot.

"Somebody order a cold one?" he asked.

She was sitting on the edge of the bed, phone in her hands, furiously typing.

He approached the bed, let the laptop fall onto one of the pillows, and set the beers on the nightstand. He tossed his hat onto a corner chair and ran a hand through his hair. Then he glanced over her shoulder, expecting to find her firing off a text or seven. But she was in her notes app.

"What are you doing, Doc?" he asked, letting the nickname slip.

She either didn't care or was too busy to notice.

"Making a list," she said. "Or *lists*, I guess. After learning the software, I'm going to acquaint myself with the kitchen staff—let them know they probably shouldn't let me near the food unless it's an absolute emergency. Then I want to meet the guest room staff and get a list of any vendors I should call in the morning. Oh, and Gran's going to be released today, so somewhere in there I have to work out how to get her home, situated, and pick up any medication she might need. I could take her car and do it, but I should probably be here, shouldn't I? Wait, what if she was already released while I was sleeping?" She shook her head vigorously. "Carter would have called, right? Also, there's the night staff for me to meet. I know it's only a few people, but I'll need to bring them up to speed."

He furrowed his brow as he saw times next to each event on the list. All the way at the bottom of the second column, at 3:00 a.m., it said Sleep (maybe). And then at 5:00 a.m. Wake up and start my first full day.

"Who are you, and what did you do with the woman I met three weeks ago? She didn't have a planner or lists. And the *only* thing that kept her from a good night's sleep was *me*," he said.

She gave him a nervous smile, swiped at her screen a few times, and then turned the phone toward him.

It was a note that said Vacation Agenda Day One in bold with a list beneath it, each item marked with an asterisk. His eyes widened as he read.

*Coffee with Gran

*Go for a ride at Meadow Valley Ranch

*Shower

*Relax

*Dinner with Gran

*Meet Carter at tavern (do NOT flirt with rancher if he's there)

*OR, if you flirt with rancher, make sure he knows you don't do more than flings.

Ben made a move to swipe at her screen, but she yanked the phone away.

"Aw, come on," he teased. "I want to see what happened to your list once you decided to flirt with the rancher."

She rolled her eyes. "You flirted first."

He raised his brows. "Sure did. And you shot me down—but then decided you couldn't resist me. That's usually how it goes."

This time she groaned. "Aren't you supposed to be teaching me how to run this place?"

He held out his hand, palm up.

"What?" she asked, finally looking up.

"Hand over the phone first," he said with gentle authority.

"But if I don't write it all down..."

"One thing at a time, okay? This isn't New York City. It's Meadow Valley. Things work a little differently around here. The phone's not ringing off the hook. There's not a two-hour wait for a table at the inn's café. Slow and steady, Doc. No one's going to beat you to the finish line."

Her throat bobbed as she swallowed, but she gave up the phone.

"I just want everything to be perfect when Gran gets home. I don't want her to worry or overextend herself when she's supposed to be healing." She sucked in a shaky breath. "What was she thinking going up a ladder by herself?"

Ben pocketed her phone, grabbed the two beers, and sat next to her on the foot of the bed.

"She was thinking she was going to do something she does all the time, something that she's completely capable of doing. But accidents happen."

He handed her a beer, and she took a long, slow sip.

"It's different when it's someone you know—someone you *love*. Kids come into the office every day, some sick and some hurt. I can apply the science, and I can detach. It's easy. I thought I could do the same with Pearl, but seeing my grandmother like that?" She shook her head. "I wasn't prepared for it despite everything I know about broken bones and healing and... She's the closest person in my life."

Ben narrowed his eyes. "Three thousand miles away is close?"

She laughed. "I mean *closest*." She pressed a hand over her heart.

He thought for a second and took a sip of his own beer.

"What about your parents? Friends back in New York?" he asked.

"My parents have never been much for stability. They're more the wanderlust type, which meant dropping me in Meadow Valley most summers while they traveled the globe, building up their photography business's reputation. These days they're overseas more often than not, which means they miss a lot of stuff going on at home." She cleared her throat. "Like my grandfather's funeral, but that's a whole other story."

"I'm sorry," Ben said. "About your grandfather."

She shrugged. "It was a long time ago."

But Ben could tell from the way her eyes glassed over that time hadn't healed all.

"New York is where my residency took me," she continued. "And because I found a great job with a great practice and stability *is* my thing, I never left. But residency, internship, getting hired at a practice, *and* keeping up with every new advancement and trend in pediatrics—it doesn't leave a lot of time for things like lasting friendships." She blew out a breath. "Look, I appreciate you trying to do the whole talk-about-my-feelings thing, but I have medical journals and conference recordings and even a few podcasts to set my mind at ease. And all that is beside the point. I need to learn how to run this inn, like, right now."

"You got it, Doc," he said, setting down his beer and grabbing the laptop.

"*Charlotte*," she reminded him. "I'm Charlotte. You're Ben. I think these next several weeks will go a whole lot better if we use proper names only from here on out."

He opened the laptop, the appointment calendar still on the screen.

"Okay, *Charlotte*, this is the—" He shook his head. "Nope. Can't do it. I'm sorry, but I called you Doc for a full two weeks. Until you blew back into town, I don't think I ever said your given name out loud. Charlotte is . . . *weird*."

She scoffed. "It's my *name*. And I actually like it."

Ben laughed. "That's not what I meant." Her hair was in a ponytail, but one auburn lock had fallen free and hung down the side of her face. He wanted to tuck it behind her ear, to do something that had once felt so natural but now seemed wrong. "It's just hard to transition."

She blew out a breath and nodded. "I get it. But it's what we have to do, isn't it?"

He set the laptop down again and stood, arms crossed over his chest.

"If that's what you want."

She blew the piece of hair out of her face. At least, she tried to, but it only fell right back where it was. Then she stood and started pacing. "Don't get me wrong. I had a lot of fun during the time we spent together, not to mention the stress relief, but stress or no stress, I'm not here to blow off steam, Ben. I don't have time for fun, and I don't have time for . . . for anything other than taking care of Gran and her inn."

Ben raised his brows. "You mentioned the time thing. Twice. And the fun thing too."

She waved him off. "Because fun doesn't factor into the

equation anymore. Fun isn't why I'm here. Fun is...that was all it was, for both of us. The perfect commitment is one where you don't have to commit to anything but the fun part, right?" She stopped so she was facing him, hands in the pockets of her jeans as she rocked back and forth on her heels.

That was what he'd said to her on the day they'd met, not because he was an ass but because they'd both wanted the same thing. Now she used his own words against him, and she wasn't exactly wrong to do so. But there was still something between them. He could feel it bubbling beneath the surface. He wouldn't push though. If it was there today, it'd be there tomorrow, right? After she got settled and realized that maybe, possibly, the next several weeks didn't have to be all work and no play.

"Right," he finally said. "Our time was fun. I should let you get to work."

She held up her beer. "This is good. I could use another. My last chance to blow off some steam before I'm officially on the job twenty-four-seven." Her cheeks turned pink. "I didn't mean blowing off *steam* as in...you know. Just a drink. And then business as usual."

He grinned. He could always help when it came to blowing off steam—even if it wasn't the way he'd initially intended.

"I can do you one better. I know you *know* just about everyone in town. But you need a squad. You know Ivy and Casey. And I can introduce you to Delaney. She's pretty tight with them now..."

Instead of laughing, this time she snorted and narrowly escaped spitting out her beer.

"A squad?" she said after swallowing. She swiped her

forearm over the corner of her mouth where a tiny dribble
of beer had leaked out.

He squared his shoulders. "We have this family with
a couple of teenage girls who checked in the other day.
All they talk about is texting their squad and sharing pics.
They don't even say the whole word—*pictures*." Good
Lord. He was about to be thirty, not seventy. When did he
start talking like a curmudgeon? "Whatever. What I was
going to say was I could text Ivy, Casey, and Delaney
and get you that much-needed girls' night before all hell
breaks loose tomorrow."

Charlotte nodded slowly. Then she cocked her head to
the side and looked at him like she'd never seen anything
like him before. He wasn't sure if that was a good sign or
a bad sign.

"You'd do all that for me?" she asked. "Even though I
said we can't...you *know*."

"Sleep together?" he asked, going for blunt because
why dance around the subject?

She coughed on her next sip of beer, then nodded.

"Geez, Do—*Charlotte*. Give a guy some credit. I can
do something nice for someone without there being anything in it for me."

Sure, it shocked him too—wanting to do something
for her just because—but it didn't mean he was incapable
of such an act.

"Sorry," she said. "I didn't mean anything by it. This
is just new ground for me, I guess. Are we becoming
friends?"

His brows drew together for a moment as he thought
about the word. *Friends*. He didn't really have any female
friends who weren't at least in other relationships. He
thought about the idea of a friendship with a woman

to whom he was still attracted and realized—oddly enough—that he'd prefer that over nothing at all.

"Sure," he said. "Friends. On one condition though. Ya gotta let me call you Doc, *Doc*. The Charlotte thing— it just feels weird."

She laughed and held out her hand to shake.

"Okay," she said. "You got yourself a deal, *cowboy*."

He smiled at that and shook her hand. "Well, it looks like we've come to an agreement."

They shook again, and her hand lingered in his. They stayed that way for a few quiet moments until the phone on Charlotte's nightstand rang.

She gasped. "What if it's someone calling to book a room? You were supposed to show me. I had a *list*."

Ben picked up the phone.

"Meadow Valley Inn, this is Ben. How may I help you?"

He strode to the dresser and woke up the laptop. Then he nodded and double-clicked on a date in the calendar and typed in the patron's name and email address. "Okay, ma'am. You'll receive a confirmation email with your reservation and a link to enter payment information. Your card will not be charged until you check out, but we require one to hold the room. We take cancellations up until twenty-four hours before your stay." He nodded. "Yes. Thank you, and we look forward to your visit."

He ended the call and placed the phone back in its cradle.

Charlotte's hands were on her hips, her eyes narrow slits.

"That's it?" she asked. "Double-click, enter an email, and wham-bam-thank-you-ma'am? I've been freaking out about how to use the reservation system, and a twelve-year-old could have figured it out?"

Ben grinned. "Would you have let me stick around

and get you situated if you didn't think I had something important to offer you?"

She opened her mouth to protest, but then blew out a breath, her shoulders relaxing.

"I'm sorry about yelling at you last night," she said. "I was so worked up about what happened to Gran that I didn't exactly know how to react when I saw you at the hospital. I was a little less than friendly, but it was only because you caught me off guard."

He winked at her. "I guess it's a good thing we're friends, now, huh? Maybe it'll help with knowing how to react next time you see me."

Her cheeks flushed, and she cleared her throat. "Right. Exactly. We can wave or high-five or whatever it is that friends do."

"Sure, Doc," he said, wondering if she was flustered because this was as new for her as it was for him. Then he held his hand up high. "I should let you get back to your lists. Up top?"

She laughed nervously and slapped his palm with hers.

"I'll see you around, friend," he said, backing toward her bedroom door.

"See you. *Friend*," she said with a soft smile.

Then he pulled her door shut behind him, shaking his head once he was out in the hall.

Did he still feel the urge to kiss her? Sure did. Old habits die hard, and this cowboy was chock-full of habits he needed to break. But something about the good doctor made him want to prove that he could.

He still held his bottle of beer and raised it in a toast to no one in particular as he made his way back up front to let Tyler off the hook.

"To friends," he said to himself, then smiled and drank.

CHAPTER SIX

"Y ou're going to be *friends* with Ben Callahan?" Casey asked. The proprietor of Midtown Tavern slipped out from behind the bar and joined Charlotte and Ivy on the other side. "Ben Callahan," she said again. "The guy who is the cowboy version of Joey from *Friends*."

Charlotte imagined Ben saying, "How *you* doin'?" and laughed out loud.

"Why is it so hard to believe? Wasn't it friend-like for him to get us all together tonight?" she whisper-shouted as if someone might hear her talking about said cowboy.

Ivy looked around the empty bar and giggled. Casey had locked the doors twenty minutes ago, but she'd topped off the other two women's pints so she could join them for her own after-work drink.

"There's no one here," Ivy whisper-shouted back to her. "And you're okay with...I mean, the last time you were here, you and Ben..."

"Had a fun vacation fling that's in the past?" Charlotte asked, ignoring the sudden flush of heat she felt at the mere mention of that week. Nothing good could come of her and Ben falling back into that pattern of...*activity*. Besides...time. She had no time for a fling. She had an inn to run and a grandmother to take care of.

Casey nodded. "Yeah. That. The fling. Friends after a fling in the close quarters of a town as small as Meadow Valley?" She whistled. "Easier said than done."

Charlotte's laughter subsided. The whole small-town thing clicked into place.

"Have either of you..." she asked. "I mean, are you both *friends* with Ben Callahan?" She winced at the tiny pang of jealousy deep in her gut. She didn't want anything more from Ben than his friendship, but she also wanted to believe that despite his reputation as a player that she'd been slightly more than a notch on his bedpost. After all, they did spend a whole two weeks together.

"No," Ivy said, shaking her head emphatically.

"You're not friends?" Charlotte asked, and Ivy laughed.

"I meant *no*, I've never...Carter's the only guy for me. And yes. Ben Callahan and I are friends. More like friendly acquaintances. His brother Sam though. *He's* the good friend type. A great friend, actually. They don't make 'em like that anymore. I mean, except for Carter." Ivy's cheeks flushed at the mention of her fiancé. "And Casey's sort of pined for Boone Murphy since high school, so I guarantee she and Ben have never...you know."

Casey elbowed her friend. "I don't *pine*," she insisted. "I just don't do the whole heartbreak thing." She turned her attention to Charlotte. "Look. Ben's a good guy. Just because he's not the commitment type doesn't mean he's a total jerk. And just because he's easy on the eyes doesn't mean every woman in town is unable to resist him."

Charlotte blew out a breath, a little surprised at her relief.

"You okay?" Ivy asked.

Charlotte nodded. "Yes. Totally. Of course. I guess it just would have been weird if all three of us had—"

A knock sounded on the tavern door, saving Charlotte from having to finish her sentence, and the three women glanced toward the sound to see Delaney Harper waving at them through the circular window.

Ivy hopped off her bar stool and let her in.

"Sorry I'm late," Delaney said, her blond hair in a low ponytail that revealed a fresh scratch on her neck. She pointed to the obvious wound and said, "Got our first foster for the shelter. And by shelter, I mean Sam's apartment until an actual building for said shelter exists. But let's just say the stray cat we found wandering around the barn was *not* a big fan of getting his claws trimmed—*or* of meeting Butch Catsidy."

Charlotte snorted. "Butch *Catsidy*?"

Delaney ducked under the bar and poured herself a beer. She nodded. "My cat. He used to be one of Trudy Davis's foster kittens." She pulled up a picture on her phone and passed it across the bar to Charlotte.

Charlotte's eyes widened. "Was he born with only three legs or was it an accident? He's beautiful, by the way. I never liked the bad rap Halloween gave to black cats. He looks a lot more like good luck to me than bad."

Delaney took a swig of her beer. "Born that way," she said, then licked the foam off her top lip. "And he's absolutely perfect just the way he is."

"You want to know what else is perfect?" Casey asked. Then before anyone could respond, she answered her own question. "This ombré dye job." She shook her hair, exaggerating the gesture like she was in a shampoo commercial. Her chin-length asymmetrical bob started as dark purple on top and gradually faded to lavender by the time the color reached her ends.

"I love it," Charlotte said. "I've never done anything edgy like that."

"Casey is *amazing* with hair," Ivy said. "If you ever want to try edgy, she's your girl."

"Maybe I should go pink," Delaney mused.

Casey waved her hand dismissively. "So easy with your light coloring. If you really want to pull the trigger, just let me know." She turned to Charlotte. "I have the best rose gold color-enhancing conditioner. I bet it would look *ridiculous* on you."

"Which means beautiful," Ivy added.

"Are you womansplaining me?" Casey asked Ivy with brows raised. Then the two burst into a fit of laughter. It was infectious, and soon Charlotte and Delaney were laughing too.

So this was what it was like to have a group of girl-friends, huh? She hadn't thought she'd been missing out, but this was actually kind of nice.

Charlotte wrapped a lock of her hair around her finger and imagined how *ridiculous* she'd look if she tried stepping outside her comfort zone—with wash-out color first, of course.

"So are you like a licensed cosmetologist, or do you just do hair for fun?" Charlotte asked.

The laughing stopped. In fact, the whole room went silent.

"O-*kay*," Charlotte said, dragging out the second syllable of the word. "I just totally messed up, didn't I?"

She'd known Casey when they were teens but couldn't remember if Casey'd had plans beyond high school or if she always knew she was going to run the family's tavern.

"Noooo," Ivy said, with both an exaggerated smile and overly happy tone.

"Actually, it's a sore subject," Casey said bluntly. "A damned sore one. But you didn't know. So I'll explain and then that will be that. I was in cosmetology school right out of high school. I was one class away from graduating and failed my color demonstration. I've obviously gotten much better, but I never went back and finished. End of story. We won't bring this up again. *Or* Boone Murphy, while we're at it. Right?"

"Right," they all said in unison. Charlotte got the idea there was more to the story than Casey was offering, but *she* wasn't going to ask. She was simply happy to be here, to be welcomed into the fold.

"Okay, subject change," Charlotte said.

"Yes!" Ivy chimed in. "How about we fill Delaney in about you and Ben going from fling to friends?"

Delaney waved Ivy off. "Awww. I think it's sweet that Ben's turning over a new leaf. And it's great that things don't have to be awkward between you two while you're back in town."

Charlotte let out a breath. Finally someone didn't think the idea was so preposterous.

Casey narrowed her eyes at Delaney. "So you're saying that after your *fling* with Sam, you could have come back to Meadow Valley and been friends?"

Delaney scoffed. "Of course not. But that's because I was in love with him. Charlotte's not in *love* with Ben."

All three women turned toward Charlotte, their eyes collectively locked on her like laser beams.

"You're not in love with Ben—right?" Delaney asked, a bit more caution in her voice.

"*No*," Charlotte said emphatically. "I barely know

him. We're friends. And that's all we're going to be. And can we have another subject change? *Please*? Delaney, tell me more about the animal shelter."

Delaney's eyes brightened.

"So Sam and I are partnering with a local vet, Dr. Eli Murphy. He's Boone's brother," she said hesitantly, then looked at Casey, who was already staring back with a raised brow. "Anyway," Delaney continued, "we're all working together to put a rescue shelter on the Meadow Valley Ranch property..."

And that was all it took to steer the conversation away from the topic of friends and lovers, possibilities and impossibilities, and any further thoughts—at least for tonight—of Ben Callahan, the man she barely knew but who'd agreed to be her friend.

So much of her life she'd felt like a nomad until finally making herself a home in New York. Tonight, though, thanks to a new friend, she felt less like a visitor than she had in a long time.

"And now, thanks to Sam, Ben, and Colt—and pretty much everyone in this wonderful town—I get a second chance at my dream," Delaney said, finishing her story. Then she held up her glass. "To second chances," she said.

Ivy and Casey lifted their pints as well, both wearing smiles that seemed to hide something behind the pleasant expression.

"To second chances," they both said, repeating Delaney's words.

Charlotte lifted her glass and thought about her grandmother getting a second chance at life after an accident that could have been much worse.

It felt a little like cheating, to drink to someone else's

do-over, but everything in Charlotte's life had gone exactly as she'd planned. She didn't need a second chance or to do anything over again. Everything was perfect just as it was.

"To second chances," she said, ignoring the unsettling churning in her gut.

All four women drank until their pints were empty, their glasses hitting the bar in rapid succession.

"All right, ladies," Casey said, producing four shot glasses and a bottle of whiskey. "Time for the good stuff."

"Yeehaw!" Delaney shouted, and Ivy and Casey gave her a collective look. "What?" she protested. "I live in cowboy country now. I can *yeehaw* if I want to!"

Casey shrugged and poured each of them a shot. "When in cowboy country, then..."

All four of them *Yeehawed* before they drank, and then Charlotte swiped her forearm across her mouth and burped.

"Another!" she said. "Yeehaw! Or whatever."

They all laughed.

Because everything was perfect just as it was. Charlotte didn't need to tell herself twice.

Even if she did.

CHAPTER SEVEN

Ben woke at the crack of dawn—not because he needed to, but because his body just wanted to get busy living its best life, and apparently sleeping in was not part of the deal. He lay in bed for several minutes trying to convince his brain that he wasn't on shift until 9:00 a.m., but he lost the battle and decided to shower and find some coffee instead.

After throwing on a navy Henley and a pair of jeans, he strolled down the quiet hallway of the guest quarters. No one stirred, not a single sound from any room. Even Jessie was snoozing at the front desk. He didn't blame her. Poor kid moonlighted at the ranch while also working as a Meadow Valley firefighter.

He tiptoed past the desk—knowing she'd have an alarm set to wake her before any guests headed out for their day—and stepped out into the crisp early morning air.

He turned to head toward the dining hall and saw their produce supplier's truck parked out front, which meant Luis, Meadow Valley Ranch's one and only chef, was awake and would have a pot of coffee going even though breakfast didn't start for another two hours.

Ben strolled around to the back entrance and heard them before he saw them.

"Parsnips?" he heard Luis say, incredulous. "I'm making *carrot* soup and you bring me parsnips?"

Ben creeped up to the screen door but didn't step inside.

Anna brandished a handful of parsnips, holding them by their greens. "These are the *sweetest* parsnips you will ever taste. Make the soup with these. You'll thank me."

Ben shook his head and laughed. Looked like it was another day ending in *y*. Hell, even before the two were dating, this had always been their MO. Coffee or no coffee, Ben didn't want to get in the middle of a heated root vegetable argument that would likely end in the two of them making out against the door of Anna's truck.

Speaking of making out—or perhaps a temporary resident with whom he used to lock lips—the only other place in town where he could get coffee before 7:00 a.m. was Pearl's. Pre-injury, you could find Pearl in the kitchen helping prep breakfast, which meant her replacement—a certain doctor who was now a new friend—would be on breakfast duty instead.

Ben whistled to himself as he headed back toward his own vehicle for the short ride to town.

He hopped out of his truck, kicked the dust off his boots, checked his hair in the reflection of the window, and shrugged. The sun wasn't high enough to warrant his hat. Plus, he'd only take it off once he walked inside. And what was a little bedhead between friends?

He took the steps up to the front porch two at a time, bypassed the main entrance, and headed straight through the café to the kitchen, offering hellos and good mornings to the usual crew.

"Anyone seen Charlotte?" he asked the room.

Responses came in the form of shrugs and blank stares.

"Okay...Let me rephrase," Ben said. "Has anyone *met* Charlotte North, Pearl's granddaughter, who will be running things around here while Pearl recuperates from her accident?"

This time, instead of shrugs, he was met with a small chorus of head shakes.

"Uh-oh," he said. This wasn't good. He remembered her list from the afternoon before, how she'd barely left herself two hours to sleep. She knew to be up early.

Ben shook his head and laughed. He'd enjoy giving her a good ribbing for oversleeping her first day on the job.

He strode into the small lobby and back toward her room. When he reached 7A, he hesitated before knocking.

Maybe she was about to walk through that door, polished and ready for the day, and wouldn't appreciate Ben showing up and thinking she wasn't up to the task. To clarify, that *wasn't* what he thought. Everyone overslept now and again. The time difference was probably still catching up with her. But he could see how him showing up and checking in on her *again* might be misconstrued as such.

Aw, screw it. It was 6:30 a.m., and the kitchen was in full swing. If she wasn't up, she'd sure as hell want to be.

He knocked. "Doc? Are you in there?" he asked.

There was no answer, so he knocked again—more like pounded—and waited. After a few seconds he heard a whimper and then a moan.

"Doc?" He pounded on the door again. "Doc, I just

want to make sure you're okay. Kitchen's up and running, and I thought you might want to join in the fun."

"Coming," she said, but the word sounded worse than the moan he heard before.

He heard the click of the handle turning, and then the door swung open.

His eyes widened and it took everything in him not to burst out laughing.

Some of her hair was still fastened with a ponytail holder, but said ponytail was sticking off the right side of her head while the left side looked more like an auburn bird's nest that was still under construction. Dark circles ringed her eyes. Or maybe that was makeup. And all she wore was an inside-out T-shirt that barely covered her underwear.

"You know, we really need to stop meeting like this. Would it be too much to ask if we could take a selfie?" he asked, unable to stifle the laughter this time.

She squeezed her eyes shut and shook her head. "*Why* are you shouting?" she whispered.

"Oh wow," Ben said. "What happened last night? I'm guessing nothing that ends with *hashtag squad goals*."

"Whiskey," she said, her voice scratchy. Her eyes were still shut. "Lots of whiskey."

She stumbled back a step, then braced her hand against the door frame.

"Gotta open those eyes, Doc. Makes balancing a whole lot easier."

She shook her head. "Can't. Nauseous. Headache. Light hurts. *Why?*"

He chuckled. "You *have* been hungover before, right?"

She wavered again, and this time Ben caught her by the elbows. Her head fell against his chest.

"I am *never. Drinking. Again*," she said.

"Famous last words, Doc. Now let's get you into the shower. Then we'll head to the kitchen for some greasy scrambled eggs and a nice tall glass of Coke."

"Coke?" she croaked.

"Yes, ma'am. Folks like to call it the red ambulance. I'm betting you'll be one of those folks soon. The carbonation will help settle your stomach, and the caffeine will wake you up faster than you can say *I'm never drinking again*— again. And the sugar?" He whistled. "Well that'll pull ya right outta hell and back to the land of the living."

She lifted her head and winced. "Ow. Also, there will be no *getting me into the shower*. I can make it there on my own, thank you very much." She stepped back and tugged the bottom of her T-shirt lower.

"Oh, come on, Doc. It's nothing I haven't seen before. And it's not like I'm asking to join you—unless you want me to."

He winked, and she narrowed her eyes at him.

"Just a little teasing between friends. But I'll take that as a no," he said with a grin. Then he nodded toward the bathroom. "Go on, then. Might not hurt to brush those pearly whites while you're in there either."

She covered her mouth, eyes wide now.

"That's not what I meant, Doc," he said, but he couldn't help laughing. "I'm just saying—based on my own experience—that hangover dry mouth can taste like the bottom of a boot after it steps in a cow pie. You get yourself all minty fresh, and you'll feel like a whole new person. Trust me."

She crossed her arms, attempting, he guessed, to look indignant, but with her less-than-formal attire and hair that looked like it got sucked into a Dyson and then spit out again, it was hard to take her seriously.

"You'd like me to leave?" he asked, interpreting her glare.

"Yes, please," she said, polite but firm.

He nodded. "You promise you're steady on your feet? You're not going to fall and hit that pretty head of yours, are you? What kind of friend would I be if you needed my help and I wasn't here?"

Her hand went to her head, and she winced as she felt the nest that was her hair.

"Your *usually* pretty head," he amended.

She groaned and pointed toward the door. "*Out.*"

Ben held his hands up in surrender. "I'm going. I'm going." He turned toward the door. "You're welcome for the wake-up call, by the way."

She cleared her throat. "Thank you," she said. "You won't have to do it again. And please don't mention any of this to my grandmother. The last thing I need is for her to think I can't handle this on my first full day. She's not awake, is she?"

Ben shook his head. "Believe it or not, looks like she's following doctor's orders and staying in bed her first morning home. She did okay last night?"

Charlotte nodded. "I waited until she was asleep to go to Midtown, which I'm *never* doing again. Have I mentioned that?"

Ben laughed.

"I'll leave you to it, Doc."

Satisfied that she would make it safely to the kitchen in a matter of time, he left. Only when he was outside her room with the door pulled closed behind him did he let out a long breath.

Not too long ago, she might have said, "Why don't you join me, cowboy?" And he'd have been naked and in that shower in record time. But today, despite her being half dressed, he found himself wanting to be there *for* her rather than simply naked *with* her. Not that he'd have said no if there had been a naked invitation. But still, this friendship thing was...odd.

For a second he felt like he'd gone over the steep drop of a roller coaster, and his stomach rose in his throat. *Great*. He was developing a sympathy hangover. This was a first. That was the only logical explanation.

His stomach settled, and he shrugged off the strange sensation as he headed to the kitchen. Looked like they could both use some scrambled eggs.

"I'm here! I'm here! I'm here!" Charlotte called as she ran into the kitchen twenty minutes later. She'd thrown on her Los Angeles Kings T-shirt and a pair of jeans and had piled her wet hair into a bun. It was far from glamorous, but at least it wasn't the tornado it had been when Ben knocked on her door.

Ugh. How had she messed up so royally on her very first morning? Oh right—her newfound *squad*. Not that she wasn't grateful for a few allies, but the field of cotton that was the inside of her mouth felt otherwise.

She halted midstep and narrowly escaped knocking a woman straight into the pot of hollandaise sauce she was stirring.

"Hey, hey, *hey*!" the woman yelled. "Thanks for the announcement, but do you know anything about kitchen safety?"

Charlotte winced. She knew exam room protocol and how to administer an injection, but kitchen safety hadn't turned up in any of her oft-read journals.

"Um...don't run?" she said.

The other woman—maybe a decade older than Charlotte, her brown hair in a net-covered ponytail—rolled her eyes. "That's a start." She pulled the spoon from the pot and set it on a nearby plate. Then she turned toward a shelf above the counter opposite the stove, pulled a binder off the shelf, and dropped it into Charlotte's hands.

Charlotte pitched forward with the weight of the book but righted herself before she face-planted onto the tile floor.

"Meadow Valley Inn: Kitchen Procedures and Regulations." Charlotte read the title on the cover out loud.

"We appreciate what you're doing for your grandmother," the woman said. "But if you want to do the job without harming yourself or others, I suggest you read up. I'm Val, by the way. Not sure we've ever officially met."

Charlotte shook her head, hugging the book to her chest with her left arm and holding out her right.

Val shook her hand. "Callahan's got some eggs and coffee waiting for you in the café. Looks like you could use a little pick-me-up."

Ha. Pick-me-up. That was the understatement of the year. Charlotte needed to turn back time and just say no to a second, third, and possibly fourth shot of whiskey. Heck, she'd go so far as to stop before having any at all.

It had been fun though. Being one of the girls and talking about boys—well, they were *men* nowadays—it was everything she never knew she missed about high school and college.

And speaking of boys or men or whatever they were, Ben Callahan waiting for her with breakfast was about as strange as dogs and cats walking on their hind legs and speaking like humans.

The transition to friends was good. It was what she

wanted. But there was an intimacy to friendship that hadn't been there when they were...well...not friends. Now he was waking her from the depths of a hangover and fixing her breakfast—or having Val fix her breakfast. Either way, it was an adjustment that seemed seamless for him while she was pretty much a hot mess who had answered her door in a T-shirt and panties two days in a row.

"Thanks," Charlotte finally said, then headed through the door that led to the café seating area.

Only one table was occupied this early other than the one where Ben Callahan sat, a cup of coffee in one hand and a pen in the other as he stared intently at the newspaper crossword puzzle.

She'd been so flustered at oversleeping—and being royally hungover—that she hadn't had a chance to fully appreciate the view. After all, friends could appreciate another friend's aesthetic, couldn't they?

His hair was a little rumpled, probably from sleep, but oh how that blue shirt hugged his lean torso. He set down his coffee, his brow furrowed, and tapped his pen against his chin.

In the handful of mornings they'd woken up together, she'd never once seen Ben Callahan read the morning paper or do the crossword puzzle. She remembered not wanting to be attracted to his brain because the physical specimen was hard enough to resist. But the scene before her was pretty darn attractive.

"Can I help?" she asked as she approached.

Ben's head shot up, and his lips parted into a smile when he saw her.

A strange warmth spread through her at such a greeting. It was nothing more than a smile, something she'd seen him do countless times for countless others. That was Ben Callahan's charm. He used it for good *and* for mischief. She'd seen it in action. But something about this smile made her feel like it belonged to her and her alone.

"That depends," he said. "Do you know a four-letter word that means *speak hoarsely*?"

She dropped the kitchen binder on an empty chair and sat down in front of a plate covered with scrambled eggs, bacon, and toast. Suddenly nothing looked better—not even the cowboy across from her—than the food she was about to inhale.

She shoved a piece of bacon in her mouth and groaned with pleasure.

"Rasp," she said. "The word you're looking for is *rasp*, and this might be the best bacon I've ever tasted."

He scribbled the word, his eyes lighting up.

"Nice work, Doc. My coffee's still kicking in, but look at you—completely hungover yet still a whiz with words."

She narrowed her eyes at him and shoveled a forkful of eggs into her mouth. But he was right, and the eggs tasted even better than the bacon, which meant she couldn't even pretend to be annoyed.

She slumped into her chair and swallowed. "My God, was the food always so good here?"

He nodded toward the perspiring glass of cola next to her plate.

"Coffee's good, but try washing it down with that," he said.

She took a sip from the glass. Then another, and another after that. She couldn't get enough. The abundance of ice in the glass cut the carbonation, making it easy to down the whole beverage before coming up for air.

When the glass was empty, she wiped her napkin across her mouth.

"Oh my God," she said, eyes wide. "Ben Callahan, you're a genius!" Then, before she even knew it was coming, she let loose a burp the likes of which she'd never heard from her own person before.

She gasped, throwing a hand over her mouth, and Ben burst into a fit of laughter.

"Now *that*," he said, still laughing, "is a side of Dr. Charlotte North I haven't seen before."

Her cheeks burned, but she was determined to maintain a shred of dignity. So she squared her shoulders and held her chin high, scooping another pile of eggs onto her fork.

"Friends take the good with the bad," she said haughtily. "If you want to be friends with me, you have to accept the prim and proper along with...other stuff."

She went for it and inhaled her next bite. With her mouth full, she could pretend she hadn't failed miserably at the whole dignity thing. Come to think of it, after the morning started out with her hungover and half dressed, dignity didn't have a chance from there on out.

She downed half the glass of water that sat beside the glass once filled with Coca-Cola, and even the water tasted like the nectar of the gods.

Finally, because he was still laughing and it was contagious, she laughed too. Soon, her belly ached she was laughing so hard, but it was an odd sort of ache, one that felt good even when it hurt.

"See, Doc?" he finally said. "You let loose, learn how to laugh at yourself, and life is good. Bet they don't teach you that in medical school."

He was right. Maybe this whole squad thing—

Delaney, Ivy, Casey, and now Ben too—was exactly what she'd been missing in her life. Too bad she couldn't bring the whole squad back home with her when she left California.

"You ever been to New York?" she asked, not sure where she was going with the question, but it just sort of came out.

He shook his head. "Never even stepped foot in L.A. and never been farther east than Carson City. I'm quite happy in my little corner of the world. You like the big city, huh?"

How different their life experiences had been, yet how similar the two of them were. Charlotte spent a semester at Imperial College in London studying biology and had completed a summer internship at a research facility in Rome. She'd seen parts of the world Ben seemingly had no interest in seeing, yet hadn't she done the same thing in settling into her own little corner out east? Aside from still being famished and epically dehydrated, Charlotte was as relaxed in his company as she was with Gran. She wasn't sure she could say that about anyone she knew back in New York.

"I grew up in L.A., which is a big city, but it still has that sunny California vibe. There's a zen to it even when it seems larger than life. New York is gritty and real and loud and perfect. It's everything I never knew I was missing in L.A. But I didn't see that until I accepted that it was home. Then everything sort of clicked into place."

He leaned forward, elbows on the table. "And how about Meadow Valley, Doc? Is it your home away from home? Are things clicking into place on your first day?"

She laughed. "No. But after hanging with three amazing women last night..." She cleared her throat. "Thank you, by the way, for setting that up. Even though it was a less-than-stellar morning after, last night made it easier to admit to myself that I'm here for the long haul and that even though it scares the pants off me, I'm going to be okay."

And maybe this friendship thing with Ben helped too. He'd already proven he had her back by getting her hung-over butt out of bed this morning, which further proved they'd made the right decision to keep things platonic from here on out.

"*Taciturn*!" he shouted, grabbing his pen and scrib-bling down another word. "It was on the tip of my tongue. Whew! Wouldn't have gotten that one without your *rasp*."

Charlotte scoffed. "I give you the closest thing to an emotional outpouring, and you're still doing your cross-word? Also since when are you left-handed?"

Ben slapped his pen on the table and held up his hands. "I was listening, Doc. My eyes were on you the whole time. If we're splittin' hairs here, I guarantee you are much more fun to look at than a bunch of words. But when genius strikes, it strikes without warning."

Charlotte balled up her napkin and tossed it at him, nailing him square in the chin.

He chucked it back—again with his left hand—catching her on the cheek.

"Okay, okay. Truce," she said.

"And to answer your question, I've been a lefty all my life, darlin'. Looks like *you* were the one not paying attention to me." He stole her last piece of bacon and popped half of it in his mouth, even though he had three on his own plate.

"Hey!" she said. "What was that for?" She stole a piece back from him for good measure.

He shrugged. "Every time you break a little piece of my heart, I'm collecting a tax. Being left-handed is part of my identity, and it's painful to know you never noticed."

She opened her mouth to throw a barb back at him, then second-guessed herself.

"Wait, really? If I hurt your feelings—"

He burst into laughter, and she pelted him in the chest with the napkin.

"Wow, Doc," he said between full-on belly laughs. "These next two months are going to be a hell of a lot of fun."

She stewed in her embarrassment, but only for a few seconds. Soon they were eating and chatting like it was something they did every morning. And by the time she finished her last sip of coffee—because one Coke did not equal her daily requirement of caffeine—and *Ben's* last piece of bacon, she'd moved to the chair next to him, the two of them hovered over the crossword puzzle in a race to see who could solve the clues faster. *Not* that anyone was keeping score. Okay, maybe Ben figured out one or two more words faster than she did, but she wasn't going to admit that out loud.

This was good. Comfortable. Nice. A warmth spread through her that hadn't been there the first time around. Sure, the guy was good-looking—drop-dead gorgeous if she was being honest—but he was a good man. Maybe even a better one than she'd initially given him credit for. She was glad she got to see this side of him now. And despite the lingering attraction that was maybe, possibly, still there, she knew now that if they didn't cross that line again, their friendship might even last after these next several weeks.

Sure, that welcoming smile might make her stomach

flip, but it would pass. Her body was simply working from muscle memory. In time it would catch up with her brain, wouldn't it?

"You really saved my butt this morning, Callahan. I owe you one," she finally said.

He grinned that Ben Callahan grin, and she silently willed the butterflies in her belly to stay dormant.

"I'll hold you to it, Doc," he said.

And she hoped he would.

CHAPTER EIGHT

Ben, Sam, and Colt and their horses emerged from the trail into the clearing. The horses whinnied, and Ben knew all three were ready for a snack. So the men hopped down and tied them off at the short expanse of fence they'd installed for this very purpose. Then Ben pulled the bag of apples from his saddle pack and tossed them on the ground for the animals to feast.

A little over a week ago, this had simply been a clearing at the end of a short trail with the abandoned beginnings of a new home. Now it had the potential to be the place where Ben truly started his new life.

"Well," he said to his brother and friend. "This is it. I mean, not *right* here, but down the hill toward the road. The foundation's already there, ready to go. I'm thinking a small stable so I can ride Loki back and forth. And I don't know, three bedrooms? Four? What do you think?"

Sam took his hat off and swiped his forearm across his brow. "Who's going to be sleeping in all those rooms?" his brother asked. "You're going from a guy who only needed a bed—whether it was yours or someone else's—to someone who wants to build what sounds like a family home. I'm just trying to wrap my head around this one-hundred-and-eighty-degree turn you're doing here."

Colt gave Ben's shoulder a good-natured squeeze. "I get it," he said. "When the time is right, I'm going to build a place big enough to be spilling over with kids of my own."

Sam laughed. "I'm assuming there's going to be a woman involved in all this baby-making? Because I can't recall the last time you introduced any of us to—"

Ben backhanded his brother on the upper arm. "Give the guy a break. It's *only* been five years since Emma turned him down. A guy needs at least a decade to get back in the game." He stifled his own laugh.

But Colt shrugged it off. "Dish it out all you want, Callahans. I'm the only one here who has any clue how to commit to a woman, and I sure as hell am not apologizing for taking my time before I do it again."

He had them both there. Colt had proposed to his high school sweetheart after they'd dated for nearly a decade, only to find out she no longer wanted to have children. He respected her choice, but for a guy who grew up bouncing from one foster home to the next—separated from his sister until she was eighteen—it wasn't the life he wanted. He wanted the family he never had and had been holding out for it ever since.

"Hey now," Sam said defensively. "I went all the way to Vegas to tell Delaney I was ready to commit to her. One day—when we're ready—we'll expand my place to include room for a family. But baby steps, Morgan. Give a guy some credit for moving in a new direction." Then he narrowed his eyes at Ben. "But you? I feel like maybe you're taking these steps out of order."

Ben shrugged. "Look. I'm the first to admit I don't know what the hell I'm doing. But I've been going with the flow for so long that I feel like I gotta commit at least to my life here in Meadow Valley, and what better way to do that than with a home?"

Colt raised a brow. "And this has nothing to do with you having coffee with Pearl's granddaughter this morning? Trudy Davis said she saw you two looking pretty cozy in the restaurant. Walked by with one of her dogs."

Sam's eyes widened. "She's leaving again," his brother said. "You get that, right? I'm as happy as you are at the reversal of your test results, but I hope you're not building a home for a woman you barely know who lives on the other side of the country. Because if you are, you're setting yourself up for a world of hurt."

Ben rolled his eyes. "We're just friends," he said. "Don't you think I can be friends with a woman I slept with and not *set myself up for a world of hurt*?" He made finger quotes around the last part.

The other two men burst out laughing, and Ben immediately regretted his decision to tell them anything at all regarding Charlotte or the house. Okay he *had* to discuss the house because he needed their help building it. But the rest was none of their damned business if they didn't think he was capable.

Sam shook his head. "I've got enough on my plate with getting this animal shelter up and running. I'm more than happy to stay out of your personal business, but I hope you're not fooling yourself into believing you can do something you've *never* done before."

Ben groaned. "Look. Now that my future looks a little

brighter than I'd thought, maybe, *someday*, I might be looking for something more real with the right woman. And *maybe* figuring out how to be friends with one will teach me how to do that. If I can commit to a friendship with Doc, a woman I'm attracted to, maybe next time it'll be the real deal."

"Doc, huh?" Colt said. "Nicknames are pretty personal, aren't they? But if you say you won't get attached—or that you aren't already—then I guess you've got this under control."

Ben wasn't going to let their ribbing get to him. What did they know anyway? Sam was in his first serious relationship as an adult, and Colt hadn't really dated in five years. They were no more experts than he was. At least Ben was going to learn how to get it right before he let his heart get involved.

"The land?" he said. "It's at the edge of our property, so technically it could be an extension of the ranch some-day if we wanted. I know we can't all work on building the place at once, but I figured I'd get 'er started, and whenever you have some free time..."

Sam groaned. "Of course I'll help. It's not like I expected you two to live in the guest quarters forever. Guess I figured we had more time before you went all family man on us."

Colt narrowed his eyes. "You sure about this, Calla-han?" he asked Ben. "Because if I say yes, and you start half-assing this job like you've been for the last six months... If you'd have *told* us about the first test results, we'd have cut you some slack, given you time to work through it."

Ben blew out a breath. He'd be pissed off if he hadn't given his brother and friend more than good reason to doubt him. But that was the whole reason for this project. To prove to them—to himself—that he could commit to something. The ranch was all Sam and Colt. Not that horses and ranching weren't in his blood. They were. But Ben would have stayed put in Oak Bluff, running their father's horse boarding business and his and Sam's contracting business on the side. He didn't much care one way or another. But he wanted to care now, wanted to show everyone who thought he was incapable that he could.

"Look," Ben said. "I know I haven't been carrying my weight. And you're right. Maybe I should have said something. It's another thing I don't have much experience with. Maybe you two can school me on, I don't know, speaking up when I'm a mess." But he was climbing his way out. Maybe, in time, he'd have done so on his own. His mother coming back into the picture, even now when their father lived in a memory care facility, would have eventually taught him that no matter how many years were left, they were worthy years. Sam had figured it out. Okay, so maybe he had some help from Delaney. She knew about the possibility of him carrying the gene and somehow made him see that his life had value no matter what the future held.

Ben was starting to realize that not speaking up when he was a mess had done nothing but leave him alone and scared. Maybe everything he was doing now—becoming friends with Charlotte, owning up to his less-than-stellar behavior toward his brother and friend—was a start to him being able to let people in.

HELP. Friend in need. Please respond ASAP.

Ben laughed when he saw the text from Charlotte—
or *Doc* as she was labeled in his contacts. He'd just
gotten out of the shower and was contemplating what
he was going to do with his night off. Usually it meant
heading to Midtown Tavern and ingratiating himself to
a tourist who might be looking for a cowboy to enter-
tain her for the evening. But the urge to do so oddly
wasn't there.

How can I be of service? he wrote back, sitting on the
edge of his bed in nothing but his towel.

Are you alone? she asked. Can I call you? I don't want
to put this in writing. Gran's eyes are everywhere.

Ben laughed before texting back, Sure. His phone rang
a second later.

"What's up, Doc?" he asked with a grin.

She groaned. "How long have you been waiting to use
that line?"

He shrugged, even though she couldn't see him.
"Didn't realize I had it in my arsenal until you called.
So what's this top-secret mission you so desperately need
me for?"

There was a long pause, long enough that he checked
his phone to make sure the call hadn't dropped.

"Doc?" he asked. "You still there?"

"A date," she blurted. "I need you to take me on a date."

This time Ben was the one who was at a loss for words.

"Gran hasn't been home a full two days and is already
on my case about *finding someone* to spend my time with
while I'm here. She thinks if she finds me the right man
that I'll up and leave New York and stay here forever,
even though she knows if I break my contract with my
practice, *no one* will hire me after that. Not to mention
the fact that they treat me really well there, and I could

become a partner physician one day. But that's beside the point." Charlotte's voice dropped to a whisper.

"Why are we whispering?" Ben finally asked.

"Because when Gran told me she had a line of suitors for me and that she was setting me up on my first date *tonight*, I told her I couldn't possibly go out with Ray from the Everything Store because I already had a date tonight—with you. And I don't want her supersonic hearing to let her know that I'm lying. But I don't *have* to be lying if you could maybe, possibly, play along and take me out tonight?"

Ben could actually hear her wince. At least he could sense it. And then something weird happened. Before he even had a chance to process what she'd said, he heard himself saying, "Sure thing, Doc. Didn't have much planned tonight to begin with."

It was only after the words left his mouth that his head flooded with questions.

Is this a real date?

Am I just picking her up and walking her around the corner so Pearl thinks she's on a date?

Why am I nauseous at the thought of Pearl setting her granddaughter up on a date or two?

Why the hell am I overthinking this?

"Really?" she said, breaking the silence. "Ohmygod you're a lifesaver. I so owe you for this."

"Twice," he said. "Now you owe me twice." But he didn't know what else to say after that without launching into his barrage of questions and likely sounding like he was off his rocker.

"Just keep a tab for me, okay?" she asked, and he could hear relief flood her voice. "And this doesn't have be like a *date* date or anything. Gran just needs to believe I'm on a date so she'll let up on the whole setting-me-up thing."

Ben cleared his throat, mentally preparing himself for the next question, yet not sure what he wanted the answer to be. "And what's to keep Pearl from setting you up the next night you have off?"

She sighed. "Maybe after we have such a nice date, I can come home and tell her that...well...that you and I are going to see each other for the duration of my stay? She knows *I'm* not looking for a commitment—as much as she wants me to find one—and she'll have no trouble believing that you'd want to keep things casual. No offense..." She paused.

"None taken," he lied. He got that he was going to have to earn himself a new reputation, but it didn't take the bite out of Charlotte's assumption.

"We'd just have to go out maybe once a week. Or every other week if that's too much. Just enough to convince her that she doesn't have to worry about me and that I'm not interested in her meddling, only in her getting well. As friends, of course. It's not like she'll know what happens on our outings."

It hit him right then and there that friends or not, he didn't want to spend the next several weeks watching her be courted by other guys. If anyone was going to court Charlotte North, it was going to be him.

Holy shit.

How was that for finally being able to commit?

Ben wanted to date her.

Ben wanted to give her a reason to stay.

Ben wanted to prove to her, to Pearl, to everyone, that he really had changed.

"Once a week," he said. "I'll take you out once a week,

and you won't have to worry about having to date anyone else." He paused. "Unless you want to."

"I don't!" she said without hesitation. "I *really* don't. Wow, Ben. You're the best. I don't know what I'd do without you."

"Pick you up in an hour, Doc," he said.

"Thank you!"

And then he ended the call.

One hour. That was all he had to show her he could pull off romantic as hell. He remembered when the fire department once hosted a picnic for the local elementary school, letting the kids climb onto the trucks to eat their sack lunches with a view from the top. All he had to do was call in a favor to Lieutenant Carter Bowen, and Ben could turn a school field trip idea into the most romantic date the good doctor had ever seen.

CHAPTER NINE

Charlotte knew she shouldn't be spying out the window, but she had to make sure Ben didn't give their secret away. And of course Gran was waiting on the porch for his arrival.

"If you're staying for two whole months..." Pearl had said, cornering Charlotte in the kitchen earlier in the morning while she helped the staff prep for the day. "You're not spending that time cooped up at the inn. I may not be able to run things twenty-four-seven by myself, but I can certainly manage enough to give you a little free time every now and then."

Charlotte had opened her mouth to protest, but her grandmother didn't give her a chance.

"Now, Eli Murphy says he still isn't ready to date, per se, but when I told him my granddaughter was all by herself without so much as a friend to share a meal with—"

"*Gran!*" Charlotte said, forcing her way into the conversation. "I *have* friends. Delaney, Ivy, and Casey have already been so welcoming and kind and— You did *not* set me up on a date with a grieving widower. Did you?"

She'd winced at the thought. Poor Eli having to take her on a pity date.

"Colt Morgan who runs the ranch with the Callahan brothers is single too. And *not* grieving. Though I do think there was a broken engagement in his past..."

"Oh. My. God. *Gran.* I came here to take care of you. *Not* to date."

Pearl rocked the lever of her motorized wheelchair back and forth as she let out an exasperated sigh.

"There's also the fire station," she said, as if she hadn't even heard Charlotte. "Your cousin Carter would be happy to introduce you to anyone in his company. And Ray who runs the store is probably free tonight—"

"I'm still dating Ben Callahan!" Charlotte had blurted. "A-and he's taking me out tonight. On a date. As people who date tend to do."

Pearl narrowed her eyes at her granddaughter. "*Still* dating Ben Callahan? I've never known Ben Callahan to *date* anyone. Don't get me wrong, sweetheart. I love those Callahan boys like they are my own flesh and blood, but you *are* my own flesh and blood, which means it's my job to protect you from getting hurt."

Charlotte groaned. "I'm a grown woman and am perfectly capable of protecting myself. Besides, there's something different about Ben since I've been back, and I'd like to get to know him better while I'm here."

That part hadn't been an act. She couldn't put her finger on it, but something had shifted in the man she'd met weeks ago. From him waiting at the hospital during Pearl's surgery to getting her out of bed and on her feet after *way* too much drinking the night before, he'd already made good on the whole friendship thing. And now he was coming to her rescue again.

"You need a man with staying power, and I'm worried that Ben Callahan isn't that man," Pearl had finally said, which made it all the more painful for Charlotte to remind her of the inevitable.

"I can't stay, Gran. You know that."

Now she watched as the man who may or may not have staying power—*not* that it mattered—hopped out of his truck. Tonight, all that mattered to Charlotte was that he'd stepped up to the plate when she'd asked him to. Whatever happened next was gravy.

Ben checked his hair in the side view mirror, and Charlotte laughed softly to herself.

Staying power or no, did Ben Callahan honestly think there was anything he could do to make himself *un*attractive in the physical sense?

Heat spread to her cheeks, and she had to remind herself that this date was a ruse, even if it was sweet to think Ben cared that he looked like he was playing the part of suitor.

She opened the inn's front door a crack, allowing herself to peek *and* listen, because now that she'd committed to spying, what did it matter if she threw in a little eavesdropping?

"Evening, Pearl," Ben said as he strode up the steps. "How's that new cast treating you?"

Her grandmother's silver hair sat in a long braid over her right shoulder, her right arm in a sling. A blanket covered her legs, one of which Charlotte knew was covered in plaster from the knee down. A warmth spread through her at Ben not only knowing that she'd been given a plaster cast after surgery but at him caring enough to ask how she was doing.

Pearl tugged at the blanket with her good hand so her toes and green cast peeked out.

"It itches like the dickens, and even though the pain isn't so bad, doctor still says no weight on it for six weeks. I love this inn, Ben, but being trapped here puts a whole new spin on things."

He bent down and kissed her on the cheek. "How about I take you for a spin tomorrow afternoon. Got the morning shift at the ranch but should be free around two o'clock."

"Let me check my mental calendar." She paused, and Charlotte wished she could see her grandmother's expression. "Yep. I'm free," she said.

"Then it's a date," Ben replied, and those stupid butterflies began dancing in Charlotte's belly.

It's an act for Gran, she reminded herself. *Ben's a good guy, but he's going overboard to sell our story. He's a good friend, but that's all this is.*

"Not so fast," Pearl said, wrapping a hand around his wrist. "I have some questions for you."

Charlotte winced.

Here we go.

"Ask away," he said. "I'm an open book." He sat down next to her on the porch swing.

"Excuse me for sounding a little old-fashioned, but are your intentions with my granddaughter genuine?" she asked.

Charlotte froze.

Ben raised a brow. "How do you mean?"

She slapped him gently on the knee. "You know I love you, your brother, and Colt like you're my own grandsons, but Charlotte's different. I'm closer with her than I am with my own daughter, and she's putting her whole life on hold for me. I'd love to give her a reason to consider Meadow Valley her home, but she's fighting me every step of the way. And please don't take this the wrong way, honey, but I don't see you being the one to do that. I just don't want to see her get attached to the wrong man."

Charlotte's heart squeezed. It was hard to be angry when she heard the tenderness in her grandmother's voice. She loved Pearl, loved Meadow Valley even, but she'd created a stable life for herself in New York. She'd committed to her practice. In *writing*. She'd committed to *science*, the most stable thing in her life. Science didn't thrust you into a life of uncertainty. Science didn't pull the rug out from under you and send your parents halfway across the globe—or your grandfather six feet underground.

And Ben... Say what you will about his past track record. She could see something different in him, even if Pearl couldn't. It didn't mean he was going to sweep her off her feet and then break her heart. They were in this together. They were friends. They could make *certain* they didn't blur those lines.

Ben rocked back and forth on his heels a couple times.

"Here's the thing," he finally said. "Remember summers when you were a teen?"

Pearl laughed. "Darlin', I barely remember *last* summer, and that was only a few months ago."

Ben leaned forward, his elbows on his knees. "I know it's autumn, and soon it'll be winter, but this thing with me and Charlotte, it's like those summers when we were sixteen, seventeen, eighteen. As soon as school's out, you know the first day of the new school year is just around the corner, but you ignore it and live each and every day like summer's never coming to an end." He wrapped his palms around Pearl's good hand and squeezed. "I like spending time with your granddaughter, and I'm pretty sure she likes spending time with me. Sure, she has a life in New York, but right now, it feels like anything is possible, and we just want to enjoy the time we have."

Charlotte's throat tightened. Who just *said* something like that off the cuff and made it sound so sincere? This was too much. Her emotions were getting the best of her, and Charlotte prided herself on keeping those in check, on keeping herself safe.

Pearl slid her hand from his gentle grip and patted his knee.

"I believe you mean well, Ben. I also believe my granddaughter can take care of herself and is certainly capable of making her own decisions."

Charlotte snorted, then covered her mouth. If Gran truly believed that, she wouldn't have tried to set Charlotte up with every eligible bachelor in town. And now poor Ben was getting the third degree because Pearl didn't believe *he* was eligible.

"It helps knowing she has someone on her team if things at the inn—or taking care of her old gran—get to be too much. But it doesn't mean I don't worry," Pearl added.

He nodded once. "Fair enough."

Pearl cleared her throat. "I wasn't finished."

Ben remained silent.

"Don't hurt her," she said bluntly. "That's all I ask."

"You have my word," he said.

And Charlotte bought the whole thing—hook, line, and

sinker—even though she knew it was fake. That meant Pearl would, too, right?

Ben was a better actor than Charlotte anticipated. A tiny voice in her head whispered how nice it would be for someone to talk about her like that for real. But *this* trip to Meadow Valley wasn't about Charlotte, so she told that little voice to keep quiet and let her focus on why she was here in the first place—her grandmother.

Pearl let out a bitter laugh. "That's what my husband said once upon a time, and then he went back on his word. I'm still working on forgiving him for that."

"I'd have liked to have met Mr. Sweeney," Ben said. "I know he was a good man."

She nodded. "As good as they come," she said. "So is our chief. Guess I'm a lucky woman, finding love twice."

Charlotte quietly clicked the door shut. She couldn't listen anymore, not if she was going to collect herself and make it look like she hadn't just violated both Ben's and Gran's privacy to the extent of almost bringing herself to tears.

I am not *going to fall for Ben Callahan.*

If she said it enough times, it would be true, right?

Ben rolled his shoulders like he was about to walk into one of his high school wrestling matches. Except Charlotte wasn't an opponent. She was his date. He spun toward the door and raised his hand to knock, then remembered this was a public establishment and he could walk inside any time he pleased.

So he did.

There she was, behind the front desk, talking to Tyler.

"Make sure you give this couple a champagne reception." She pointed at the screen of Tyler's open laptop.

"And this group arrives late morning. They're traveling all the way from Florida—a knitting retreat. Prep the kitchen staff if anything changes. Otherwise they're extending breakfast an hour so there's a hot meal when they get here. They're going to need something besides airplane food."

She spoke as if she'd been running the place for years instead of just under a week. Well color Ben Callahan impressed. Not that he expected any less of her. After all, she did save lives for a living. For someone who loved city life, she took to country living like a cowboy to the ranch.

"You got it, boss," Tyler said.

Ben cleared his throat, and Charlotte's eyes flicked up to meet his.

Her auburn hair hung pin straight at her shoulders. Her lips were painted bright red and parted in a smile that knocked the wind straight out of his chest.

He plastered on his easy grin. "Evening, Doc," he said, hoping to hide his reaction. "You look . . . Wow."

Her cheeks flushed, and Tyler made a point to avoid eye contact with either of them, focusing instead on the laptop monitor.

"I didn't know what the dress code was for the evening," she said, emerging from behind the counter. "And I figure I won't have too many occasions to get all gussied up while I'm here, so I took advantage of the opportunity. I hope that's okay."

She spun slowly, the skirt of her blue and white polka-dot dress twirling above her knees. The top of the dress fit snug against her torso, hugging her curves in all the right places. What really did it, though, was that she topped the look off with a short denim jacket and a pair of well-worn cowboy boots.

"Very New York," he said. Then his gaze trailed down the length of her body to the boots. "And very country."

She curtsied. "Why thank you, kind sir. That's exactly the look I was going for."

Everything about the look worked so well, he had to remind himself that she hadn't actually done all her gussying for *him*. It was for Pearl. All of this was for Pearl.

He held out his arm, and she linked hers right through it. She felt so familiar next to him and yet so entirely new. He wasn't sure what to make of it other than him being utterly clueless about how tonight would go. Usually he simply turned on the charm, and the night went straight to the bedroom. But starting the evening off knowing the bedroom was the last place he and the good doctor would end up meant he was up a creek without his most trusted paddle.

"Good night, Tyler," Charlotte said over her shoulder. "You have my mobile number in case of an emergency."

"No worries, boss," the younger man said. "It's all under control."

They stopped short just before stepping back out onto the front porch because through the windowed door they could see Chief Burnett outside leaning over to give Pearl a kiss on the cheek.

"We should probably give them a moment," Ben said.

Charlotte nodded, then tugged him to her right so they were just out of view of the front desk.

"You know," she said. "If this were a real date, you could greet a girl like that if you wanted to."

His eyes widened. "Is that so?"

She nodded. "I mean, you'd have to read the signs, see if the woman was open to it." She unthreaded her arm from his and clasped her hands in front of her.

Ben crossed his arms. "And how would I know if she was open to it?"

Charlotte shrugged. "She might be demure, like this." She smiled sweetly, averting her eyes, and turned her cheek toward him.

He laughed softly. "*You* would never do that, Doc."

She groaned and rolled her eyes. "Yeah, well, if you ever come to pick me up and Pearl is, I don't know, eavesdropping and/or spying, we might want to sell it better. Just in case."

He narrowed his eyes. "Who would eavesdrop *and/ or* spy?"

Charlotte's cheeks flushed. "No one, of course!" she protested. "I'm just saying that if we were afraid that *might* happen, we might have to take our little act to the next level."

Ookaaay.

"Doc..." He cleared his throat. "Are you suggesting we kiss right now for your grandmother's sake?"

She worried her bottom lip between her teeth, then let out a nervous laugh.

"No. Of course not. Not right now. I mean, if Gran were right here next to me, I wouldn't be *angry* if you did. To sell it."

He leaned closer to her and inhaled. The scent reminded him of his childhood, of the time their parents took Ben and Sam to pick oranges at a local grove, and he found it hard to pull away.

"Something innocent like this?" he said, then his lips brushed across her cheek. "You look lovely tonight, by the way."

Her cheek felt warm against his mouth. And being so close to *her* mouth made his throat dry and tied his gut into knots. But he pulled away because anything more than this would give him away.

Ben could play along. She didn't need to know that he *wanted* to kiss her. Or that he'd said things to Pearl outside he'd never say to Charlotte's face for fear of freaking her out and making her realize she'd made a huge mistake thinking she could be simply friends with him.

She cleared her throat and brushed off her skirt, not that there was anything to brush. "Yep. Great. Just like that. And look. Gran and the chief are leaving. That means if any spying did occur, we likely passed the test."

Her words came out clipped and a little breathless, and it took everything in him not to gloat. Or maybe it was that his pulse had quickened, too, and gloating might be slightly hypocritical. He could pretend he wasn't still wildly attracted to her, but his increased heart rate said otherwise.

He glanced out the window to see Pearl talking, her good arm punctuating her words with animated gestures, and the chief laughing as he slowly pushed her chair down the porch's ramp.

Ben strode back to the door and held it open for Charlotte. "After you."

"Such a gentleman," she said as she walked through.

He followed her out. "Just so you know, I'd have held the door for you whether this was a date or not. I do have a *few* polished edges."

She looked over her shoulder before heading down the stairs. "And just so *you* know, women can open doors too. We're not all damsels in need of saving."

He shook his head and laughed. If there was one thing he was sure of, it was that Charlotte North was completely capable of saving herself should the occasion arise.

She walked right up to his truck, then burst out laughing when he left her standing at the unopened passenger door and rounded the cab so he could hop into the driver's seat.

She climbed in next to him, and he bit back a grin.

"Touché, cowboy."

He shrugged. "You want to open your own doors. Who am I to stop you?"

She buckled her seat belt and turned to him with a grin. "So, where are you taking me?"

Ben made a quick U-turn, drove one block, then parallel parked in front of the Meadow Valley fire station.

"We're here," he said. "Need help with that door?"

CHAPTER TEN

W e're...*where*?" Charlotte asked.

She'd expected him to take her to Midtown Tavern, the only place other than the inn where you could order food off a menu—even if it was pub fare. Sure, she'd dressed up to make this look real, and maybe Ben had done the same, but once Pearl and the chief left the inn, Charlotte and Ben could have simply wandered down the street to the tavern to do what they both would have done separately anyway. Instead, he'd actually *planned* something?

"Should I have eaten before you picked me up?" she asked. "Because I've been at it with the inn since sunup, and I don't think I've had more than a cup of coffee and a banana. So I should just warn you that when I get hangry, I kind of lose my filter and say things I shouldn't."

He laughed. "As much as I'd like to see what that looks like, there's plenty of food involved tonight—as long as Meadow Valley has no major emergencies."

He leaned over, one hand braced on the edge of

her seat while the other reached across her torso. For a second, he was so close she thought he might kiss her for real this time, not just that sweet peck on the cheek that had still sent her mind off to places it shouldn't go. Her belly flip-flopped, and she held her breath only for him to open her door from the inside.

"It's a compromise," he said, straightening. "I get to be a little chivalrous, and you get to exit the vehicle on your own accord."

She exhaled. "Compromise. Right. Okay." *Come on, Charlotte. Full sentences. You're not going to let a little chivalry get to you.* "You still haven't explained why we're not at Midtown or having Pearl's kitchen staff cook us dinner. Once she and the chief were gone, we could have even gone our separate ways." Though she wouldn't admit out loud that she was relieved they hadn't.

He scoffed, the gesture exaggerated. "You think I'd say yes to taking you on a date and feed you what you eat every day? Or worse, *not* take you out at all? I didn't know you thought so little of me, Doc."

Her mouth hung open for a second. "I'm...I'm sorry," she stammered. "I wasn't insinuating you weren't good for your word."

"Seems to be a touch of that going around," he said. "People not sure to trust me at my word."

Her heart sank. She'd hurt his feelings, or his pride at least.

He hopped out of the vehicle, so she did the same, meeting him in front of the cab.

"Ben, I really didn't mean..."

He waved her off and plastered on his most charming grin, but she could still see the flicker of pain in his blue eyes.

"You ever picnicked on top of a fire engine under the stars?" he asked.

Her eyes widened. "Is that allowed?"

He held out a hand, and she threaded her fingers through his. Again her belly did that flipping thing. She'd have to explain to it later that this was nothing more than Ben doing her a favor and her going along for the ride.

"It is when you're friends with the lieutenant—and his girlfriend helps get everything together on an hour's notice. Ivy would kill me if I didn't give credit where credit was due."

"You did all this for me? Simply because I asked you to?"

He winked. "What are friends for?" he asked.

Right. *Friends.* But he'd pulled out all the stops when he didn't have to, which made this one of the most romantic dates she'd ever been on, and it had only just begun. Even if it wasn't real, Charlotte could still enjoy the effort he went to. She could still feel a *little* special, couldn't she?

She bit her lip and grinned. Screw it. Even if the effort wasn't truly for *her*, Charlotte was going to enjoy herself.

"Thanks...friend," she said. "And I will be sure to thank Ivy for her help tomorrow," Charlotte said.

Ben led her onto the fire house's property, but instead of heading for the main doors, he pulled her around the corner to where a bright red engine sat parked outside.

"Wow," Charlotte said. "That thing is huge. I've never seen one up close."

Ben gave her hand a squeeze. "Now that's what a man likes to hear."

She laughed and backhanded him on the shoulder. "Do all grown men still have the sense of humor of a thirteen-year-old?"

He nodded. "Every single one of us."

On the back of the engine was a small set of stairs leading to the top, but the stairs themselves were a good two and a half feet off the ground. In tennis shoes and jeans, it would have been no problem. But she'd gone and gotten gussied up, and while she was glad for the reaction it had elicited from Ben, she was not dressed for climbing.

After standing and staring at the engine's rear for long enough, Ben finally broke the silence.

"Something tells me you might need some assistance. Would it be all right if I provided said assistance?"

Ugh. She never should have made the comment about opening her own door.

She groaned. "Yes, Ben. I might be in need of some assistance."

Looking at it now, she swore that small set of stairs was a full *three* feet off the ground. And once up there, it didn't lead all the way to the top of the truck. She'd have to do some jumping or shimmying or some other maneuver where she had a very good chance of winding up with her rear end hanging out of her dress.

He unthreaded his fingers from hers and crossed his arms. "You want me on top or bottom?" he asked with a devilish grin.

She shook her head. "You really are just an adolescent child in a grown man's body, aren't you?"

He arched his brows. "What's it going to be?"

She weighed her options. If he went up first and helped her from above, she had the best chance of her dress keeping her covered, but if she fell... well, there'd be no one to catch her. If she went up first, he'd be getting quite the view, but he'd also catch her if she lost her footing.

"I'll go up first," she finally said, realizing it wasn't him sneaking a peek that had her tied up in knots. It wasn't anything he hadn't seen before. It was that this date that wasn't a real date *felt* like a real date. And she wasn't sure if that thrilled her or made her want to run for the hills. Right now the only place she could run was up the ladder of a very large fire engine.

"Note to self," Ben said, perfectly clear so she could hear. "The lady likes it on top."

She didn't dignify his comment with any sort of a response but instead approached the four stairs that started three feet off the ground. There was a railing, but it only extended as low as the second stair so that when she grabbed it, her arm was fully extended, leaving her practically dangling with only the toes of her boots left on the ground.

"May I?" Ben asked from behind her. Then he pulled the skirt of her dress against her thighs and wrapped his arms around her knees so that she was basically using his shoulder as a chair.

She laughed nervously as he set her down with ease on the first step.

"Wow. Kind of felt like I was the cheerleader on top of the pyramid." She glanced over her shoulder at him. Forget climbing the engine. Ben Callahan's easy smile could knock her on her butt at any second.

Run for the hills, Charlotte.

But she was sort of stranded now.

"Still got the uniform?" he teased.

She made it to the small landing at the top of the four steps and managed to hoist herself onto the vehicle's roof.

Ben was next to her in seconds flat, hopping onto the rig as easily as he hopped onto the back of a horse.

"I wasn't *actually* a cheerleader," she told him.

He gestured toward the front of the vehicle and helped her maneuver her way to where a red-and-white plaid blanket lay over the unencumbered area above the cab. On top of the blanket sat two pillows that looked like they were stolen from a couple of deck chairs, a picnic basket, and a bottle of wine chilling in a bucket of ice.

"Let me guess," he said, holding her hand as she lowered herself onto one of the pillows before taking the spot next to her, their backs against the cab. "A dancer? Color guard? Oh! Maybe marching band? Had a crush on a flute player back in the day."

She spread her skirt over her knees and looked him straight in the eye. In those stupidly beautiful, long-lashed blue eyes.

"Not a cheerleader. Not a dancer. Not anything involved in football games or basketball games or whatever. I never actually went to any of my high school's athletic events."

He was in the middle of removing the bottle of wine from the bucket and stopped short.

"Not *one*." He said it more like a statement than a question.

She shook her head, and because he wasn't moving things along, grabbed the wine from him. Thankfully, it was a screw top—a sparkling rosé with a label that read CROSSROADS VINEYARD from Oak Bluff, California. She'd heard of the town but didn't know it had a winery.

"I know I said I'd never drink again, but that was then, and you said it yourself—famous last words." She could use a little liquid courage to settle her nerves. So she unscrewed the top and searched their limited surroundings for something in which to pour the bubbly.

Ben flipped open the basket and produced two red Solo cups.

"Classy," she teased.

"Nothing but the best for you, Doc."

She poured them each what she hoped was the equivalent of *one* glass of wine and set the bottle back in the bucket.

She took a sip and waited for the bubbles to spread through her, then let out a long breath. She glanced up at the star-studded sky on this beautiful night and allowed it all to sink in. The date that wasn't a date that sure as hell felt like a date. And the nickname. Ugh, the nickname she tried to get him to stop saying that he made a term of their friendship.

"Sorry," he said, breaking the silence. "I will try to get used to the whole *Charlotte* thing if that's really what you want. Old habits die hard, I guess."

She shook her head, not sure what was more unsettling—that he was practically reading her thoughts or that she *didn't* want him to break the habit.

"It's not that. I mean it is, but...no one has ever given me a nickname before," she said. "Not even my parents. And I guess *maybe* I like it? I mean, it's kind of sweet. Something that's just for me—unless, of course, you call all the girls *Doc*, in which case the joke's on me."

He knocked the bottom of his cup against hers. "Nope. You are and have been the only *Doc* in my life. Can I ask though? Does becoming the doc that you are have anything to do with missing four years of athletic events in high school?"

She rolled her eyes. "It's not like athletics is the be-all and end-all of school experience."

He raised a brow. "True. So...debate team? Model UN? You weren't some hermit, were you?"

Her pulse quickened. They hadn't done this before, this getting to know each other. Talking about personal stuff.

"Why do you want to know about my uninteresting teen years?" she asked, trying to sound breezy.

He shrugged. "I'm a little inexperienced, but isn't that how this friend thing works? You tell me stuff about you...I tell you stuff about me. Come to think of it, it's really not as complicated as I thought."

Right. Friends. He was really good at reminding her of what she was beginning to forget.

Her stomach tightened. This wasn't the carefree cowboy she met when she first came to town—before Gran got hurt. He was someone else entirely, someone she was starting to care about as a friend. Or more. She didn't know and didn't want to think about it because either way she could feel herself getting attached, and this was a really sweet date that he didn't have to take her on and *ugh*. Why couldn't she just enjoy it?

Charlotte sighed. "I never made it to a football game or basketball game or school play or Model UN or any big event because I was too busy with my club, Future Medical Professionals of America," she said.

His brows drew together. "I didn't know there was such a club, but then again, I went to a pretty small high school. We just had the basics."

She let out a nervous laugh. "We didn't exactly have such a club either. I founded it, convinced my biology teacher to sponsor it, and it was basically six of us who got together and did medical research."

"For...fun?" Ben asked. While there was no judgment in his tone, she could tell he was holding something back. A laugh? A pitiful grin for her missing out on what he thought was the crux of the high school experience?

She nodded, desperately wanting to drain her Solo cup before she continued, but she kept herself from doing it. Maybe she had missed out—on connecting with people, on sharing her hopes and her fears—but the trade-off had been worth it, hadn't it? She was good at what she did—really good—and her patients were better for it. And even though she technically wasn't practicing medicine in Meadow Valley, who better to take care of Gran during her recovery than Charlotte?

"Kind of?" she admitted. "My grandfather had one other heart attack before the one that . . . you know."

Ben nodded but let her continue.

"I love my parents. Don't get me wrong. But he and Gran were different. They were nurturing in a way my parents weren't, a way I needed. Life always felt safer with them. More stable. Anyway, when we first found out about Gramps's heart condition, I learned all I could about it to make sure he was doing everything possible to stay healthy." She let out a nervous laugh. "I know he had doctors looking out for him, but they didn't care about him like *I* did. They didn't love him." Her throat grew tight, and she stopped to collect herself.

"Doc," Ben said. "It's okay. You don't have to say any more."

But she shook her head. "I like talking about him. It's just hard sometimes." She paused. "Okay. *All* the time."

"Can't say I know loss like that," Ben said. He knocked his shoulder softly against hers. "So keep going if you want, but stop if it's too much, okay?"

She nodded and swallowed the lump in her throat that was only partly for Gramps. The other part had a cowboy's name written all over it, a cowboy she wasn't expecting when she came back to Meadow Valley—at least, not this version of him.

"There's not much more to say. The first heart attack was a shock because Gramps was pretty fit. The second one happened when he overdid it on a hike, trying to be even healthier. By the time the ambulance arrived at the hospital, he was gone. I started my little medical club at school two weeks later."

Ben set his hand gently on Charlotte's knee.

She cleared her throat and straightened her shoulders, blinking a few times to will the tears away.

"I knew then that medicine was the only choice of career for me. I thought I'd go into cardiology, but when I did my peds rotation, I realized that working with kids would be like hitting the ground running, you know? Teach them healthy habits when they're young and give them the best shot at growing old."

And because she didn't know what else to say after that, she let the rosé ease the ache of the memory—and the mild panic about having just shared all of that with Ben.

She stared straight ahead, afraid that if she made eye contact she might actually come undone. And Charlotte didn't know how to do undone, nor did she want to scare off her new friend who'd taken her on such a lovely date—that wasn't a date.

She nibbled on the rim of the Solo cup once it was empty.

Ben's hand hadn't moved from her knee.

"My father's been living with early-onset Alzheimer's for several years now. I'm sure you remember when we briefly lost him during the fall festival. When he first got sick, none of us knew what was happening and it messed everything up. His job. His marriage. And eventually his ability to care for himself. Sam and I made a deal that we were just going to live our lives and not get tested to see if we had the gene. I convinced myself that I was going to enjoy the ride until it was my turn to get off, but a little over six months ago, I went to visit our father, and he had no idea who I was. Things got heated, and he had me thrown out of the facility, claiming I was there to steal his identity. Never told my brother about it, but it scared me enough that I went and got tested for the gene. The results were positive." He let out a bitter laugh. "I thought his future was *my* future. So naturally I turned into even more of a prick than I already was. But the joke was on me."

He laughed again, but there was a bitterness to it, and Charlotte finally turned to face him, absently placing her hand over his.

His eyes were dark and his jaw tight, which was more emotion—more *real* emotion—than she'd seen since she'd met him. She wasn't prepared for this, not tonight and maybe not ever. Charlotte could deal with facts and figures without missing a beat, but *feelings*? Feelings were messy, and they were supposed to keep this neat and tidy, weren't they?

So she did her best to mask her expression, to remain professional like she would when talking to any patient—or in her case, often the parents of patients. This was why she was good at her job. She learned to distance herself from the emotion of it. Gran had caught her by surprise. Even after spending the entire cross-country plane ride talking herself out of reacting emotionally, Charlotte wasn't prepared for seeing Pearl in that hospital bed, bruised and bandaged and connected to an IV.

She wanted to tell Ben that everything would be okay—something she never did—even though she knew it wouldn't. These were her emotions talking, and they made no sense. Charlotte liked sense. She *needed* sense. Which meant she had to remind herself about the safety of distance even when a person was close enough to touch. And kiss.

"But it's *not* your future?" she asked, confused.

He shook his head. "For six months I was convinced it was—until I went with Sam to get his results and found out there was *another* Benjamin Callahan in Plumas County being tested for the same thing."

Her jaw fell open. So much for keeping her cool. "They gave you the *wrong* results?"

He raised his brows and then nodded.

"Okay. That's it." She scooted herself to better face him and pulled her skirt over her legs so she could cross them. "This is no longer a date. It's a celebration." She peered into his empty cup, then tapped hers against his. "Bartender—another round for me and my friend." Then, heeding her own request, grabbed the bottle of bubbly and emptied the rest of it into their cups.

He laughed, and she let out a relieved breath. She could handle a smiling Ben, especially when it was directed at her.

"To Ben Callahan," she said, holding her cup high. "May he get all that he wants out of this amazing second chance now that he's healthy as a horse."

He raised his glass as well. "And to Charlotte *Doc* North." He winked, and something fluttered in her belly. "May her time here be well spent and in the company of good friends, and may her grandmother refrain from any and all matchmaking from here on out."

She snorted, then gasped, but Ben just kept on grinning. Good *Lord* that grin.

"Cheers to *that*!" she said, tapping plastic against plastic, wondering if in another time and place, she might have already met her match.

She tilted her head toward the star-speckled sky and downed the effervescent liquid, willing it to go straight to her head, to cloud thoughts she certainly shouldn't be thinking.

They slammed their empty cups down in unison.

Charlotte hiccupped.

Ben gave her a pointed look. "Why do we say that, anyway? Healthy as a horse."

The night air was cool and crisp against her cheeks, but inside Charlotte bubbled over with warmth.

"Horses are remarkably healthy animals," she said. "They eat well, exercise often, and are sociable creatures, which is great for mental health. And a healthy mind helps promote a healthy body." Heat rushed to her cheeks. "Sorry. That was Dr. Charlotte talking to one of her six-year-old patients. Sometimes it's hard to turn it off."

Ben grinned, and his shoulders relaxed. "I'd love to see you at work. I bet you're great with those mini humans."

She snorted *again* and silently cursed the rosé for working *too* well, then covered her mouth in embarrassment. She shook her head and laughed. He'd already seen her at her worst two mornings in a row this week. What was a little snort after that?

"I'm great with kids," she admitted. "Way better with them than grown-ups."

He shrugged. "You seem to be doing okay with me, and I'm *almost* a grown-up."

She smiled at him. "You should give yourself more credit than you do."

"And *I* should really give you some food," he teased, knocking his knee against hers.

Her pulse quickened.

A flash of heat rushed through her. Why was this man—

this night—making her so nervous? It was like she'd lost control of her body's reaction to his touch, his teasing, and just the close proximity of him.

"I'm famished," she admitted, then lifted one of the picnic basket flaps, and he gave her hand a playful smack.

"Hey. I worked hard letting Ivy help me put this together." He gave her a mischievous grin. "At least let me surprise you with what's in there before you go grabbing at everything like a toddler in a candy store."

He opened the basket to reveal two foil-wrapped sandwiches, a container of what looked like potato salad, and another that *definitely* looked like dark-chocolate-covered strawberries.

Charlotte's mouth watered, and it took everything in her not to inhale the entire contents of that basket—and maybe the basket itself.

"Ivy said these were her favorite. She snuck them out of the inn's café thanks to Val. She snuck everything out, actually. I can't take credit for much more than getting the food here unharmed."

He handed Charlotte one of the sandwiches, and she unwrapped it like it was the first present from under the tree on Christmas morning.

"PB and J and *Brie*?" she exclaimed, and then the crispy corner of the grilled sourdough bread was already in her mouth. "Oh my *God*," she said as her teeth sank into the sandwich, her favorite of her grandmother's recipes. She swallowed her first bite and licked a warm glob of peanut butter from the corner of her mouth. "It doesn't matter how many times I try to make this back in New York. It never tastes the same as when it comes from the Meadow Valley Inn kitchen."

Ben hadn't even taken a bite of his yet. He'd unwrapped it but was just staring at it, brow furrowed.

"Looking at it is fun," Charlotte said. "But you're not going to mouthgasm without tasting it."

Ben met her gaze, his expression still wary. "But it's peanut butter, jam...and *cheese*."

She rolled her eyes. "It's not like it's nacho cheese. It's *Brie*. And Brie goes amazingly well with something sweet." She broke off a gooey piece of her own sandwich and pinched it between her thumb and forefinger. "Do you trust me?" she asked. And when he opened his mouth to reply, she popped her shared piece of heaven between his lips, a shiver running through her as her thumb swiped the tip of his tongue.

Charlotte snatched her hand back as Ben's eyes widened and then fell shut. He let out a deep moan—which sent *another* shiver from the tops of her ears to the tips of her toes.

She blew out a shaky breath. "See?" she said, fighting to maintain composure while Gran's tried-and-true favorite suddenly felt a little less wholesome. Maybe she shouldn't have used the word—

"Mouthgasm," Ben said after swallowing his bite. "You weren't kidding, Doc."

She stuffed a big hunk of said mouthgasm past her lips and nodded, figuring she'd better refrain from speaking until she wasn't thinking about a certain cowboy's tongue touching her thumb or the countless places that tongue had been weeks before but wouldn't be going any longer because friends didn't do those sorts of things and...and...*Why* did he have to take her on such a sweet date and be such a sweet and vulnerable guy behind that playful exterior? He made it too easy for her to open up too. Everything about being with him was easy. And *that* was terrifying.

It looked like he'd taken the hint because they ate in silence after that, polishing off every last crumb of their sandwiches along with the container of potato salad until Charlotte was sure she was going to give birth to a food baby at any second.

"Save the strawberries?" Ben asked.

She nodded. "You read my mind. Funny how quickly hangry turns into food coma."

He laughed. "How about we pack up and I walk you home? It's not too cold, stars are out, and the inn's practically across the street."

"That sounds nice," she said. "And an awful lot like something a couple would do on a real date."

He shrugged. "This kind of has been a real date, hasn't it? I picked you up, bought you a free dinner, made you a picnic under the stars. Even if we're only doing this for Pearl, there's no reason not to end it with a quiet walk home. Hell, I might even let you hold my hand if you play your cards right."

Only doing this for Pearl.

Had her flashes of heat and chills been one-sided all night? Maybe she needed to take her temperature when she got back to the inn. She could be coming down with a bug and confusing that for feelings that were highly inconvenient.

"Or we could take the truck," he said when she still hadn't responded. "I didn't mean to step over any invisible boundaries, Doc."

She brushed crumbs off her skirt and rose to her knees. If he could play it cool, then so could she. "No. Sorry. I spaced out there for a minute. Let's walk back. That'll be nice. Not sure about the hand-holding thing though," she teased. At least she hoped it sounded like teasing. She couldn't tell anymore.

She climbed down the engine's ladder first, getting down a bit easier than she got up. When they made it out to First Street, it was quiet and dark save for the few streetlamps.

"Wait until you see this place come Christmas," Ben said as they crossed the street and headed toward the inn.

"The holiday light parade?" Charlotte asked, remembering when she was a kid and her parents still came with her on trips to see her grandparents. On Christmas Eve, every storefront on First Street would turn on their holiday decorations in quick succession, sending a ripple of light up from the bookshop all the way to the town hall in the village square. "Wow. I haven't seen that since I was maybe ten years old."

Ben shoved his hands in the front pockets of his jeans. "That's right," he said. "I keep forgetting that you probably know this place better than I do."

"It's fun," she admitted. "Seeing it through your eyes."

He placed a hand on the small of her back as they crossed the street to the inn. It was nothing more than a light touch, a small gesture from one friend to another, yet she still held her breath until they reached the curb on the other side of the street.

He threaded his fingers through hers as they approached the steps that led to the inn's front porch.

"In case we have an audience," he whispered when she stared down at their interlaced hands.

"Right," she said, heat coursing through her veins. "Good move."

But what would his next move be? Would there *be* a next

move? How should she react if there was? Then she spotted Pearl through the window in the door and decided someone had to make a move soon or risk blowing their cover.

"Gran!" she whisper-shouted, nodding her head in the same direction. "She's right inside. We should play this whole good-bye part up, you know? For her sake." *And maybe for mine.*

Ben raised a brow. "Are you suggesting a kiss good night, Doc?"

She smiled nervously. "Would...you...be open to such a thing?"

"For *Pearl*," he said.

She nodded. "Of course. For Pearl." She wasn't sure what frightened her more—if he went for it or if he rejected her.

"Actually," he said, "if this *had* been a real date, I'd have had the good night kiss all planned out. Would you like to hear how it would have gone?"

She nodded, feeling light-headed.

He stepped past her and over to the porch swing, where he sat down and patted the spot next to him.

She peeked back inside the inn and saw Gran still sitting in her wheelchair, talking to Tyler at the front desk. She was *definitely* checking up on them, and Charlotte wasn't ready to walk in there and tell a bold-faced lie to her beloved grandmother, not when she'd already lied through her teeth about the date in the first place.

Charlotte took no pleasure in deceiving the woman but also didn't want to spend the next seven weeks dodging her grandmother's attempts at securing her betrothal to the next available Meadow Valley suitor she could find. So she followed Ben to the swing and sat beside him, heart thumping in her chest.

"We were going to sit here, laugh at the drunk folks stumbling out of Midtown, and then I'd come up with something really romantic to say..."

"Like *what*?" Charlotte blurted.

He turned toward her and tucked a lock of red hair behind her ear, his blue eyes intent on hers.

"I'd say something like...Doc, I thought you were beautiful the moment I met you over at the stable, but I didn't know then what I know now."

"Which is what?" she asked, her throat suddenly dry.

"That I envy you. How selfless you are to come here and do what you're doing for Pearl. That I can learn a lot about becoming a better man from the good woman that you already are and have probably always been."

She swallowed. "Ben, I—"

He raised a brow. "I wasn't done."

She made a motion of zipping her lips, terrified yet desperate to hear what he said next.

"I'd wrap your skirt around your legs and then pull them over my knees like this." He demonstrated, and now she was sitting perpendicular to him, her knees over his, and her heart ready to burst from her chest or stop beating altogether.

How was it that only weeks ago she was fine knowing nothing more about this man than what it was like to sleep naked pressed up against him. For the record, it was really, *really* nice. But now she found herself fantasizing about what would happen after they woke up together the next morning. Would they indulge their physical needs and then go their separate ways like they'd done before, or would they linger with their legs entwined as he peppered her neck with soft kisses and told her about his hopes and dreams?

"And then," he continued, bringing her back to the

moment, "I'd tell you that I never talked to anyone before the way I talked to you tonight. That you make me feel seen in a way no one ever has before. That maybe I *can* be better at this whole grown-up thing if you believe I can."

Her eyes widened, and her breath caught in her throat. Didn't he see what a good man he already was and maybe had always been? She wanted to tell him, wanted to *show* him, and that was when all thinking went out the window.

She grabbed his shirt collar in her hands and tugged him toward her, her lips crashing against his.

This was the only way to keep her from admitting to him that this didn't feel like a game or playing pretend. It didn't feel like they were doing this to appease Pearl so that she wouldn't worry about Charlotte for the time she was here. Every touch of his lips against hers simply felt *right*.

She parted her lips, and he slipped his tongue inside, and she could have sworn it was the Fourth of July instead of the preface to a California winter.

He slid his hand up her thigh, and a chill rocked through her all the way to her bones.

"You're freezing," he said, and she only pulled him closer.

Logic told her that it had been a mild evening, temps still in the high fifties. But goose bumps peppered her skin despite the warmth in her belly.

"Come here," he said softly, and pulled her fully onto his lap. Then he grabbed the blanket Pearl left folded on the swing and wrapped it around them. "How's this?" he asked.

She nodded, her forehead leaning against his. "It's good," she said. "Really good."

"It really is," Ben said.

He kissed her again, then shifted their position so her

head was snuggled into the crook of his neck, which was an immediate cure for her shivers.

"There," he said, and she could hear a smile in his voice. "Now you only owe me once more."

She laughed but didn't respond, not sure if it was wise to discuss how she might repay him for the second favor he'd already done for her.

They stayed that way for a while, no kissing or talking or anything other than his body molded around hers.

It was easy, just like talking to him about her grandfather had been. Easy because they were friends now. And nothing more. This was all for show.

Or maybe this was what it felt like to have Ben Callahan as a friend—easy, comfortable, warm. With just a touch of her heart doing an extra pitter and maybe an extra patter.

She shifted to the side, putting the tiniest space between them, giving herself what she hoped was room enough to settle her pulse *and* her breathing before heading back inside.

Ben must have gotten the hint.

"Good night, Doc," he finally said when someone had to say *something*. "We should do this again sometime. But I suppose I'll see you tomorrow afternoon or evening for the First Street Trick-or-Treat. Looking forward to seeing you in costume."

"Wait, what?" she asked, her mental faculties now on full alert. "Costume? Trick-or-treating?" She pulled out her phone and checked the date. He was right. Tomorrow was, in fact, Halloween. "No one told me anything about..." She trailed off as she scrolled through her Notes app, looking for one of her many lists. Then she gasped. "Get candy for First Street Trick-or-Treat." Her eyes widened as she sprang up from the swing. "I didn't get the candy. I have to go. I have to find someplace outside of town that's still open. I have to..." She leaned down and kissed him again. "Good night! Thank you for the...the date and the wine and the— Good night!"

And she ran back into the inn, slamming the door behind her, squeezing her eyes shut and leaning against it to catch her breath.

"Nice night?" she heard her grandmother say, then opened her eyes to see Pearl *and* Tyler staring at her.

She nodded. "Great. Perfect. A dream come true. But I forgot tomorrow was Halloween!"

She ran past them toward her room to grab the keys to Gran's car.

Despite being totally unprepared for tomorrow's holiday, she was grateful for a task that needed completing.

Go to store. Buy candy. Bring candy home.

That was simple. *Simple* she could handle. Like prescribing an antibiotic to cure an infection. What she couldn't handle was the thing that was becoming more and more abundantly clear.

Charlotte North had some bold-faced feelings for this cowboy that couldn't be explained in her favorite medical journals. How the heck was she going to cure that?

CHAPTER ELEVEN

The ranch only had one family with young kids, and Ben had volunteered to be the one to take them to town for the festivities.

"I am *not* going to fight you for this one," Sam said as they helped clean up the dining hall after dinner. They'd pushed dinner service an hour earlier to save daylight for anyone going to town even though they knew the streets would be lit and shops open late to dole out candy to any and all who came by.

"But if anyone's giving out Heath bars," Delaney chimed in, "*please* bring me one—or twenty—back. They're my favorite. And oh my gosh they are so amazing crushed and sprinkled over some good vanilla ice cream. Do we have any ice cream? I *so* have a taste for ice cream right now."

She looked at Sam imploringly, and he laughed.

"You sure are sexy when you're ravenous," he teased. "I think Luis might have something hiding in the freezer we can borrow."

"Not the homemade stuff!" Luis called from across the kitchen, where he was packing up unused produce from the evening. "That's for guests only! You can grab the store-bought I keep for backup."

Sam laughed and headed toward the cooler. "Wouldn't think of skimming from the good stuff," he called back, then winked at Delaney and kissed her on the cheek. "I'm totally skimming from the good stuff."

Delaney laughed, and her cheeks turned pink.

"Okay," Ben said to her. "Honest opinion on the costume?"

He'd come to dinner ready to head straight to First Street as soon as he, Sam, and Delaney helped the kitchen staff clean up. They'd been so busy that no one had said a word about what he was wearing.

Delaney narrowed her gaze. "You're wearing a costume? I guess I just thought you had some sort of shady business meeting after dinner."

Ben rolled his eyes and she laughed.

"Okay. Okay. Um . . . is it from a movie?" she asked.

He grinned.

"Oh! I got it! Neo from *The Matrix*. I guess I didn't take you for a sci-fi fan, but I like it!"

He groaned. "I *do* like sci-fi, especially if George Lucas is involved, but no. Not *The Matrix*. Think more twenty-first century. More big franchise. More . . . villain." He raised his brows.

She stared at him again, her expression blank for several long moments.

"Um . . . Professor Snape?" she guessed.

"Wrong again," he said. "Forget it. I have to head out." He hadn't worn a Halloween costume since middle school, so it was either pull what he could from his closet or go as a rancher, which wasn't exactly a costume at all. For the first time in who knew how long, Ben Callahan was putting forth effort and trying to get into the damn spirit of the thing.

"At least give me a hint," Delaney said, trying to suppress a laugh, which only made him more irritated that he'd put any effort forth at all.

"Good night, Delaney," he said, rather than giving her the satisfaction of an actual reply. "Make sure Sam doesn't get lost in the cooler."

"Say hi to Charlotte!" she called after him as he pivoted toward the door that connected the kitchen to the dining hall and promptly left—almost tripping over his brother's dog, Scout, who was curled up just outside the door, along with Sam and Delaney's cat, Butch. "Where the hell did they come from?" he mumbled to himself as he headed out the main door and to his truck, where Mr. and Mrs. Hastings—along with their six-year-old son and eight-year-old daughter—were waiting for a lift into town.

"Evening, Hastings family," Ben said with his patented customer-service grin. Then he dropped to a squat in front of the two children.

"Let me guess," he said to Kyle, the young boy, who wore a bright yellow onesie, replete with a pointy-eared hood. "Pikachu?"

Kyle's cheeks turned bright pink as he nodded bashfully.

"And you are..." He studied Kara, Kyle's sister, who wore jeans, a flannel shirt, the cutest little cowboy boots he'd ever seen, and the straw cowboy hat he'd given her the day before at her riding lesson. "Are you the new trail rider we hired earlier this week? Because you look just like a rancher to me."

If Kyle had blushed when Ben guessed his costume, then Kara went full crimson.

"Can I, Mom?" she asked, turning to look up at Mrs. Hastings. "Can I get hired as their new rancher?"

The woman laughed. "Maybe, sweetheart, when you're a little bit older."

Kara pouted for a brief moment until Ben opened the door to the truck's back seat.

"You come back here when you're old enough for the job, Kara, and we'll have a position waiting for you," Ben said as he helped her into the cab.

She beamed as she buckled her seat belt and her brother climbed in after her.

"I think she has a little crush," Mrs. Hastings said. Then she looked Ben up and down. "Professor Snape!" she said. "We *love Harry Potter*!"

He resisted rolling his eyes at yet another wrong guess and simply said, "Sure. Snape," before climbing into the front seat along with Mr. Hastings.

It was a quick ride into town, only a few minutes, but the comment brought him right back into the kitchen with Delaney.

He wasn't sure what was eating at him more, her teasing him about his barely-a-costume costume or the fact that she knew he'd put forth whatever effort he had for the good doctor.

Last night had been…unexpected. He'd been prepared to woo, under the guise of putting on a show for Pearl. But it hadn't exactly been a guise for *him*. Not that Charlotte needed to know that. Still, she'd gone and opened up to him, making it so easy for him to do the same, like it was what they'd been doing all along. How much of that was her trying to fill the minutes, and how much of it was simply *them*?

That kiss last night. That *kiss*. He'd had to hightail it

off that porch before he did something stupid like drop to one knee and propose.

He was quickly learning the difference between telling himself he was ready for something more and actually starting to *feel* that something more.

Ben wasn't prepared for the lines between fiction and reality to already feel blurred. Tonight he'd get a handle on things. Tonight he'd remind himself that whatever was happening between himself and Charlotte was simply an arrangement, much like the one they'd made the first time they met. He'd promised Pearl he wouldn't break her granddaughter's heart, but it wasn't Charlotte's heart he was worried about.

All the way into town, he told himself that kiss wasn't real no matter how spectacular it had been. When he parked his truck in front of the inn, he let the Hastings out to start their trick-or-treating. Then he looked in his rearview mirror and said the words out loud.

"Not real, Callahan. Not. Real."

Local trick-or-treaters lined First Street, where shop owners had kept the lights on, the doors open, and buckets full of candy for the taking.

Ben and his guests agreed to meet up in ninety minutes to head back to the ranch. After allowing himself only a few seconds of hesitation, he strode up the steps to the inn, where a woman clad all in black, including knee-high black boots that hugged her calves over tight black jeans, stood doling out full-sized candy bars to a posse of Disney princesses, her auburn hair hanging loose at her shoulders.

He crossed his arms as he watched her greet each child, complimenting them on their costumes, her red lips parted in a smile that—were he not aware that the two of them were only playing at being a couple—would have knocked the wind straight from his chest.

She noticed him only after the princesses scampered back down to the sidewalk and began to laugh.

"Loki from the New York scene in *Thor: Ragnarok*?" she asked, incredulous.

He raised a brow. "And Black Widow from any Marvel film ever."

Her eyes widened. "Do you know how many people have been asking me if I'm Trinity from *The Matrix*? Has no one seen anything new in the past twenty years? I mean, no offense to some good ol' late nineties philosophical sci-fi, but come on."

Ben laughed and glanced down at his own attire. "Happy Halloween from—according to everyone else— either Neo or Professor Snape."

She pulled a Kit Kat from a jack-o'-lantern bucket that was slung over her wrist and offered it to him.

"Compensation for a valiant effort gone awry?" she asked with a half-smile.

That *smile*. He'd seen it before and it had even been directed at him. But it was different now. The smiles she'd offered him the first time around usually happened after he'd brought her to the height of pleasure and she'd done the same for him. Smiling and offering him chocolate when all he'd done was show up? It somehow felt better earned, which sort of scared the hell out of him.

"Only if you share it with me," he said, accepting her offer and then making himself comfortable on the porch swing. This was uncharted territory that made him feel unsteady on his feet. He needed to sit. To get his bearings. So he patted the spot next to him, but his mind brought him right back to last night—Charlotte in his lap, her arms wrapped around his neck.

This wasn't helping.

Come on, Callahan. It's nothing more than sitting on a porch swing with a woman you like. You've sat next to attractive women before. Plus, there are plenty of children around to remind you that you and said attractive woman are NOT alone. So stop thinking about her lips and your lips and how well they fit together.

He shook his head and laughed quietly to himself, warding off the urge to put on a repeat performance, this time for quite a large audience.

We should do this again sometime, he'd said, when what he'd really meant was *We should do this* all *the time, Doc.* Tonight. Tomorrow night. And all the nights to come until he convinced her that maybe he was worth more than two months of her life. That maybe *they* were worth more than their original no-strings-attached arrangement or a pretend relationship for the benefit of Charlotte's grandmother.

Wait, wait, wait, wait, *wait.*

This was not how to mentally persuade himself to take a step back. This was...it was...He had *feelings* for her.

Oh shit.

"Did I miss something funny?" she asked, sliding into her reserved spot and knocking her knee playfully against his.

He unwrapped the Kit Kat, broke off half, and handed it to her.

"This is just weirdly easy, isn't it?" he asked, taking a bite. Because the hanging out part was. They'd fallen into what felt like a real friendship in a matter of days. Ben just had some extra emotions, it seemed, tied into said friendship.

"Eating chocolate?" she asked, biting off a piece of her share. "Can't think of anything easier. I truly don't understand people who say they don't like it. Chocolate is the best thing next to, I don't know, really spectacular sex, I guess."

He almost choked on his candy.

She laughed. "Sorry. I couldn't think of a better comparison. But come to think of it, I've probably had chocolate that was better than some of the physical encounters I've had."

This was a hint, right? She was hinting this all felt different for her, too, that she was thinking about more than just kissing because that kiss . . . had he mentioned that kiss?

Good Lord, he was losing his mind and with it *all* of his game.

He shook his head and chuckled, then rocked the swing back and forth with his heels.

"No, Doc. I wasn't talking about the chocolate. I was talking about this." He motioned between the two of them. "Us. Sitting here in our stupid costumes that no one gets—except *us*—eating candy and talking about the merits of chocolate and sex. Though I'm going on the record to say that nothing rivals spectacular sex."

She raised her brows. "Not even, say, Nutella?"

He crossed his feet on the porch in front of him and grinned. "Correct me if I'm wrong, Doc, but couldn't those two work hand in hand for an entirely different sort of spectacular experience?"

She cleared her throat, and her cheeks turned pink. "You were saying something about us sitting here . . ."

He laughed. She wasn't easily rattled, but he sure did enjoy when he was successful at it.

"I was just wondering," he said, "if you like this friendship thing between us as much as I do. I mean,

I'm already game for taking you to dinner on the regular and making sure Pearl doesn't try to marry you off. But the kissing part of last night's make-believe wasn't too shabby, if I do say so myself."

She nodded, a nervous smile spreading across her face.

"That kiss was *miles* away from shabby," she said. "I couldn't even *see* shabby from where we were last night."

"Right," he said. So they were on the same page. Maybe. But the only way to know for sure was to up the ante on their game of pretend. "So..." he continued. "Since we both seem to be fans of activities that are *not* shabby, we *could* make these dates that aren't dates a little more authentic if, let's say, I kissed you when I picked you up. For Pearl's sake, of course. And since we know from experience that she waits up for you to get home, it only makes sense that I should also kiss you good night. Each time. Again, for Pearl's sake." There, how was that for a little honesty, even if it was *partial* honesty at best? So he *wanted* to kiss her. Isn't that what two people did on a date if they both liked one another? And if Pearl believed them all that much more, then who was it hurting if they both enjoyed it?

She popped another piece of Kit Kat into her mouth, her brow furrowed, as they continued to rock in the swing.

When she finally swallowed, she shifted to face him.

"People always say relationships are better when your significant other is also your best friend. I mean, I'm not saying that we're *actually* significant others, but we're playing the parts for now, right? So I don't see why starting and ending our 'dates'"—she made air quotes around the word—"with a kiss would be anything less than mutually beneficial." She blushed, and he felt a little proud that simply talking about kissing him made her do that.

"But our friendship is important. Being with you *is* easy. And real, you know? At the risk of sounding completely pathetic, I'll admit that I don't have a lot of friends in my life. Time and circumstance—and maybe a little of my own hang-ups—have sort of made things that way. But spending time with Ivy and Delaney and Casey...spending time with *you*...I guess I'm starting to realize what I've been missing." She raised her brows. "How about this? I'll agree to your kissing proposal if you can promise me that no matter what happens these next several weeks that when I go back to New York, we'll still be...friends."

Right. New York.

They could pretend all they wanted while they were here, but one big, irritating piece of reality would always be there.

New York.

But Ben had six months of training himself that the future didn't exist, that all that mattered was today. Maybe he'd turned over a new leaf, but that didn't mean he had to erase *all* of his selfish bad habits at once.

He tapped what was left of his chocolate against what was left of hers.

"To far from shabby kisses," he said.

She smiled. "To kisses hello *and* good night," she said. "And we've already missed one. *Hello*, Ben," she added, then surprised him by leaning over and brushing her lips softly against his.

That was twice now that she'd initiated those good night kisses, not that he was keeping score, but it looked like he had some catching up to do.

CHAPTER TWELVE

Ben shook Casey's hand as she stood to leave. "Thank you for coming on such short notice," he said. "I know the tavern's about to pack up with the dinner rush."

She tucked her violet hair behind her ear as Ben stood too.

"You're really doing this?" she asked. "Building a home for yourself, putting down real roots in our little town?"

"You don't believe I'll go through with it?" he asked.

She shrugged. "I'm still trying to figure you out, Callahan. You've always been a bit of an enigma. But whatever this change of heart is, it looks good on you," she said, then strolled out the door.

Ben sat back in Sam's office chair and crossed his boots on the desk in front of him. His stomach growled, and he told it to hold its horses. He'd be heading to Midtown soon enough for a burger and a pint.

Technically the office belonged to all three of them—Sam, Ben, and Colt—but Sam had always managed the business side of things. Today, though, Ben had business of his own.

In his hands he held a stack of signed and notarized loan documents for his very own piece of land. Colt was in the process of securing building permits for him, and Sam made a few adjustments to his blueprints to fit the plot of land better. It meant tomorrow, on his day off, he'd start building the frame. If he cut out sleep, he could finish the place by spring.

This was the final piece to the puzzle—really and truly committing to the life they'd started here in Meadow Valley. He'd show his brother and Colt—and his parents—that he wasn't all talk, that this adulting thing was for real.

This was...huge. He wanted to tell someone. To celebrate. And his first instinct surprised him.

He pulled out his phone and scrolled to Charlotte's name in his contacts—*Doc*.

But she'd be heading up the inn's dinner rush, and he wasn't selfish enough to interrupt that.

Life at the inn and at the ranch had taken hold, and he hadn't been alone with her since Halloween, since she'd kissed him *again*, yet both of them insisted on calling this thing between them friendship. Sure, they'd seen each other in passing, in groups where he had to do everything in his power not to scoop her into his arms and find whatever private corner was closest. Right now he didn't care what they called their arrangement. All he cared about was spending time with her when he could and figuring out when he could kiss her again.

If he was smart enough to admit it, he might call what they were doing—going on dates that might end in kissing (some *really* amazing kissing)—a relationship.

"How's that for commitment?" he said to no one in particular.

"What's that now? Also, would you mind getting your boots off my desk?"

Ben's eyes shot up to see his brother leaning against the door frame.

"And here I thought we all owned an equal share of the ranch—which includes the desk," Ben said, leaving his boots where they were, only because he knew it pushed his brother's buttons.

"And here I thought you were a grown man," Sam said, his eyes narrowed and expression grim.

Ben lowered his feet, then had the decency to look chagrined when he saw the flecks of dried mud that had fallen from his boots onto the desk. He quickly blew them away.

"See?" he said. "Good as new. Don't you want to know why I was in here with Casey for the past thirty or so minutes?"

A muscle in Sam's jaw twitched. "Did you not get my text this morning? Because I'm guessing it wasn't updating the website to allow guests to book volunteer time in Delaney's animal shelter. We're already booking into next fall, and she'll be up and running by the end of winter."

And now Ben was chagrined for a whole new reason.

"Right. The website. I did get the text. I just got sidetracked."

"I thought you didn't do that anymore," his brother said with a sigh. "And by a pretty woman, which is also nothing new. Casey's a friend, Ben. You mess that up, and there goes my first draft being on the house."

Ben stood and brandished the stack of documents at his brother.

"Casey's a notary. I just closed on the property. Thanks

to you and Colt, everything's zoned. Permits are just about approved. Since I'm simply continuing what was already going to be a residential structure—and because Nora at the courthouse has a soft spot for me—I can get started whenever I want." He shrugged. "I have tomorrow afternoon off. Thought I'd ask if you had some free time and wanted to come by and break ground with me."

"Can't," Sam said. "Luis is short help in the kitchen tomorrow, so I'm on meal prep at dawn and on call to help with lunch and dinner if he needs. And while I appreciate your enthusiasm for this little house project of yours, the ranch comes first. But congratulations on making it official. I hope you know what you're in for."

Ben brushed nonexistent dust from his jeans.

"Sure thing, big brother," Ben said, trying to read too much into Sam's tone. Eventually someone would believe that he was in this life for the long haul, that he was ready to carry his weight even if he was a little self-ish, still, with his free time. "Excuse me while I go and grab myself one of those on-the-house drafts and unwind after a long day."

Sam shook his head. "Sorry, brother. But you're not off the clock yet."

Ben went through his mental checklist. He'd finished the last scheduled trail ride an hour ago. Horses were set for the night. Luis had a fajita bar going for dinner, and Colt was on dinner duty. All that was left was the bonfire, which was on *Sam's* docket for the night.

"I'm pretty sure I am as soon as I take care of the website, which will be fifteen minutes tops," Ben countered. "But if you'd like to enlighten me as to what I'm missing, I'll be more than happy to oblige." No, he wouldn't. He was tired and hungry and ready for that beer.

"I just got a frantic phone call from Pearl Sweeney," Sam said.

Ben's pulse quickened. "What happened? Is she okay? Is Doc—I mean Charlotte— What happened?"

Sam's brows drew together, and he rested a firm hand on Ben's shoulder.

"Wow," Sam said. "Maybe you are starting to walk the walk. Well, if you care about what goes on over at the inn as much as it seems like you do, then you won't mind waiting tables this evening."

Ben's eyes widened. "Wait, what?" There was caring what happened with Pearl and Charlotte and then there was trading a couple hours on a bar stool for the dinner rush.

"Tracy, Pearl's best server, just went into labor three weeks early. Said she wanted to work right up until the baby came and, well, baby's on its way and Pearl can't get a replacement until tomorrow, maybe not even until Thursday. She said she'd pay you for your time, but I told her that wouldn't be necessary. You'd be happy to help out."

Ben opened his mouth, then closed it.

He knew horses and riding. He knew building something from nothing. And if he remembered to do it, he could even update the ranch's website.

But waiting tables? In the early days of opening the ranch—when they hadn't booked enough guests to warrant Luis cooking in bulk—they'd tried to do the whole make-your-food-to-order deal with less-than-stellar consequences. Ben still had nightmares about carrying a tray of drinks only to spill them all down his torso and pants when he was just a foot away from the guests.

"How hard could it be?" Sam asked, as if he were reading his brother's thoughts.

"I don't suppose you want to trade and give me the bonfire?"

Sam shook his head and gave his brother's shoulder a reassuring squeeze.

"Delaney just took in an abandoned mutt from Dr. Murphy's clinic. She's working on socializing her with Scout and Butch Catsidy tonight, so I should stay nearby. In case of emergency."

Ben rolled his eyes. Delaney was an animal whisperer. He was certain—and he was sure Sam was too—that she'd have no trouble hanging out with two dogs and a three-legged cat tonight.

"You know, you sound ridiculous saying Butch Catsidy," Ben muttered.

Sam shrugged. "You know, I thought so too at first. But Delaney loves all the animals, especially that cat. And I love her. Guess it goes with the territory, and I'm all good with that. Dr. Murphy said he's expecting a few goats next week that are coming from some outdoor yoga studio that went belly-up. Something about doing yoga with goats? Guess I wasn't aware that was a thing. Anyway, the owner is looking to offload the livestock, and Delaney's taking them in as well. We're going to have ourselves a full-on petting zoo soon."

Ben crossed his arms over his chest, his sheaf of papers still in hand.

"You and Delaney *are* going to adopt those animals out, right? Or are we eventually going to be a ranch plus zoo?"

Sam laughed. "A shelter's a shelter. Means animals in need of a home will live here as long as they need to. If we end up keeping them . . ." He trailed off.

Ben raised a brow.

"I know," Sam added with a laugh. "You're just jealous of my growing four-legged family."

Ben didn't care if Delaney ran a shelter or a petting zoo. Not when he saw his brother laugh more than he'd done so in years. Maybe he liked giving Sam a hard time about a pet's name or whatever else he could come up with, but the truth was, seeing his brother happy made a small part of him happy, too, not that he'd ever admit that to Sam. He'd lose all teasing power if he did.

But Sam might have been right—about the jealousy part. Maybe he and Delaney weren't rushing to the altar or anything like that, but in the span of a month Ben had watched his brother go from lone wolf to one of the happiest people he knew. How had he gotten his life together so quickly while Ben still felt like a fish out of water?

"You better go," Sam said. "Pearl sounded pretty desperate."

"I don't get to shower or change? Or eat?" His hunger was already bordering on hanger.

Sam stepped out of the doorway to give his brother room to exit.

"I'm sure you can grab some scraps after your shift," he said with a chuckle.

Ben brushed past his brother, then pivoted to face him.

"You're enjoying this, aren't you?" he asked.

"A little bit," Sam admitted. "I'm just sorry I won't get to see you in action. Maybe only carry one drink at a time just to play it safe."

Ben left with a parting gesture that, instead of a wave, included only one finger.

He muttered to himself all the way to his car and into town about the cold beer and hot meal that were no longer in his immediate future.

He was still muttering when he strode up the inn's steps, through the main door, and into the kitchen. But then he saw the chaos. Dishes clanged onto counters and into the sink. The small kitchen staff yelled order numbers to each other across the room while Ben swore he smelled something burning. To his left, prepared plates lined two silver carts, and Charlotte rushed in from the café to grab two of them before rushing back out again.

"Oh, thank the stars," he heard from over his shoulder.

He spun to see Pearl on a new motorized wheelchair rolling out of the walk-in cooler with a sealed white tub of *something* resting precariously on her lap.

"Butternut squash soup," she said, nodding toward the item. "Already sold out of what we cooked up before opening." She tapped her temple with her index finger. "With the temperature dropping today, I had a feeling. So we made extra this morning, just in case."

"What do you need me to do?" he asked, feeling like an ass for pouting about the extension of his day. Clearly Pearl needed more help than Charlotte was able to manage on her own.

One of the kitchen staff took the tub of soup, and Pearl maneuvered her way to the rapidly filling carts.

"Get this food out there before it turns cold. Or before the sandwiches and salads go warm. Or before—"

"I'm on it!" he said. He rushed to the sink and gave his hands a good scrub. Then he lined his right arm with three plates and marched into the café. "Okay!" he called out, his voice booming, and all the patrons—and Charlotte—froze and gave him their attention. "I've got a Cobb salad, a chicken sandwich, and my favorite, PB and J Brie panini."

"I've got the salad!" one woman called out.

"Chicken's mine!" said a man one table away from her.

"I've got the panini with Brie!" another woman said with a flirty grin. She sat at a table with three other women, all of them around Ben's age. One in particular wore a sash that said *Here Comes the Bride*. "You can have a bite of mine if you want ... since it's your favorite."

He passed the plates out in that order.

"Thanks for the offer," he said with a wink as he handed the woman her sandwich. "But no eating while I'm on the clock."

She raised her brows, patted her knee, and then yanked on the belt loop of Ben's jeans. Because she'd caught him off guard, he lost his footing—and fell right into her lap. The rest of the women at the table exploded into cheers and applause as the woman wrapped her arms around Ben's neck. "You can meet us at the tavern later if you want, cowboy. Plenty more to try there."

"I have to work, ladies, but I'll tell you what," he said, gently unclasping her hands from behind his head and turning his attention to the whole table—*still* on the woman's lap. "I'll call my friend Casey at Midtown and make sure she gives you all a round of drinks on me. Sound good?"

There was more applause, more cheers, and even a catcall or two.

Phew. He still had a bit of game left in him, even if this table of strangers wasn't who he wanted to impress with it.

Out of the corner of his eye, he saw Charlotte watching the whole transaction, mouth agape.

Ben simply grinned, stood, and backed away from the table, then brushed off his hands and addressed the entire café once more.

"Okay, folks! We're a little short-staffed tonight, but I promise we're going to get you everything you need. I'm Ben and this is Charlotte..." He nodded toward the woman who was his coworker for the next few hours or so. "We're going to make sure you're well taken care of. We just ask for your patience as we sort out all the orders due to our best server having to duck out early to have herself a baby."

The rest of the café, along with the bachelorette party, erupted in a chorus of *Aws*.

"Thank you for your understanding, and we'll have your food out to you shortly," he added.

Ben strode back into the kitchen. He had this in the bag.

He was ready to pile another string of plates on his arm when he heard Charlotte's voice.

"How did you do that?" she asked, and he detected a hint of annoyance in her tone.

He spun to face her and was less than prepared for her glare.

"Did I do something wrong?" he asked. "Because you have a room full of smiling faces out there. You're welcome, by the way."

He flashed her the same customer-service grin he'd given to the café patrons, but it didn't exactly have the same effect on her. In fact, the glare seemed to grow with intensity.

"I've heard nothing but whining and complaining since the first orders went in. *Miss, I ordered my iced tea without ice. Miss? Is this going to take much longer? We're supposed to go see Shakespeare in the Park.* Since when does Meadow Valley have a Shakespeare troupe? And it's like forty degrees out there."

"High school drama club," he said. "They're practicing

for some state competition coming up. I hear they're pretty good."

"I burned my hand on a pot handle," she continued, holding up a bandaged hand, Shakespeare no longer her concern. "And that bachelorette party that apparently wants *you* to be their evening entertainment keeps ordering shots and then asking me to take their picture as they get more and more drunk, as if I don't have anything else I need to do." She groaned. "I'm beginning to think the reason I holed up with my doctor club in high school was as much about avoiding social interaction as it was curing heart disease. Newsflash: I can't do what you do."

"What do I do?" he asked. Then he gently took her bandaged hand in his and inspected the dressing. She hissed in a breath through her teeth.

"You should ice this," he said.

"I know," she admitted. "But I don't have time."

He fought the urge to press the bandaged hand to his lips and instead walked her toward the ice machine, where he unwrapped the gauze, winced at the blister already forming in the middle of her palm, and then scooped a lone piece of ice onto it before replacing the bandage.

She let out a breath, her shoulders relaxing.

"Okay," she said. "Yeah. That feels really good."

He smiled and kissed her forehead, a friendly peck even if to him it felt like more.

"Now tell me what it is that I do that you can't do. Because I'm pretty sure you can do anything, Doc."

She rolled her eyes at this, but he knew it was true.

"Schmooze," she said. "Charm the pants off every woman in the room—figuratively and possibly literally as well. Make people forget their selfish needs because they just can't help but smile when you so much as spare them a glance. I thought it was cute when I first met you, but now it sort of makes me hate your guts a little. I don't relate like that to, well, *anyone*, but you don't have the ability to turn it off. People fawn over you, dopey grin and all." One corner of her mouth fought its way to a crooked grin. "See? You're even doing it to me!"

He laughed. "Doing *what*? I'm just standing here."

"I know, but it just oozes right off of you. You flash that grin at people, and it's like they'll do whatever you ask without hesitation. Like that drunk woman from the bachelorette party pulling you onto her lap."

Was that *jealousy* in her tone? He could tell she was more exasperated than really upset, but how much of that exasperation resulted from seeing a stranger's arms around his neck?

Her cheeks were flushed, but that could be from running herself ragged since the café opened for dinner. He liked to believe it was partly to do with him. He *liked* that she *didn't* like another woman's hands on him.

He waggled his brows. "Will *you* do whatever I ask without hesitation?"

She opened her mouth to offer what he was sure would be a smart retort, but they were both interrupted by Pearl.

"Can you two save the foreplay until *after* the kitchen closes?" she barked.

They spun to find her sitting in her chair at the end of the prep counter, her head held high and shoulders back. Her good hand gripped the armrest, and even though the woman was seriously injured, she looked very much like the queen of Meadow Valley that she was. That wheelchair might as well have been an iron throne.

"Right!" Charlotte yelped. "Sorry, Gran."

"Okay, then," Pearl said. "You get the food out, and *you*"—she pointed to Charlotte—"go table to table and check on drinks. Refill what needs refillin' and clear what needs clearin'."

Ben nodded once. "Yes, ma'am."

"On it!" Charlotte added.

From there on out, the kitchen and café were a frenzy of activity. While Ben did his best to deliver the correct orders to patrons, Charlotte poured and refilled pitchers of water and iced tea, cleared empty plates to make room for full ones, and, thanks to another round of shots, endured watching—more than once—as Ben received a smack on the ass from the bachelorette party's maid of honor.

His path crossed Charlotte's on his next trip back into the kitchen. She was on her way out with a pitcher of iced tea but stopped when she saw him.

"So...everything going okay out there?" she asked.

He nodded, looked over his shoulder at the tables of satisfied patrons and then back at her. "I might have a knack for this after all," he said.

Charlotte worried her bottom lip between her teeth.

"What is it, Doc? Did I mess up an order? Tell me what I did wrong. I can take it," he said. And he realized he *could* take the criticism if it was coming from her because she'd let him down easy, like a good friend would.

She groaned. "Did you...like it?" she asked hesitantly.

His brow furrowed. *Like* it? Like—

Realization bloomed, and he laughed softly.

"Doc?" he said gently. "Are you jealous of that handsy drunk woman out there?"

"*No*," she insisted, then winced. "Maybe. I don't know. Forget I said anything." Then she groaned again and strode past him and back out to the café.

Despite Charlotte's embarrassment, Ben felt like he'd just won the lottery.

His pulse sped up as he tried to figure out what to say when their paths crossed again.

"Crème brûlée cart for table six!" one of the kitchen staff called out, and Ben grabbed the dessert-laden cart to wheel out to Charlotte's favorite table, the bachelorette party.

"How are we doing, ladies?" he called out as he pushed through the door and into the café.

The table of women responded with whoops and hollers.

"Better now that you're here, cowboy," one of them replied.

"Are you sure you don't want to come to the tavern with us?" another one asked as he rounded the table, passing out each individual dessert.

Out of the corner of his eye, he caught Charlotte glancing in his direction while filling a patron's glass—until iced tea spilled over the top of said glass and down her hand and arm.

"I'm sorry, ma'am," she said to the patron, who'd absorbed some of the overflow.

"Ugh!" the woman yelled at Charlotte. "I'm *soaked*!"

"Excuse me, ladies," he said, dropping off the last crème brûlée and then dashing into the kitchen to grab a couple towels and a slice of Pearl's famous carrot cake.

"On the house," he said to the woman, setting the cake down in front of her and handing her one of the towels. "The cake and the extra iced tea," he added with a smile.

The woman blushed—much to the chagrin, it seemed, of her husband sitting across from her.

"It's no problem, really," she said with a giggle.

Charlotte rolled her eyes as Ben handed her the other towel and then set the pitcher down on the empty cart next to table six. Then he led Charlotte toward the door leading back to the kitchen.

"Now your charm is just getting annoying," she mumbled as she dried off her arm.

He blew out a breath. "You know it's just flirting, right? None of that means anything. It's all in good fun."

"I *know*," she said. "It just makes it feel less special when you flirt with me, and it shouldn't matter because this?" She motioned between them. "It's pretend. It's so my grandmother doesn't worry about me. It's so I don't have to go on a bunch of awkward dates with men who could never be more than a two-month distraction anyway, so why even bother, right? It's...it's all those things."

She twisted the tea-stained towel in her hands.

She was right. It was *all* those things. Which meant what? *He* was nothing more than a two-month distraction. But that was what he'd signed up for, so it shouldn't be an issue. She shouldn't care about his flirting, and he shouldn't care if it made her feel less than special.

But the problem was, he *did* care.

"Doc..." he started. "Do you *want* my flirting with you to mean more? Because from the way you describe it, I'm nothing more than the friend who saved you from all that awkwardness, which is what I'm supposed to be, right?"

She nodded, then squeezed her eyes shut and groaned.

He couldn't help but laugh. She was adorable when she was exasperated. He just didn't understand *why* she was exasperated.

"I feel like there's a *but* coming..." he said, and she nodded again, then opened her eyes.

"I get it," she said. "You're this tall, dark, devastatingly sexy drink of water who couldn't turn off the charm if he tried. Before, when I was here for..." She cleared her throat. "Um...*pleasure* rather than business...I was secure enough to know that I was pretty good at the pleasure part of our arrangement and that even though you turned heads the second you stepped out the door, *I* had something to offer you that no one else did—that you'd be in *my* bed that night and would *not* be disappointed." She shook her head and let out a nervous laugh. "It's stupid. I know it is. But it felt good. It felt, I don't know, special. And powerful, that you wanted me and no one else."

Jesus. Now he was the one squeezing his eyes shut, trying to will away visions of her in his bed. Trying not to admit to himself that even back then, when they were enjoying a no-strings-attached arrangement, he hadn't wanted anyone else but her. The fact that she felt any less special now simply because she wasn't *pleasuring* him?

"Is that what you really think, Doc? That the only thing that made you special or unique in my eyes was what we did each night?" he asked.

She shrugged. "*And* some mornings." Then she forced a laugh, trying to make light of the situation that basically spelled out what a complete ass he used to be—and maybe still was.

"You were *always* more than just a good roll in the hay, Doc. But I'm crap at showing it." Because he'd only been thinking about himself. Even now, when he could finally admit to himself that he cared about her—as a friend or more or whatever they were or could be—he still didn't know how to put someone else first.

"Ben, you don't have to say that," she insisted. "I'm fine. I shouldn't have said anything."

He shook his head.

That was it. He'd not only put her first but he'd also put her on a damned pedestal so everyone knew that even if they were only friends, Dr. Charlotte North had quickly become one of the best damned parts of his newfound appreciation for life.

"Come here," he said. He grabbed the towel from her hands and threw it over his shoulder. Then he wrapped his hand around hers and nodded back toward the patrons in the café.

"What are you—"

But he gave her a gentle tug and grinned.

"Putting you first," was all he said before leading her to the center of the room.

Slowly, he turned her to face her.

"With your permission, Doc, *I'm* going to initiate some lip-locking this time."

Her eyes widened, and she swallowed. Then she nodded her assent.

He cradled her head in one hand and wrapped the other around her waist. Then he dipped her and kissed her like he hoped she'd never been kissed before.

She held tight around his neck and wrapped one leg around his waist. This was a good sign that hopefully he hadn't messed up everything between them. So was her opening her mouth, inviting him in, letting him taste the sweetness that could only be described as Charlotte North.

He straightened, hooked a hand around her other thigh, and lifted her in his arms.

She nipped at his bottom lip, and he growled softly

against her mouth. Then she deepened this kiss, all the while squeezing him tight as if her life depended on her never letting go.

Or maybe that was *him*.

For a few glorious seconds, he let his selfishness slip back in, let himself forget they had an audience and that the woman in his arms was only meant to be his friend—only meant to be a temporary part of his life in Meadow Valley.

For a few seconds, he dared to imagine what it would be like if she stayed.

But that kind of thinking was almost as selfish as the way he'd treated her the first time around.

Their lips finally parted because eventually they had to breathe—and face whatever came next.

What he faced was a smile spread across Charlotte's face that was so big it made it hard for him to breathe.

"Sorry, ladies," he said to the table of bride and bridesmaids—who stared at him and Charlotte with mouths agape—but the matching grin on his face revealed he wasn't sorry at all. "The kitchen's closing, and it seems I've got plans for the rest of the evening. If you'd all kindly settle up your tabs, we'll be happy to assist with whatever you need. We'll be back open for breakfast bright and early tomorrow morning."

He tipped his nonexistent hat and sauntered back toward the kitchen, his partner in crime still smiling triumphantly and wrapped around him like this was how she always exited a room.

Once through the kitchen door, he set her down gently. For a second he—the man who always knew the right words to charm his way in or out of any situation—had no idea what to say next. The kiss was *way* beyond the borders of shabby. That much was certain. And he was pretty damned sure that any patron he'd flirted with as a matter of "customer service" was clear where they stood in relation to one very kissable doctor.

But had he just royally complicated their *situation*?

The kitchen was a blur of movement around them— the small staff washing dishes and closing down shop. And he and Charlotte should probably be back in the café collecting payment as guests closed out their tabs, but they had to debrief after what they'd done, didn't they?

"So..." she said, quickly looking at him but then averting her gaze.

"So..." Ben echoed. "I'm...*sorry*?" he said, wincing.

Her head snapped up, and her eyes locked on his.

"What?" she asked. "Why? Did you *not* want that to happen because you kind of started it."

His eyes widened. "What?" Jesus. He needed to stop repeating her and come up with his own words. "No," he added. "I mean, *yes*. Shit. I don't know what question I'm answering. I *wanted* to kiss you, Doc. I wanted you to know that even when we weren't playing whatever game we're playing now, that it was more than sex that had me in your bed or you in mine each night for two weeks. I'm not sure how much you've heard about me, but that first time we met was the most committed I've been to any relationship. *Ever*."

She crossed and uncrossed her arms, then rolled her eyes.

"*That* wasn't a relationship," she said.

He ran a hand through his hair. "I know," he admitted. "But it doesn't change the fact that when I *wasn't* with you, I looked forward to the time I would be and that when I *was* with you, I didn't want you to leave."

She scoffed. "Well, maybe I looked forward to the time we spent together too! *Maybe* I still do!" She was practically yelling.

"Are we fighting?" he asked, unsure if she was happy about her realization or not. Because it really felt like *not*.

She threw her arms in the air. "I don't *know*. I keep telling myself that we're doing all this for Pearl, that friendship is good because it's safe and we're both so good at safe. But that *kiss*? What the hell was *that*?"

He blew out a breath. "*Not* safe."

A throat cleared behind him, and Ben spun to see Pearl in her wheelchair, eyes narrowed.

"Charlotte, sweetheart, there's probably some folks waiting to close out their tabs. Be a dear and go check on that. Being as crowded as we are, I don't want to run over anyone's toes or get in the way."

Charlotte looked at her grandmother, then back at him. "We'll finish what we were talking about later," she said, her expression unreadable. "Consider yourself off duty for the rest of the night while I finish up here."

Yep, he was in trouble all right, but as she brushed past him, she slipped her hand in his, and he felt cool metal pressed against his palm.

He squeezed his hand shut as Charlotte strode back out of the kitchen door.

Pearl rolled close enough to him that her wheels were inches from the toes of his boots.

"*What* was that?" she asked, jutting her chin toward the café.

Ben's eyes widened. "You saw?"

Pearl rolled her eyes. "Honey, the café walls are *windows*. All of First Street saw you two. It was unprofessional," she said coolly.

"I know. I'm—"

"Uncivilized," she added.

"But—"

"*And*," she interrupted, "downright uncouth. This is a place of business, not a Hallmark movie."

He was ready to agree with her but was pretty certain she'd cut him off again, so he waited to make sure the ball was in his court.

"*But...*" she continued. Because there was always a *but*. Wait, he was already in trouble, so was a *but* good in this case? "But that was also just about the most romantic thing I've ever seen. Next to being able to see my late husband one more time, I can't think of anything better than the smile you put on my granddaughter's face."

Ben's shoulders relaxed. "So, I'm not in trouble?"

She leaned forward and patted his knee with her good hand. "I don't like admitting when I'm wrong, but I think I was when it comes to you, Ben. Maybe you *do* have staying power. And maybe you'll show Charlotte that there's more to life than trying to take care of everyone else. Every now and again, we all need to be taken care of ourselves." She gave his knee another pat. "But let me remind you of my earlier request," she added.

He hesitated to speak, but then she raised an impatient brow.

"Anything," he said, grateful he at least wasn't in hot water with *both* grandmother and granddaughter.

"Don't break her heart."

Then she spun her chair back toward the lobby and rolled away without waiting for his reaction.

Looked like their little charade had worked. Only problem was Pearl hadn't considered the alternative— Charlotte having the power to break his.

He opened his palm to find a key—*Charlotte's* key—which had left marks where the metal teeth dug into his skin.

This was nothing new, being given a key to a woman's room. Hell, he'd been given a key to *this* woman's room a time or two before. They'd been here. But she was angry at him, wasn't she? He'd somehow messed up with that kiss, and now she was sending him to her room?

He didn't get it, but he also knew he wanted to fix whatever he'd broken, so he waited until Pearl was out of sight before following her path out toward the lobby and back in the direction of Charlotte's room.

He paused when he got to her door.

"Face it, Callahan," he mumbled to himself. "One way or another, you're in deep, and it's time to either sink or swim."

He could disappear back to the ranch, ignore what happened tonight and do what he did best by putting his walls right back in place. Or he could cross the threshold of self-preservation and see what happened next.

For several long moments, he flipped the key between his fingers. Then he opened her door and stepped inside.

CHAPTER THIRTEEN

It wasn't difficult closing up the café. Apparently the very public display of affection Charlotte and Ben had put on for the guests expedited the process.

"You two are just the sweetest," one woman had remarked. "See?" she'd added, turning to her husband. "The stuff I read in my books *does* happen in real life. How about more of *that* before our vacation is over?"

The bachelorette party settled up their tab first. "I'm really sorry," one of the bridesmaids whispered to Charlotte on the way out. "We didn't realize that, you know, that he was your boyfriend. We were just being silly and having some fun. And probably crossing a line or two. Not appropriate no matter how much alcohol is involved. I really do apologize."

"Oh," Charlotte said. "We're not...I mean, it's okay," she added, deciding not to correct the woman one way or another. And then she and the rest of the bachelorette crew filed out of the café.

This had been a night, to say the least.

That word, *boyfriend*, was still bouncing around in her head as she washed her hands and double-checked the locks on the café doors and on the walk-in cooler in the kitchen.

Ben Callahan wasn't her boyfriend. Not for real, at least. But—if she was going to get all middle school about it—he was a *boy* and, now, her friend. Her friend that was either waiting for her in her room or had run for the hills. She wouldn't blame him for the latter. But if he *was* there, what came next? She'd needed time to think, time to clear her head, but she was as confused now as she was when he'd walked her back through the kitchen door, her legs still squeezed around his waist.

She moved hesitantly through the kitchen's swinging door and into the lobby, creating a mental list of possibilities for what might happen if Ben had stayed—and what it would mean if he'd left. She yelped when she found her grandmother perched regally in her wheelchair tapping the fingers of her good hand on the armrest.

"Gran!" she said. "You scared me."

Pearl Sweeney raised her brows, which made Charlotte feel like she was eleven years old again and had just gotten caught after sneaking a piece of her grandmother's famous carrot cake out of the cooler at midnight—a cake that was supposed to be served *whole* for an engagement party being held at the café the following evening.

"I didn't eat the cake," she blurted, sounding about as convincing as she had two decades ago when all her grandmother had to do was wipe the cream cheese frosting from the corner of Charlotte's mouth with her thumb and brandish it as proof.

"Maybe not," Pearl said. "But about a half hour ago, I saw Ben Callahan striding toward your room with a key in his hand."

Charlotte rolled her eyes. "Gran, I love you. But I'm a grown woman. Have been for a long time now. If I want to give a man the key to my room, I'm not going to apologize for it."

Pearl's face softened. "Oh, sweetheart. Is that really what you think I'm worried about? I've got a fire chief waiting in my room this very minute because if you think a broken ankle and wrist is going to stop me from enjoying the pleasures—"

"Okay! Okay! Okay!" Charlotte interrupted. "You're not shaming my choices. I get it. But just because I said I'm a grown-up doesn't mean I'm mature enough to hear about my own grandmother's sexual exploits."

Pearl laughed, but then her expression fell serious again.

"If you really care about him, and I think you do, then *why* won't you consider staying for good? Meadow Valley was once your second home. You *fit* here. And now that it's more than your cousin and me who'd love to have you around . . ." She trailed off.

Carter and Gran. In one place. Two of her favorite people. And then Ben. *Not* that he'd asked her to stay, but what if he did?

Dammit. She'd only wanted to appease Pearl, but she and Ben had done so well playing their parts that her grandmother was back at it, trying to rearrange Charlotte's carefully planned life.

She squeezed her eyes shut and shook her head, then blew out a breath. "Gran, you know I can't up and leave the practice. Not if I don't want to be blacklisted from every other practice in the country if I break my contract.

I've worked so hard and so long to get where I am. It's not that easy to simply up and start over, you know."

Her grandmother shrugged. "Sweetheart, you can up and do anything you want to do. The only one who ever tells you no is yourself. Maybe your mama was too big for her small-town britches, but that isn't you." She paused. "I have enough help tomorrow. Why don't you take the day off and think about that." She flipped a switch on her chair and pivoted away from Charlotte. "Now, if you don't mind, I have some—what did you call them?— *exploits* to attend to."

Charlotte shuddered as her grandmother rolled away, but then she laughed. Losing her grandfather was hard. She couldn't even begin to imagine what it had been like for Pearl. It was easier to be far away these days knowing, at least, that her grandmother had found love again. That she had Carter here and—as always—a whole town that would do anything for her.

With her heart a little lighter, she made her way back to her room. But the lightness only lasted until she was in front of her door.

What if he was in there? What if he *wasn't*? Pearl might have seen him head this way, but he could have changed his mind. She hadn't yet figured out what to do about how real that kiss felt or how it had made them admit that the week they'd first met had meant more to both of them than they'd initially let on.

Well, this was *her* room. She had to go in there and deal with whatever lay beyond her door.

"Just pretend it's a patient," she said softly. She could walk into an exam room and talk to a kid with tonsillitis or a parent concerned about a fever like it was no one's business. She knew why too. It was because she had all the answers—or at least, most of them. But science and journals and all her go-to resources had nothing on what was about to happen when she walked through that door. Still, a little pep talk couldn't hurt.

"Just a patient. Just a patient. Just a patient."

She whispered her mantra as she squared her shoulders and opened the door.

"Listen, cowboy. I need to—".

She stopped short.

On her bed, wrapped in nothing but a towel from the hips down, was a very handsome, *very* sexy, very likely naked-under-said-towel, and very *sleeping* Ben Callahan.

Somehow, seeing him like that—quiet and vulnerable and without any sort of mask of bravado—Charlotte had her answer without any sort of data to back it up.

Their kisses were far from shabby, and her heart was miles away from safe.

Since Ben had helped himself to a shower, Charlotte decided to do the same. A few minutes under the soothing spray of hot water might not have cleared her head, but it at least loosened some of the tension her body had been holding on to since she bumped into her grandmother in the lobby.

Charlotte opted for her navy-blue silk robe that hung on the back of the bathroom door. Ben was sleeping. She'd just crawl into bed next to him and—if she could shut off her brain—join him. No talk of feelings or the future. Just your average, everyday, good ol' night of sleep.

She did little more than towel-dry her hair and run her fingers through it before taking a deep breath and throwing open the door.

Of course, though, Ben was no longer asleep. He was propped up against the headboard on a couple of pillows, his arm behind his head and a big, beautiful, megawatt grin spread across his face.

"Evening, Doc," he said. "Hope you don't mind me using your shower. Was feeling pretty ripe after an extra-long day." But there was something different in the sound of his voice—different from all the other times he'd said those exact same words. The words sounded weighty, like he knew just as well as she did that crossing a line tonight would mean a hell of a lot more than it had before.

"Evening." Her voice was hoarse, so she cleared her throat and tried again. "*Evening*," she said again, fully enunciating the word.

He patted the spot on the bed next to him.

"Unless you really like that spot outside the bathroom," he teased.

She pressed her lips together and nodded, but as soon as she took a step forward, she pivoted right instead of left and made her way to his side of the bed, balancing on the edge so she could face him.

She wanted to take the reins. She wanted some semblance of control, some pretense of the safety and stability she'd learned to rely on as she built her life and her career.

"That kiss was . . . *wow*," she admitted. "And I appreciate what you were trying to do for my fragile little ego."

"Doc," he said. "I wasn't—"

"I'm not done," she interrupted, holding on to those reins. He made a motion like he was zipping his lips, and she couldn't help but laugh.

"I know you didn't do it to get me into bed," she added. "And I know that this is all for my grandmother, so she won't worry or meddle, and you have done a bang-up job playing your part, mister. We sure fooled her." She huffed out a shaky breath. "I like you, Ben. I like the way I feel when I'm around you, and when you're not here, I wish that you were. And tonight, when you came to my rescue after Tracy went into labor, I realized how hard I've worked to not need anyone to take care of me—but how good it felt when someone actually did. I don't want to cross any lines we shouldn't cross, but what if we—"

"Pretended this was real?" he asked, breaking his vow of silence and stealing the words right from her mouth. If they continued to call it pretend, then they could stay safe, couldn't they?

She worried her lip between her teeth and nodded, knowing that safety had left the building the moment she'd given him the key to her room.

She had no right to ask him this, not when she couldn't promise they wouldn't end up hurt. And then there was her grandmother. How much would it hurt her if this all went up in flames and she knew Charlotte and Ben had been lying to her?

Yet here she was, asking for more than she could give, risking the hearts of everyone involved, because just this once she wanted someone to be there for *her*.

"Are you sure this is what you want?" he asked.

She nodded again.

I want to pretend we're real.

I want to pretend we could have a future.

I want to pretend I won't fall for you or hurt you if you fall for me.

But instead she said, "Only if it's what you want too," hoping that if he said yes, it meant they were on the same page.

"I want *you*, Doc. Only you."

That was all she needed to hear.

She untied her robe and let it fall from her shoulders, where it pooled around her waist.

"Wow," he said.

She laughed. "You've seen me before. *All* of me." But her heart beat a little faster now, and her stomach clenched a little tighter—reactions she couldn't control, reactions that were definitely *not* make-believe.

He nodded. "I know. You're beautiful, Doc. I always knew that." He cupped one of her breasts in his palm and swiped a thumb over her pebbled flesh.

She gasped.

"I feel like I've been wading through fog for years."

She skimmed her teeth over her bottom lip. "And now?" she asked.

"Now it's lifted, and I can finally see what's been missing."

He pulled her to him and kissed her, her chest bare against his.

She got it—living in a fog or the bubble of work, sleep, repeat or whatever you wanted to call what kept her safe. What kept her *heart* safe. She'd never truly thrown caution to the wind. But that was exactly what they were doing now. She knew the label meant nothing. They could call this pretend, but the wanting was real. How much they wanted and how much they were both capable of giving was another story, one she couldn't worry about tonight.

Not when his skin was on her skin, his lips on her lips, and there was nothing she could do but ride the wave to wherever it took her.

She undid his towel and slid her hand between his legs. He hissed in a breath as she stroked him from root to tip.

She nipped at his bottom lip as she did it again, and he let loose a low growl that sent her heart racing.

Control. She needed to stay in control if she had any hope of ensuring she'd make it out of this intact. At least, that was what she told herself.

"Touch me," she said, sliding over his torso and sprawling out on her back next to him.

"Yes, ma'am," he said with a grin. "The pleasure is all mine."

He lay down next to her, propping himself up on one elbow. For a few seconds, all he did was stare.

"What is *with* you?" she asked with a nervous laugh.

He raised his brows. "I'm just drinking it all in, getting used to seeing you in this new light."

"You like what you see?" she asked with as much bravado as she could muster.

"I really do," he said.

Her stomach flipped, and heat rose from her core all the way to her cheeks.

"And who's in charge right now?" she added.

"You, Doc. One hundred percent you."

"Well, I'm not going anywhere, so how about less lookin' and more doin'?"

For a second, they were both quiet. Because she *was* going somewhere. In little more than a month. Knowing it and dealing with it, though, were two entirely different things. And the last thing she knew either of them wanted to do right now was *deal.*

She grabbed his free hand and placed it on her breast.

He laughed, breaking the tension.

"Does doin' include kissing?" he asked, sliding his hand out of the way and kissing said breast.

She let her eyes fall shut and nodded.

He peppered her with kisses from her chest, up her neck and to her waiting lips. His kisses were soft yet strong. And with each touch of his lips on hers, his fingers traced circles on the sensitive flesh of her inner thigh.

"I could do this—*just* this—all night long," he said, his lips still on hers.

Her eyes shot open, and she snorted. "You could *not*."

He grinned at her, and her stomach flip-flopped again. "You don't think I could enjoy just kissing and touching you all night long? Because if that's a challenge, Doc—"

"No!" she cried. "Not a challenge. I believe you!"

Then they both burst out laughing.

Maybe he could do it, which in all honesty was super sweet and kind and even melted her heart. But she wanted to *be* with Ben tonight, all of her and all of him.

The laughter faded, and with it so did his smile.

"One more chance to back out," he said. "We can go right back to what we were doing before tonight, and I'd be okay if that was what you truly wanted."

What she *truly* wanted was more than she was willing to admit out loud.

"I'm all in if you are," she said, wondering if he could hear the *more* anyway. It was right there, on the tip of her tongue and in the rapid beat of her heart.

"I'm *all in*, Doc," he whispered, and then the fingers that had been tracing those teasing circles on her thigh slipped between her legs and inside her.

She gasped as her back arched and he kissed her.

Hunger and heat replaced the gentle care of when she first crawled into bed with him. His lips moved down her jaw, her neck, and to her breasts while his fingers—wow those fingers—moved inside her like he'd been given a secret map pointing him exactly where he needed to go to drive her absolutely mad with need.

He nipped at the hardened peak of her breast, and she cried out.

It wasn't enough. She needed more. Needed him closer.

She wrapped her hand around his length and stroked. He hummed with pleasure.

"Please," she said, urging him to where his palm was pressed between her legs, his fingers working their magic.

"Do you have—" he started. "I mean, I didn't bring— I didn't come here tonight expecting this."

She nodded, then gripped his wrist so he had to slow his movement inside her. Otherwise she wouldn't be able to speak.

"I'm...protected," she said. She'd had the IUD for a couple years now. "And before you, before our first time around...Let's just say it had been a while. And previous partners have always, you know, covered up." She laughed nervously. Nothing like bringing up past lovers to kill a mood.

He laughed as well. "I always cover up, too, Doc. Not to sound like a broken record, though, but are you sure?"

She nodded. She wasn't sure about what came next or what damage would be done when they said good-bye in a matter of weeks, but she was sure about this. About him. About tonight.

"Are you?" she asked.

He nodded too.

She cleared her throat and gave his wrist a gentle tug.

He slid his hand from between her legs.

"Then I guess we have an agreement," she added.

She pressed gently on his shoulder, a silent request for him lie on his back.

"You're in charge, Doc," he said with a grin, and she crawled over him, letting him nudge her opening.

He hissed in a breath, and she bit her bottom lip, realizing both of them were throwing self-preservation out the window.

She sank over him, and she gasped as something guttural tore from his chest.

He pressed his strong hands to her hips and lifted her up so she could descend on him again.

"Oh my—" she started. "I mean, this is—"

"I know," he said. "Come here."

She lowered herself over him, and he rolled her so they were both on their sides, his leg hooked over hers, and kissed her as their bodies found a rhythm that hadn't been there before.

Equal ground.

Either they were both in control or neither of them were. She wasn't entirely sure. All she knew was that everything was better when Ben Callahan was kissing her and that *this* was something she could do all night long. And other than a break to steal snacks from the kitchen or take a cat nap here and there, that was exactly what they did.

When she woke up, it was nearly 10:00 a.m., and Ben was gone. There was a note on the inn's stationery, though, resting on top of her pillow.

Hey, Doc. Had an early morning trail ride and didn't want to wake you. Figured you needed the rest with how hard you've been working. I'm off at about 3:00 today. I'd love you to stop by this address if you have the time: 1 County

> *Road. If you need incentive to show up, there's*
> *a whole lot of kissing in it for you.*
>   —*Ben*

She smiled—a big dopey grin she was glad no one else could see—and pressed the letter to her chest.

She pretended not to think about what would happen in five weeks when she left.

She pretended like they'd be able to keep up the charade—for Pearl *and* for themselves.

And she pretended she wasn't falling for her the man she realized had been taking care of her from the moment she stepped foot back in town.

Charlotte *liked* her life in New York. Maybe it was lacking in family nearby—or a cowboy in her bed—but it was a life she was proud of, and she wouldn't just walk away from it. She *couldn't*. Not without jeopardizing her career.

Eventually, she'd *have* to walk away from Ben, though, and it would be the hardest thing she'd ever do.

CHAPTER FOURTEEN

B en was grateful for the cooler November temperatures. Made working outside more bearable than summer. But this afternoon, it had already dropped to forty degrees, and it would steadily decline as the sun dipped beyond the horizon. So he needed to get in as much work as possible to get a decent portion of the frame done before they lost daylight.

"I owe you one, buddy," Ben said to Colt, who was holding a beam of wood in place while Ben manned the nail gun.

Colt laughed. "I'm using my free time to build *your* house so you can leave me alone in the guest quarters. You owe me a heck of a lot more than *one*."

"You name it," Ben said, securing the final nail and straightening so they could move on to the next part of the frame.

Colt dusted off his hands, then blew into his palms.

"I think it's time for gloves," he said. "And as far as cashing in, how about we start by you taking my bonfires the weekend after next. Dr. Murphy has a calf he's been treating for shipping fever. She'll be good to head back home by then, but the owner has another heifer close to calving and is afraid to leave her. I could use a long solo drive if you can cover me. I'll be back by the following Monday in time for Thanksgiving."

Was it nearing Thanksgiving already? They'd purposely closed the ranch to any bookings for the holiday. With their mom back in the picture, Sam thought it was best the family was together since there was no telling how many more family gatherings were in their future. So the three men were preparing a feast—not that Luis was thrilled about handing over his kitchen, which was why he insisted he and Anna join and help out.

Ben blew out a long breath as he remembered all the nights and weekends his brother and Colt covered for him when he'd been far less considerate as far as *asking* for the time off.

"Yeah. Sure," he said to Colt. "You got it. Though I was hoping you were asking for time off for something a little more exciting than four hours in a truck with a calf trailing behind."

Colt raised his brows. "No calf on the way home. Just me, myself, Northern California out my window, and country music on the radio."

Ben laughed and shook his head. For all of Colt's talk about building a house of his own big enough for a whole brood of kids, he seemed so content on his own. Sure, it took time to get over proposing to your girlfriend and having her turn you down, but five years? Nowadays he'd swear his friend preferred his solo existence. Or maybe it was just the easier path. Ben sure as heck wasn't one to fault another for choosing easy over the possibility of loss. But at least he was trying now—building this house, putting down roots that went deeper than the day-to-day operations of the ranch.

"You got it, friend," Ben said, holding out his right hand for the two men to make the deal official. "It's the least I can do."

Colt laughed again. "You're right. The *very* least. And I plan to cash in more when and if I need to. But right now I'm headed to the truck to grab my work gloves. Remind me again why you're building a house in winter?" he asked as he hopped off the frame and started to back toward the truck.

"It's not winter yet!" Ben called after him. "November is still considered autumn!"

Colt waved him off and turned toward the truck.

They'd both grown up in Oak Bluff, farther south from Meadow Valley and on the coast. They didn't see much in the way of winter down there, but Ben liked the change of seasons, something to mark the passage of time, to remind him—especially now—how lucky he was to have another day, another year. His future had infinite possibilities, and he couldn't help but wonder what that meant for him and Dr. Charlotte North.

"Speak of the devil," he said to himself as he squinted toward where Colt had parked the truck along the street.

There she was, hopping out of Pearl's car and staring up the hill to where he stood on one of those infinite possibilities—a home he hoped to share with someone like her.

She strode toward him, hands plunged in the pockets of a short navy-blue coat, her auburn hair bouncing against her shoulders as she quickened her pace.

"This address doesn't even *exist*," she said when he

was in earshot. "When I asked one of the nurses at the hospital, he said there's nothing on this road for miles and miles."

Ben grinned and hopped onto the grass to greet her, leaving the nail gun behind.

"And yet you found me," he said. "Wait, why were you at the hospital? Is Pearl okay? Are you okay?"

"Everyone's fine," she insisted. "I was checking on Tracy's new baby girl, Kayla, as a favor to my grandmother. She's healthy and happy—well, as happy as someone can be who was still in the womb twenty-four hours ago."

"Look at you being all doctor-ish and stuff," Ben said, taking a step closer.

She smiled. "Yeah. You know, at first I was a little annoyed at Gran for scheming to get me to do it, but I've been so crazed with the inn these past few weeks that I didn't realize how much I missed my job."

He leaned in close and whispered, "Bet you didn't realize we have all that doctor stuff here in Meadow Valley too."

She surprised him by taking a step back.

"Whoa. What did I say?" he asked. "I was just teasing you, Doc. That's what we do, remember?"

But maybe, somewhere beneath the surface, there was a bit of wishful thinking to the comment. Would that be so bad?

"Sorry," she said. "I didn't mean to react so strongly. Today, checking on Tracy's baby? It was wonderful. But it was Pearl setting me up to show me exactly what you just said, as if I didn't know there were doctors all over the country. But my career is in New York. Even if I wanted to leave—which, right now there's no reason for me to do that—I can't. I signed a contract. And I'm happy there."

Ben nodded. "I never suggested otherwise."

"I know," she said. "It was just bad timing, I guess. Felt like maybe you were pressuring me too."

He swallowed, but his throat was unexpectedly tight, and it felt like trying to choke down a bitter pill without any water. She'd made it abundantly clear that New York was home for her.

And the ranch was home for him.

"No pressure, Doc. I'm not the pressuring type." He held out a hand, and she threaded her fingers through his. "Now can we try this again?"

She smiled one of those smiles he knew was just for him, and her shoulders relaxed.

When they were like this, he could almost forget that she was leaving, that the first woman he could fall for might also be the first to take a little piece of the heart he'd protected for so long.

"So, why am I here?" she asked.

Over her shoulder, he saw Colt on his phone by the truck. Either he was giving them a minute alone or something had come up. Ben was simply happy for a few minutes with Charlotte before having to explain anything to his friend.

"Okay," he said, realizing how this would look now. "So, my brother and I, before we moved here and built the ranch, we built other stuff, like houses and barns. Or we did remodeling projects. We're contractors, basically. And now ranchers."

She nodded, but he could still tell she was hesitant.

"Back home we lived with and took care of our father, which never quite suited my selfish lifestyle. Nor did visiting him at the facility where he lives now—not when I thought it was where I'd end up in a matter of years." He cleared his throat. "I never really wanted a place of my own because...I was afraid I didn't have enough time to enjoy the kind of life you're supposed to enjoy in a home. So I slept where I could find a bed, and for a lot of years that was enough." He shrugged. "I'm not exactly proud of who I was, but I'm trying to change."

"And *this* is you changing?" she asked, dropping his hand and stepping past him and up to the unfinished frame, running a gloved hand along a freshly nailed beam.

"Now I want all the things I didn't let myself want. And before you think this is me pressuring you again, I've had my eye on this land since we got here over two years ago. Just never thought there was any point in putting down roots—emotionally speaking, of course. What was the sense in building a home when I never thought I'd be filling it with anyone other than myself? Now, I don't know what the future holds, and for the first time I'm okay with that. But I needed to do something to prove to myself—and to everyone else who thought I wasn't capable—that I can commit to *something*. And for now that something is this."

Would it really be so bad if *she* saw him in a different light now too? Maybe they were still calling this a game, whatever was happening between them. But that didn't mean he wanted her to see him as the same selfish ass he was a few weeks ago. He cared what she thought of him, maybe more than he'd like to admit.

She nodded again. "Okay. I guess that makes sense," she said hesitantly. "Can I...can I see?"

"Yeah," he said. "There's not much to see yet." It was a start though. Ben knew he was good at what he did.

But this wasn't a job. It was *his* design. *His* home. *His* commitment to being a better man. He wanted her to see that, even if it was just the little he'd done so far.

He climbed onto the beginnings of the frame and held out a hand to help her up. She walked past him, inspecting the work they'd done so far before turning back to face him.

"It's hard to tell what it will look like, but it's a start. It'll be slow going since I'm borrowing my labor from the ranch." He gestured toward Colt at the truck. "I wanted you to see what I do when I'm not leading trail rides or giving riding lessons. Maybe it's crazy to think it matters, but I feel like you had this notion of me in your head when we first met, and you were probably right about a lot of it."

She pursed her lips. "What is it you *think* I thought of you?"

He raised a brow. "That I was maybe...irresponsible. That I was *definitely* selfish. That the only commitment I had was to the ranch, and even that was shaky at best. I guess I just wanted to show you something you didn't know."

She took the few steps to close the distance between them and shook her head.

"It's not crazy. It's— I'm glad you wanted to share this with me. You're building a home. It's wonderful. Whoever gets to share it with you is very lucky."

She blew out a shaky breath and wrapped her arms around his waist. He let his forehead fall against hers.

There it was. The reality that it *wouldn't* be her.

"Why the hell do you have to live in New York?" he asked, trying to tease but knowing he was failing miserably.

"Why the hell do you have to live in California?" she asked right back.

And why did it even matter when neither was willing to admit this was anything more than pretend?

"I know my grandmother's not anywhere close to where we are and that she can't see us..." she said with the hint of a smile.

But Ben didn't want to finish her thought. If she wanted to do what she was hinting at, she had to say it so he was sure. So he furrowed his brow, stepped back, and crossed his arms.

"I don't follow, Doc," he said, fighting the urge to grin.

Charlotte rolled her eyes. "Yes, you *do*," she insisted. "I *thought* our little arrangement said something about our comings and goings, about how a man might greet a woman he's dating."

His expression remained impassive.

She groaned. "Colt is still over by the truck. *He* might see us not doing what he thinks we should be doing, and...and then what if he reports back to my grandmother?"

Ben raised his brows.

"Are you suggesting that Mr. Morgan might blow our cover if we don't do—I don't know—something to make him think we're an item?" he asked innocently. "Because I'd hate to invite you out here only to ruin everything we've done to make this thing between us look rock solid."

"You know, I was ready to kiss you to make up for reacting harshly when you first showed me the house. But now I don't think you deserve it," she said, clearly annoyed.

He finally cracked a smile and let loose a soft chuckle.

"You're so easy to rile up, Doc. You know that?"

She jutted out her chin. "If you don't *want* to kiss me, all you have to do is say so." Then she spun on her heel. But she wasn't fast enough.

He grabbed her hand, and she turned back to face him, unable to hide a smile of her own.

"I don't take kindly to teasing, Mr. Callahan," she chided.

He laughed. "I forgot you're an only child. See, with me and Sam, teasing is how we— I mean, growing up it was— And *now* . . ."

Jesus. He had no clue how to use words to express that she meant *something* to him, even if there was no definition for *what* they were.

She sighed. "I care about you, too, cowboy. Now lay one on me already."

Saved by the kiss.

Because when his lips touched hers, he didn't have to think of the right thing to say. He could simply pull her close and hope she understood that teasing or no, he always *wanted* to kiss her. And if she wanted to use the prying eyes of Colt or Pearl or anyone in town as the reason to do it, far be it from him to disagree.

His phone buzzed in his back pocket, and he reluctantly broke away from her to check the message.

Speak of the devil.

Colt: Looks like you don't need me anymore today. Mind if I head back and you can get a ride from the doctor?

Ben quickly responded with Sure. Thanks again, and thought that would be the end of it, but then he saw those telltale three dots that said Colt wasn't done with the conversation.

Colt: Just friends, huh?

Right. He hadn't exactly told his brother or Colt that they were dating. Or pretending they were dating. Because the last thing any of the men at the Meadow Valley Ranch cared about was who was kissing whom or whether or not Pearl believed their charade.

But maybe he'd better play it safe. For Charlotte's sake, of course.

"What is it?" Charlotte asked as Ben just stared at his screen.

"Nothing. Colt needs to head back to the ranch. Think you can give me a ride after I clean up here?"

Ben wouldn't be completing the frame today, but he was suddenly in no rush to get to the finish line. Even after their kiss, her words still echoed in his head.

Whoever gets to share it with you is very lucky.

The only problem was that when he pictured the completed house, he kept imagining *her* in it, which was ridiculous. That was never going to happen.

"Sure," she said, interrupting his thoughts. "I can drive you back."

He nodded and texted Colt back one more time.

Yes. Friends. Sort of. But if anyone asks, we're dating.

Colt: Who's going to ask?

Ben: No one. I don't know. Pearl, okay?

Three dots appeared to let Ben know Colt had more to say on that matter.

Colt: So you're lying to Pearl or to yourself? Or both? Either way, my friend, be careful.

He didn't answer but instead locked his screen and shoved his phone back in his pocket.

"Hey," he said. "Pearl got you working on Thanksgiving?"

She nodded. "Sort of. We're pretty booked up, but it's mostly with out-of-towners coming to see family, so they won't be at the inn for Thanksgiving dinner. But Gran's head cook always prepares a feast and brings her husband and kids to the inn. The chief is coming too. Ivy and Carter. She still invites my mom and dad every year even though they're barely on speaking terms, but they're always out of town. Even I've been out of the picture since getting wrapped up in school and my residency and— I'm rambling. Sorry. What was the question again?" She laughed nervously.

"Sam, Colt, and I are doing it up big at the ranch— just friends and family. We're not calling it until late afternoon/early evening, so everyone who is *not* a Callahan can hit up their respective family gatherings first. Ivy and Carter said they'd stop by—I'm guessing after the inn. Casey's going to drop in after she's done with her family. And in case you're worried about our skills in the kitchen, our head chef, Luis, is helping run the show along with his girlfriend, Anna, our produce supplier. I swear the night will be worth it just to listen to the two of them argue. It's an interesting dynamic." He took a steadying breath. "My parents will be there. You could stop by if you want, after you're done at the inn."

"You want me to meet your parents?" she asked, her eyes wide and her voice wavering. "That's a big deal, right? Like, people only do that when they're *actually* dating."

She had a point, but so did he.

"Wouldn't Pearl think it was strange if I *didn't* invite you? Come to think of it, why hasn't she invited me?"

Charlotte swallowed. "She asked, but I sort of told her that since we were both having our family dinners at the same time that we'd probably just meet up after."

Ben took a step back and crossed his arms. "But you didn't know what time we were doing our dinner."

Charlotte winced. "I *panicked*. It's one thing to lie to my grandmother with our dating life off camera, so to speak. It's quite another to do it right in front of her. What if we mess up? What if she realizes... And now you want to do the couple thing in front of *your* whole family?"

Her cheeks were flushed, and there was a vein pulsing in the middle of her forehead Ben swore he'd never seen before.

"Okay," he said, holding his hands up. "You don't have to come. I can stop by Pearl's after and stuff my already stuffed gut with whatever desserts are left over. Nothing formal. But enough to show her that we're real— in her eyes, of course—to celebrate part of a holiday together. Just know the invitation stands... in case you change your mind. I can't promise *our* crew will save any dessert though." He winked at her. Ben hid his nerves behind the humor and charm. He'd always worn the traits like a mask, using them to hide his anticipation, his hope, and his fear. He crossed all his fingers and toes it still worked with her.

The thing was, his parents would like her—really like her. Maybe he and Charlotte weren't in it for the long haul, but he knew it would make his parents—his father especially—happy to see both his sons happy. What was wrong with putting on a show for them just like they were doing for Pearl?

Maybe she was right, that it was a risk to try to perform for *everyone*, let alone her grandmother. The thing was, until rationalizing it in his head right now, Ben hadn't given his initial invitation a second thought. He'd simply wanted her to be there, so he'd asked. Now he had to reconcile that want with the knowledge that she didn't want the same thing.

"I'll try to stop by," she finally said, getting him—thankfully—out of his head. "When things die down at the inn. But promise it will be low key, that no one's going to be all up in our business or anything like that."

He couldn't help but laugh. "No pressure, Doc, I promise. And I'm fine either way. Not holding my breath or anything."

Except . . . *maybe* he sort of was.

CHAPTER FIFTEEN

Charlotte held a hand over the boxed cake in the passenger seat—her grandmother's carrot cake (and Charlotte's favorite)—that Pearl insisted she bring after she practically kicked her out of the inn.

"The man you're *dating* invited you to meet his family," Pearl had said when Ivy and Carter asked if Charlotte was going to join them at the ranch.

"But I'm here, and you're *my* family," Charlotte had offered as a feeble argument.

Pearl had simply scoffed. "As soon as we're done straightening up here, you're officially banished from the inn until further notice. Or until your next shift."

And true to her word, as soon as the dishes were cleared and coffee was served, she'd sent Charlotte off to the ranch with a belly full of turkey, stuffing, sweet potatoes, and a whole lot of nerves.

This was ridiculous. She and Ben were friends. Friends who kissed. And maybe had some really spectacular sex every now and then. So she was meeting his parents. Big deal. This didn't *mean* anything. It wasn't like either of them had admitted to anything more than caring about each other. They were both doing a great job at convincing themselves that for all intents and purposes, it was still a pretend relationship—one so Gran wouldn't worry or meddle. Now she and Ben were *pretending* by spending one of the biggest family holidays together—after which they'd keep on pretending they would never have to say good-bye.

No. This wasn't going to be stressful at all.

She parked right outside the ranch's dining hall, her slightly trembling hand still acting as a seat belt for the cake. She couldn't decide if it was due to the car not having time to warm up on the short ride or the butterflies in her stomach. Probably a healthy dose of both.

She stepped out of the vehicle and smoothed her coat over her sweater-covered flannel shirt and jeans. She was getting used to pulling on her boots instead of a pair of heels. And the last time she'd put on a dress? It had been weeks since Ben had taken her on their first "date." She'd fallen into a rhythm here, but even that wasn't real. Even if she forgot it from time to time, Gran would be on her feet sooner rather than later, and Charlotte would return to the life she'd built.

She could see all the smiling faces inside—Carter and Ivy, Sam and Delaney, Colt, Casey, an animated couple she guessed were Luis and Anna, and a slightly older couple she knew were Ben and Sam's parents. And then there he was, her vacation cowboy.

Her throat tightened, and her belly flipped. She told herself it was nothing more than general nerves about joining a family gathering where she was the outsider, that it didn't have anything to do with seeing Ben Callahan smile, even from a distance.

She reached back into the car and grabbed the cake, then closed the door with her hip. After one more steadying breath, she squared her shoulders and marched toward the door.

Wait...Did she knock? On any other day, this was a public dining hall—at least, public enough for the guests of the ranch. But everyone in there was family or friend, someone who definitely belonged in this scenario, while—standing in front of what she was sure was an unlocked door—Charlotte still felt so very far from either of those labels.

She squeezed her eyes shut and gave herself a silent pep talk.

You can do this. In fact, you just *did at the inn. It's food and people, one of whom is the man you can't stop thinking about, one is his brother, and two are his parents, and everyone else are the closest people in his lives here in Meadow Valley. Piece of cake!*

She should really just go back to the car.

"Are you...meditating?" she heard someone ask. It was a man's voice she didn't entirely recognize. "I do it every morning," he said when she didn't respond. "Helps me center myself into my day. I'm guessing you need some centering before heading into the lion's den, huh?" He chuckled, and she heard the door click shut, so she opened her eyes.

"Colt," she said, putting a face with the voice. "I was just— I mean, it was sort of meditating in the way that you might look at freaking out as meditating?" She laughed nervously as the handsome, golden-haired cowboy flashed her an easy grin. Good *Lord*, a girl could get used to being greeted by gorgeous ranchers on a daily basis.

He laughed again. "Nothing to freak out about in there other than trying to find an extra stomach or two to put away all food we still have." He raised his brows at the box in her arms. "Looks like you brought more. Come on in. He'll never admit it, but there's someone inside who's been checking his phone every ten minutes. I think he might be a little anxious to see you."

Anxious to see her? It should have eased her mind, but instead it just made her more nervous.

Her palms were sweating. Oh God. Was she going to leave handprints on the cake box?

"Yeah. Great. Excellent. Let's, uh, go inside!" she said with way too much gumption to sound natural.

"After you." Colt pushed open the door and held it so she could walk through.

She was ready for the chatter to screech to a halt like a needle being dragged across a record, for everyone to stare at the party crasher who was *technically* invited yet still felt like a twelfth wheel, but the revelry continued without interruption.

Except for the dark-haired, blue-eyed cowboy who looked awfully sexy in a formfitting dark green sweater, jeans, and his ever-present dusty boots. He strode toward her like she was the only person in the room.

It was like there was a spotlight on her now, which should have made her freak out even more. Instead the biggest, dopiest grin took over her features as he greeted her with a bone-melting kiss.

"Happy Thanksgiving, Doc," he said softly, his lips parting in a smile against hers.

She cleared her throat. "I...um...I brought cake," she said, taking a step back and nodding at the box still in her hands, the one they somehow avoided smashing with what she considered a greeting to end all greetings. "I didn't make it. Pearl did."

Ben raised a brow. "That wouldn't be her famous carrot cake with the best cream cheese frosting I've ever tasted, would it?"

"I heard that!" a man called out from behind Ben, and they both turned to see who Charlotte assumed was the ranch's chef, Luis, staring daggers in Ben's direction.

Ben laughed. "Don't mind him. He's *very* protective of his reputation, but everybody knows that when it comes to baked goods, no one holds a candle to your grandmother." He took the box, which she relinquished with pleasure. "I'll go set this with the other desserts and then introduce you to—"

"*There* you are!" Ivy exclaimed, appearing behind Ben. "Come on. You need a glass of champagne. Sam's about to make some big toast, and a toast isn't a toast without a glass of bubbly." She grabbed Charlotte's hand. "I may have had a glass or two of bubbly already," she said with a giggle.

Charlotte shrugged as Ivy dragged her away from a grinning Ben, who simply shrugged right back. Ivy led her to a table that had a couple of bottles sitting in a bucket of ice on one side and a cooler full of canned and bottled beer on the other, a table that was, conveniently, out of earshot from the one where everyone had been eating.

"Bubbly!" Ivy said, and filled a champagne flute for Charlotte.

It was a little more upscale than the Solo cups Ben had used for their first date—something more akin to what she'd grown used to back home in New York. Yet she could have sworn the plastic cups added a little something extra that night. A little something more Ben Callahan.

"Okay, *spill*," Delaney said, coming up behind them and refilling her own flute.

Suddenly Casey was there too. "Yeah, Doctor. You want to tell us what's up with that kiss? You know I'm the last one to get up in anyone's business—"

Ivy snorted. "You run a *pub*," she said. "The only pub in town. You are up in *everyone's* business whether you like it or not."

Casey narrowed her eyes at her friend, and Ivy waved an olive branch in the form of a freshly poured glass of champagne. Casey cleared her throat, and Ivy groaned, setting down the bubbly and reaching instead for a frosty bottle from the cooler.

"Now *that's* more like it," Casey said, popping the top off on the table's edge. She turned back to Charlotte, who was watching the whole exchange with a mixture of amusement and relief. She figured, though, that the spotlight was back on her.

"Hi," Charlotte said, her nerves returning. "Happy Thanksgiving?" The greeting came out like a question, one she hoped asked, *Can I get away with just saying that?*

But the other three women stared at her, brows raised.

"Hey," Delaney said, her voice gentle and maybe a little hesitant. "I know firsthand what it's like to get swept up in the whirlwind that is Meadow Valley. I fell in love with this town before I ever met Sam."

Charlotte nodded, but she wasn't really following. "I'm no stranger to this place," she said. "Spent my summers here until I was a teen."

Delaney nodded. "Yeah. I know. But there are Callahans here now. That changes things a little. And I think what Casey was trying to say about that kiss—"

"Is that I've given and received plenty of kisses hello.

From relatives. From...*friends*..." Casey said. "And that—what just happened between you and one of those Callahans Delaney was talking about—was a far cry from *friendly* and just as equally far from that little no-strings-attached thing you had going the last time you were here." She raised a brow.

Ivy bit her lip and nodded. "He's barely been able to sit still all night. I can't even tell you how many times he found some excuse to get up and peek out the window or take a step out onto the porch."

"Seven," Casey said bluntly. The other three women stared at her. "What? Don't judge. You all go home to someone in your bed at night while I, apparently, live vicariously by being up in everyone else's business. Ben stepped out onto the porch after I walked in and again when Luis and Anna started going at it about whether or not his wedge salad—prepared with Anna's grape tomatoes and blue cheese—would have been better complemented with the balsamic glaze she suggested or the homemade blue cheese dressing Luis prepared. Plus his five trips to the window, and that's just since I showed up."

Everyone's eyes widened, and Casey groaned. "Fine," she relented. "I *am* in everyone else's business. Ugh. When did *that* happen?" She took a long swig from her beer.

"You really like him. Don't you?" Ivy asked. "And if Casey's mild stalking is correct—"

"Hey!" Casey said with a pout. "I didn't say I was proud of my behavior."

"Then it looks like Ben feels the same way," Delaney added. "We didn't mean to ambush you, by the way. It was just really hard to miss that kiss."

Really strong like. That was all this was, right? Friends *liked* one another. And she liked Ben. A lot.

Good Lord. She sounded like a middle schooler even in her own head. The truth was she'd be lying to her friends and to herself if she tried to brush off her feelings for Ben as *like*. There was certainly an L-word involved, though, and if she said it out loud, then what? She'd resent Ben if he pressured her to stay when he knew she couldn't. Wouldn't he feel the same if she asked something that monumental of him?

"I—"

She was saved by seeing Sam standing at the main dinner table, awkwardly tapping a fork against his champagne flute.

"A toast!" Charlotte blurted instead. "We should head back over."

"Um...sorry, folks, if I'm interrupting," he called out to everyone still at the table as well as the women still by the makeshift bar. His deep voice only somewhat masked his apparent nerves. "I'm not usually one for speaking in front of an audience, but I kind of wanted to do something I haven't done in a good long while." He motioned toward the group of women. "Vegas, how about you and your friends join us?" he said with an easy grin, his eyes on Delaney.

Charlotte grabbed a bottle of beer and—not being as adept as Casey—used the bottle opener to remove the cap. Then the four women made their way to the table. Ivy slid into her chair next to Carter and Casey took the seat on her other side. Delaney found her spot next to Sam, and Charlotte blew out a breath as she took the one remaining empty seat in between Ben and her cousin. Hey, that was right. She *wasn't* entirely the odd woman out. She had family here too!

"What's happening?" she whispered to Ben, handing

him the beer and finally taking off her coat and tossing it on the back of her chair.

"I have no idea," he whispered back. "Buckle up, though, because my brother has been full of surprises lately." He tapped her champagne flute with the bottom of his bottle. "Thanks for this, by the way."

"When Ben and I were kids," Sam continued, not giving Charlotte a chance to respond, "Thanksgiving was a big deal at our house. It was a time when all four of us were in one place. Mom and Dad would spend the day in the kitchen together preparing all of our favorites—everything we tried to re-create tonight—and the table would always be surrounded by family and any friends who didn't have family nearby." He glanced around the table. "Kind of like this. And even though Ben and I always groaned about it— because it meant we had to wait for dessert—I think we both sort of enjoyed the tradition, one I'd like to reinstate. Where we go around the table and share one thing we've been the most grateful for in the past year." He leaned over and kissed his mother on the cheek and then took his seat between her and Delaney. "And because it's my game, I get to go last. So, Mom, what do you think?"

The older woman swiped at a tear under her eye and nodded. She linked both arms around the man sitting next to her, Sam and Ben's father. "I'm just so grateful to be here, doing this, with my family—that we found our way back to each other." She looked specifically at the older Mr. Callahan. "And that we did it while there is still time."

She kissed her husband. Wait, was he her husband? Ben had mentioned her leaving and then coming back, so maybe they weren't married anymore, but they looked every bit the loving couple.

"I guess it's my turn, huh?" Ben's father said. "I'm Nolan, for anyone who doesn't know." He winked at Charlotte, and her stomach tightened. Had Ben mentioned her before she arrived? "And heck, I'm grateful I escaped the home for the day to be with you all."

"*Dad*," Sam said with amusement in his tone.

"Okay, fine," Nolan replied. "They *let* me out. And since I'm sensing my son wants me to share something a little more meaningful, I'll say this. I may not remember tonight up here in the not too distant future." He tapped his temple with his index finger. "But sitting here with the love of my life and my two boys—my two *healthy* boys with their whole lives ahead of them..." His voice cracked on the word *healthy*. "I will *never* forget how that feels *here*." This time he tapped the left side of his chest but didn't say any more.

It was quiet for several seconds until the thirtysomething dark-haired woman next to Nolan threw her hands in the air. "Well how am I supposed to follow that?" she asked.

Luis nudged her lightly with his elbow. "Just tell everyone how grateful you are for my *perfecto* blue cheese dressing on the wedge salad, and we'll call it a day."

The woman, who Charlotte now realized must be Anna, responded with a flurry of Spanish that Charlotte didn't understand, and suddenly the chef and produce supplier were arguing animatedly in another language about salad dressing.

Ben waved them off. "Ignore them, folks. This is simply foreplay. But if they aren't going to participate in family time..." he said, his tone teasing but also with a hint of *Hey, knock it off*.

The couple stopped arguing and stared at their audience.

Anna groaned. "I am grateful that my job brought me to this ranch so that I could meet this man who drives me up the wall and down again." She placed a palm on Luis's cheek. "And I wouldn't have it any other way."

A dopey grin spread across Luis's face, and he laughed an equally dopey laugh. "What she said," was his only response. And then it was Ben's turn.

"Uh...yeah," Ben said. "Kind of thought I was going to have more time to put my thoughts in order, but I don't want to keep you all from dessert, so here it goes." He took a sip of his beer and then slid his left hand under the table, linking his fingers with Charlotte's.

Her heart stopped and sped up all at the same time, which wasn't possible, but there you go. She was some sort of medical anomaly.

"Wow, this was easier to do as a kid," he said with a nervous laugh.

She squeezed his hand.

"Something happened a little over a month ago. I found out I'd been given a second chance at a future. And I realized two things. One, that I better make the most of this chance, and two, that I was a selfish ass for the way I'd been living up until then." He looked at his parents. "I saw what I thought my future might be, and I bailed— mentally and emotionally—when I should have been grateful for whatever time I had to live the life I wanted. I'm not proud of how I behaved as a son...a brother...or a friend." He glanced at Sam and Colt, respectively. "I'm going to do better. I'm going to appreciate what I have for however long I have it. And I'm going to stop bailing when things get tough." He cleared his throat. "Okay, so that sounded more like a New Year's resolution, but there you have it."

He raised their clasped hands and kissed hers.

She gasped.

"Also," Ben said, staring straight at her but directing his words to the rest of the table, "for anyone who doesn't already know, this is Dr. Charlotte North, Pearl's grand-daughter. She's taking care of Pearl and the inn until just before Christmas, and I plan to spend every second I'm not working the ranch or building the house showing her that I can be the man I think I can be."

Wait. What?

She was prepared for some generic Thanksgiving toast. *Maybe* something for his parents. But that? He'd never said— That wasn't what he was really doing.

Was it?

And then he answered the questions swimming through her head by kissing her to a chorus of gasps and *Aws*, which was a good thing because she had no idea what to say after that, and she wasn't sure three more weeks would be enough to figure it out.

"Great," she heard Sam say with a chuckle while Ben's lips were still on hers. "How the heck am I supposed to propose after that?"

That shut everyone up quickly.

She and Ben broke apart to see Delaney with her hand over her mouth and tears in her eyes—and Sam Callahan down on one knee.

"Sorry to steal your thunder, little brother," he said to Ben with a wink. "But I kind of had a plan for tonight."

"Go get her," Ben said, then wrapped an arm around Charlotte's shoulders and pulled her close.

"Vegas," Sam said, grabbing her free hand and kissing it. "I had a quick chat with your parents and your sister before I stole you back from your hometown—though you and I both know you've always been a small-town girl at heart."

She nodded.

"I told them that if I was lucky enough to win you back that I was going to marry you—if, of course, that was what you wanted too." He smiled.

Delaney finally dropped her hand from her mouth. "That was less than two months ago."

He grinned. "I don't need much time to know when something's right. And *we're* right. Even had the ring on me then but wanted to wait for the right moment. Wasn't expecting my brother to upstage me." He glanced at his brother, and the whole table laughed. "I messed up once," Sam said. "And I'll probably do it again because, let's face it, I'm still figuring this all out. But I want to figure it out with *you*—if you'll have me. I love you, Delaney. Marry me?"

He produced a small blue box and opened it to reveal a beautiful princess-cut diamond solitaire ring.

Charlotte's throat went dry as Delaney burst into tears with an emphatic "Yes!"

She should be happy for her new friend. And she was. But Ben wasn't the only one realizing two things about his life tonight. Charlotte had come to two conclusions as well. One, that she'd never get a proposal like that from a Callahan cowboy. She couldn't. It was impossible. She understood that. But then there was that terrifying number two.

Maybe she wanted the impossible.

Everybody rose from their seats and erupted into applause as the newly engaged couple kissed.

Charlotte downed the contents of her champagne flute, but it didn't help.

"I need some air," she said, stepping around her chair and striding toward the door.

She hoped everyone was focused on Sam and Delaney so as not to notice. She wasn't trying to make a scene but simply looking for room to breathe.

It was colder outside than she'd remembered, and she regretted leaving her coat behind. But when the cool air filled her lungs, she no longer felt like she was suffocating. Her heart stopped threatening to pound straight out of her chest.

When she finally had the guts to turn and see if anyone noticed her abrupt exit, the only one looking back was Ben.

"I'm sorry," she mouthed through the glass.

And then she headed toward Pearl's car and the only safety she knew—being alone.

CHAPTER SIXTEEN

Ben offered his brother and new fiancée his congratulations as more bottles of champagne were popped open and glasses were filled. But when he saw the headlights of Pearl's car turn on, he slipped out of the melee and into the night.

He wasn't sure what he was going to say if he made it in time to stop Charlotte from running off, but he understood why she'd left. He'd promised her no pressure, and then he'd gone and kissed her there in front of everyone, which would have been enough. But Sam with that damned proposal—not that he wasn't happy for his brother, but a heads-up would have been nice.

She'd already put the car in drive by the time he got there, so he slapped his palm against the windshield. He knew all too well how easy it was to run when things got too real. They'd both been doing it the whole time they'd been "together." As long as they called it make-believe, they could ignore the truth—that somewhere along the way, their friendship had grown into something much bigger than either of them had bargained for. And rather than stop it, they'd run from the truth—right into each other's beds.

Ben didn't want to run anymore. If *she* did, fine. But at least he was going to grow up and face it.

She startled, slamming on the brakes, barely avoiding rolling over his boot, and somehow turned on the windshield wipers at full speed. If it wasn't for his quick reflexes, he might have had no choice but to become a righty.

She put the car in park and threw her hands in the air, shouting something that sounded like Charlie Brown's teacher through the muffling of the glass.

He tapped his ear and shook his head, then crossed his arms and waited.

Finally, the engine went silent, and Charlotte threw open the door.

"Are you crazy?" she asked as she hopped out and slammed the door. "I could have run you over!"

"And sliced off a finger or two," he said with a laugh.

She glanced at the windshield, wipers stalled sticking straight up over the glass.

She gasped, but when she turned back to him, her jaw was tight, eyes narrowed.

"I didn't ask you to come after me," she said, voice even now. "I just needed some air."

He nodded. "There's getting air and then there's taking off with your coat still inside."

She squinted at the dining hall window and then shrugged. "I'll get it tomorrow."

"Come on, Doc," he said softly, taking a step closer. When she didn't run for the hills, he blew out a relieved breath. "I know this evening turned a bit more dramatic than I'd anticipated, but it's not like *I* proposed. I promised you no pressure, and I think I've kept up my end of the bargain. So what's got you spooked?"

She blew into her hands, then rubbed her palms up and down her arms.

"You're freezing," he said, wanting to wrap her in his arms, but since she was already spooked, he hesitated to make another move.

"I am not," she lied, rubbing her palms together and then dropping her hands to her sides when she was caught in the act.

"Do you really need air?" he asked.

She nodded.

"Well, you're not going to get it inside a car. If I run back inside and grab your coat, I can take you somewhere you can really get some space—even from me if that's what you need—but do you promise not to run off?"

She skimmed her teeth over her top lip and then nodded again.

He narrowed his eyes at her and held out his palm. "Keys," he said. "I feel like I need a bit of insurance."

She rolled her eyes but handed him the keys.

"Ninety seconds," he promised, wrapping his fingers tight around the keys. "Tops."

She shoved her hands in the pockets of her jeans. "I can still walk. *Fast*," she threatened, but she was finally smiling. "Eighty-nine, eighty-eight, eighty-seven..." She raised her brows, and Ben started backing up toward the dining hall. *Fast.*

He made it back in less than a minute, barely having to make an excuse for his exit amid the celebration going on inside. He kissed Delaney on the cheek and congratulated her, gave his brother an equally congratulatory slap on the back, and then grabbed Charlotte's coat.

"Just taking a quick walk!" he called over his shoulder on his way back to the door.

It was *mostly* the truth.

When he made it back outside, he held Charlotte's coat open, and she eagerly slipped her arms inside. He took the opportunity to wrap his arms over her shoulders, kiss her softly on the cheek, and whisper in her ear, "Let's head to the stable."

"The what?" she asked, spinning around to face him. "It's forty degrees out here."

He raised his brows. "Thirty-eight last I checked. But we'll get you in some thermal riding gloves, and you'll be good to go."

Her brow furrowed, but when he wrapped her hand in his, she nodded and let him lead the way.

Black Widow nickered softly when they approached her stall.

"I think she remembers you," he said.

Charlotte's lips parted in a smile as she gave the mare a scratch behind her ear.

"I rode her the day we met," Charlotte said.

Ben nodded. "You almost beat me around the arena."

Charlotte laughed. "That seems like a million years ago," she said wistfully. "Hey, girl," she said to the mare that had been as taken with the good doctor as he'd been back then. "I think she does remember me!" she continued, her enthusiasm building. "But...isn't she tired? I don't want to give her a workout after a long day."

Ben shook his head. "No guests until Saturday, which means all horses had the day off and then some."

She worried her lip between her teeth. "Are you and Loki coming out there with me?"

Ben laughed, realizing they'd both dressed up as the horses' alter egos for Halloween. He couldn't tell if that was an invitation or quite the opposite, but he guessed she needed a bit of time on her own.

"Thought I'd let you warm up the arena first. On your own."

Her smile widened, and whatever else happened from here, he'd consider tonight a win.

"You want a saddle?" he asked, but Charlotte shook her head. "All right, then. I'll grab you those gloves and a bridle while you two get ready."

He strode toward the tack room, realizing that he was grinning about as big as she was. All those things he'd said at the table before Sam went and proposed to Delaney? Ben had meant them. He wanted to be a better son, a better brother, and a better man. Maybe finding out he was healthy was the catalyst for his change, but he'd turned over plenty of new leaves in years past and gone right back to the man he'd always been—one who looked out for himself above all else.

But this time was different. Charlotte was different than any woman he'd known. And *he* was different with her.

He grabbed the bridle and gloves and an extra pair for himself, just in case, and headed back to find Charlotte already on Black Widow's back, ready to head outside.

"She's all yours, Doc," he said, handing her the gloves and then bridling the horse.

She put them on and nodded. "Thank you—for knowing what I needed."

He lifted a lever on the wall next to the open doors, and the arena lights lit up the night.

He heard her breath catch in her throat, and then she

tapped her heels lightly on Black Widow's sides, and they were off.

He climbed onto the arena fence, taking a front row seat to the event.

Good Lord the woman could ride. She sped past him, her body low against the mare's, the two of them finding a rhythm he rarely saw with ranch guests. That kind of connection only existed for those who truly loved both the sport and the animal. And as much as he'd planned on taking Loki for a spin—maybe challenging her to a rematch—for the first time in the arena, he was enjoying being a spectator more than a rider.

She and the horse cantered for several more laps while he remained perched on the fence, the rider's only—yet biggest—fan.

They slowed to a trot on the next lap, and by the time she made it back to Ben again, she was tugging the reins, bringing the horse to a halt.

"You get all the air you needed?" he asked.

Charlotte nodded. "I'm sorry about in there." She motioned toward the dining hall.

He laughed. "Doc, if the tables were turned, and you'd ambushed me with your whole family, including bearing witness to an unexpected proposal, I'd have peeled out of that dusty drive so fast the tires would have left burn marks in the dirt."

She narrowed her eyes at him. "I'd have believed that a little over a month ago, but I don't know, cowboy. What you said in there? And goodness I could *feel* the love oozing out of everyone's pores. I don't know what to do with that. I mean, I'm not equipped—" She groaned. "Do you want to know what Thanksgiving was like at my house growing up?"

He shrugged. "I don't know. Do I?"

She let out a bitter laugh. "If we were in town, I'd beg my parents to make the drive to Meadow Valley. But because they worked most weekends, it barely happened. When I got older, they started using breaks from school to book jobs out of town. Many Thanksgivings we spent in motels in other states eating fast food and watching whatever cable station we could all agree on. They called it an adventure, but I don't know. I always felt so disconnected. And now I'm here tonight with your family, who is back there talking about being grateful for second chances or proposing or saying they're going to be better men when they're already one of the best men I know. I felt...I felt *connection*, Ben. It's bad enough I've grown attached to you. I don't want get attached to *them* too."

And here he thought *he* was the one ready to admit the truth.

She averted her eyes after that last remark, and Ben had to grab the fence beneath him. This woman threw him off balance at every turn, and it was time she knew.

"I didn't ask you to come here tonight to ambush you, Doc."

She nodded. "I know. But sometimes the best of intentions can only go so far."

He hopped off the fence and dared to approach her and Black Widow. The mare snorted and took a couple of steps back.

"Looks like you've got yourself a bodyguard," he said.

Charlotte cleared her throat. "Do I need one?"

He rested a hand on her thigh, and neither she nor the mare protested, so he took the sign as encouragement.

"Do you think I'm going to hurt you?" he asked

warily. Because if there was one thing he knew for sure, it was that she had the power to obliterate him.

She gripped Black Widow's reins tighter but shook her head.

"Do you think *I'm* going to hurt *you*?" she countered.

He nodded without hesitation, and her mouth fell open.

"I don't think I really knew what I was doing until you showed up," he said. "But once you walked through that door, I knew I wanted you there tonight—for the unintentional ambush," he said with a chuckle. "And so that you'd know beyond a shadow of a doubt that this isn't a game for me anymore. No more pretending. No nothing. Just two people who maybe, in another place or time, could have had something pretty damned fantastic."

He watched as she stared at him blankly, hoping that she was processing what he'd said in her own way.

She dropped her head back and stared up at the star-speckled sky.

"Why?" she asked, and he wasn't sure if she was talking to him or to the stars—not that the stars could have done anything to piss her off.

"Should I...answer that?" he asked.

She dropped her head, her gaze meeting his. "*Why* couldn't you have just stayed my vacation cowboy?" she asked.

He grinned, and she rolled her eyes. How he loved to push her buttons.

"Because I don't want to be that guy anymore," he admitted. "I don't want to take the easy way out." He paused for several seconds. "I want more, even if that more means only a few weeks."

He gave Black Widow a pat on her side. "Is there room

for two up there?" he asked, knowing that the mare could handle two riders but not sure if Charlotte could.

She nodded slowly, and in mere seconds he was seated behind her, arms around her waist and hands gripping the reins.

"I want you, Doc," he whispered in her ear, the closest he could get to the truth.

She leaned back and kissed him. "I want you, too, cowboy." Then she kicked her heels against Black Widow's sides, and they took off across the arena.

As long as they never left the arena, they could pretend a little while longer. Not for Pearl. Not for his folks. Not for anyone this time but themselves. So for now they simply rode, and rode, and rode.

"I don't have to be at the inn until lunchtime tomorrow," Charlotte mentioned as they closed the stable up for the night. "Gran is...um...The chief is off duty tomorrow, so he's spending the night and wants to help out in the morning."

He smiled at her and planted a soft kiss on the tip of her nose—which felt like kissing an icicle.

"We need to get you inside." He glanced back toward the dining hall and noticed his mom's car and Casey's truck were missing. "Looks like things are winding down in there anyway. How about I meet you at the guest quarters?" He pulled a key card out of his pocket and slipped it into her gloved palm. "First floor, last room on your left. You can do whatever you need to do to warm up, and if that doesn't work..." He winked. "I'll be there in ten minutes."

She laughed, but then her expression grew serious. "I should come say good-bye to everyone. I feel like a jerk for my dramatic exit. I didn't even really get to meet your parents."

He waved her off. "Looks like they already left. And everyone else you'll see tomorrow or the next day. I should have eased you into this, and I didn't. Sorry about that."

She wrapped her arms around his waist and stood on her tiptoes to kiss him.

He hummed against her as her lips touched his.

"How about we go visit your dad together? I have Monday night off if you're free and *if* you'd want me there. I didn't mean to just invite myself."

He laughed. "Monday evening is perfect. In *fact*, it's family game night as well as *my* night to pick. Hope you like Uno."

Her green eyes shone in the sliver of moonlight.

"I am an Uno master," she said with glee. "And I am not above tossing a Wild Draw Four your way, so watch out."

He raised a brow. "Competitive much?"

She jutted out her chin. "Don't pretend like this is brand-new information. If you hadn't hitched a ride on *my* horse, I'd have done the same with you in the arena."

Like she'd tried the first day they met.

Had that only been a couple months ago? He couldn't wrap his brain around how much had changed in so little time.

"I look forward to your ruthless competition," he teased.

She gave him a teeth-chattering grin.

"In*side*, Doc." He pointed toward the guesthouse.

"Is that an order?" she asked, teasing him right back—as much as she could while shivering. "Okay, fine," she relented. "I'm going. See you in ten minutes."

* * *

It hadn't taken long to clean up, especially when Luis and Anna insisted on staying behind and wrapping the leftovers as well as ensuring that Luis's kitchen was left exactly as Luis liked it.

"Mom and Dad cut out early?" Ben asked his brother as he headed toward the door.

Sam nodded. "Dad said something about a headache. Mom thinks it was overstimulation. Either way, it looked like he'd had enough for the night."

Ben shrugged. "Looks like things are under control here, so I'm going to call it a night too. Charlotte's sorry about the…uh…abrupt exit. I think she was a little overstimulated too."

Before Ben made it out the door, though, Sam and Delaney cornered him. Well, it was more Delaney, considering she stretched her arm across the door right when he'd reached to open it.

"Does she know?" Delaney asked, not giving him a chance to protest about his blocked exit.

"Know what?" both men responded in unison.

Delaney rolled her eyes. "That you're in *love* with her," she directed at Ben.

"You're in love with her?" Sam asked, then turned to his new fiancée. "He told you he's in love with her?"

This time, Delaney groaned. "Do you guys really not *see* these things? He invited her to Thanksgiving dinner, practically paced the room until she arrived, *greeted* her with an unquestionably romantic kiss, and then took off with her for the rest of the evening. Your brother is head over heels for that woman, and if we all know, I think she should know too."

"Okay. Hold up a second." Ben brought his hands

together in the *time-out* gesture. "No one knows *anything* because I haven't told anyone anything about any sort of feelings I may or may not be...feeling." He blew out a breath.

"Is word repetition your tell?" Delaney asked him. "For when you're lying?"

Sam's eyes widened. "It is!" he exclaimed. He turned to Ben. "Remember when you were thirteen and you and Colt stole the horses Dad was boarding and rode them up to the school track? Sheriff had to trail you two back to the stable, and even when you rode up on the evidence, you still tried to talk your way out of it." Sam laughed. "Told our father he was only borrowing the Thorough-breds to give them some exercise. You went on and on about *borrowing* for at least ten minutes."

Ben half smiled and half frowned at the memory. It was right after their parents had split, his mom having moved out the week before. He'd convinced Colt they could take a midnight ride and make it back with no one the wiser. He'd been wrong.

"Dad could have pressed charges if he'd wanted to teach us a lesson," Ben admitted. "But he knew one more strike would have sent Colt to a juvenile detention center, which would have also meant him losing his placement with his foster family."

Delaney's eyes widened. "Colt? Juvie?"

"Someone call me?" Colt popped his head out from the kitchen.

"No!" all three of them called back.

Colt held his hands up in surrender. "Yikes," he said. "I'll just go back to taking all the leftovers."

He slipped back through the kitchen door.

"Colt?" Delaney whisper-shouted this time. "He seems

like—I don't know—some sort of golden boy or some-thing."

Ben chuckled. "He grew up, but don't let the good-boy persona fool you. He'll always have a wild streak. He just keeps it in check these days. Mostly. And fine. Maybe I have a tell or whatever, but that doesn't mean I need you two to get the small-town rumor mill going about me and the doc. The situation is under control," he lied, making a point *not* to say the word *control* in any way, shape, or form for the rest of this conversation—which meant he needed to leave before he dug himself any deeper. "Can I trust you two not to go all town crier on whatever it is you think you might know that you don't actually know?"

Dammit. Two *know*s.

He gently removed Delaney's arm from where it was still blocking the door.

"Good night," he said with enough finality that she willingly stepped aside. "And congratulations with the whole engagement thing."

He slipped out the door, but he could feel both of them staring after him as he did.

What if he *did* tell Charlotte how he felt? What if he was simply honest and put himself out there and took a stupid chance—a *real* chance—at happiness? Best-case scenario was she loved him too and they'd figure this out. Worst case? The worst case would likely knock him on his ass, but he'd get back up eventually. Wouldn't he?

He weighed the pros and cons in his head the entire walk to the guest quarters and all the way down the hall to his room.

"Get it together, Callahan," he whispered to himself before knocking on the door. Then he convinced himself he'd know what to say when he saw her.

She answered the door wearing an old, gray T-shirt of his that said CALLAHAN BROS. CONTRACTING across the chest in a faded white font, a shirt she must have found strewn over a chair or at the foot of the bed since that was basically how he "put away" clothes.

Her legs—her beautiful freckle-dotted legs—were bare. And in her hand she held one of several DVDs he'd unearthed in case the night ended with just him and his laptop.

The Empire Strikes Back.

"Doc, I..." The words were right there, on the tip of his tongue, but he faltered, or freaked out, or simply forgot how to speak. The man who was never at a loss for anything to say suddenly couldn't get his mouth to form three simple words.

She nodded, an understanding smile spreading across her face.

"I know," she said.

His brow furrowed. Wait. Did she just Han Solo him? And if she did, did that mean... Did they both?

His brain was going to short-circuit the longer he tried to figure her out. But maybe that was the thing with them. They could feel how they felt without saying it, without one of them pressuring the other to uproot his or her life.

He scooped her into his arms and threw her legs around his waist. She yelped with laughter, the DVD flying to the floor.

"I'm not sure you do," he said, his voice low and rough. He kissed her and then tossed her onto the bed.

She took off the T-shirt and then wiggled out of her pale blue, lacy, low-cut briefs.

His eyes widened as he drank in the vision of her. She was beautiful and vulnerable and *his*.

"I think you might have to demonstrate or something," she said. "Just so I'm sure."

He nodded. "Yeah. I think I do."

He kicked off his boots and pulled his sweater and T-shirt over his head. She leaned up and unbuttoned his jeans, gently tugged his zipper down. She watched, grinning, as he let the pants fall to the floor, stepping out of them and his socks at the same time. Two seconds later, gone were his black boxer briefs.

"There," he said, crawling over her in nothing but his skin. "We're even."

She skimmed her teeth over her bottom lip and wrapped her warm hand around the base of his erection.

He hissed in a breath as she urged him down and between her legs, his tip nudging her opening.

She was ready for him, and in case he hadn't gotten the message, she rocked her hips forward so he slipped partially inside.

"Who's showing who here?" he teased, and she answered by wrapping her arms and legs around him, taking him all the way in.

"Right," he ground out as he buried his face in the crook of her neck. "I forgot. You're in charge."

He tilted his head up and smiled at her, then kissed her hungrily, greedily, and was grateful when she did the same.

It didn't matter that they'd been doing this for weeks now or that they were getting really good at it.

Okay, who was he kidding? They were always fantastic together.

"I'm better with you," he said when he came up for air, slowly rocking his body against hers.

"Mmm-hmm," she said, her back arching so that he had to dip his head to allow his lips to greet her breasts.

But he didn't mean just now. Here. In his bed.

He was a better man with her. Period.

The following morning, they still lay entwined with each other and the sheets. He buried his face in her hair.

"I love it here. I swear I could stay like this forever," she said, her voice breathy and light.

In Meadow Valley? Had she decided to stay? What if all she needed to know was that he wanted the same thing? What if—

"Don't go," he whispered, without thinking it all the way through.

She hummed softly. "I'm not," she added dreamily. "Told you I don't need to be back until lunchtime."

"To New York," he clarified after only a second of hesitation. "Wait, did you not mean *here* as in Meadow Valley?"

She went still in his arms, and he knew he'd messed up. But it was out there now.

Dammit.

"Sorry," he said. But then he stopped himself. "No," he decided out loud. "I'm not sorry for telling you that I want you for more than just a handful of weeks. If that makes me an ass, then so be it. But I'm tired of tiptoeing around this."

He tilted his head back so he could see her, and if they weren't so close, he might have flinched.

Her jaw was set, and her wide-eyed gaze somehow doubled as a fiery glare.

"Are you trying to kill me with your eyes?" he asked, trying to lighten the situation. "I'm just wondering if I should duck and cover."

Her mouth didn't even twitch.

"I'm going to take a shower," she said, sliding out of bed and taking the sheet with her. "At my place."

She gathered her clothes and dressed in a flurry of movement, then tossed the sheet back onto the bed. He ignored it and got up, one hundred percent naked.

"Come on, Doc. Can we at least *talk* about this?"

She opened her mouth to say something, then closed it, then opened it again.

"Are you building that house for me?" she asked, not fazed in the least by his naked form.

"No," he said, his knee-jerk reaction. "I mean, I don't know. Maybe? Would that really be so bad? I know there'd be a ton of logistics to figure out, but dammit, Doc, am I such a bad guy for picturing us here—together?"

She groaned. "I've worked so hard to gain control of my life, to give it the stability I always needed. I went to New York because I was accepted into one of the top residency programs my school had to offer, and I stayed because I was hired by one of the best pediatric practices around. My life. My decision. My one way to control the outcome. To keep myself safe."

She sucked in a breath. "I *know* Gran is okay without me. That she has a life with the inn and the chief. But knowing how much she wants me here for good, when I can't just up and leave the life I've built, it breaks my heart every time I have to tell her no. And now you, the guy who was supposed to get it, who was supposed to understand, you're building me a freaking house." She shook her head. "We were supposed to just be friends. This kind of emotional attachment wasn't part of the deal."

Ben took a step toward her, and she reacted by grabbing his jeans from the floor and tossing them at him. He caught them, very strategically, in front of his morning wood, then let out a bitter laugh. "Doc, you're talking to the king of emotional distance, but I have news for you. You've got about as much control of that part of yourself as you do a bronc at a rodeo."

"I can control prolonging the hurt though. We both can." Her shoulders sagged. "Pearl gets her cast off in two weeks. I'll be back in New York before Christmas." She hesitated, and for a second he thought she might not go. But then she said, "I'm sorry, Ben. I really am."

And then she was gone.

He stood there, dumbfounded and naked, his balled-up jeans still held between his legs.

He'd somehow gone from having the most spectacular night of his life to losing the woman he loved for being honest about how he felt. At least telling her he wanted her to stay made it clear how he felt. Didn't it?

He showered, got dressed, and stormed out of the room. He could still fix this, still make things right. Except that now it was practically noon, and she was on the clock, which meant he had an entire day to figure out what to say. Or...maybe he should give her some space. What was the right answer? He didn't have it. Seemed like he never did.

So he headed down to the house in progress. One thing was for sure: When in doubt, take out your frustrations on a pile of lumber—with the appropriate power tools and safety gear, of course. If there was one thing Ben Callahan knew well, it was how to protect himself from getting hurt.

CHAPTER SEVENTEEN

Ivy backed up while Charlotte leaned over the top of the ladder, hanging the last strand of icicle lights over the porch of the Meadow Valley Inn.

Now that it was Monday, she took stock of how she'd spent the rest of the weekend since walking out on Ben—doing everything she could to stay busy, even if that meant freezing her ass off on a ladder. The more she worked, the more she thought she could fill the cavernous pit in her stomach.

But it was still there—a dull ache when she was busy and pretty much abject misery when she wasn't, which had made sleeping quite the challenge. She hated the thought of Ben feeling this way, too, but it wasn't like she could heal the wound she'd already caused—or that they weren't going to break each other's hearts when her time in Meadow Valley was up.

"Got it!" she called out, the ladder wobbling below her.

"Whoa!" Delaney said, holding tight to the base. "Is this the same ladder Pearl fell from?" she asked, looking up as Charlotte climbed down.

She brushed her gloved hands together and then looked at her handiwork with a satisfied grin. "Not bad for a first-timer, eh?" she said to the other two women.

Ivy danced back and forth, her hands plunged into the pockets of her white down vest. "You...you haven't plugged them in yet," she said through chattering teeth.

Gone was the surprise heat wave from her early October visit. It felt like full-on winter now, especially as late afternoon turned to dusk. *Not* winter in NYC, where people got snowed in for days on end, but she still kind of hoped it would snow before she left. It had been years since she'd been in Meadow Valley for the holidays, and the place was as picturesque as a postcard when it snowed.

"What happens if I plug it in and it doesn't work?" she asked.

Delaney and Ivy stared at her. "Wait, have you never put up your own lights *ever*? Like, even indoors?" Delaney asked.

Charlotte shook her head. "I've only ever lived in an apartment since living on my own, and holiday lights for one always seemed so—"

"Sad?" Ivy asked, her voice soft with pity.

Charlotte took off one of her gloves and threw it at her friend. "No!" she laughed. "I was going to say *pointless*."

"Whoops," Ivy said, wincing. She tossed the glove back to Charlotte. "My bad."

Charlotte shrugged. "I guess I didn't see the point of the lights if I was the only one who would see them."

"The point is..." Delaney started, then strode to where they'd run an extension cord from the lobby through one of the front windows. Charlotte nodded, and Delaney plugged in the lights, the whole front of the inn now shining with bright white twinkling icicles.

All three of them gasped.

"*That*," Delaney added. "That's the point. Add some snow—and I mean *real* snow and not that one little dusting we had a few weeks ago—and we are looking at some serious holiday spirit, ladies."

Ivy hooked one arm through Charlotte's and pulled her toward Delaney so she could do the same with her. "Now can we get inside and warm up? I was told that if I helped string lights there would be warm, boozy drinks involved."

Charlotte forced a laugh. "There've been warm boozy drinks all afternoon. Pearl's having an Irish coffee and hot toddy reception in the lobby area until six. It's her new Cyber Monday tradition. She figures if she can liquor up the guests, it'll keep them from holing up in their rooms, shopping on their laptops."

Ivy let Charlotte's arm go and pushed open the inn's front door.

"Do you mean I could have been sipping whiskey and coffee this whole time?" she asked as the other two women strode through. "And next year tell your gran to start this tradition a few hours earlier. Might throw a little extra business to some of the local shops." She coughed. "Like mine."

Charlotte felt a pang in her gut at realizing she likely wouldn't be in Meadow Valley for the holiday season next year. She worked for a good practice with doctors who understood a family emergency. But still, she'd insist on working the holidays—Thanksgiving at least— as a show of good faith for the favor they did for her. She probably wouldn't travel at all next year.

She sighed as they entered the inn where a small gathering of patrons and locals mingled in the small foyer, hands wrapped around steaming beverages. Pearl sat in her chair, a hot toddy in her hands, next to a small buffet lined with mugs.

"There they are," she said as the three women approached. "My holiday decorator trio. What'll it be, whiskey or whiskey?"

Charlotte reached for an Irish coffee while Delaney and Ivy both went for a toddy.

"There's an extra plate of white chocolate cranberry cookies in the kitchen if you girls want some quiet."

Ivy's eyes widened over the rim of her glass mug.

"Are you sure you're okay on your own for a little while longer?" Charlotte asked her grandmother, but Pearl waved her off.

"Chief's in the kitchen making the next round of drinks. He's not due back at the station until early tomorrow morning." Pearl waggled her brows. "Which means...I'm not alone."

Ivy winked at the woman. "Atta girl, Miss Pearl. Ain't nothing like a handsome firefighter to keep you company."

Delaney giggled, and Charlotte rolled her eyes. *Not* because she had any sort of issue with her grandmother and the company she kept—but because it had been three whole days since she'd woken up in Ben's bed and then left him standing there naked and dumbfounded after she'd freaked out on him not once but twice.

And it had been radio silence ever since.

It was fine. Better, actually, because now leaving wouldn't be so hard. There were no more blurred lines or assumptions about people staying in places that weren't their home and...She needed to focus on the hot drink in her hand and to stop said hand from trembling every time she thought about Ben Callahan.

"You okay?" Delaney asked as they headed into the kitchen to grab that extra plate of Pearl's cookies.

"What?" Charlotte asked. "Yeah. I'm fine. So fine. Totally fine."

She wasn't fine.

"What are we talking about?" Ivy asked, trailing behind them. "Oh, hey, Chief," she said when she saw that Pearl's companion was putting the finishing touches on two more Irish coffees.

He lifted them both in a gesture of cheers.

"Evening, Ivy," the older man said. "Delaney. Charlotte." He nodded toward the counter where the plate of cookies waited. "I'm guessing you're looking for that. Knock yourselves out," he added, then exited toward the lobby.

The three women made a beeline for the cookies, Ivy setting down her toddy and hopping up on the counter right next to them.

"I like a close human-to-baked-goods proximity," Ivy said, snagging the first cookie and tearing off a bite. "STOP everything you two are doing right now." She held out her partially eaten treat like it was a police badge.

Charlotte and Delaney froze, hands outstretched for their own cookies.

"I'm going to need to confiscate these along with my toddy and retire to the closest guest room," Ivy added.

Delaney slapped her hand away and grabbed her own cookie.

"Nice try," she said. "But you need to share."

Ivy pretended to pout and went back to nibbling her cookie, clearly savoring it rather than devouring it.

"*I* was just asking Charlotte if she was doing okay," Delaney added. "I mean, aside from kicking butt with your first set of holiday lights, you seem a little...off?

This doesn't have anything to do with Ben's trip to the ER on Friday, does it?"

Charlotte gasped.

"Uh-oh," Ivy said. "I don't think she knows."

"Wait. What?" Delaney asked. "I thought you and Ben— I mean, Sam didn't say..."

"Wait...*what*?" Charlotte parroted. "I *didn't* know. Emergency room? For what? How have I not heard about this? I thought news spread every time someone sneezed around here. And how do you two know but I don't?"

Ivy shrugged. "Carter was there when they stitched him up. Said Ben made him swear on doctor–patient confidentiality that no one would hear about it. Of course, he did tell *me*."

Charlotte scoffed. "Carter's *not* his doctor. Plus, he's *my* cousin, dammit. If there's anyone he should have told, it's his own flesh and blood, especially when I'm Ben's...I'm..."

Delaney raised a brow. "This should be interesting. You're Ben's *what*? Because if you didn't know about the accident, that means you haven't seen Ben since Thanksgiving..." She paused for effect. "*Or*...the morning after, which means *something* is up."

Wow. They hadn't even taken their coats off yet, and they were *here*.

"Is he okay?" Charlotte asked, her throat tight and that cavernous pit in her gut somehow twisting itself into a knot. The medical stuff she could handle. She at least needed to know that he was all right before the conversation veered back to the scary stuff—what Ben Callahan was to her. Judging by the way her insides were turning into a pretzel, she was not going to be able to bluff her way out of this one.

Delaney nodded. "He's fine. But he's going to have quite a scar right through that pretty right eyebrow of his. I guess he was working on the house, took a shortcut climbing through a window frame with his arms full and lost his footing. Caught his eye—or just above, luckily— on an exposed nail."

Ivy winced. "Now that the cat's out of the bag, I guess it's okay to tell you that Carter said it looked pretty bad. Couldn't believe Ben drove himself to the hospital. I should have told you," she said. "I'm really sorry, Charlotte."

Ben was alone. And had gotten hurt. Charlotte had to remind herself that in this context, he was just a patient. That was all they were doing, discussing a patient. A patient who was fine and who didn't want her to know about the accident in the first place. So she tamped down the growing urge to march over to the ranch and see for herself that he was, in fact, okay.

"Did he get a tetanus shot?" she asked, working harder than usual to keep her voice even.

Both of the other women shrugged.

"Didn't think to ask," Ivy said.

"Yeah. Me neither," Delaney added. "It's pretty standard, though, in this sort of situation. So I wouldn't worry about it."

Charlotte set her Irish coffee on the counter and very calmly, very deliberately smoothed her hands over her coat.

"Well," she said, then cleared her throat. "If neither of you can verify whether or not a tetanus shot was involved when there could have been some very dangerous bacteria on that nail, then it's my duty as a doctor to make sure the proper measures were taken to ensure the patient's well-being."

Delaney rolled her eyes. "Or you could just admit that you care about him and that no matter what happened after Thanksgiving dinner, he's important to you and you want to make sure he's okay."

Sure. She could admit all of those things. But that would also mean admitting that Ben wasn't so off base for asking her to stay and that the real reason she freaked out was because part of her wanted desperately to do just that.

"Is he at the ranch today?" she asked, ignoring Delaney's comment.

Delaney nodded. "He was in the dining hall with Luis and Sam when I left. But I think he was taking off soon for game night with his parents at Nolan's facility."

Game night. Shoot. She totally forgot.

She felt around in her pocket and found the keys to Pearl's car.

"I need to go," was all she said.

The other two women nodded.

"We know," Ivy replied. "But we will give you hell for it later. Expect much adolescent teasing—but only because we're rooting for you two. And you know, it's okay to turn off that overactive brain of yours and think with this every now and then." She pressed a hand over Charlotte's heart.

Charlotte's throat grew tight. Was it okay? Because right now thinking with that organ hurt. A lot.

Charlotte hugged them both. "Save me a cookie?" she called over her shoulder as she headed for the door.

"I can't make any promises!" Delaney called in return, and Charlotte bit back a smile.

She pulled up to the dining hall right as Ben was getting in his truck, so naturally she parked perpendicular to the truck's bed, making it next to impossible for him to reverse.

She flew out of the vehicle and up to the driver's side, where he sat in the seat, the door still open.

"You know that's not a parking spot," he said evenly, his face not fully turned toward hers.

She cradled his cheeks in her hands and urged his full gaze on hers, then hissed in a breath.

"C'mon, Doc," he said coolly. "I know you've seen worse."

She squeezed her eyes shut, remembering when she first saw her grandmother post-surgery, lying helpless in that hospital bed. It was so much harder to pretend it was *just a patient* when it was someone she loved. And now here was Ben, his maddeningly perfect brow split into two uneven parts by a gash held together by dark thread, the surrounding skin slightly purple and bruised.

Wait...*loved*?

"Hey," he added, interrupting her revelation, his voice gentler now. "I'm okay."

When she opened her eyes, she could feel that her lashes were wet.

"*Hey*," he said again, swiping a finger under one of her eyes. "I'm guessing you just found out. I didn't think— I mean, I would have told you if..." He trailed off.

"If I hadn't made you think I wouldn't care," she said flatly.

He shook his head. "No. Geez, Doc. No. *I* pushed when I told myself I wouldn't. I asked you to do what was easiest for me, and that wasn't fair. Not by a longshot. I might have confused a signal or two and thought I was on the right track, but it doesn't change the fact that I messed up." The corner of his mouth turned up. "Of

course, you messed up pretty royally, too, running out on
me like that."

She threw her head back and laughed. It was either
that or burst into tears. God she needed that, a break in
the tension—and Ben's forgiveness.

"You were right, okay? I tried to shut it off—the
emotion part—because I wanted to save both of us from
whatever is going to happen when I head back home. But
I failed. Miserably." She shook her head. "There isn't an
easy solution here. I thought I was saving us both by not
prolonging the inevitable."

He shook his head. "Nah," he teased. "That solution
hurt like hell."

Her chest ached realizing *she'd* caused that hurt.

"Then we'll make these last days count," she said. She
couldn't stay, and she'd never ask him to leave. But this
was better than wasting the time they had left, wasn't it?
"If you're up for it," she added.

He shrugged and gave her his most irresistible Ben
Callahan grin—which was basically *every* Ben Callahan
grin. "Only 'cause it's you, Doc."

She blew out a relieved breath, the cavern in her
stomach almost all the way refilled. But there was something else missing. "If it's all right with you, cowboy, I'm
going to kiss you now."

"What are you waiting for?" he asked. He slid out
of the truck so they were standing face-to-face, his body
pressed against hers. "I've been wanting you to do that
for three days."

She rose onto her toes and draped her arms around his
neck. And when she felt his warm lips against hers, his
rough stubble along her chin, she was home.

"This is better, right?" she said against him, not sure

which of them she was trying to convince more. "Being together while we can and then…Do we talk about *and then*?"

Do we tell each other how we really feel?

Why was she still holding back?

"Doc," he said, interrupting her. His hands slid down to her rear, and he gave her a gentle squeeze.

"Yeah," she squeaked.

"I know this might be remnants of the old me talking, but I'm going to let it slide and kindly ask that we stop talking and keep kissing. We'll get to the rest later."

She nodded. "Just one more thing though."

He groaned, but it was with a smile.

"Am I still invited to game night?" she asked. Maybe she couldn't get the words out, but she could show him that despite whatever the future held, this wasn't pretend for her anymore. Maybe it never truly was.

He let out a long, shaky exhale. "Why do you think I waited until the last possible second to leave? Give or take a few to kiss you senseless."

"Okay, then," she said, and did her best to kiss *him* senseless for every extra second they had.

When they entered his father's facility, they signed in at the lobby and then Ben led her straight to the game room. His parents were already there, his mom typing away at her phone while his father shuffled a deck of Uno cards, both of them sitting at a round wooden table.

In addition to the cards, there was an assortment of canned beverages on the table, along with a bowl of M&M's.

"There you are," the older woman said, rising to greet them. "I was beginning to worry you forgot."

Ben kissed his mother on the cheek. "That was the old me, Ma. Sorry. Just had to tie up some loose ends at the ranch." He pulled Charlotte in close. "And now I get to formally introduce you to Dr. Charlotte North." He winked at her, and heat rose in her cheeks.

"It's nice to officially meet you, Mrs. Callahan," she said, extending a hand. But the other woman waved her off.

"Nonsense, sweetheart. It's family game night, which means you get greeted like family. And please, call me Barbara Ann." Then she pulled Charlotte in for the warmest hug she'd had since...she couldn't remember when.

Charlotte sank into the embrace a little more than she should have. And maybe she should have let go a little earlier than she had. But God it felt good to simply let go for a few seconds.

She cleared her throat and backed away.

"Mr. Callahan," she said as Ben's father continued to shuffle. "We met briefly at the fall festival in October—and again at Thanksgiving. I was the one who took off in the middle of all the beautiful toasts?" She let out a nervous laugh.

He didn't look up.

"Hey, Dad," Ben said. "Charlotte and I—"

The older man held up a hand and shushed his son. "I need to concentrate, Benny." Then he tapped his index finger against his temple. "Keeps me sharp. Keeps the memory...keeps..."

He looked up then, brow furrowed as he glanced from Ben's mom, to Ben, to Charlotte.

"Benny?" he said. "When did you start growing facial hair?"

Charlotte's heart sank. She slipped her hand through Ben's and gave him a reassuring squeeze.

"I'm going to be thirty in a few weeks, Dad." He forced a laugh and scrubbed a hand over his jaw. "Facial hair's been here for quite some time."

Ben's mom sat down next to his dad and rested a hand over his.

"It's game night, Nolan. Ben brought his friend Charlotte for game night."

The older man looked down at the cards on the table, half of them still in his left hand.

"Right," he said with a nervous laugh. "Game night. I remember."

Charlotte swallowed the lump in her throat. Nolan Callahan might have been old enough to have two grown sons, but he wasn't an *old* man by any means. He was good-looking like his sons, just with salt-and-pepper hair and a laugh line or two. She doubted he was much over fifty. She couldn't wrap her head around what it had been like for Ben to imagine the same future for himself while also watching his father continue to appear healthy as his brain invisibly deteriorated.

Charlotte sat across from Nolan while Ben took the seat next to his father.

"Remember the ranch, Dad?" Ben asked hesitantly. "Sam and I built the ranch in Meadow Valley. We all moved out here, Colt too."

"Of course I remember," Nolan snapped, going back to shuffling. Then he took a deep breath and made eye contact with his son. "I remember," he said again, his tone gentle this time. "How's the eye? Mom told me about the accident."

"I'm good, Dad," Ben said softly. He reached a hand over and set it on Charlotte's knee. "Real good."

Nolan turned to look at Barbara Ann. "I'm damn proud

of our boys, especially now that this one comes to see me more." He nodded back at Ben with a smirk.

"And he's back," Ben said, clapping his dad on the shoulder. "How about shuffling and getting this game going?" He grabbed a handful of M&M's. "Are these peanut, or have you started experimenting with other flavors?"

Nolan scoffed. "There is no other flavor worthy of consumption and you know that."

Ben laughed, then nudged the bowl toward Charlotte. "The man does have a point."

She took a handful herself and popped one in her mouth while Ben's father started to deal. "I couldn't agree more."

After that, the game was underway. As cards were thrown, Nolan and Ben began ribbing each other like she guessed fathers and sons did. Soon she saw Ben's shoulders relax and his hesitant smile creep closer to his eyes. Charlotte was having so much fun, she'd all but forgotten about her good-natured threat to kick Ben's butt in the game.

But when Barbara Ann threw down a Reverse card and changed the color from red to yellow, Charlotte had no choice but to throw the card she'd been saving at a smiling Ben, who only had two cards left in his hand.

Wild Draw Four.

"Uno," Charlotte said, holding nothing but a red four in her hand.

"Oooh," Nolan said with a sly grin. "I think she just upset your almost win."

Ben narrowed his eyes at her and drew his four cards.

"But what color should I throw?" he asked, his words more of a taunt than a question.

She laid her card flat on the table so as not to

accidentally give herself away and stared at him with a vacant expression. She was a doctor, after all. She could put on a poker face when needed.

"Green?" Ben asked.

She remained unmoved.

"Blue?" he tried, but she didn't falter.

He organized his six cards and glanced at her again, then groaned when he couldn't get a read on her.

"Sorry, Dad," he said. "But it's the best move I've got right now." Then he threw a Draw Two. A *red* Draw Two.

She held her breath as Nolan chose his two cards and then threw down a red six. Barbara Ann followed with a red two.

Charlotte held on to her composure just long enough to flip over her card and then whooped and clapped at her victory.

"In your face, Callahans!" she shouted, then sprang up from the table into a not-at-all-embarrassing victory dance. When she realized she was dancing alone—which wasn't quick enough—she abruptly stopped. "Oops," she said sheepishly. "I'm guessing maybe Ben should have warned you that I have a competitive streak."

For several seconds, they all stared at her. Then Nolan burst into a fit of laughter, and Ben and Barbara Ann were quick to follow. Soon all four of them were up and out of their seats, mimicking her sweet moves like "stirring the pot" and "the running man." Somehow all her dance skills came from the '90s and sort of got stuck there.

The few other residents in the game room were watching, as was the female check-in attendant who snuck in from the lobby, and soon it was a full-on dance party in the game room.

Charlotte thought that *this* was what family must feel

like—laughing and dancing and looking ridiculous but not even caring. At one point, Ben—breaking out of a silly yet sexy booty shake—wrapped his arms around her and pulled her into a kiss.

"Thank you," he said when her bones had turned to Jell-O and she thought she might not be able to stand if he let go.

"For what?" she asked, then kissed him one more time for good measure.

"For being you," he said, then kissed her cheek. "For being here," he added, then kissed the other. "If I'd have known that all it would take for you to let that guard down was me almost losing an eye, I'd have done it weeks ago."

She backhanded him on the shoulder.

"Real cute, cowboy. You know, I may not be the best at saying how I feel, but I can show it—with the right person."

He dipped his head so his lips were next to her ear. When his breath hit her skin, goose bumps rippled up and down her arms.

"Are you saying, Doc, that what you're *feeling* is that *I'm* the right person?"

Her breath hitched. But before she could squeak out a yes, Barbara Ann's voice broke through the haze.

"Nolan? Nolan, are you okay?" she asked.

Ben released her, and they both spun to see Nolan Callahan no longer dancing but instead standing with both hands over his ears and his eyes squeezed shut.

"Is it another headache?" Ben's mother persisted when Nolan didn't respond.

"How often has he been getting headaches?" Charlotte asked as Ben helped his father back into his chair.

"Thanksgiving was the first that I know of," Ben said. "He said it felt like a tiny explosion in his head, but after some ibuprofen and rest, it seemed to go away."

"Mr. Callahan?" Charlotte asked, squatting down next to him. "Is that how it feels this time too? A little—" She cleared her throat. "A little explosion?"

He nodded, eyes still squeezed shut, then said something that sounded like *Yesh*.

"We need to get him to a hospital," she said to Ben. "I'm assuming the facility has emergency vehicles?"

Ben stood there and blinked for a second, then nodded.

She placed a hand on his cheek. "Stay here with your dad. I'll be right back."

Seconds later, she returned with two male nurses, one of whom was pushing a wheelchair. Outside the main entrance, an ambulance was already waiting.

Nolan Callahan was no longer gripping his head like a vise. Instead, he sat in his chair, the left side of his mouth drooped lower than the right, and his left arm hanging slack at his side. Ben's mom was still squatting next to him, whispering soothing words as her voice shook.

"What the hell is going on?" Ben asked as the nurses explained in calm voices to his father that they were going to help him into a different chair and then take him outside.

He ran a hand through his hair, tugging at its roots, and Charlotte put on her best poker face as she took in a calming breath. This was the first time she'd truly been terrified in a medical scenario—terrified for what Ben could lose. But he was already frightened enough. She needed to be his lifeline, and the only way she could do that was to stop being *Doc* and be Dr. North instead.

"Your father is presenting signs of a CVA, or

cerebrovascular accident," she said, her tone clinical. "A sudden intense headache, numbness or paralysis on one side of the body, slurred speech—"

"In *English*, Doc. Jesus. Talk to me like I'm your boyfriend, not like I'm the family of one of your patients."

Dammit! She'd already made things worse when all she wanted was to keep it together in the hopes of keeping Ben—her *boyfriend*—from falling apart.

"I'm sorry," she said. Then she grabbed one of his hands and pressed it between hers. "I'm either a doctor or your... I've never had to be both. I'm just trying to help you understand... I'm trying to tell you without upsetting you that—"

The nurses were wheeling Nolan Callahan toward the door now, with Ben's mother right behind. Ben was backing out of the room and toward the exit.

She stopped midsentence, her mouth hanging open. There wasn't time to process or react, just to be up front with him.

"A stroke," she finally said. "I think your father is having a stroke."

Ben swore under his breath, then looked over his shoulder at the ambulance, his father now strapped to a gurney.

"There's only room for your mom in there," she said. "We can follow behind them. Do you want me to drive? You might be too emotional to get behind the wheel."

He didn't say anything, just pulled the keys from his pocket and held them in his open palm. She squeezed his hand in hers before taking the keys. She couldn't tell him that everything was going to be okay because it very likely wouldn't be. "I'm here," was all she said instead, hoping that would be enough for now.

Once in the truck, she tried again to explain the symptoms and the possibilities. She couldn't help it. Knowledge comforted her. It gave her direction, even if it was a frightening direction. Maybe it could do the same for Ben. *Maybe* the more he knew, the better he could process the situation.

"There is a possibility it was only a transient ischemic attack, or TIA. It's *like* a stroke, and likely the warning sign that an actual stroke is imminent, but a TIA passes quickly and usually doesn't leave any lasting damage. You mentioned something about a headache on Thanksgiving night though. *That* might have been the TIA. Often a stroke happens within a week of a transient ischemic attack and—"

"Dammit, Doc, please. Just *talk* to me. Like a person. I don't want to hear doctor jargon or clinical speak or whatever it is you're doing over there. Is my father going to die?"

Okay. So, she was wrong.

Charlotte's hands gripped the steering wheel tighter. This was the only way she knew how to talk about life-threatening scenarios, in jargon and clinical speak. She could understand the science of the situation and work from there. But the emotion of it—if she let herself step outside of what she knew to what she felt or what Ben must be feeling, then she didn't have the answers. And that was terrifying.

"I don't know," she said softly. There were no three words she hated more. Her right hand twitched with the urge to release her death grip on the wheel and take his hand in hers or rest it on his knee. *Something* to make this better, to make up for not being able to give him the answer he needed.

But her expertise had always been in facts. Sure, there were times her patients and their parents needed words of reassurance that came with a soothing voice, but she always used knowledge as her jumping-off point. *Here's what we know, and here are the possibilities.* Ben wanted definitive answers, and she didn't have them.

"I'm sorry, Ben," was all she could add. "I wish I knew more."

By the time they made it to the emergency room desk, Nolan was about to be whisked away for testing. Ben sprinted to his father's side and quickly grabbed his hand.

"We're here, Dad, okay? It's me, Ben. Mom and I are here, and we're going to call Sam, and you're going to be fine." Charlotte swore she saw the man nod at his son, or maybe it was wishful thinking, but then the paramedics gently pushed Ben out of the way and continued down a hallway until they were out of sight.

Ben's mother sat in the waiting area, a clipboard on her lap and a pen in her hand, but she wasn't writing anything.

"Mom?" Ben said, rushing to the chair next to her. "What did they say? What's going on?"

She patted the chair next to her, and Charlotte stayed put, suddenly feeling out of place when thirty minutes ago she'd felt like she'd found a new family. She was still in earshot yet felt like any more physical proximity would be an intrusion.

"I need to tell you something," the older woman said. Then she looked up at Charlotte. "Come here, sweetheart," she said, motioning for Charlotte to sit too.

Her stomach tightened, and she told herself not to speak, not to throw out any doctor talk unless she was asked.

She nodded and took the seat next to Ben.

Barbara Ann Callahan set down her pen and grabbed each of their hands, squeezing tight. Charlotte's palms began to sweat.

"He was alert in the ambulance," she started. "Alert and here, you know? Fully present. Knew me. Knew what was going on when the paramedics asked him questions. His speech wasn't so good, but I could understand him."

Ben cleared his throat, and Charlotte held her breath.

"He told me," she continued, then sniffed as her eyes filled with tears. "He told me that if this was the last night, it was one of the best and that he was okay with that."

Ben pinched the bridge of his nose. "Jesus, Mom. It's not his last... it's not—" He sprang up from his chair. "I need to do something. Where did they take him? I can't just sit here and wait." He started pacing.

Ben's mother let Charlotte's hand go, then gave her knee a pat.

"I'm okay," she told her. "Really. Sam and Delaney are on their way. Why don't you take him for a walk, get some coffee or something. I'll text him if there's any news."

Charlotte nodded, then took a leap of faith and leaned over to give Ben's mother a hug.

"Thank you," the other woman whispered as she hugged Charlotte right back. "For helping make tonight one of the best."

CHAPTER EIGHTEEN

Ben didn't know where Charlotte was taking him, but moving felt better than standing still.

"I don't want coffee," he said flatly.

"I know," she said.

"And I'm not hungry. So screw the cafeteria, okay? I need to go somewhere I can get answers. I need to—"

"We're here," she said, then pushed through a glass door that led outside.

Or, *not* outside. Because outside was thirty-eight degrees, and though he could see the sky and the stars, he didn't feel the cold bite of the winter air. An atrium.

"I didn't even know this was here," he said. It wasn't big, maybe the square footage of a large master bedroom. But there were wooden benches, a couple trees, and a glass ceiling and walls that extended to the top floor of the hospital.

"I found it when Pearl was in recovery after surgery," she said softly, then let out a nervous laugh. "I'm not good with waiting either."

Ben spun to face her. "I'm sorry I snapped at you in the truck," he said.

She shook her head. "You don't need to apologize for a natural reaction to a scary situation. I just...I don't know what to say about a patient if I'm not trying to make a clinical diagnosis."

There were at least four feet between them, but he felt like they were miles apart.

"I'm not a patient," he said softly.

She nodded. "I know."

"What my mom said out there?" He squeezed his eyes shut and shook his head. "If this is the last night..."

"Ben, don't. We don't know if that's the case. It might not be a stroke, and the percentage that are fatal—"

"Stop," he said softly. He opened his eyes and swallowed despite the tightness in his throat. "I don't want to know numbers and percentages, okay? We're talking about my father, and while he may have made his share of mistakes, especially before we knew he was sick, he's still my father. Not a statistic." He said the words as gently as he could, but he felt them in his gut. He felt the years he wasted worrying about himself when he could have been a better son, when he could have been more help to Sam in taking care of the man who raised them. He felt how still—even in the past two months—he'd thought he'd grown so much, but he was still the selfish ass he'd always been. Here he'd been planning a future, finally committing to his life at the ranch—and to Charlotte. But he'd barely scratched the surface of being there for his parents. He'd let himself get so wrapped up in a relationship that was never meant to be real when he could have spent every second of his free time with his father.

He could have done more to make up for the time

they'd already lost. And now there might not be any time left.

"I'm sorry," Charlotte said. "I didn't mean to insinuate that I thought of him like that."

He stepped toward her, not knowing what it would matter if he told her now, because his father was possibly dying, and she was leaving, and he was going to be right back where he was six months ago when he thought he'd tested positive for the early-onset markers.

Broken and alone.

He grabbed her hand and pressed her palm to his chest where his heart hammered with worry. With anticipation. With the hope he had of figuring out a way for them to be together disintegrating. He didn't deserve her, didn't deserve this type of happiness when he'd failed everyone else he loved.

"It was one of the best nights for me too," he finally said. "That's what I wanted to tell you."

She pressed her lips together and nodded. Then she stood on her toes, wrapped her arms around his neck, and held him. No mind-bending kiss. Just his body pressed to hers.

He let out a long, shaky breath and squeezed her tight, like it was the last time he would.

His phone vibrated in his pocket.

He pulled it out, the screen lighting up with a text. Sam. It was only two words but that was all it took.

He's gone.

Sam had questioned whether or not they could afford to close the ranch for Thanksgiving. Now they'd hired on extra help for the following couple of weeks so they could settle their father's affairs without having to cancel their upcoming registrations.

Ben had spent the week helping his mom clean out Nolan's rooms at the facility, while Sam had taken care of all the necessary paperwork. Charlotte had called more than once offering to help in what little spare time she had, but Ben found every excuse in the book to turn her down.

"It's a small space, barely enough room for me and my mom to begin with," he'd said the first time she'd asked. Then, "I think they only let blood relatives past the lobby," the next time she tried. It was an obvious lie, and despite the hurt he heard in her response when he'd said it, he'd felt nothing but relief when she didn't offer again.

The pain of losing his father was already too much to bear. And the guilt of his absence from Nolan's life for the better part of the time they'd been in Meadow Valley? He wasn't sure he'd ever get over that. The only choice was to do better. To *be* better. He'd never be the kind of man Charlotte deserved—not with an entire country between them—not if he still hadn't learned how to truly be there for his family, the people who'd been there for him his entire life.

So he'd done what he did best—retreated.

Even now, five days *after*, he still felt like his throat was closing and that he couldn't breathe.

"We'll make it up," Sam was saying to Ben and Colt, the three of them sitting around the table in Sam's apartment behind the registration building. Ben couldn't even remember what they were talking about.

All he could think was how misplaced they all looked,

three men in dark suits with a sprawling ranch just outside.

"Don't worry about the money right now," Colt said, his hand on Sam's shoulder. "Just be there for your mom. For each other. Nolan was the closest thing I had to a father of my own. He was a good man."

Colt glanced at Ben, but Ben avoided eye contact, pushing his chair from the table and standing.

Even when Sam had feared ending up like their father, he had never faltered in his care for Nolan Callahan, especially after they'd moved to Meadow Valley. *Ben* had been the selfish one, the one too scared to face the man he thought he'd become. It was too late to make up for lost time, and Ben only had himself to blame.

"You two stick around for Delaney and Mom. I think I'd like to head over on my own," he said.

He didn't wait for either of them to respond but instead strode for the door, nearly tripping over Sam's dog Scout, who sprang to her feet at his approach, likely guessing it was time for a walk.

"Not now, girl," he said, sidestepping the pit bull and practically sprinting through the attached registration area and finally outside.

The cold air burned his lungs, but he didn't care. He gulped for more, feeling like he'd never get enough.

There wouldn't be a traditional funeral, his parents both deciding long ago to be as environmentally conscious as possible and opting for green burials. It meant his father's remains had been interred within twenty-four hours of passing.

Today, though, they were heading to the burial site where a sapling would mark his grave rather than a headstone. Immediate family—plus Colt and Delaney—only.

And after dinner convened at the ranch's dining hall, Luis and Anna would stay late to provide refreshments for those who wanted to stop by and pay their respects or— as his mom kept saying—celebrate Nolan's life.

His hand was on the door to his truck when he heard wheels crackling up the drive.

He turned slowly to see Pearl's Escape idling behind him, Charlotte at the wheel.

She lowered her window.

"Your mom called the inn," she said. "Invited me to..." Then she trailed off. "I thanked her but declined. I'll be there tonight. But I thought— I mean, I wanted to make sure you were okay since I haven't seen you all week." She groaned and shook her head. "I know you're not okay. My studies on grief say that the heavy mourning period lasts at least thirty days, and after that it can take up to six months for..." She swiftly closed her mouth and shook her head. "I'm doing it again. Sorry."

He found himself slowly moving toward her car, not realizing he was doing it until he was at the passenger door.

His chest tightened at the nearness of her, but it was so much better than the hollowness he'd felt moments before.

"If I let you drive me there," he started, "do you promise not to mention percentages or statistics?"

She nodded and crossed her finger over her heart, and he climbed inside.

"Hi," she said softly when he closed the door.

"Hi," he echoed. Had it only been five days since that night in the hospital? It felt like months.

"I was...um...worried about you. That's what I was trying to say when I started, you know, doing my statistics thing." She smiled and rested a hand on his knee. "*That's* why I came."

He sucked in a deep breath and then covered her hand with his own.

"Thank you," he said, his chest tight as his heart warred with his logic. He hadn't realized how much he needed her here, but it didn't change that soon she'd be gone.

His heart won out for the moment, and he leaned over, resting his forehead against hers. "Thank you," he said again. Then he allowed himself the comfort of kissing her, of having some sort of lifeline when everything felt turned upside down.

Her lips on his were like a beacon, leading him out of the woods and to solid ground. He wasn't there yet, but he was closer.

"How did you know where I was?" he asked. "I've been pretty MIA this week. I'm s—"

"Oh no you don't," she said, interrupting him. "You don't get to apologize for processing this in whatever way works best for you. I'm just glad I'm here now, even if the only thing I can do to make this easier is to get you to where you need to be."

He pressed his lips to hers once more. It was the only time he didn't feel the ache of loss.

"I'll take it," he whispered against her. "I'll take whatever I can get until... you know."

Until she left to go back to New York next week.

"Yeah," she said, her breath warm on his lips. "I know."

He gave her directions to the burial site, and Charlotte drove, her hand in his as they left the ranch grounds and pulled onto the main road.

"Pearl gave you the day off?" he asked.

She nodded. "Took her for some X-rays yesterday,

and things were looking so good that they switched out the plaster cast for a walking boot, which means no more wheelchair. Also means she's officially phasing me out." She let out a nervous laugh. "It's a relief, you know. That she's recovering so well."

"Happy to hear it," he said. And while he meant the words and wanted nothing but the best for Pearl, now that Charlotte was here, the selfish part of him had secretly hoped there'd be some sort of delay. That Pearl might need her granddaughter to stay on a little while longer just so he wouldn't have to say good-bye.

They pulled off the road and onto a winding path, where they were greeted by the sign that read LAKEWOOD CEMETERY. She pulled to a stop at a fork in the winding road, each branch seeming to extend into uncultivated land.

"How do we know which way to go?" she asked.

He pulled out his phone and opened the email containing the directions to his father's burial site.

"Left," he said. "For about a quarter of a mile. Then we should see a sapling in between two mature trees, both maples. Uh...right side of the road."

She nodded and continued on. And there it was, exactly as the directions said.

"Should we wait for everyone else?" she asked.

He shook his head. "I want a few minutes alone." He turned to face her. "You coming?"

Her eyes widened. "You want me— I mean, of course. I just didn't think—" Then she looked him up and down. "You don't have a coat."

He shrugged. "I'll survive."

She shook her head. "That won't do. While you technically can't catch a cold from being in the cold and the risk of frostbite is low to none..."

He gave her a look that said *You're doing it again*, because she paused and narrowed her eyes at him.

"What I was getting at is that it just plain sucks to be cold."

He laughed softly. "Like I said, I'll survive."

"Yeah, well, maybe I want more for you than that."

She held up a finger for him to wait, then pulled the key from the ignition, undid her seat belt, and got out of the car. After a short rummage in the trunk, she was back with a wool blanket folded in her arms. She opened the door and stuck her head back inside. "Come on," she said.

Side by side, they made their way to the young tree under which his father was laid to rest. She opened the blanket and draped it over his shoulders, and he held his arms wide, inviting her inside.

Together they simply stood there, cocooned in their own little world, much like they'd been for the past several weeks. And despite the hell of the past week and the knowledge that this time next week she'd be gone, he felt safe from the grief. From reality. From losing again.

Later that night, the dining hall was anything but somber. Bottles of beer and wine abounded, and it truly was a celebration of Nolan Callahan's too-short life.

"What do you want to do, Mom?" Sam asked when the three of them found a moment alone. "What can *we* do to make this easier?"

Barbara Ann Callahan took a final swig of her beer and then set it on a nearby table. She linked her arms with her sons and sighed.

"I know I can't make up for the time I was gone, for leaving your father when I did…"

Ben shook his head. "He cheated. And even if it was all tied to him being sick and none of us knowing, it doesn't change how much that must have hurt you."

She nodded, but her eyes filled with tears. "And it doesn't change how much my leaving must have hurt the two of you." She took a steadying breath. "Now let me say what I want to say before I lose my nerve, will you?" she asked with mock impatience.

Both Sam and Ben laughed softly. "The floor is yours, Mom," Sam said.

"I'm so glad your father and I found our way back, even in what was the most challenging part of our lives together. He was sick," she said, her voice cracking. "But when he was himself, he made it clear that he was also very, very happy. And so proud of you two for taking his legacy and turning it into your own dream." She pulled them both closer. "I miss this—*us*," she said. "Just being on the ranch, knowing our horses, Ace and Barbara Ann, are right over there in the stable, makes me feel closer to him. To the life we used to have. Plus, I miss riding. I was wondering if maybe you'd take on a fourth investor in the ranch and possibly put me to work."

Sam's eyes widened, and Ben took a step back so he could see her more clearly. He realized now that the part of today that hit him the hardest wasn't just saying good-bye to his father but worrying about what life after all of this would mean for her.

"Is this really what you want, Mom?" Ben asked, unable to contain a grin.

She nodded, tears streaming down her face. "It really, truly is. Tahoe was never home, you know? It was an escape. But I found my way back. Home is where the people I love most are, and that's here."

He gave his brother a look, and one nod between them sealed the deal.

"You're in," Ben said. "Welcome home."

Losing Charlotte would be almost as hard as losing his father, maybe even harder knowing she was still out there somewhere, moving on with her life, without him. But this was it, his mom coming home was his chance to be a better man and do right by his family, like he should have been all along. He'd have to hope for himself and for Charlotte that time would do its job and heal.

CHAPTER NINETEEN

Charlotte sat on her suitcase as she pulled the zipper the rest of the way. Other than what she was wearing right now and tomorrow morning when she left, she'd somehow fit two months' worth of her life back into one rectangular box.

Even after zipping it shut, she still sat there, staring at her room and remembering that first day when Ben set her mind at ease with a bottle of beer and the promise to help her through the next two months, the promise to be a friend when she truly needed one.

Should she have told him in the hospital? Or at the burial site? She should have said *something* so that he knew that even if it was over, she loved him with every bit of her heart.

But how would that have helped? How would that have made anything easier for a man who'd already been through so much?

"I'm so sorry about your dad, but—just so we're on the same page—I love you."

It seemed like maybe, probably, not the best moment to toss that little nugget of information into the mix. Plus, she read a psychology article once that claimed you could fall in love with anyone just by answering a series of questions that promoted intimacy. Maybe their intimacy was merely thrust upon them because of proximity, and from there they simply went through the stages of lust, attraction, and attachment. It could have happened with any two people in their position.

She needed to logic her way through this day. It was the only way to make it out of Meadow Valley and back to New York with her heart intact.

As she sat there on top of almost two months of her life, a folded piece of paper, just inside her door, caught her eye.

Was that there when she'd started packing?

She slid off the suitcase and bed and approached the paper with caution. It wasn't like it was a checkout statement or anything like that. And her grandmother certainly didn't communicate through written correspondence.

The toe of her boot nudged the paper, as if that would suffice as a test for safety.

She groaned. "Just pick it up," she mumbled.

So she did, and immediately recognized her favorite cowboy's scrawl.

Hey, Doc. I know tonight's going to be a little strange. But I hope it's okay if I still come to Pearl's farewell dinner for you. We have an hour before it starts. If you're up for it, meet me at the new house? I have something to show you. I'll understand if you don't come. But I hope you do.

—Ben

Had he been at the inn? Or did he put someone up to leaving the note? Either way, she was a jumble of nerves. Leaving was going to be hard enough, but if he was going to show her this amazing home that he was building and ask her to stay again, she might not be able to say no. And she *had* to say no. She'd worked too long and too hard building the life she wanted, where she could make sense of her world with science and statistics and facts and... She could do this. She could go down there, say no to whatever he offered, and they'd both be better for it.

Eventually.

She gave the room one last glance, then folded the note and stuck it in the back pocket of her jeans before throwing on her coat and striding out the door.

Pearl was chatting with a guest in the lobby. Her arm was still in a sling for a few more days, but she was standing on her own two feet.

A lump rose in Charlotte's throat, and she had to remind herself that Pearl would be okay. Bones heal with time, and her grandmother would be good as new the next time she saw her.

That was how the body worked when it came to broken things. Time made everything better.

She waved to her grandmother. "Be right back," she said. "And I'm taking your car."

"Don't be late for dinner!" Pearl called after her, and Charlotte couldn't help but smile, even if there was a sadness to the gesture. Everything was returning to normal, to how it was before she flew across the country and headed straight to the hospital emergency room—and found Ben Callahan waiting in the lobby.

She drove the short distance to the home site that still didn't exist on a map, but she knew the way now.

When she pulled up behind Ben's truck, she could see him walking around inside the house—or what would be a house in the coming months. It was already dusk, and she was ready to raise hell if he was working under less than optimal light, especially after his recent injury.

But when she reached the structure, she found him carrying a small trash bag out of the space where there would one day be a front door.

The front door to a house where he would live with someone else.

She exhaled, watching her breath cloud before her in a tiny puff of condensation, readying herself for whatever came next.

"Hey there," he said, a soft smile spreading across his face when he saw her. He hopped down to the ground—no front porch yet—and dropped the bag at his feet.

"Hey yourself," she said.

"I wasn't sure if you'd come," he said nervously.

Really? You can't tell I'm out of breath because I sprinted out the door the second I read your note?

But she couldn't say that.

"And I didn't think you'd come tonight—let alone invite me out for a secret rendezvous," she said instead, aiming to tease but unable to hide the tremor in her voice.

What was this? Why did he want her here, and what did it mean that he did—if it even meant anything at all?

There was no answer that could change so much that was standing in their way—her fear of admitting her feelings when she knew she'd still get hurt, him pushing her away since the night his dad died, and the most insurmountable of them all—the fact that he'd still live here and she would be in New York. So she stared into his deep blue eyes, throat tight, knowing that there wasn't a solution where both of them won.

Which was why it took her several seconds to feel it—a tiny blast of cold on her nose and then another on her cheek. It must have registered with Ben at the same time, because they simultaneously broke into incredulous laughter, tilting their heads up at the sky as snow fell softly on their skin.

"Oh my God," she whispered. Snow was nothing new to her after years in New York. But it was new here. Now. With him.

"I know," Ben said. But he wasn't looking up anymore. His eyes were focused on her. Then he grabbed her hand. "Come here. This is what I wanted to show you."

She bit her lip as he led her to the back of his truck. He lowered the tailgate and pulled out a large lawn sign with white letters posted on a red background that read FOR SALE BY OWNER.

Her breath caught in her throat. "You're selling it?" she asked, voice shaking, though she wasn't sure why.

He nodded, expression unreadable. "Sam, Colt, and I will finish building, but I rushed it," he said.

She shook her head. "No, Ben. You can't sell this place because of me."

"It's not you . . . It's me." He laughed softly. "Sorry. Bad relationship joke. But it really is about me. It was pretty foolish to think that just because I decided one morning that I wanted my life to go a certain way that I could make that happen at the drop of a hat." He scratched the back of his neck. "I've been beating myself up the past couple weeks about all my should-haves. I should have been a better brother. I should have been a better son. I should have just been there, period, for the people in my life instead of putting myself first. This"—he motioned toward the house—"That was more of the same."

Her throat felt tight, like it might strangle her if she spoke. It wasn't as if she knew what to say. She couldn't tell him to keep it, not if this was what he wanted.

"You just worked so hard already," she finally said. "And there's so much more to do."

"And I'll work hard on another one someday. When it's the right time. I bet I can find a buyer who'd love to see the job through, put on their own finishing touches. But right now it's time for me to put my heart into the ranch instead of simply treating it like a job I could take or leave. I need to show Sam and Colt that I give a damn. And now that my mom is signing on to stay, I need to count my lucky stars that I still have another shot at being the kind of son I want to be."

He lifted his knee and shut the tailgate.

She pressed a palm to his cheek. "You were a good son to your father, even if you made mistakes. You loved him, and he knew that. I could see that after only one night with you two."

He covered her hand with his. "I can be a better son to my mom. A better man. I *need* to be a better man."

"Nothing I say is going to make you believe you already are, is it?" she asked, and he kissed her palm, lowering her hand back to her side.

"I wish you could, Doc. I really do. But I need to figure this out on my own." He glanced down at the sign he was balancing on his feet with his free hand. "I wanted you here to make this official. I hope that's okay."

Whatever he needed. For this last night, she'd give him whatever she could to help him on this path he thought he needed to follow.

"Let's do it," she said. "Together."

They carried the sign to the edge of the property about ten feet from where the grass met the road. Ben kicked the toe of his boot against the snow-speckled grass and laughed.

"I probably should have made this decision in the spring after the thaw, but I never was good with timing."

She forced a smile.

Timing.

Would there have been a better time for them to have met? She guessed this would have always been the way it ended. Knowledge, though, didn't make it any easier. There was a first. She and Ben were victims of more than just time. There was circumstance and distance and it all added up to a relationship doomed to fail, yet *knowing* the facts, for the first time, didn't give her the comfort it was supposed to.

He raised the sign and jammed the posts hard against the ground, then stood on the horizontal bar between the posts to drive them farther into the frigid earth.

"There," he said, crossing his arms. "It's official."

And that was exactly how it felt—like the finale to a show she always knew would end, yet she somehow hoped for one more scene before the credits.

"I feel like we should shake on it or something," she said, wanting to fill the space between them with the words she *could* say, instead of the ones she couldn't. She held out her hand.

Ben offered a bittersweet grin and grabbed her hand, but instead of shaking, he pulled her in for what she knew was their last kiss, under the Northern California snow.

* * *

"Dinner was fantastic as always, Pearl," Delaney said, scraping the last of her redskin garlic mashed potatoes from her plate and closing her eyes in what looked like ecstasy as she licked her fork clean.

They all sat around the table in the inn's private dining room, the one used only for small events and family dinners, like this one. Charlotte's heart swelled as she glanced at everyone who'd made the past seven weeks better than she ever could have imagined.

Sam and Delaney. Ivy and Carter. Casey, Chief Burnett, her grandmother, and beside her, Ben.

"Thank you, sweetheart," Pearl said to Delaney, taking a sip of her red wine.

Sam laughed. "I already got an earful from Luis for eating 'off grounds' tonight, especially when I told him it was an early holiday dinner due to Charlotte leaving. 'I want a detailed menu breakdown for what Pearl serves for a holiday meal. Whatever your favorite dish is, I'll top it,'" Sam said, quoting his talented yet competitive chef.

"Potatoes," Delaney said, stealing a forkful from Sam's plate.

"Hey there," he said. "That's theft."

Delaney laughed and stole some more.

Charlotte drew in a shaky breath. She wasn't one for speeches or sentimentality, but she felt like something ought to be said. She'd fallen for so much more than Ben Callahan. She'd fallen for all of them— Delaney, Ivy, and Casey. Sam and Colt. Having Carter here was beyond amazing. And Gran—Gran who'd always been the most special person in her life. It was like she was leaving Oz to go back to Kansas, her real home. Only instead of waking from the dream to find her loved ones still there, she was going to be alone.

"Thank you all for coming," she started. "I'm not really great at sharing how I feel. But I want you all to know how much your love and friendship have meant to me and Pearl. I know I always had my grandmother, but now I feel like I have a whole family to come back to the next time I visit." She was grateful for Ben sitting beside her so she didn't have to look him in the eye. With a forced smile, she added, "And I hope Luis will forgive me for pulling you all away and for the fact that I know my grandmother will *never* divulge her recipe for her mashed potatoes, which means there's no way he'll be able to top them."

Pearl laughed. "Even if he had the recipe, he wouldn't top me. Not with that attitude. Good food—un*beat*able food—comes from the heart. It's the same with anything you do whether it's riding horses, rescuing animals, tending to sick children, or trying to pull the wool over your grandmother's eyes. If you put your whole heart into it, you can't fail."

She gave her granddaughter a pointed look, and Charlotte's breath caught in her throat. She could feel Ben looking at her but didn't dare give herself away by looking back—even though she was pretty sure their deception had already been found out.

"Laying it on a little thick, aren't you, Gran?" she asked with a nervous laugh.

Pearl shrugged. "Honey, I'm your *grandmother*, and I simply want the best for you, which means your happiness. And if that means laying it on as thick as my secret recipe mashed potatoes to make you see what you need to see, then so be it."

Charlotte opened her mouth to say who knows what, but nothing came out.

"You know, I feel like that should be a toast," Pearl said, holding up her glass. "So how about it? To laying it on thick and seeing what needs to be seen."

Soft laughter and mumbling sounded around the table, but everybody raised their glasses, so Charlotte had no choice but to follow in kind.

"To laying it on thick and seeing what needs to be seen," everyone else said.

Charlotte downed her whole glass without coming up for a breath.

"Now, who wants my also unbeatable apple crisp?" Pearl asked with a wink, and Charlotte knew Sam and Ben would drive Luis crazy with details of her grandmother's fabulous feast while that over-the-top toast would sit like an anchor in her belly for the rest of the night.

When the last of the dishes had been washed and dried and Charlotte had been hugged too many times to count, Pearl cornered her before she could make it out of the kitchen.

"Did you really think I didn't know?" her grandmother asked, brows raised.

Charlotte could play dumb, but where would that get her? At the end of the day, she'd tried to lie to her grandmother, and she'd been found out.

She cleared her throat. "How long have you known?"

Pearl scoffed. "That you were *pretending* to date Ben Callahan to get your meddling gran off your back or that you'd fallen in love with him and are too damned scared to admit it?"

"I— I mean *we*..." she stammered. Then she groaned.

"So, the whole time is what you're saying." It wasn't a question. Of course Pearl had known. She'd always known.

Her grandmother narrowed her eyes. "What is so wrong with admitting how you *feel*?" she asked.

"This visit wasn't about my *feelings*," Charlotte said, exasperated. "I came here to take care of you. I came here to take care of the inn. This was never about *me*."

Pearl jutted out her chin. "The town would have rallied to fill in for me. You didn't *have* to come back. You didn't have to lock yourself into a longer contract in New York on my account. I would have survived."

Charlotte huffed out a bitter laugh. Her grandmother sounded just like Ben had the day of his father's burial.

"Maybe I want *more* for you than that," she said, echoing her own words. "Maybe I want to be here for you when Mom can't. Maybe I want to take care of someone I love just because I can. Is there anything wrong with that?"

Pearl's gaze softened, and she grabbed Charlotte's hand. "Oh, sweetheart," she said. "Don't you get it? I know you think I meddle and maybe even pressure you a little bit, but it's only because that's exactly what I want for you too—more than just surviving. If you're happy—*truly* happy with your life and you won't regret leaving him behind, then that's all that matters to me." She gave Charlotte's hand a squeeze. "Tell me you're happy with your life," she said.

Charlotte *was* happy—with her job. Her apartment. And her best-coffee-in-the-world bodega.

"That's a long pause," Pearl said.

"I—" she started, ready to argue. But her shoulders fell. "I need to get ready for bed."

Pearl nodded. "I think you have one more guest to say good-bye to before you do."

Then she let go of Charlotte's hand and backed out of her way.

Charlotte found Ben in the lobby, quietly pacing.

"I thought you might have left with Sam and Delaney," she said, his back facing her.

He stopped and turned toward her.

"I thought maybe I should have," he said. "Didn't seem like the smart thing to do—hanging around. Guess I couldn't quite bring myself to leave. Not yet, at least."

She let out a relieved breath.

"Do you have an early call time tomorrow?" she asked.

He nodded. "Breakfast duty. Sam and Delaney are headed out to Dr. Murphy's clinic to pick up a stray puppy who needs fostering, and Colt is headed back to Oak Bluff to visit his sister for Christmas and New Year's. So I can't pull any of my old stunts and not show up."

She smiled. "I don't think you'd do that even if you could."

He smiled right back. "Maybe you're right," he said.

This was usually the part where she invited him back to her room or he invited her to his. But this was no usual night. And as much as she'd love to wake up with him one more time, she could tell that would make all of this so much harder than it already was.

"Why *did* you stay, Ben?" she asked, as if he'd been part of the conversation she was having with herself in her head.

He let out a nervous laugh, then ducked behind the registration desk and came back with a rectangular gift wrapped in plain pink paper.

"Someone once told me that friends buy each other gifts for special occasions. So...I got you a going-away gift," he said, holding it out for her.

Her breath caught in her throat as she clasped what felt like some sort of book between her palms.

"You can't open it until I leave though," he added. "I don't think I could take it if you hate it—and I also don't think I could handle it if you love it. So in my last selfish act, I'm going to save face and get while the gettin' is good." He grinned, but then his jaw tightened. "Thank you, Doc," he said softly, then brushed a kiss across her cheek. "For everything."

She held the gift against her chest and stared at him, unable to speak for fear her words would melt into tears.

He pressed his lips into a sad smile and nodded once, then slipped out the inn's front door.

It took her several seconds to realize he wasn't coming back and several more to remember the package in her hands. But when she did, she tore off the wrapping and burst into a tearful laugh when she saw what lay beneath.

The List Maker's Journal:
A List for Every Day of the Year

He bought her a book of to-do lists!

She opened it to a random page where it said *List five things that make you laugh.* Then she flipped to another that asked her to list her favorite sounds. And another made her wonder about her favorite sandwiches—not *food*, but sandwiches specifically—PB&J and Brie had always topped the list, but now the reasoning was two-fold. It was ridiculously delicious but it was also what

Ben had fed her on their first date. That wasn't a date. But really, she guessed it sort of was.

With a start, she threw open the door, thinking he might still be waiting on the other side. But there was no sign of Ben or his truck. No sign that what she held in her hand was anything more than what he'd said it was— a good-bye gift.

As she closed the book, a folded piece of paper fell out through the fluttering pages, and she caught it before it hit the floor. She blew out a shaky breath, unfolded it, and read.

> *Didn't have the heart to say good-bye, Doc. Not the actual words. So I'm not going to. Because we'll see each other again someday. We have to. You still owe me one. So for now I'll simply say, "Until then."*
>
> *Until then, Doc*
> *—Ben*

Well...who knew Ben Callahan could be such a romantic?

Charlotte. Charlotte knew.

CHAPTER TWENTY

Ben paused to take stock. So far he'd accidentally slammed his hand in his truck door—bruised, not broken (he hoped); punched the head of the drill through the drywall; sawed off the tip of his glove (and almost his index finger); and spilled hot coffee on his jeans trying to open his thermos. If he tried hard enough, maybe he could trip over the cord from the work light and give his other eye a matching scar.

Things were *not* going well.

"Can't get any worse, right, Callahan?" he mumbled to himself. He just needed to get his head screwed on straight so he could focus on the job.

Not on her.

Except now he was focusing on her.

It was time for a break. He grabbed the thermos and strode through the front door opening, hopped down, and sat on the ledge.

There was just enough coffee to justify a coffee break, so he poured what was left and drank.

Charlotte had been gone two weeks. Somehow he'd muddled through the holiday without his father, telling himself he had to put on a brave face for his mom. But the emptiness in his gut went deeper than that, and it was getting harder and harder to ignore.

"You look like you've been through the meat grinder a time or two."

Ben looked up to see his brother standing in front of him.

"Where the hell did you come from?" he asked. Then, still wearing his torn glove, he held his small cup of coffee up in a gesture of cheers before throwing it back like it was a shot of whiskey.

God he wished it was a shot of whiskey. He needed to start spiking his coffee.

"Same place you did," Sam said. "Drove over from the ranch. But it looks like you're in your own little world here."

He glanced past his brother into the house, where the visibly damaged piece of drywall hung for all to see.

"Looks like things are going well," Sam added with a wry smile.

Ben offered him a one-fingered salute.

"You know," his brother said, "you don't have to work. It *is* New Year's Eve. Colt's got dinner duty. Mom is over the moon to host the bonfire. And Delaney is curled up with a book and a three-legged cat in her lap."

"Sounds like you two have quite the New Year's bash going on," Ben said flatly.

"Hey," Sam said. "I'm not saying I won't have a beer or two before falling asleep on the couch."

"Party animal," Ben said with a quiet laugh.

Sam shrugged. "I've got seven and a half hours before I need to pop the top off a cold one and kiss my fiancée at midnight, so what do you say I buy you a drink? Consider it a pre-birthday celebration."

Ben scrubbed a gloved hand over his jaw.

He'd been in such a fog he hadn't even realized that tomorrow was his thirtieth birthday.

"I'm not really in the mood for a celebration," Ben said. "But a drink or two sounds a heck of a lot better than drilling a hole through my own flesh and bone."

Sam's brow furrowed. "Wait, did you—"

Ben shook his head. "Almost though. More than once." He pulled off his torn glove to show his brother his bruised hand. "This is courtesy of the truck's door, and I'm wearing most of my thermos. I'm thinking *maybe* I shouldn't be handling power tools for the rest of the evening."

Sam nodded. "I'm thinking you're right. Come on. I'll help you clean up, drink your troubles away, and then I'm driving. You can pick your truck up in the morning."

Ben set his coffee down and held up both hands in surrender. "You're not going to get any argument out of me."

Sam grinned. "Good." Then he produced two metal flasks from an inside pocket of his coat and held them out to his brother. "Courtesy of Casey at Midtown. You got your choice of bourbon or bourbon," he said.

Ben snagged the flask in his brother's right hand. "I think I'll have the bourbon." Then he shook the bottle slightly. "How much is in here anyway?" This flask was much healthier in size than others he'd seen before.

Sam gently knocked the bottom of his flask against Ben's. "Enough that you might need the morning off tomorrow. Good thing it's a national holiday. Welcome to your pre-birthday celebration, little brother."

* * *

The two men sat on the plywood floor, their breath clouding before them. Sam held up his flask to take another swig, his eyes growing wide.

"Whoops," he said, shaking it around and listening intently. "I just about finished it. That wasn't supposed to happen." And then he burped. "Looks like we're both coming back for our trucks in the morning."

Ben laughed and took another sip of his drink, then fell softly onto his back, staring up at the not-yet-drywalled ceiling.

"I know you think I'm full of it, but I had goals for turning thirty." His laugh turned bitter. "I was supposed to have more time to get it right. With Dad, I mean. I was going to be better. I *could* have been better."

Sam sighed, then slowly lowered himself next to his brother.

Ben closed his eyes for a few seconds, remembering nights as a kid in their backyard in Oak Bluff—he, Sam, and their parents lying on their backs and staring up at the sky waiting for a meteor shower. Everything was perfect. The future was nothing but possibilities. Now he felt like he'd missed his opening. Or worse—that he'd had it and blown his shot.

"What do you think Dad would have done?" Sam started. "A man like him who prided himself on his achievements, on being self-made, on building a life for himself and his family. What do you think he would have done if he knew in his twenties that before he turned fifty his brain was going to rebel against him and continue to do so until he stopped trusting his wife or forgot that his sons were grown?"

Ben blew out a long, cloudy breath, watching the condensation disappear over his head.

"That would have been tough for him to swallow." He shrugged. "He'd have probably done something to convince himself he was stronger than the disease. And because he was a Callahan, that thing might have been a little selfish. Maybe reckless."

Out of the corner of his eye, he saw his brother nod.

"You mean like cheating on Mom?" Sam asked. When Ben didn't respond, his brother kept going. "I'm not justifying what he did, but think about it. His memory was starting to play tricks on him, and he had no explanation for it. He acted out like you did. Like I did. I think about how scared I was for so many years, and I *knew* what I might be up against. He had no idea. And once he did, Mom was long gone." Sam pulled himself to sitting again, then climbed to his feet, *not* without a struggle. "There's never going to be enough time, so stop wallowing and get on with it. *Do* something with the time you still have."

Ben groaned. "If I wasn't so happy on this cold-as-hell floor, I'd deck you."

Sam laughed. "No, you wouldn't."

Ben groaned again. "You're right. I've seen you at the speed bag. You'd probably kick my ass, but I would hold my own long enough to show you that there's a damned difference between wallowing and anger."

Sam kicked Ben's boot with his own. "Get up. I have another present for you, which may or may not be out of line and make you want to deck me anyway." He chuckled. "Tell you what. If my gift insults you, I'll give you one free swing *and* a head start after you take it."

Ben pushed himself up on his elbows, then to sitting. He could hold his liquor just fine, but judging from the fact that Sam looked like *two* Sams for a brief moment before his vision cleared, it probably wasn't the best time for a pissing contest he knew he wouldn't win. Finally, he made it to his feet.

"Can I reserve the right for the hit-and-run offer at a later date should I find it necessary?" he asked with a grin.

Sam reached into his coat pocket again and retrieved a long white envelope that was folded in half.

"A piece of paper?" Ben said with mock enthusiasm. "You shouldn't have."

Sam rolled his eyes. "Just don't rip it in half opening it, okay?"

Ben made a show of slowly, gently, separating the envelope's seal, so much so that Sam finally grabbed it from him and finished the job.

"You always were a pain in the ass, you know?" his brother said, handing it back to him with the contents still inside.

Ben grinned. "I'm pretty sure most people call it charm." But when he pulled out what was in the envelope, his smile faded. "What the hell is this?" he asked, looking at the cashier's check.

Sam cleared his throat. "It's your asking price for the house, which is far below market value, by the way. And a little extra to—"

"I don't understand," Ben interrupted, his throat tight. "You don't have this kind of money. *We* don't have this kind of money."

His brother nodded. "Mom does. I mean, she and Dad did. The divorce settlement combined with his life insurance payout...He never took her off as sole beneficiary. This is her investment in the ranch."

Ben's head was spinning. It still wasn't computing. He wasn't sure if it was the bourbon or the shock or a combination of both.

"Mom wants to live in a four-bedroom home by herself?" he asked.

Sam laughed. "No. She doesn't. But she wants to kick me and Delaney out of the apartment the second this place is done, which is going to have to be sooner rather than later. Turns out we've got more than a wedding to plan. Delaney's pregnant."

Ben's eyes widened, and Sam continued.

"Before you say anything, let me lay it all out on the table. The offer to throw an upper cut my way still stands." Sam glanced around the unfinished house that—for a while—Ben thought might be his home. "Colt is going to help, as are Carter and a few other guys from the station. The extra bit is me and Colt buying you out." Sam jutted out his chin. "Go ahead. Take a swing."

Ben stared at the check, then up at his brother, then stared at the check again.

What the hell was Sam doing? Ben was committing to this life they'd built. He was going to be the brother, son, and friend he should have been all along.

"Are you firing me?" he asked, thinking a lot more seriously about taking that swing.

"Everything we've done since we were barely old enough to do so has been my idea," Sam said. "Fixing up homes to put some extra money away, then turning a side hustle into an actual business. That was all me. The ranch?" He ran a hand through his hair. "Hell, the ranch? I dove headfirst into that one as soon as we found the facility for Dad, and then I roped you and Colt in for the ride. Maybe it's what you wanted. Maybe it wasn't. But I kind of get the feeling you've been along for the ride this whole time because it's been the easy way out, and maybe it's time for you to figure it out the hard way."

Ben opened his mouth to say something, then closed it. He paced the unfinished floor of what would one day be a living room filled with his brother and Delaney and their unborn child, and he—he needed to *do* something. To feel something. To *hit* something.

Stop thinking. Stop thinking. Stop thinking.

He spun on his brother and threw a left hook at his brother's jaw, but Sam pivoted out of the way and defended himself with a jab straight to Ben's gut.

Ben doubled over and went down on one knee.

"What the hell was that?" he asked. "I thought I had a free shot!"

Sam doubled over, too—laughing. "It's a reflex. I can't help it. And to be honest, I didn't think you'd actually hit me." He laid a hand on his brother's back. "Are you okay, or are you going to lose your liquor?"

Ben struggled to his feet, one hand over his abdomen and the other still clutching the check.

"I'm not losing anything," he said, straightening. "Except my stake in the ranch, I guess."

Sam threw his hands in the air. "Tear up the damned check, Ben. If that's what you want. But I'll tell you this much. Whether I'm in that little apartment or in this house or wherever Delaney and I end up raising our family, it's going to be home because she's there and Scout's there and that stupid three-legged cat I'll never admit in public is my little buddy. I'd have stayed in Vegas and told you and Colt to figure out the rest if she wouldn't have come back with me."

Ben let out a bitter laugh. "That's a crock if I ever heard one. You'd have never left the ranch. Or Dad."

"Fine," Sam said. "But I had the luxury of falling for a woman who loves this place as much as she loves me.

Maybe even more than she loves me. I'm not asking, just to be safe. The point is, you can be a rancher anywhere if that's what you really want. There's nothing keeping you here."

Ben's breath caught in his throat. "And Mom?"

"She's exactly where she wants to be. What do *you* want?"

Even if he had been along for the ride, Ben loved the ranch. *And* Meadow Valley. But the thing was, he *could* be a rancher anywhere he could find a ranch. And this didn't have to be good-bye for good. Just for now. Because if anyone asked *him*, Ben would tell them that there was one thing—one *person*—he loved more than everything he had here.

Ben swallowed. "To sober up and get my ass on the first plane to New York."

"Good. You've got just enough time to do it." Sam laughed and clapped his brother on the shoulder. "I booked you on the red-eye. You leave at midnight."

CHAPTER TWENTY-ONE

Charlotte knew it was pointless and maybe a little sad to hang holiday lights on New Year's Eve, but when she'd gotten off the subway yesterday evening after work, she couldn't help but notice the Walgreens window advertisement about decorations being half off. Somehow that compelled her to march inside, buy too many boxes of various strings of lights, and take them home to turn her apartment into something that now resembled a cross between an overzealous teen's bedroom décor and the Griswold house at Christmastime.

Icicle lights dressed the few windows she had while colored lights were tacked to the ceiling and ran down the walls of her living room/dining room. It was, in a word, hideous.

But it reminded her of her grandmother's inn. Of drinking Irish coffee with Delaney and Ivy. And of a certain cowboy she was never supposed to miss once she left Meadow Valley.

She poured herself a glass of red wine and stuck a frozen meal for one in the microwave.

It's just a drop in dopamine levels, she reminded herself. Missing someone was simply a chemical reaction. It was like going through withdrawal from a drug. Once her body chemistry regulated, she'd be fine.

Never mind that at least four times in the past two weeks, she'd googled "How long does it take to get over a breakup?" and had read posts on everything from personal blogs, to *Cosmo*, to Bustle, finding—surprisingly—that they all pretty much agreed that the timeframe was somewhere around three months.

Except she and Ben hadn't actually broken up. *Until then* meant someday. Maybe. When the timing was right. Right now, though, it felt like she was hoping for the impossible again, and the more she hoped, the more it hurt.

The microwave beeped, and at the same time, someone pounded on her door.

She startled, wine sloshing over the top of her glass and onto her light gray T-shirt.

"Coming!" she called out, her heart inexplicably leaping at the thought of who might be on the other side of that door.

She set the wine on her counter and grabbed a paper towel, rubbing furiously at the stain that bloomed like a rose between her breasts.

She glanced through the peephole, then exhaled, heart sinking back into her gut.

She undid the chain and top lock, throwing open the door to find her next-door neighbors, Jason and Megan—recent newlyweds—decked out in all-black cocktail attire. Megan even had a HAPPY NEW YEAR headband on. She smiled at Charlotte with painted red lips.

"See, sweetie?" Megan said to her husband. "I told

you she was home." Megan peered inside Charlotte's apartment and gasped. "Oh my God. What. Happened? Did one of those holiday stores throw up in here? And—" She gasped again. "Your shirt? Oh no. This won't do."

Jason let out a nervous laugh. "She's trying to invite you over. It's just a few friends. Some music. Food. Plenty to drink. We'd love to have you."

Megan nodded earnestly. "You need to slip on a little black dress—I *know* you have one—and come to our place. Quick. You are *not* spending New Year's Eve alone." Megan kissed Jason on the cheek, leaving a crimson smooch mark on his skin. "I'll help her get ready. Why don't you get the sushi platter out of the fridge?"

"You got it, babe," he said, then planted one right on her lips. Her cheeks flushed when he pivoted and strode back to their apartment. Then, without technically being invited, Megan strode straight through Charlotte's front door.

Megan sniffed, then wrinkled her nose. "Why does it smell sad in here?"

Charlotte rolled her eyes. "It's a Trader Joe's broccoli and cheddar quiche. It's perfectly suitable as a meal for—"

"Nope," Megan interrupted. "Nope, nope, nope. I don't want to hear anymore. I know we don't know each other well, but I feel like if we did, we'd be friends."

Charlotte forced a smile. "That's sweet of you, but I work long hours and do most of my patients' paperwork at night. I really don't have time for much else. It's nothing personal."

Megan waved her off. "Honey, I'm in law school, and Jason is a fifth-grade teacher. We pretty much only see each other on holidays and in the summer—and every night in bed." She laughed. "That helps. A lot." She shrugged. "We can be friends even if we only see each other when one of us is saving the other from starting the New Year alone. The rest of the time you can just know I'm here if you need something, and I'll do the same."

Charlotte felt a strange yet familiar warmth in her chest, one much like she'd experienced while hanging her monstrosity of lights. She opened her mouth, then closed it, not sure how to respond.

"This is the part where you say, 'Thank you, Megan. I'd love it if we were friends, especially if you'd style me for your fabulous New Year's Eve party tonight.'"

Charlotte looked down at her stained T-shirt and laughed.

"Thank you, Megan. I've never been great at the whole friend thing." But then she thought about Delaney, Ivy, and Casey, how easy they'd made it for her to open up. She thought about Ben. Maybe what they'd had wasn't exactly a friendship in the traditional sense, but she realized now how closed off she'd been before she'd left and how she was falling back into old habits now that she was back home. "You know, scratch that. I *used* to really suck at letting people into my life, but I don't want to be that girl anymore. I *don't* want to be alone on New Year's Eve." She laughed nervously. "Sorry. You asked for thank you, and I gave you word vomit. Is that too much information for a new friendship?" She winced at her own awkwardness.

Megan grabbed her hand and pulled Charlotte toward the only other room in the apartment other than the bathroom, her bedroom.

"You want TMI?" Megan asked. "How about my mother taking me and my bridesmaids out for lunch and telling all of us how she and my stepfather go on annual swingers retreats?" Megan covered her ears and shook her head. "I'm as sex positive as they come. Believe me. But it never gets easier hearing about your own mother's—"

"Or grandmother's—" Charlotte interrupted.

"Sexual exploits," they said at the same time.

And just like that, after the two most unlikely words, Charlotte realized she wasn't the same woman she was two months ago. She could do this. She could start letting people into her carefully planned life because where had those plans gotten her other than stringing holiday lights alone a week after the holiday was technically over?

Charlotte *did* have the perfect little black dress and an equally perfect pair of red suede pumps to give the look the pop of color it needed.

"All we need is to lose this ponytail," Megan said, sliding the rubber band from Charlotte's hair. "And..." Megan rummaged through Charlotte's makeup bag and pulled out a lipstick as ruby red as her own. The shade she wore on her first official date with Ben when he made her a picnic on top of a fire engine.

Charlotte swallowed. "No," she said. "I'm good with just some gloss." She grabbed her tube of sheer, pale pink gloss and applied it to her lips before Megan could protest.

Her neighbor shrugged. "Whatever works for you. Let's go!"

Despite a fabulous sushi platter, endless bottles of prosecco, and finally feeling like there might be more to her life than work, eat, sleep, repeat, Charlotte made her way to Megan's door at precisely 11:50 p.m. She almost made it *through* said door when she felt a hand on her shoulder.

"You're not seriously leaving before midnight, are you?" Megan asked as Charlotte turned to face her.

Charlotte forced a smile. "I am." She was ready to throw out her patented excuse—an early day at the office tomorrow. But even pediatricians took a couple of holidays off throughout the calendar year. Tomorrow was one of those days, and the second was her regular day off, so she had some wiggle room to...to what? She went for honesty, which surprised even herself. "The thought of watching everyone kiss at midnight, it...I mean, I don't have someone to..." She groaned. "There's this guy, and I might love him—and there is an entire country and my own stubbornness between us." She covered her mouth with her hand.

Was it really that simple?

"How did you know?" she asked Megan. "About Jason. That it was real. Did you wait until the dopamine spikes subsided? Did you spend time apart to determine if absence made your...your feelings wane over time?" She groaned. "I mean, when were you sure that you wouldn't suffer the physiological manifestations of loss if you broke up or something happened to one of you or—"

Charlotte had been reading quite a bit about said physiological manifestations of loss since she'd returned home. She needed something to explain this intense feeling of missing someone she hadn't even known mere months ago—something that could tell her how to heal a wound she couldn't even see. But so far she hadn't found the answer.

Megan pushed Charlotte out into the hall and pulled the door closed behind them.

"I'm going to make this short and sweet, neighbor, because I need to get back in there and kiss my husband at midnight." She shook her head and laughed. "Maybe there is a physiological response to finding the right partner, and *maybe* with time apart, that response may dissipate or fade or disappear altogether. But at some point, you have to get out of your head and your textbooks and medical journals and take a leap of faith—or across the country—because you don't *want* to know how the science of it all works. You just want that person, by your side and in your corner, for however long you can."

"But," Charlotte said, "that's—"

"Terrifying?" Megan interrupted. "Of course it is. But if the alternative is red wine on your shirt and a quiche in the microwave, which is worse? If you're happy and fulfilled on your own, then I'm happy for you. But if something is missing? If *he's* the something, why wouldn't you do something about it if you could?"

Because doing something about it would mean uncertainty.

Doing something would mean putting herself out there and possibly getting her heart stomped—theoretically, of course.

Doing something would mean admitting that she didn't have all the answers and that maybe, someday in the distant or *not*-too-distant future—if things didn't work out or something happened to Ben that was beyond her control—she could ache more than she did right now.

"Think with this," Megan said, tapping the left side of Charlotte's chest just under her shoulder. "And not this." She did the same against Charlotte's temple, and it brought Charlotte back to the night she found out Ben had been hurt when Ivy had tried to get her to do the exact same thing. To game night. To the night he lost his father and she realized that all the medical training in the world couldn't give him back what he'd lost.

She cleared her throat. "The heart is actually more centrally located than most people think, and while it is a muscle that performs very important bodily functions, it can't truly *think*, and—" She stopped herself short and blew out a breath. "Right. It's a figurative thing. I can do figurative. I can...I can go back to California and say what I should have said weeks ago."

Through the door they could both hear the partygoers starting to count down.

"Go!" she and Megan both said at the same time.

Megan slipped back into her apartment, and Charlotte barreled through her own door, kicking off her pumps and rummaging in her closet until she found her cowboy boots. She threw on her wool coat, grabbed her cell phone and her purse, and unplugged her tangle of holiday lights. Then she ran back into her room and reached up to the high shelf in her tiny closet, the one where she'd hidden Ben's going-away gift because she'd been too afraid to look at it again. After that she was out the door and in the elevator before she had time to rethink her plan—or lack thereof.

She didn't want red wine spilled on her T-shirt or Trader Joe's quiche for one. Though it was a really good quiche, which she could totally share.

She didn't want safety or science or all of the answers. Not if that meant Ben Callahan would be nothing more than a memory that made her throat tight and her chest ache.

She wanted him. She wanted a happily-ever-after even if there was no guarantee how long it would last.

When she burst out of her apartment building—onto

the empty-as-hell New York street on New Year's Eve—
she simply started to run.

She could take the subway to the Howard Beach
station and then hop the AirTrain to JFK. There had to be
a flight out to California sometime in the next few hours,
right? Direct. Not direct. It didn't matter as long as she
was moving.

And for the next hour, she was. She made it all the way
to JFK, to her favorite airline's ticket counter, and asked
for the first flight out to Northern California.

"I'm sorry, miss," the sleepy ticket agent said, her
disheveled bun and smeared eyeliner making it clear that
she'd worked more than her regular shift today. "But the
next flight out isn't until late this evening." She tapped
away at her computer, then looked up. "That's including
us and other airlines."

Charlotte shrugged, then realized she had *no* luggage
and an entire day to spend at the airport. There was no
way she was going home. She'd lose her nerve. So she'd
just have to make a day of it. And figure out what she
would tell the office tomorrow if she didn't make it back
by the third.

"I'll take the ticket," Charlotte said.

The other woman nodded and offered a tired smile.
"Will that be one way or round trip?"

Her breath caught in her throat. Well, then. Here was a
decision she wasn't prepared to make. All she knew was
that she had to see Ben, to tell him what she felt regard-
less of whether she could back up those feelings with
any sort of scientific guarantee. She loved him. She *loved*
him. And the more she thought it, the simpler it became.
But what came after that? At the end of books and
movies, what came after the happily-ever-after? Because

no matter which way you sliced it, one of them was going to have to give something up.

"If it helps, miss," the ticket agent began, "I can book you on an open-ended return. It's less expensive than two one-way tickets but a bit more than a round trip. It's good for a full year."

She could figure her life out in a year, right? All she knew right now was that life meant being a doctor and loving a man who somehow made it okay to not have all the answers. But she could at least have these two and figure out the rest from there.

"I'll take it," she said, then slapped a credit card onto the counter like she was in some big grand gesture scene at the end of a movie. But it was just Charlotte and Rita, the ticket agent who had to work overnight on New Year's Eve.

Rita smiled. "I'm going to need a photo ID as well. Any bags to check?"

Charlotte shook her head and handed over her driver's license. In less than two minutes, she had a boarding pass in her hand.

"Happy New Year!" she said, stowing her cards in her purse in a rush. Then she ran in the direction of her gate.

It didn't take long to get there considering she was the only person at the TSA PreCheck line. Once there, she found the only open shop and stocked up on bottled water, a bag of dried fruit, some chips, a chocolate bar, an airplane pillow, a pile of magazines and a couple of *New York Times* bestsellers, and a small tote bag in which to carry it all.

She guessed she had some luggage now.

Then she promptly situated herself in a chair at the gate, neck pillow resting on her shoulders, her list journal open in her hands to the page that read, *List five things that truly make you happy*.

1. *My job.*
2. *My bodega.*
3. *My family.*
4. *My friends.*
5. *Being okay not having all the answers.*

And next to each one, she'd written *and Ben Callahan*. Because her life was good, but without him in it, she was doing little more than surviving. *With* him, though, it all came together into one perfect word—*happiness*.

She fell asleep after that, satisfied that of *all* her lists, this one was the best.

"Doc?"

Charlotte heard the word, the nickname no one had called her in two weeks, and squeezed her eyes shut. She didn't want this dream to end.

"Doc," she heard again. "Open those green eyes or I swear I'm stealing that giant bar of chocolate."

She bolted upright in her chair, the threat of losing her sweet treat enough to raise her from the dead.

Except instead of finding her stash of goodies in danger, she found Ben Callahan sitting in the chair next to hers. His eyes were bleary and his jaw lined with scruff, but that million-dollar smile still made her heart leap into her throat.

"Going somewhere?" he asked, nodding at her overflowing bag of travel goodies.

She nodded. "California," she said. "I needed to tell you something."

He tucked her hair behind her ear, and she shivered at his touch. God she'd missed that touch.

"Does it have anything to do with that list you made there?" he asked, the sound of his voice better than any song or piece of music composed, and she'd seen *Hamilton*. Twice.

"Wait," she started, then realized she was still wearing her pillow and ripped it off. She wasn't going to declare her feelings with a travel pillow wrapped around her neck. "What are you doing here?"

He shrugged matter-of-factly. "My brother and my mom seem to think I'm better suited finding work on an East Coast ranch. They bought my house and my third of the business right out from under me. Of course I agreed willingly. Signed a contract and everything. And I already have a few contacts at some upstate ranches and even a horse farm in Connecticut. Might mean only seeing you on my days off to start, but that's a hell of a lot better than you being across the country. And I—"

"I love you," Charlotte blurted. "I can't believe I left without telling you. Maybe it would have made you realize that you didn't need to become a *better* man because you were already the *best* man I knew. But I couldn't do it. I couldn't say it. I was so damned scared." She cleared her throat. "I *am* scared. And I have no idea what I'm doing. At. All. The only thing I know is that I love you, Ben Callahan."

"I love you, too, Doc."

She nodded. "I know," she said with a soft laugh.

"You *did* Han Solo me. On Thanksgiving night." Now he was laughing too.

Then he leaned in and kissed her. Everything and nothing made sense at the same time because she knew without a doubt that this was right, that *they* were right. But hell if she could find any evidence in a book or journal to back that up, and for once she didn't care.

"Happy New Year, Doc."

"Happy birthday, cowboy."

His smile—as if it could get any bigger, broader, or more blindingly beautiful—grew.

"Tell me again," he said. "One more time."

"Happy birthday?" she teased.

He shook his head.

"Oh," she said with a grin. "You mean the part about being in love with you? Because I am. I love you. And I really like saying it."

And then he said the only two words he could have possibly said to let her know she'd made the right decision betting on him.

"I know."

EPILOGUE

Ten and a half months later...

Ben watched, unable to hide his grin, as Charlotte tried in vain to zip the suitcase they were both sharing.

"I'd offer to take something out to make it easier on you, Doc, but all I've got in there is my suit for the wedding and a couple of other changes of clothes."

She stood and climbed on top of the case, jumped a couple of times, and then lost her footing. Ben leapt toward her and caught her under the arms before she crashed to the floor.

"Saved your life," he whispered in her ear. "Looks like you owe me."

She let out a breathy laugh as he lowered her safely to the floor; then she spun to face him. "Good thing I'm in no rush to get rid of you," she said. "So I have time to dole out my payments."

He kissed her on the nose.

"You overpacked," he said.

"I *didn't*," she insisted. "It's my dress for the wedding, a different dress for brunch the next day, casual clothes, something to sleep in, gifts for the baby, and maybe four pairs of shoes."

She mumbled the last bit, but he heard it loud and clear.

"*Four* pairs of shoes? Doc, I don't even own four pairs of shoes. And where we're going, all you need is one. Cowboy boots go with everything."

She laughed, flipped open the case, and pulled out *three* of the four pairs, and then zipped it shut with no problem.

"Strappy heels for the wedding, boots for everything else." She clicked her heels together because said boots were already on her feet, looking all sexy poking out from the frayed bottoms of her jeans.

"Should we tell them before or after the wedding?" he asked.

Charlotte skimmed her teeth along her bottom lip. "Let's wait until after. This is *their* moment. Not ours."

He clasped his hands around her waist. "You haven't even told your grandmother?"

Charlotte grinned and shook her head, proud at having kept their secret. "Which part? That in about eight months I'll be proud owner of Meadow Valley Pediatrics when Dr. Grady retires, or this?" she asked, flashing the diamond ring on her left hand in her fiancé's face.

He laughed. "Both." Then his smile faltered. "I'll stay here forever if that's what you want," he said.

She nodded. "I did want it. I mean, I still do—being the best doctor I can be. But I want more," she said.

He raised a brow. "More than your career and *me*?" he teased.

"Yep," she said with a smile. "I want everyone we love to be only minutes away—Gran and Carter; Sam and Delaney; your mom..." She paused. "And for me and Black Widow to kick your and Loki's asses in that arena."

He threaded his fingers through hers, rubbing his thumb over her engagement ring. "You know, you can't wear that thing to the wedding," he said.

She pouted. "But—"

"You said it yourself—it's Sam and Delaney's weekend." He kissed her. "And *then* we can tell them I'm going to be the future Mr. Doctor Ben Callahan."

She snorted. "You *don't* get the title of doctor just by marrying me."

He scoffed dramatically. "Then *why* am I doing this again?"

She grinned and nipped at his bottom lip. "Because you love me. And you can't live without me. And we're finally going back where we *both* belong."

He raised his brows. "Right," he said. "All of those things. Just out of curiosity, why are you marrying me?" he asked.

She shrugged and pulled him tight. "Because you're sweet." She kissed him. "And sexy." She kissed him again. "And you're my best friend." With this kiss, her lips lingered on his, and he smiled against her.

"How much time before our taxi comes?" he asked.

"Thirty minutes."

He scooped her into his arms and piloted her toward the bedroom.

She yelped with laughter. "What are you *doing*?" she asked.

He strode straight through the door and dropped her onto the bed. *Their* bed. He loved that word—*their*. He loved all the words that meant the life they'd built was one they'd committed to share.

Even through the windows, he could hear the sounds of traffic outside—horns honking and motors revving as a light changed from red to green. He'd grown used to the strange harmony of traffic and construction, to the ninety-minute drive to and from the ranch where he worked upstate, to all of it. For now, this was *their* home, Ben and Charlotte, which made everything worth it.

He grinned at the woman who would one day be his wife. His *wife*. *His* best friend. He still couldn't get over how lucky he was. The least he could do was show his gratitude.

"Thirty minutes is plenty of time," he teased. "To show you just how good a friend I can be."

DON'T MISS THE NEXT
BOOK IN A.J. PINE'S
MEADOW VALLEY
SERIES!

*ONLY A COWBOY
WILL DO*

AVAILABLE SPRING 2021

ABOUT THE AUTHOR

A librarian for teens by day and a romance writer by night, A.J. Pine can't seem to escape the world of fiction, and she wouldn't have it any other way. When she finds that twenty-fifth hour in the day, she might indulge in a tiny bit of TV when she nourishes her undying love of vampires, superheroes, and a certain high-functioning sociopathic detective. She hails from the far-off galaxy of the Chicago suburbs.

You can learn more at:
AJPine.com
Twitter @AJ_Pine
Facebook.com/AJPineAuthor

KEEP READING FOR A
SPECIAL BONUS NOVEL
FROM BESTSELLING AUTHOR
SARA RICHARDSON:

HOMETOWN COWBOY

Jessa Mae Love is done with relationships. No matter how tempting he might be, she cannot—will not—fall for a man like Lance Cortez. The outrageously handsome cowboy is practically a living legend in Colorado, as famous for riding bulls as he is for breaking hearts. What would a big-time rodeo star like him see in a small-town veterinarian who wears glasses, rescues animals, and cries when watching rom-coms? Turns out, plenty.

Raising bulls, riding the circuit, and looking after his ailing father, Lance never stands still for long. Yet Jessa catches his attention, and the more she tries to resist him, the more he wants her. When she agrees to move to the ranch to keep an eye on Lance's dad, Jessa tells him they have to keep it professional: no flirting, no sweet talk, and definitely no kissing. But with Jessa now living under his roof, that's easier said than done...

Prologue

Funny how you can remember every detail about the most significant day of your life. Not the best day of your life necessarily, but the day that shaped you, the day that you were forced to find your strength.

Lance Cortez wandered to the bay window in his living room and stared out at the land that had been in his family since the Spaniards had crossed the mountains into Colorado and founded the town of Topaz Falls.

From his house situated on the valley floor, it seemed he could see every acre, from the razor-edges of Topaz Mountain to the pointed tips of the evergreens that studded the steep slopes. Even in the dimness of that eerie space preceding the dawn, he could make out the stables up the hill, the bullpens across from the pasture, and the house farther on down the hill where his father still lived. The house where he'd grown up. It was a ranch style, built from the logs of those trees on the mountain. Anchored by a wraparound porch.

Sixteen years ago, before dawn, he'd stood on that porch right there and watched his mother walk out of his life. He didn't know what had woken him that day. Maybe the sound of the dog barking or the door creaking. But when he'd stumbled down the hallway, he'd caught her dragging her suitcase across that old porch.

"Where are you going?" he'd asked, not liking the weakness that had started to spread over his body like a dark shadow. Something in him already knew. She'd been distant for months, there but not.

His mother had paused on the sidewalk at the bottom of those porch steps, but she hadn't looked at him. "I have to go away for a while," she'd said. "I can't do this anymore."

He'd wanted to ask why, but couldn't. He couldn't open his mouth, couldn't unfist his hands. She was leaving them. And he wondered if it had anything to do with the underage drinking ticket he'd gotten two days before. At fourteen, he knew he was a holy terror.

Or maybe it was the fact that his father was away so much, traveling to the rodeos, giving all of his time to a sport his mother hated.

"I'm sorry, Lance," his mother had said. There were no tears in her eyes, but her voice caught. "I'm so sorry."

That word gathered up the sadness that had weighted his bones and spun it into a whorl of anger. If she was sorry then why was she going?

"I hope you'll understand someday."

He didn't. Sixteen years later, he had yet to understand how a mother could walk out on her husband and three boys who needed her. He'd been fourteen. He could take care of himself. But what about Lucas? At ten, he'd only just started the sixth grade. And Levi. Hell, he was still wetting the bed at seven.

Without another word, she'd walked away and hauled her suitcase into the old pickup. Energy had burned through him, tempting him to run down those steps and somehow force her to stay. He couldn't, though. He knew it. He saw it in her eyes.

She'd already left them behind.

The engine had started and the tires ground against gravel. Lance had watched until the darkness swallowed the taillights and she was gone.

When he'd stepped back into the house, he was a different kid. Refusing to shed even one tear, he'd made himself a cup of coffee and omelets for his brothers. When his father came back that afternoon, he'd told her she was gone.

They'd never said another word about it.

In the months and years that followed, he'd tried to make up for her abandonment. He'd quit being such a delinquent. Watched over his brothers when their father was out searching for something to remedy his own pain. Became a bull-riding champion in his own right. But he couldn't undo the damage she'd left in her wake. It took seven years after she left for things to fall apart.

He wished he would've been watching Levi that night he'd set the fire. Wished he'd been able to stop it before it killed the livestock. Wished he could've stopped it before it ruined them all. Lucas had wanted to take the blame, to protect their younger brother just like he always did, and Lance let him. They'd made a plan. Kept quiet about it. He'd been so sure Lucas would get off easy.

But he'd been wrong. Even though his brother had been

only seventeen, they'd charged him as an adult and sent him to prison.

Nothing had ever been the same after that. Levi threw himself into bull riding and hadn't been home in years. After Lucas got out of prison, he refused to come home. He'd gone on to work for a stock contractor down south and hadn't been home since.

All because of one day. One rejection. One person who was supposed to care for them turning her back instead.

Funny how you remember the details of days like that. The words, the sounds, the feelings that'd turned your body cold. Funny how you spend every day for the rest of your life trying to forget them.

Turning his back on the view of that porch, Lance headed for the kitchen.

It was time to put the coffee on.

Chapter One

"Sorry, sir." Jessa Mae Love threw out her arms to block the heavyset man who tried to sit on the stool next to her. "This seat is taken."

He eyed her, the coarseness of his five o'clock shadow giving his face a particularly menacing quality. Still, she held her ground.

"You been sittin' there by yourself for an hour, lady," he pointed out, scratching at his beer belly. "And this is the best spot to watch the game."

"It's true. I have been sitting here for a while." She smiled politely and shimmied her shoulders straighter, lest he think she was intimidated by his bulk. "But my *boyfriend* is meeting me. We have an important date tonight and I know he'll be here any minute." She checked the screen of her cell phone again, the glowing numbers blaring an insult in her face. Seven o'clock. *Seven o'clock?*

Cam was never late. He'd been planning this date for

more than a week. Since she was coming straight from the animal rescue shelter she owned, they'd agreed to meet at the Tumble Inn Bar for a drink before he took her to the new Italian restaurant on Main Street. "He'll be here," she said to the man. "Cam is *very* reliable."

"Whatever," the man grumbled, hunching himself on a stool three down from her.

Signaling to the bartender, she ordered another glass of pinot. "And why don't you go ahead and bring a Bud Light for my boyfriend?" she asked with a squeak of insecurity. But that was silly because Cam would be there. He'd show up and give her a kiss and apologize for being so late because...his car broke down. Or maybe his mother called and he couldn't get off the phone with her.

"He won't let me down," she muttered to cool the heat that rose to her face. He would *never* stand her up in this crowded bar—in front of the whole town.

Everyone considered the Tumble Inn the classiest watering hole in Topaz Falls, Colorado. And that was simply because you weren't allowed to throw peanut shells on the floor. It was nice enough—an old brick auto shop garage that had been converted years ago. They'd restored the original garage doors and in the summer, they opened them to the patio, which was strung with colorful hanging globe lights. Gil Wilson, the owner, had kept up with the times, bringing in modern furniture and decor. He also offered the best happy hour in town, which would explain why it was so crowded on a Wednesday night.

She stole a quick glance over her shoulder. Were people starting to stare?

Plastering on a smile, she called Cam. *Again.*

His voice mail picked up. *Again.*

"Hey, it's me." She lowered her voice. "I'm kind of worried. Maybe I got the time wrong? Did we say we'd meet at six? Or seven? I guess it doesn't matter. I'm here at the bar. Waiting for you…" A deafening silence echoed back in her ear. "Okay. Well I'm sure you're on your way. I'll see you soon."

She set down the phone and took a long sip of wine. Everything was fine. It was true she hadn't had very good luck with men, but Cam was different.

She drummed her fingers against the bar to keep her hand from trembling. Over the past ten years, she'd been *almost* engaged approximately three times. Approximately, because she wasn't all that sure that a twist tie from the high school cafeteria counted as a betrothal, although her seventeen-year-old heart had thought it to be wildly romantic at the time. Little did she know, one year later, her high school sweetheart—the one who'd gotten down on one knee in the middle of the cafeteria to recite one of Shakespeare's sonnets in front of nearly the whole school (did she mention he was in the drama club?)—would go off to college and meet the Phi Beta Kappa sisters who'd splurged on breast implants instead of fashionable new glasses like Jessa's. Breast implants seemed to get you more bang for your buck in college. Who knew?

She pushed her glasses up on her nose and snuck a glance at the big man who'd tried to steal Cam's seat earlier.

"Still no boyfriend, huh?" he asked as though he suspected she'd made up the whole thing.

"He's on his way." Her voice climbed the ladder of desperation. "He'll be here soon."

"Sure he will." The man went back to nursing his beer and tilted his head to see some football game on the television screen across the room.

She was about to flip him off when an incoming text chimed on her phone. From Cam! "It's him," she called, holding up the phone to prove she wasn't delusional.

"Lucky guy," Big Man muttered, rolling his eyes.

"You got that right." She focused on the screen to read the text.

Jessa, I left this morning to move back to Denver.

Wait. *What?* The words blurred. A typo. It must be a typo. Damn that autocorrect.

"What's the word?" Big Man asked. "He comin' or can I take that seat?"

"Um. Uh . . ." Fear wedged itself into her throat as she scrolled through the rest of the words.

I didn't see a future for me there. In Topaz Falls or with you. Sorry. I know this would've been better in person, but I couldn't do it. You're too nice. I know you'll find the right person. It's just not me.

Yours,

Cam

"Yours? *Yours?*" Ha. That was laughable. Cam had never been hers. Just like the others. Hadn't mattered how *nice* she'd been. She'd been jilted. *Again.* This time by her animal rescue's largest donor. And, yes, the man she'd been sleeping with . . . because he'd seemed like a good idea at the time. Women had slim pickings around Topaz Falls, population 2,345.

"Is he coming or not?" Big Man asked, still eyeing the empty stool.

"No. He's not coming." A laugh bubbled out, bordering on hysteria. "He broke up with me! By text!"

A hush came over the bar, but who cared? Let them all stare. Poor Jessa. Dumped again.

"It's not like he's a prize," she said, turning to address them all. "He's a technology consultant, for God's sake. Not Chris Hemsworth." Not that she knew what being a technology consultant meant. But it'd sounded good when she'd met him after she found his stray puggle wandering downtown six months ago. Peabody had pranced right up to her on the street and peed on her leg, the little shit. Now, Jessa was a dog person—an *animal* person—but that puggle had it out for her from day one.

When Cam had come in to retrieve his little beast from the shelter, stars had circled in her eyes. He was the first attractive man she'd seen since all those bull riders had passed through town three months ago. So unfair for those smokin' hot cowboys to gather in town and get the women all revved up only to leave them the next day.

In all honesty, Cam was no cowboy. Though his slight bulk suggested he spent a good portion of every day sitting in front of a computer screen, his soft brown eyes had a kind shimmer that instantly drew you in. He'd been good to her— taking her out to fancy restaurants and buying her flowers just because. Also, because she'd saved his beloved varmint from the potential fate of being mauled by a mountain lion, he'd made monthly donations to the shelter, which had kept them going.

Now he was gone.

"I can't believe this. How could he break up with me?"

Everyone around her had gone back to their own conversations, either unwilling to answer or pretending they didn't hear. So she turned to Big Man. "I guess you're happy about this, huh? Now the seat's all yours."

He didn't even look at her. "Nope. I'm good right where I am, thanks."

Oh, sure. After all that, now he didn't want to sit by her? "Fine. That's fine. It's all fine." Raising the glass to her lips, she drained the rest of her wine in one gulp.

"You know what?" she asked Big Man, not caring one iota that he seemed hell-bent on ignoring her. "I'm done." This had to stop. The falling in love thing. It always started innocently enough. A man would ask her out and they'd go on a few dates. She'd swear that this time she wouldn't get too attached too soon, but before she knew it, she was looking up wedding venues and bridal gowns and honeymoon destinations online. She couldn't help it. Her heart had always been a sucker for romance. Her father had said it was her best quality—that she could love someone so quickly, that she could give her heart to others so easily. He got it because he was the same way. Her mother, of course, labeled it her worst quality. *You're simply in love with the idea of being in love*, her wise mother would say. And it was true. Was that so *wrong*?

"Hey, Jessa."

The gruffness of the quiet voice, aged by years of good cigars, snapped up her head. She turned.

Luis Cortez stood behind her, hunched in his bowlegged stance. Clad in worn jeans and sporting his pro rodeo belt buckle, he looked like he'd just stepped off the set of an old western, face tanned and leathery, white hair tufted after a long ride on his trusty steed.

"Hi there, Luis," she mumbled, trying to hold her head high. Luis was her lone volunteer at the shelter, and he just might be the only one in town who loved animals as much as she did. He'd also been her dad's best friend and since she'd come back to town last year to settle her father's estate, she'd spent a lot of time with the man.

Maybe that was part of her problem with finding the love of her life. She spent most of her free time with a sixty-seven-year-old man...

"You all right?" Luis asked, gimping to the stool next to her. Seeing as how he was a retired bull-riding legend, it was a wonder he could walk at all.

"Uh." That was a complicated question. "Yes." She cleared the tremble out of her voice. "I'm fine. Great." She would be, anyway. As soon as the sting wore off.

"Thought you and Cam had a date tonight." Luis shifted with a wince, as though his arthritis was flaring again. "Where is he anyway? I was hopin' I could talk him into puttin' in his donation early this month. We gotta replace half the roof before the snow comes."

Cam. That name was her newest curse word. *Cam him! Cam it!* Feeling the burn of humiliation pulse across her cheeks, she turned on her phone and pushed it over to him so he could read the text. "Cam broke up with me." Luis had obviously missed the little announcement she'd made earlier.

He held up the phone and squinted, mouthing the words as he read. The older man looked as outraged as she was, bless him. "Man wasn't good enough for you, anyways, Jess. He's a damn fool."

"I have a knack for picking the fools." Just ask her mother. Every time she went through one of these breakups, Carla Roth, DO, would remind her of how bad the odds were for finding true love. Her mother had never married her father. She didn't believe in monogamy. *One person out of six billion?* she'd ask. *That is highly unlikely, Jessa.*

It might be unlikely, but the odds weren't enough to kill the dream. Not for her. Neither was the lack of any significant relationship in her mother's life. Jessa had grown up being shuffled back and forth—summers and Christmas in Topaz Falls with her father and the rest of the year with her college professor mother who didn't believe in love, secretly watching old romantic classics and movies like *Sleepless in Seattle* and *You've Got Mail* with wistful tears stinging in her eyes.

"Don't worry, Jess," Luis said in his kind way. "You'll find someone."

Big Man snorted.

Before she could backhand him, Luis gave her shoulder a pat. "My boys ain't married yet," he reminded her, as if she would *ever* be able to forget the Cortez brothers. Every woman's fantasy.

Lance, the oldest, had followed in his father's footsteps, though rumor had it this would be his last season on the circuit. He trained nonstop and had little time for anything else in his life, considering he left the ranch only about once a month. The thought of him married almost made her laugh. Over the years, he'd built quite the reputation with women, though she had no personal experience. Even with her father being one of his father's best friends, Lance had said maybe five words to her in all the years she'd known him. He seemed to prefer a woman who'd let him off the hook easily, and God knew there were plenty of them following those cowboys around.

Then there was Levi. Oh, hallelujah, Levi. One of God's greatest gifts to women. She'd had a fling with him the summer of their sophomore year, but after that he'd left home to train with some big-shot rodeo mentor and rarely came home.

There was a third Cortez brother, but Luis didn't talk

about him. Lucas, the middle child, had been sent to prison for arson when he was seventeen.

"Sure wish I'd see more of Levi," Luis said wistfully. "He ain't been home in a long time."

Her eyebrows lifted with interest. "So, um..." She pretended to examine a broken nail to prove she didn't care too much. "How is Levi, anyway?"

"That boy needs to get his head out of his ass. He's reckless. He's gonna get himself killed out there."

Jessa doubted that. Levi Cortez was making a name for himself in the rodeo world.

"Lance, now, he's the only one of my boys who's got his head on straight," Luis went on. "He always was a smart kid."

From what she'd seen, the oldest Cortez brother had never been a kid, but she didn't say so. After their mom ditched the family, Lance took over a more parental role. Not that she had any right to analyze him. "He's handsome, too," she offered, because every time she did happen to run into him, his luscious eyes had completely tied up her tongue. Yes, indeedy, Lance happened to be a looker. Though it was in a much different way than his cocky brother. "He looks the most like you," she said with a wink.

Luis's lips puckered in that crotchety, don't-want-to-smile-but-can't-help-it grin she loved to see. Her dad used to have one like that, too.

"Anyway...," the man said, obviously trying to change the subject. "What're we gonna do with Cam gone? I assume he didn't leave any money behind for the shelter."

"Not that I know of." Apparently, he hadn't left anything. Not even the toothbrush she'd kept at his house, Cam it.

"You got any other donors yet?"

"Not yet." She'd been so preoccupied with the most recent love—infatuation—of her life that she hadn't exactly made time to go trolling for other interested parties. Her dad had a big heart, but he'd always hated to ask for money, so when she'd come to take over, the list of benefactors had been...well...nonexistent. In one year, she'd already used most of what little money he'd left her to purchase supplies and complete the critical repairs. She could live off her savings for a couple more months, and at least keep up with the payroll, but after that things didn't look too promising. She'd probably have to lay off her night shift guy.

With Cam's generosity, she hadn't been too worried. Until now, of course.

"Don't you worry, Jess. Somethin'll work out." Luis's confidence almost made her believe it. "You're doin' okay. You know that? Buzz would be proud."

She smiled a little. Yes, her father definitely would've been proud to see his old place cleaned up. When she'd finished veterinary school and started on her MBA, he'd been so excited. He'd owned the rescue for thirty years but had never taken one business class. Which meant the place never made any money. He'd barely had enough to live on.

She had planned to change all of that. They'd planned it together. While she worked her way through business school, they'd talked on the phone twice a week, discussing how they could expand the place. Then, a month before she finished school, her father had a heart attack. He'd been out on a hike with Luis. Maybe that was why the man felt the need to take care of her, check in on her, help her fix things up around the house.

Familiar tears burned. She'd never blame Luis, though. That was exactly the way her dad would've chosen to go. Out on the side of a mountain, doing something he loved.

"We'll find a way, Jess." Pure determination turned the man's face statuelike, making him look as pensive as his eldest son. "All we need is some inspiration." Which he always insisted you couldn't find while stuck indoors. "I'm headin' up the mountain tomorrow. You wanna come?"

She brushed a grateful pat across the man's gnarled hand. "I can't, Luis. Thank you."

As much as she'd like to spend the day on the mountain, drowning her sorrows about Cam and the rescue's current financial situation in the fresh mountain air, she had things to do. This breakup had to be the dawn of a new era for her. She was tired of being passed over like yesterday's pastries. To hell with relationships. With romance. She didn't have time for it anyway. She had walls to paint and supplies to purchase and animals to rescue. Which meant she also had generous donors to find.

She shot a quick glance down at her attire. Might be a good idea to invest in herself first. Typically, she used her Visa only for emergencies, but this could be considered disaster prevention, right? She needed a new wardrobe. Something more professional. How could she schmooze potential stakeholders looking like she'd just come from a half-price sale at the New Life Secondhand Store?

"You sure you don't want to come?" Luis prompted.

"I'd love to but I have to go shopping." Right after their book club meeting, she'd enlist her friends to help her reinvent herself so she could reinvent her nonprofit.

By the time she was done, the Helping Paws Animal Rescue and Shelter would be everything her father dreamed it would be.

It would keep the memory of his love alive.

Chapter Two

"Easy, now, Wild Willy." Raising his hands in stick-'em-up surrender, Lance eased closer to the barn stall, where his favorite training bull was backed against the wall, snorting and pawing at the ground like he was seeing red. *Fuck.* Sweat soaked the bull's brown coat and for some reason those horns looked even more lethal in the dim light.

On a normal day, he didn't enjoy standing eye-to-eye with one of his bovine athletes—especially before he'd finished his coffee—but this mean bastard had given him no choice.

Just as the coffeepot had started to hiss, Tucker, the stable manager and training wrangler, had come barreling into Lance's kitchen hollerin' about how Wild Willy had gone ape shit in the field. Seemed his favorite cow was flirting with another bull. In the process of proving his manhood by charging Ball Buster, Wild Willy had stepped in a hole and come out of the debacle with a limp. Which meant Lance had the pleasure of assessing the injury to see if they had to call out the vet.

"All over a woman," he muttered. Last he'd checked, he was a bull rider, but some days he felt more like he was stuck on an episode of *The Bachelor*.

"Trust me, fella," he said, easing closer to Wild Willy, who'd calmed some and was now chawing on a bundle of hay. "She's not worth it." Relationships in general weren't worth it. "You're better off alone." Why put in all of that effort when almost every relationship ended with two people walking in opposite directions? Or two cows, in this case. "All right, Wild Willy. Let's get a look at that hind leg." Keeping a safe distance on the outside of the pen, he tested the bull with a sweep of his hand down its flank, which only riled it up again. The dumbass jolted away, slamming its rear end into the wall.

Shiiiiit. Whipping a bandanna out of his back pocket, Lance mopped sweat from his forehead. "You're not gonna make this easy on me, are you?" he asked, backing off to give Wild Willy some space.

The bull tossed its head and snorted a confirmation.

"Don't forget who feeds you. I *own* you." And he needed this big guy right now. Only a few weeks until World Finals, and he had a hell of a lot of work to do to get ready. This season had pretty much sucked. Only one title and a whole lot of back talkin' from fans about how he should've retired two years ago.

"Well, maybe I'm not ready to retire," he said to the bull. Hell, he was only thirty. He could still go out on top. Even with his joints creaking the way they did. He'd ignored pain before, especially when he had somethin' to prove. This wouldn't be the first time.

But it might be the last.

No. Couldn't think about that. Couldn't think about how everything he'd worked for his whole life would likely end after this competition. What would he have after it was over?

Instead of dwelling on that fun question, he faced the bull. He'd rather face a lethal bull than uncertainty any day. "Steady now." He ripped the bull's halter off a nearby nail in the wall. "Don't make me get the tranquilizer—"

"Lance?" A woman's voice echoed from outside the stall. Not just any woman, Naomi Sullivan, the ranch's book-keeper and all around caretaker of the whole lot of them. "Are you in there?" she called again. And she didn't sound calm.

Raising a finger to Wild Willy's snout, Lance tried to match the crazy in the bull's eyes. "This is not over." He tossed down the halter and stepped outside into the early morning sunlight. The sky was still pink. It cast a bluish haze over the hand-hewn log buildings that made up the Cortez Family Ranch. Smoke still puttered out of the main house's chimney from the fire he'd started in the woodstove last night. That's how early it was. Too damn early for another crisis, but from the looks of Naomi's bedraggled reddish hair and wide green eyes, something had her panties all bunched up.

Naomi had been a family friend forever. The sister they'd never had. So he could tell when she was stressed. And now would be one of those times. "What's up?" he asked, think-ing of nothing but the steaming hot coffee waiting in his kitchen.

"Sorry to bother you." She was heaving like she'd run all the way up the hill from her house. She lived with them on the ranch. After her husband had taken off and left her with a baby girl ten years ago, Lance had offered her a job and invited her to move into the guesthouse on the property. Not that she was a charity case. She was damn good with numbers. Always had been. However, she did tend to run high in the drama department.

He gave her a smile to simmer her down. "You're not bothering me. Everything all right?"

She looked around as though torn. "I'm worried about your dad. I haven't seen him since yesterday." In addition to doing the books for the ranch, she kept an eye on his father, which had become a heroic task as of late. As if she hadn't already proven herself a saint, the woman had offered to cook and clean for Luis. She was the one who made sure he took his blood pressure meds.

"He said he was going for a hike and wouldn't need dinner," Naomi went on. "But when I brought over his breakfast this morning, he wasn't around."

Of course he wasn't. Because lately his dear old dad had taken to wandering off without bothering to tell anyone where he was going. If he wasn't volunteering at that animal shelter in town, he was somewhere out on the mountain, head in the clouds as he relived better days.

Naomi wrung her hands in front of her small waist. "I noticed his backpack was gone. Along with his sleeping bag." She reached into her pocket and held up a prescription bottle. "But he left his medication behind."

Which meant a thousand things could've happened to him out there. He could've gotten disoriented. Could've passed out. Could've lost his balance and fallen off a cliff. He was sixty-seven years old, for shit's sake. A fact Lance had to keep reminding him of over and over. He didn't belong out on that mountain alone.

"I'm worried about him." Naomi was on the verge of tears now, and if there was one thing he hated more than having to act like his father's babysitter, it was a woman crying. "Should we call out search and rescue?"

Hell no. He didn't say it, but he wasn't about to call out search and rescue. They'd called those guys six times in the past year, all because Luis Cortez had taken to wandering off alone somewhere on the three thousand acres they owned. God only knew how much of the taxpayers' money they'd already wasted. Not to mention he didn't want to put any lives at risk for a man who was probably just out for an extended stroll.

Lance laid a hand on Naomi's shoulder and steered her back toward her house. Looked like his training would have to wait. Again. "I'm sure Dad's fine. Probably just wanted a night under the stars." That's what he usually said when Lance dragged him back home from one of his impromptu camping trips. A new layer of sweat burned his forehead. If the man kept wandering away he swore he would implant a GPS chip into his father's arm so he could start tracking the old coot.

"What if he's hurt?" Naomi asked, grabbing his arm like she needed support. "Oh God, Lance. I should've checked on him last night. After everything he's done for me, I hate to think of him out there alone."

"Hey." He stopped and turned her to face him. She seemed to worry about everything. Everyone. And he knew the weight of that burden. She didn't need it. She had a daughter to raise. Much as she mothered him, he took it upon himself to protect her, to make sure she didn't have to worry.

"He's *fine*. Don't forget, he does this all the time." His father was worse than an untrained Labrador the way he got distracted and roamed away. "I don't want you to worry, got that? I'll take care of it." The same way he always did.

"How do you even know where to look?"

"I don't. But Jessa might." She spent more time with Luis than pretty much anyone. If it was any other woman, he'd worry she was on a gold-digging expedition, but Jessa didn't exactly scream temptress.

Naomi's face brightened. "Great idea. Jessa will know how to find him."

"Sure she will." He prodded her up the porch steps. "Now you go on in and take care of Gracie. Tell her we can do a riding lesson this afternoon, if she's up for it." Naomi's ten-year-old was currently the only female he chose to spend time with and that was just fine with him.

Naomi shook her head with a wide smile. "*If* she wants to? Are you kidding? You should hear her bragging to all of her friends about how she has the most handsome riding instructor in the whole wide world. She actually told them all you look like Ryder from *Tangled*. You should've heard the squealing." She trotted up the steps to her modest guesthouse and turned back to him with a smirk on her face. "Me? I'd take Gerard Butler. No offense."

"None taken." They'd determined long ago that they'd be a bad fit. Course, he'd be a bad fit with pretty much anyone.

"See you later." Naomi waved him off. "Tell Jessa I said hey. And be nice to her, Lance. I saw her at book club..."

He happened to know that book club was a fancy way of saying wine and chocolate club, but whatever.

"She got dumped again."

Shiiiiit. Wasn't this his lucky day? "As long as she's not crying," he muttered, heading down the road. Boots pounding the packed dirt, he passed the main house, passed that steaming hot cup of coffee waiting in his kitchen, and kept right on movin' until he'd reached his truck, cursing the whole way.

* * *

This couldn't be right. Jessa turned to get a profile view of her body. *Hello!* When she saw that the label on the bra said Bold Lift, she'd had no idea what it meant. In a matter of two minutes, she'd somehow gained at least two cup sizes. She gawked at herself in the mirror. *Wow.* Those babies were really out there. When she looked down at her toes, her chin practically hit her cleavage. Not to mention the straps were already digging into her skin. Why did satin and lace feel so itchy compared to cotton?

Turning her back on the spectacle in the mirror, she gazed longingly at an old cotton bra hanging on the knob of her closet door. But no. *No.* It was time for her to kick it up a notch. She had a lot to offer and she was about to show it to the world.

When she'd called her mother last night to inform her that she'd lost her main donor (carefully omitting the fact that he'd also happened to be her boyfriend), the woman had gotten right down to business. "You'll only appear as professional as you feel," she'd said. Then she'd advised her on how to build a wardrobe that would help her "dress for success."

Jessa had written everything down.

Expensive undergarments. Check! Even though the bra squeezed her tighter than a corset, she'd wear it. Along with the new thong she'd bought to match. Because smart, stylish women apparently wore uncomfortable undergarments.

Carefully avoiding a glance at the backside of her body, she backed out of her bedroom and into the small bathroom. When it came to how she looked in a thong, she subscribed to the ignorance-is-bliss mentality.

After doing her makeup the way she'd learned on Pinterest last night, she dashed to the closet to select one of the new outfits she'd bought. Today was a big day. She'd set up meetings at the local real estate office, the bank, and the town chamber to see about developing some partnerships with businesses in town. Not that any of them had seemed particularly excited to talk to her, but she'd change their minds. Which meant she had to look her best.

To her credit, her mom had never nagged her about the way she dressed, though it was obvious that style had never been important to Jessa. It'd never mattered what she wore, seeing as how she spent her time with animals. She'd been bled on, vomited on, pooped on, peed on...so she'd never actually had a reason to wear nice clothes. Most of her life, scrubs, yoga pants, and T-shirts had suited her just fine.

But Dr. Carla Roth was refined, elegant, brilliant, and incredibly sophisticated. Even as a professor, her mother wore beautiful silk blouses and wrap dresses with heels. At a cocktail party, the woman glittered like royalty. She'd won three of the university's largest grants by simply charming old men at various university functions.

Unlike Jessa, her mother had never had her heart broken. Not once. And that was exactly the kind of woman Jessa needed to become.

Her book club friends—Naomi Sullivan, Cassidy Greer, and Darla Michelson—had been all too eager to help her craft a new look.

The whole group had led her down Main Street, parading

through the clothing boutiques, arms full of adventurous new garments for her to try on.

But now, hanging in her closet, the skirts and brightly colored tunics didn't appeal to her the way they had last night when everyone was oohhhing and aahing at her in the dressing rooms.

She snatched a flowery blouse off a hanger. What did that go with again? Was it the blue skirt? The red capri pants that her friends swore made her look exactly like Katharine Hepburn? All the new colors and patterns in her closet started to blur together in a whorl of confusion. *Whoa.* This could take a while. She needed coffee. Stat.

Leaving the clothes behind, she dashed through the living room to the kitchen and scooped heaping tablespoons of coffee into the French press. The familiar scent of her morning routine soothed the mounting tension from her hands. She could do this. She could match a shirt and shorts, for the love of God. It wasn't rocket science. She had an MBA, Cam it!

After filling the kettle, she set it on the stove and cranked the burner. It was the flowery shirt that went with the capris, right?

Shit. She had no idea. It was time to call for backup. Snatching her cell phone off the counter, she summoned her mother.

"Hello?" Her mother sounded a bit out of breath, which meant Jessa had probably interrupted her morning yoga practice.

"Hi, Mom," she said, glancing down at her body. Come to think of it, she might benefit from a morning yoga practice, too. The only morning practice she embraced regularly involved pastries.

"Jessa?" her mother wheezed. "Is everything all right, honey?"

"Everything's good!" she said, trying to sound chipper. "I bought all those clothes you told me to get."

"That's wonderful! I'm so happy for you." Her mother sounded more relieved than happy. "You're *finally* investing in yourself. It's going to make such a difference. You won't believe what new clothes can do for your self-confidence."

"Yeah. Um. It's pretty exciting." But it'd be even better if she could actually *dress* herself in the new clothes. "So listen. I have some important meetings today and I'm not sure what top to wear with my red capri pants."

"Hmmm..." Her mother mused as though this decision ranked right up there with purchasing a house. "Were you able to find a white asymmetric blouse?"

"Uh—" What was an asymmetric blouse again?

A knock sounded. At the front door. Yes, that would be the door, which was neatly centered between the two large bay windows a mere twenty feet from where she stood. In the kitchen. Wearing only a bra and thong.

Okay. She edged her back against the refrigerator. Sheer curtains had seemed like a good idea when she'd picked them out last year, but she was starting to regret that decision. Clearly, she hadn't thought through the implications of what would happen when she wanted to make herself a cup of coffee dressed only in a thong and Bold Lift bra.

"Jessa?" her mother said loudly. "Did I lose you?"

"No. I'm still here," she whispered.

Another round of hearty pounding pried a squeal from her lips. What the hell was happening? Who'd knock on her door before seven? Was her house on fire or something?

"Honey? Is everything all right?" her mother asked.

"Yes," she hissed. "But I'll have to call you back." Before her mother could answer, she clicked off her phone and set it down. Holding her breath, she stood perfectly still and quiet—minus the loud drumbeat of her heart.

The knocking didn't stop.

"Hello?" A man's deep rumbling voice sent her heart off to the races again. There was something vaguely familiar about it...

"It's Lance Cortez. I need to talk to you."

Lance! Oh. Holy. No. This was *not* happening. She gazed longingly at the other side of the living room to the safe darkness of the tiny hallway that led to her bedroom. There was no way she'd get through there without him seeing *some*thing. Like her ass, maybe. Cam it!

Get the front door with the windows, the ignorant Home Depot salesman had advised. *It'll let in the most light.* Yes, and now it would also give Lance a clear view of a very full moon.

She flattened her body against the cabinets, craning her neck, and sure enough, he stood right there on her front porch, now peering through that lovely window on the door.

Oh, God. Her lungs heaved so hard it felt like the Bold Lift Bra was about to bust at the seams. *Calm down*, she instructed herself. *He'll go away.* He had to go away.

"Jessa! I know you're in there. Your car's here," he called again, rapping the door with that big manly fist of his. "I need to talk to you. It's an emergency."

Tell me about it! Maybe she could call 9-1-1 and have him escorted off her porch...

Footsteps thudded on the front porch, moving closer.

Sweet lord! Lance Cortez was peeking through the bay window!

"Hang on a sec!" she yelled, then hit the deck, pressing her body against the wood floor. Lifting her head, she assessed the distance to the hallway. It might as well have been twenty miles.

Okay. Think. What would Naomi do? That was an easy one. She never would've gotten herself into this situation in the first place because Naomi had the ability to get dressed without the assistance of coffee.

"Jessa, I really need a word," Lance called again.

"Be there in a minute!" Despite the fact that she was basically naked, sweat itched on her back. Her room. She had to get to her room. And there was only one way. She'd have to army crawl. As long as she stayed on this side of the couch, Lance probably wouldn't be able to see her from the window. It was risky, but what other option did she have? He obviously wasn't going away.

Here goes. Trying to remain one with the floor, she squirmed forward, shimmying past the bookshelf. *Squirm, pull, squirm, pull.* She edged against the couch, bare skin grazing the cold wood planks.

Yes. Yes! It was working. Almost halfway now...

A scratch stung her hip as something sharp caught the delicate strap of her thong.

Uh oh. Contorting her body, she tried to get a better look. A loose staple from the re-upholstery job she'd done on the couch had hooked her adorable brand-new panties. *Cam it!* She should've known a staple gun wasn't enough to hold a couch cover together. *Thanks a lot, Pinterest.*

"Jessa!" More pounding.

"Hold on! Give me a minute!" she called, trying to wring the panic from her tone. What the hell was his problem, anyway? Couldn't he take a hint? She pushed onto her side to free herself from the staple, but her legs smacked into the end table. The whole thing toppled over with a deafening crash. *Ow! Shit!* She rolled over, gripping the backs of her calves. At the same time, the thong stretched, ripped, and snapped, falling to the floor underneath her.

"Jessa?" Lance yelled through the door. "What was that?" The doorknob clanged like he was trying to get in. "Is everything okay?"

Hot tears filled her eyes. "Fine!" Minus the throbbing in her legs and the fact that she'd just shredded a fifty-dollar thong.

"Are you sure?" he persisted, the sonofabitch. "That sounded bad. Is the key still out here?"

The key? Oh, dear God, the key! Her dad had always left a house key underneath the flowerpot...

A new wave of terror surged, blinding her with white-hot fear.

The sound of metal clanged in the lock.

"No!" She squealed, scrambling to hide herself behind a small square throw pillow from the couch. "Please! Don't come—"

The door sprang open.

Right as Lance stepped around the couch, she shifted the pillow to cover her lower hemisphere.

"What're you—?" He halted like he'd been shot, his gaze bouncing from her eyes to her bra and then, sure enough, down to the pillow.

"Turn around! Cover your eyes," she wailed. For the love of God! Humiliation curdled into anger. "Why'd you have to come in? Who just barges into someone's house, huh?" Why couldn't he have waited on the porch like she'd asked?

"Uh..." He seemed to be frozen in place. "Sorry. I heard the crash. Thought you were hurt..."

Was he gawking? His lips had parted with surprise. And then there were his eyes. Wide and unblinking. Men didn't usually look at her like that...

"What the hell happened?" he asked, finally finding the decency to turn around and stare out the bay window.

Securing the pillow against her lower abdomen with one hand, she covered her Boldly Lifted chest with her arm in case he decided to peek again. "I had a bit of an accident." She should make something up. Something really exciting. Something like she and a mystery man were playing this kinky game...

"Are you hurt?" Lance asked, his head swiveling toward her again.

She kept herself covered. Oh, yes. She was hurt. On more than one level. "I'm fine," she choked out. "Can you get my robe? It's hanging up in the bathroom at the end of the hall."

"Right. Your robe." He sort of side-shuffled his way down the hall and back, before tossing the robe at her without turning around.

Clutching her salvation, she scurried up to a standing position, the backs of her calves still aching, and wrapped the fabric around her, tying the belt securely at her waist.

Lance peeked over his shoulder as if to check on her, then turned all the way around.

She wasn't sure if she was out of breath due to the terrible thong ordeal or to the fact that the elusive Lance Cortez looked so different up close. She's seen him around town since she'd been back, but she'd never *looked* at him that closely. He'd never looked at her the way he was now, either.

Eyes open slightly wider than a normal person's, lips parted like he couldn't remember what it was he'd wanted to say.

Yes, well, neither could she. Not with the sight of his dark hair, which curled slightly at the edges. It was mussed like he'd been nervously running his hand through it all morning. And those eyes. An arctic blue-gray. Cutting. He wore a dark red flannel shirt with the sleeves pushed up over his bulky forearms. His jeans were faded and worn like he worked hard, which she'd heard he did.

"So..." His voice had this deep soothing reverberation that made her want to curl up against him. "Did you fall or something?"

Or something. "I was in the kitchen making coffee," she informed him, trying to smooth her hair into soft waves like it had been before she'd gone to battle with the couch. "Wasn't expecting anyone to show up at my door..." Especially the enigma that was Lance Cortez. "So I panicked and was trying to get back to my room without giving you a show." Which was clearly too much to ask from the universe.

"Oh." His gaze seemed to fixate on the leopard-print thong that lay a mere two feet from his boots.

As swiftly as possible, she swiped it off the floor and shoved it into the pocket of her robe. "Um. Did you need something, Lance?" Because her humiliation meter was about tapped out for the day and it wasn't even seven o'clock.

"Right. Yes." That intense gaze pierced her eyes. "Dad spent the night out on the mountain and I need you to tell me how to find him."

The news shocked her into stillness. "He spent the night out there?" Luis hadn't said a word about camping when she'd talked to him Wednesday night. Though he did camp occasionally, he usually told her his plans.

"I'm sure he's fine," he went on. "His sleeping bag is gone, which means he planned on being out all night. But he didn't bring his meds."

Though she tried not to panic, her mind hopped on a runaway train car of worst-case scenarios. So many things could've happened to him...he could've taken a fall. He could've gotten turned around. He could've had a heart attack like her father...

Lance's weight shifted. He cleared his throat. "So, have you seen him?"

"Not since Wednesday." It was hard to swallow past the emerging rock formation in her throat. Because Luis had asked her to go up the mountain with him. And she'd said no.

"Are you okay?"

"I'm..." What if something had happened to him and he was all alone because she didn't go with him?

A shrill whistle sliced into her thoughts.

Lance looked around. "You got water on the stove?"

Blinking fast enough to sop up threatening tears, she nodded quickly. "I was making coffee..."

"Coffee sounds great," Lance said. And if that wasn't shocking enough, he sat himself down on her couch.

Heat blanketed her, making the robe feel like a fur coat. He wanted to sit and have coffee with her? While she wore her robe? "But...um...maybe...well...okay..." The words stumbled over one another, mimicking the erratic beat of her heart. *No. Don't you dare*, she told that stubborn thing.

No matter how beautiful Lance Cortez was, she was done with romance.

Chapter Three

He'd only stayed for the coffee, so he'd best stop looking at Jessa like she was on the menu.

Lance did his best to reel in his tongue and crank his jaw closed. But...*damn.*

It had to be the thong. And the bra. And the robe. Who knew Jessa Mae Love owned sexy lingerie? Not him. It would've been better if he'd known, if he'd been prepared to see her like that—all half naked and done up like a no-strings-attached fantasy. Her legs were much longer than he'd ever realized. Long, tanned, and defined. Lethal combination. Must be all of that hiking she did.

Though he knew better, his gaze followed her to the kitchen. Yes, Jessa had spent every summer in Topaz Falls for as long as he could remember. He'd known of her, even a little bit about her, considering their fathers were more like brothers than friends. He'd seen her around the ranch, but he'd never looked at her too closely. How could he have ever missed that bust, which he'd gotten a nice view of before he remembered his manners and turned away. He may not get out much, but he was still a man. And he had perfect eyesight. He noticed things like that. Somehow on Jessa, he'd missed it until the moment he'd seen her lying on the floor. All of a sudden, there they were, two perfect breasts staring him in the face, and he was awake on a whole new level. Even without coffee.

The unrecognizable woman in front of him—could he even call her Jessa anymore?—worked quickly in the kitchen, clutching the top of the robe like she wanted to bolt it together. He almost wished she could.

After she'd removed the screaming teakettle from the stove and poured water into a French press, she sort of scuttled past him. "I should go change," she said in a huskily sexy voice that didn't seem to fit her. Or at least it hadn't. Before the lingerie...

"I'll throw on some clothes," she went on, nervously shifting her eyes. "Then we can talk about Luis."

Yes. Clothes. That would be best. Because if she put on more clothes, maybe he could focus on something besides these details he'd never noticed about her. Like the soft way her blondish hair cascaded past her shoulders. Or the way her earnest, unsure, brown-eyed gaze had stirred something inside him. Instead of answering her, he simply averted his eyes and nodded, giving her permission to go, giving himself space to get his shit together. Because he'd just spent a good five minutes checking out Jessa Mae Love. Town animal activist. Best friend to his sixty-seven-year-old father. Which was weird.

God, this was so weird...

"Um. Be right back." Her skin blotched bright pink before

she whirled and scampered down the hall, that short robe riding up enough to make his eyes pop open wider so he could get a better look before he checked himself again. Jessa Mae Love. He tried to picture her the way he'd always seen her—wearing tan hiking pants, a T-shirt, hair pulled back tightly into a ponytail, and those eyes obscured by thick-rimmed glasses. But the image kept morphing back into sexy robe babe. No way would he get her out of his head now.

He pushed off the couch and did a lap around her living room to get the blood flowing somewhere besides his crotch.

Trying to distract himself from the action happening in her bedroom down the hall, he looked around. The house was the typical 1940s bungalow. Jessa's father, Buzz, had lived there for more than thirty years. A few years ago, his father had dragged Lance to a poker game here. Back then, dark wood paneling covered the walls. A hazy smell of cigar smoke contaminated the furniture. It'd been the typical elderly bachelor pad—everything old, moldy, and most likely purchased from garage sales. But Jessa had really lightened things up.

She'd painted the wood paneling bright white and knocked down the wall that used to separate the kitchen from the small living room. There were pops of orange and turquoise in pillows and curtains. Instead of trinkets, a wall of white bookshelves was filled with academic-looking hardbacks. He paused in front of the white sofa and studied the picture that hung on the wall behind it. Jessa and Buzz standing on Topaz Mountain. He leaned in closer. She had on the typical Jessa uniform—pants and a loose-fitting T-shirt—but on closer inspection, it did appear that the woman had always been more well-endowed than he'd given her credit for...

"Sorry that took so long."

He spun, knocking his knee on the edge of an old trunk that acted as a coffee table, and held back the wince.

"I'll get the coffee. Should be done now," she murmured, nervously fisting her delicate hands.

"Sounds good." His head *was* pounding for a hit of caffeine, but the rest of his body pounded for different reasons. Apparently, Jessa had suddenly decided to start wearing shorts. Short shorts and a faded V-neck T-shirt that pointed his gaze to the very spot he'd been trying to avoid.

"Have a seat." She gestured to the couch and sashayed across the room and into the small kitchen.

For the second time that morning, he had to remind himself to close his mouth. He sank to the couch, glancing at the picture book on her coffee table instead of her ass. Which was shaped and firm, he couldn't help but notice. And if he sat here much longer, he might be tempted to do more than notice, which meant he should fast track this little meeting.

With that in mind, he shifted forward, widened his stance, and rested his elbows on his knees. "So, got any idea where my dad might be?"

"I'm not *exactly* sure," Jessa answered, working quickly to fill two mugs in the kitchen. "But if I had to guess, I'd say he's somewhere up near the north ridge."

"And the north ridge is…?" His face heated. Yes, he owned the land, but he never had time to get out and explore it. Not the way Jessa and his father did.

"It's about eight miles up the mountain." Carrying two steaming mugs, Jessa walked—no *swayed* those curvy hips—back across the living room and handed one to him. She sat on the very edge of a leather chair opposite the couch. "I saw him Wednesday," she said, her brown eyes reddening. "He asked me if I wanted to go up with him. And I said no." The last word teetered on the edge of a whimper.

Oh, shit. Don't do it. Don't cry. "He'll be fine," he said before a tear could fall.

Jessa bit into her lower lip. Something he might like to try sometime...

"I thought he'd ask Tucker to go with him since I couldn't. No one should be out there alone. Ever." A tear did slip out then, and he shocked himself by reaching over to cover her hand with his. Not because he wanted to touch her. Hell no. That had nothing to do with this. Her dad had passed away last year and it obviously still got to her, that's all. He could imagine how that would feel. Didn't know what he'd do if he lost his own father. "Dad's out there all the time," he reminded her. "He likes to be alone. And it's not your responsibility to babysit him." That burden rested solely on his shoulders. And with his training schedule, he hadn't done much of a good job of it lately.

Jessa stared at his hand covering hers like she didn't quite know what to make of it. Yeah, neither did he. So he withdrew it, lifted the coffee mug to his lips, and took a good long sip. Heaven. It was liquid heaven. Bitter but creamy. Exactly the way he made it for himself. The realization shook him up again. He set down the mug before he spilled it. "You put a tablespoon of cream in it." Real cream. None of that fake flavored shit.

Jessa startled, her eyes worried. "You don't like it?"

"No. I mean...yes." He paused to unscramble his thoughts. "That's exactly how I make it." But she hadn't asked him if he wanted cream.

A soft smile plumped her lips and made them look as delicious as the coffee. "That's how Luis drinks it every day at the shelter. I figured maybe that was how you liked it, too."

"Good guess." He sipped again, hoping the caffeine would clarify his thoughts, because they kept wandering and now was not the time to get distracted by a woman. He had to find his dad so he could get back to the ranch and take care of Wild Willy. Otherwise he wouldn't be able to resume his training and then he'd be five hundred miles up shit creek.

"So he didn't tell you where he planned to camp?" Jessa asked, crossing those long legs. Her voice had a formal ring to it, like she was about as uncomfortable with the current situation as he was.

He focused on his coffee. "No. But he does this all the time." Definitely more than Jessa knew about.

"He can't sit still," she said through a fond smile. "He hates to be confined."

"Yeah, well, if he doesn't start sitting still more often, I'll *have* to confine him." He couldn't watch the man 24/7. Not with Worlds coming up.

Not that he needed to have that discussion with Jessa. He'd already said too much.

Lance finished off his coffee and plunked the mug onto the trunk. "So can you tell me how to get up there? To the north ridge?"

"There's really no easy way." She stood and collected their mugs, rushing them to the kitchen. "You'll have to take the ATV up most of the way," she called as she rinsed them in the sink. "Until the talus field. Then you go on foot about another mile or so until you see the outcropping."

The what huh?

She traipsed back to her chair and sat. "Then you run

into the boulder field." Her eyes glittered with excitement. "That's where it gets fun."

"Sounds simple." Yeah, about as simple as getting his body to behave when he took his gaze to the point of her V-neck shirt. Holy hell. This was gonna take him all day.

"It's actually pretty complicated. I'll have to come with you," she murmured, the rounded apples of her cheeks flushing with an intensity he'd never seen on her face. Of course, he'd never really looked before.

"You want to come?" His mouth went dry. He'd have to spend the whole day trying not to notice how sexy she suddenly was?

"I *have* to come. There's no way you'll find him on your own."

Damn it all. She was right.

* * *

Jessa did her darnedest to stuff down the worry that threatened to make her seem overdramatic. Lance was so calm about the whole thing. So sure his father would be fine. Luis went out on the mountain all the time. Sometimes alone. He knew the terrain. Knew every survival skill he'd ever need...

She gazed out at the peaks from Naomi's front porch, where she and her friend had gathered to wait for Lance to bring down the ATV. The mountains looked beautiful, powdered with snow at the very tops, the late fall sun casting a spotlight on every chiseled detail. *He'll be fine*, she told herself again, trying to mentally separate today from the trauma of last year. And yet her stomach refused to settle.

In an attempt to distract herself, she filled Naomi in on her eventful morning.

"Let me get this straight." Her friend's luminous green eyes doubled in size. "Lance came *into* your house. Sat on your couch. And had coffee with you?" she repeated for what had to be the fifth time.

Jessa's skin warmed as though the high-altitude sun was beating down right on her face, but nope, they were nice and shaded. It was simply a hearty Lance Cortez–induced blush. Not even the brisk mountain breeze could douse it, though goose bumps prickled her legs. God, she shouldn't be wearing shorts on a search-and-rescue operation. But they'd left her house in such a hurry she hadn't even had time to change into more appropriate attire.

A few feet away, Naomi's sweet daughter, Gracie, sang to herself on the porch swing.

Jessa leaned in close so the girl wouldn't hear. "*Yes*. He came into my house. And I was naked," she moaned, reliving that humiliating moment when Lance had stepped around the couch and the bottom fell out of his jaw.

Naomi's eyes narrowed in a way that quirked her lips. "Better naked than wearing your old hiking pants," she offered.

"Thanks." She'd hoped a quick chat with her friend would bolster her confidence, seeing as how she had to spend an entire day with Lance and somehow not succumb to her typical awkward ways, but so far the woman wasn't helping. "This isn't funny! You should've seen the way he looked at me." At first he'd looked shocked, then it seemed more like lust, but then, as he'd finished his coffee, his expression had looked almost disgusted. "I don't think he likes me very much."

"Lance doesn't like anyone," Naomi reminded her. "But that's why this is so perfect."

"I'm not following." This didn't sound perfect to her. She had to spend a whole day with someone who didn't like people. And he was so beautiful to look at. Which meant she was guaranteed to make a fool out of herself again.

"He's tough to read," Naomi admitted. "But it's the perfect opportunity for you to try out your new look. See if you can win him over. It'll be great practice for finding donors for the shelter."

Now it was her turn to laugh. "Win him over? Lance Cortez?" That was like a duck trying to win over a lion. "Do you know me at all? I have no clue how to charm a man."

"Well you coulda fooled me," her friend said, looking her up and down. "Seriously. You look hot. The contacts, the makeup, the hair..." She reached over and fluffed the soft waves Jessa had blown dry earlier. "You've always been beautiful, and now everyone's going to know it."

Jessa smoothed her hair nervously. "I'm not sure it'll make much of a difference."

"Trust me," Naomi insisted. "It *will* make a difference. You look great," she emphasized. "Pretty soon you'll have donors lined up down the block."

"If you say so." But after Lance came over, she canceled all of her meetings. Donors weren't her biggest concern today. Not right now. She squeezed her friend's hands, feeling her own tremble. "Do you really think Luis is okay out there?" she asked, almost breathless. Memories of getting the phone call that her father had collapsed out on the mountain bore down on her.

"I was worried, too, honey," Naomi said, not letting go of her hands. "But Lance is right. His dad is a true mountain man. He's not lost. He's not missing. He just needs to be more responsible and remember to bring along his medication next time."

"Right." She nodded as though the words had alleviated her fears.

"You and Lance will find him," Naomi went on, turning back to the driveway.

Somewhere in the distance, an engine sounded. Nerves gripped Jessa's stomach. She hoped so. She hoped they'd find Luis right away. She also hoped she could spend the day with Lance and somehow resist that dark, hot cowboy thing he had going on...

But when he came speeding around the corner on the ATV, dirt flying from the wheels, that hard body tensed and strong, her heart floated away from her again.

He skidded to a stop in front of the green lawn and pulled off his helmet.

"Uncle Lance!" Gracie squealed, launching herself off the porch and into his arms just as he stood.

Laughing, he swung her around, and that smile on Lance's face—the unguarded expression of happiness—bolted Jessa's feet right to the wooden planks beneath her. Then and there her heart dissolved into warm mush and something inside her sang. She knew she could never see him the same way again.

Lance glanced over at her, some of that messy dark hair spilling over his forehead, and their eyes locked. The singing turned into a warm hum. It was like that scene in *West Side Story*, when Tony and Maria first see each other across the dance floor. Everything else blurs into a meaningless background and it's just the two of them, staring longingly into each other's eyes. Well, she was longing. It was hard to tell what he thought.

Lance was the first to blink. "Hey, Jessa," he said casually, like the universe hadn't just exploded into a million glittering diamonds that made everything sparkle. Was she imagining it or did his voice gentle the syllables of her name?

"Hi." Jessa nearly sighed.

"All right, buckaroo." Lance set a still-giggling Gracie gently on the ground. "I've got to go. But we'll get to that riding lesson later."

The girl's eyes were sparkling the same way Jessa imagined hers still were. "Promise?" Gracie asked, hands clasped underneath her chin, the little charmer.

"Pinkie swear." He held up his little finger to finalize the deal and Jessa could've sworn her ovaries ached.

Naomi pushed her from behind, and it was a good thing because otherwise she might've stood in that spot all day long staring at Lance.

"So you two have a good time," her friend said, giving her another good nudge in his direction. "Let me know as soon as you find Luis. Tell him I'll have his lunch waiting."

"Will do." Lance looked at her. "Ready?"

No. She was clearly not ready, seeing as how she could feel her heart starting to wander away from her again. Somehow, with one look, Lance had obliterated her ambition to put romance on the backburner.

Oh God. If that had happened with one look, how would she spend the whole day with him? She shot a desperate look at Naomi, but her friend only nudged her toward the steps, her whole face beaming a calculated smile.

As if she knew Jessa was already in over her head.

Chapter Four

White-hot rays of sun cut across his vision and blinded Lance the second he turned back to the ATV. It was a damn good thing the sun blinded him, too, because *something* had to direct his attention away from Jessa so he'd quit noticing how the brightness lit her long, sleek hair. And how her hips swayed in that womanly way. Not to mention how her tanned legs tensed with her steps, shaped and strong but delicate, too.

Damn those shorts. Who the hell wore shorts on a rescue operation, anyway?

Someone with sexy legs, jackass. Not like it was a crime. The woman was allowed to wear whatever she wanted. He never used to care what she wore before. Until sexy robe babe, that is. He kept his head down and navigated the path across Naomi's lawn. *Man.* His father owed him for this mess. If the man would've stayed put, he never would've had to call on Jessa. Never would've noticed her sex appeal. *This is Jessa Mae*, he reminded himself for the hundredth time.

Blinking against the morning sun, he casually sauntered to the driveway. Jessa had already made it to the ATV, booking it down the walkway as if she could feel the snort of a pissed-off bull on her tail. Seemed she wasn't thrilled about spending the day with him, either. When she'd seen him swinging Gracie around, the woman's face had been stony and expressionless. She'd stared at him for a full minute at first, and her eyes had avoided him ever since. Kind of the way he attempted to carefully avoid looking at her. But that was about to get a lot harder because dear old Dad had taken the other ATV out for his little escape, which meant there was only one left. For him and Jessa. To ride together...

Without glancing back at him, she plunked one of the helmets onto her head and tugged the chinstrap into place. Then she swung a leg over the machine and took the handlebars in her hands, staring straight ahead.

"What are you doing?" Lance asked quickening his pace.

Jessa cranked on the handle, starting the thing up. "I'm driving," she yelled over the engine noise.

He skidded to a stop. "*You're* driving?" He hadn't counted on... spooning her from behind.

"You don't know where to go," she yelled again, handing over his helmet like she wanted to get this over with. "I bet I know exactly where he went."

He reached over her and shut off the engine. "You can tell me where to go. *I* should drive."

Jessa didn't budge, but she threw up the face shield on her helmet. "I've been up there a lot more than you have. *I* know the terrain."

"And *I* can handle the ATV," he said, before he thought

better of it. Not that he wanted to insult her, but she was pretty petite to maneuver a machine like this. Especially with the weight of two riders.

Fire filled her narrowed eyes. "I'm driving," she said, turning the key to start the engine back up. "So you can either get on the back or I'll go by myself."

"Fine," he ground out, pulling the helmet down so she wouldn't see the scowl that tightened his face.

Careful not to touch her, he eased his leg over the seat and slid on, bracing his hands against his thighs, unsure where else to put them.

Jessa glanced over her shoulder. "You need to hold on," she advised him, flicking the helmet's shield up so he could gaze into her exotic brown eyes. They flashed with determination but wouldn't quite meet his.

"I am holding on." To himself. That was much safer. He didn't want to feel her soft skin beneath his fingertips. Didn't want to feel anything for her at all.

With a slight shrug, Jessa flicked down the helmet's face shield and turned back to the handlebars.

He clamped his legs tight and secured his feet on the ATV's sturdy base. That'd be enough to hold him in place. How fast could Jessa possibly drive any—

The engine squealed then clinked, there was the grind of metal gears, and they shot off like a missile on target.

"Shit!" His arms flew up and before the momentum threw him right off the back, he wrapped them around her waist, pulling his chest against her back to steady himself.

Her shoulders tensed against him, but she kept her head straight, focused on driving, and it was a damn good thing because they must've been going twenty miles per hour straight up the side of the mountain. "You always drive like this?" he growled over the wind. He'd have to think twice about letting her and his father go up the mountain together again.

"I just want to get there," she yelled back, turning enough that he could see the worry tensing her jaw.

Right. She'd lost her father only a year ago. On the same mountain they were currently blitzing up. And he couldn't imagine that...losing his dad. He'd already lost Lucas, then Levi. One by one the people he'd cared about had walked out of his life. If he lost his dad, he'd lose everyone who mattered. Everyone he had left. Friends weren't the same. Parents anchored you to your heritage, reminded you who you were when it got hard to remember. Far as he knew, Jessa didn't see her mom much. She'd been close with her dad. An ache snuck into his chest as he peered at her profile. Beneath her helmet, her face had hardened into a mask of desperation.

He didn't like seeing her that way. Worried. A little scared. It did something to him, made sympathy prickle through him, which made his arms soften around her...more like he was holding her instead of holding on for dear life. "Hey." He leaned in close so he wouldn't have to shout so loud. "He's all right." This was Luis Cortez they were talking about. The man who'd wrestled a mountain lion off one of his horses, according to local legends. "He's probably gonna be all pissed off that we came up here after him." In fact, he knew his dad would be pissed.

The ATV slowed, then stuttered to a stop, reducing the engine noise to a low hum. Jessa glanced back at him. "Do you really think so?" she asked in a small wobbling tone. Even with the face shield in place he could see the paleness that had taken over her complexion.

"Yeah." He flicked up his face shield, then went for hers so their eyes could lock. So he could reach through her fears. "And I'll tell you one thing," he said with a smirk. "I'm riding down the mountain with *him*."

A shadow of a smile flickered across her lips. "You don't like my driving." The revelation seemed to amuse her. "That's surprising considering you ride maniacal bulls for a living."

"That's a hell of a lot safer than sitting behind you on this thing." He meant that in more ways than one. Because the sun haloed her in a mystifying glow and for the first time ever he realized she wasn't only pretty. Jessa was stunning— beautiful and real and deep.

"Hey," she scolded, her eyes narrowing. "I'm being safe. I'd never endanger—"

"I'm teasing you," he interrupted before she got her leopard-print thong all bunched. "Trying to lighten things up."

"Oh." She looked down.

"I'm not worried about him, Jessa," he said more softly. "Really. The only reason I rushed over to your place was because he doesn't have his blood pressure medication." He grinned at her. "That and I've gotta get back to my training. The sooner we find him the sooner I can get back on my bull."

"Right. Thanks, Lance." Jessa's eyes shied away from his, unsure and guarded and humble. She cleared her throat and lowered the shield to cover up her delicate face, which definitely wasn't pale anymore. Color had shaded her cheeks with the same heat he felt flickering somewhere deep.

Her scent reached him, floating into the cloud of exhaust that had started to dissipate. Some type of vanilla, but light and subtle. It'd been a while since he'd inhaled a woman's scent and a sigh expanded through him, ending in a sharp pain that descended behind his ribs. He'd lusted after plenty of women. The buckle bunnies who'd followed him around the circuit in the early days, who'd always made good on their promise of offering him a fun, uncomplicated night. That had been a different kind of ache, though. It'd never traveled any farther north than his brass belt buckle.

"Ready then?" she murmured, the words muffled. Scooting herself into position, she clamped her hands onto the handlebars again, then cranked the engine.

"Ready." Heart pulsing in small bursts of a long-forgotten desire, Lance threaded his arms around her waist again, letting her back rest against his chest, this time with no hesitation.

* * *

Heaven help her, Jessa had to start focusing on something besides the way Lance's hardened muscled chest shielded her back. The way his sinewed arms guarded her in a strong embrace. *Something else...something else...*

The cool, crisp air. The rays of sun poking through white puffy clouds overhead. Pine trees, tall and gangly. *Shit!* She dodged one that seemed to jump out of nowhere, jerking the handlebars in a way that brought Lance even closer.

"We almost there?" he asked through her helmet. And yes, she'd be the first to admit that the last twenty minutes of her driving hadn't been the best in her life. But he was the one to blame for that. Being all sweet to her. Draping his body all over hers from behind. That had made it a bit hard to concentrate on not hitting broad tree trunks or massive boulders. "Getting close," she yelled so he wouldn't hear the tremble in her voice.

She'd sworn off men, damn it. Sworn off love. All well and good in her head, but God, she wished she could cut out her heart and leave it behind. Already it had ballooned in her chest, rising higher, soaring with the same sappy emotions that had gotten her into so much trouble in the past. And who was she kidding? Lance. Lance Cortez! Bull-riding god who'd been known to shack up with the groupies who made it their life's mission to sleep with a bull rider. Or all of the bull riders. She swore those women kept a checklist in their back pockets.

That thought was all it took to deflate her heart. It couldn't take more disappointment. More pain. Lance Cortez had a certain reputation. Rumor had it that he'd never spent a full night with a woman. He'd slept with plenty of them, but he never stayed in their bed until morning. Remembering that made it easier to focus. They were out here to find Luis. That was all.

Standing up a bit, she peered over the next small rise. This was one of the trickier spots. She slowed the ATV, easing it up the side of a steep incline so Lance wouldn't be thrust into her again. They were getting close to the boulder field, the place she and Luis always parked when they hiked together.

Easing herself forward, she made a futile attempt to put space between her back and Lance's chest, leaning over the handlebars as she navigated the rocky slope. Just as they crested the rise, a smear of blue caught her eye. Luis's ATV. She plowed straight for it, then cranked the brake, skidding to stop right next to it. Hands shaky and tingling, she ripped off her helmet and let it fall to the ground. "He's

not here." She glanced around. They were high enough that
the trees had thinned; only an occasional gnarled pine tree
twisted from the snow and wind during the harsh winters.
But there was no sign of Luis. No backpack. No evidence
of a camp.

"He must've gone off on foot," Lance said from behind
her.

An ominous feeling swept over her, thinning her breath.
She stared at the boulder field, the scattered granite that
stretched all the way to the mountain's pointed summit. "I
thought we'd find him here." She'd been so sure. They'd
gone off on foot many times, but always in different directions. And there weren't many places to camp past this point.
The terrain got rocky, steeper. Less than a mile up from
this place was the spot where her own father had collapsed.
Where his heart had given out. Panic fluttered her nerves.

"He couldn't have gone very far," Lance said, coming up
beside her, seeming to assess the land. "Looks pretty unfor-
giving." For the first time gravity weighted his tone.

"It is," she whispered. She and Luis had hiked around
here. Once, she'd even gotten him to take her to the spot
where her father had died. Tears bit at the rims of her eyes.

From here, it took about another twenty minutes to hike
up to the place Luis had taken her father that day. Was that
where'd he'd gone? Did he visit the place often? Was it still
as hard for him as it was for her? Before she could stop
them, the tears spilled over in warm streaks, sadness flowing
out of her once again.

"Hey." Lance rested a hand on her shoulder. "You okay?"

"Yes." But the tears kept streaming out and she was powerless to stop them. "Sorry," she muttered, annoyed with
herself. She hadn't counted on this being so hard. "I'm

worried." And God, she missed her father. Missed being someone's little girl.

Taking her shoulders in those large manly hands, Lance helped her climb off the ATV and turned her to face him, crouching so their eyes were level. "Dad's fine. Trust me. I know."

"How?" she whimpered.

He shrugged, shook his head a little. "This'll sound crazy, but he and I have this connection. If something was wrong, I'd know. I'd feel it."

The words almost prompted a sob. Why hadn't she known? The day her father had died, she'd gone about her life, seeing her furry patients, meeting her roommate for a drink during happy hour. That's where she'd been when she'd gotten the call. She should've felt something...should've felt the loss even before she knew. He was her father.

She gazed at the boulder field, everything blurred and gray despite the bright sunshine, and once again she wondered if he'd suffered. If he'd been in pain. If he'd been scared. Luis hadn't told her much, couldn't seem to talk about it. But he'd said her father had gone ahead and was already on the ground by the time he got there.

"Don't cry, Jessa." Lance held her face in his hands and swiped away the tears with his thumbs. "Like I said, he's okay. I know it. We'll find him."

She nodded, attempting to sniffle back a year of sadness. "I believe you." And yet she couldn't get a grip, not up here so close to her dad's final moments. "It's just...my father." She swallowed so hard her throat ached. "Sometimes it's hard to be up here." God those tears burned her eyes. "I wish I would've been with him. I wish I could've been holding his hand when he..." She couldn't bring herself to say it. It was so horrible. So, so horrible to think of him out here in pain and terrified as the world dimmed and life faded from his body. Instinctively, her hand reached up to finger the necklace he'd given her. It had been his last gift. A rose gold heart with a small diamond embedded inside.

"It's real pretty," Lance said, looking down at the charm. "He give it to you?"

She nodded, tensing her throat so her voice wouldn't wobble. "I miss him. I should've been around more."

She half expected Lance to lecture her on living in the past, on not letting the regrets take over, like so many other people had done. Instead, he pulled her against him, wrapping her up in the comfort and peace of a long, sturdy hug. And despite the potential dangers, she let her head rest against him. She breathed in the calming scent of leather and coffee.

"I wish I knew what those minutes were like." The minutes before he closed his eyes and gave in. Maybe that would bring her peace. Maybe it would give her the permission to let her regrets go.

Lance moved back slightly and took her chin in his hand. She felt the roughness of his skin, the calluses, the coarseness of scabs from healing scrapes. Gently, he tilted her head up until she was staring straight at the sky. So blue, the color itself seemed alive, bottomless in its perfection. Fluffy clouds billowed and moved and floated, a fluid dance. And the sun, so bright and clear it seemed to make everything sparkle.

"That's what he would've been looking at," he murmured, the deep vibration of his voice close to her temple. "The sky, the mountains."

Jessa let her eyes soak it all in until she felt so full with the beauty and wonder of the world, she had to close them. "It's beautiful." Didn't matter how many times she saw it. This view, these mountains, that endless royal sky always struck her. And her dad had loved it, too. He would've wanted this to be the last thing he ever saw.

"It's peaceful up here," Lance said, looking up, too. "Maybe a little what Heaven's like."

The words held a gift, a surprise ray of hope that penetrated her doubts. "You believe in Heaven?"

Those lips quirked in a small smile, and even though he was so dark, with that mussed hair and tanned sun-drenched skin, his eyes were lit with energy. "I like to believe there's something more."

More. The word spread over her like a healing salve, alleviating the lingering throb from the wounds of loss. All these years, she'd been wrong about Lance. She'd thought him to be closed off and grouchy, a man of few words who got annoyed easily, but now she realized she'd misjudged him. He might not do small talk, but a seven-word sentence from Lance meant more than paragraphs from most people.

Her eyes opened and color flooded in. The first thing she saw were his lips, right there, inches from hers. The tendons that threaded her joints together loosened and sparks crackled in her heart. She inhaled his musky scent, let her gaze rest in his. Such beautiful clear eyes. Deep and wise. And yes, she seemed to be moving in closer now but she couldn't fight that pull, couldn't stop the hard cry of need and desire that pushed her into him. Her palms came to rest on his chest as her lips grazed his. But that one light touch wasn't enough. Wasn't nearly enough... so she went for it— a full-on kiss, lips fused to his, sighing, searching...

Except his chest tensed and he seemed to step back. An

icy realization splashed her face, dousing the passion that had ignited. Lance didn't want to be kissing her. He'd offered her a kind word because she was upset. That was all.

That was all.

Throat thick and pulsing, she slowly eased back, the warmth that had bathed her lips turning cold.

Lance stood stock-still, his own lips parted, arms out as though he'd lost his balance, chest suspended like he wasn't sure if he should breathe in or out.

"Oh my God." Invisible flames of humiliation licked at her cheeks. "I'm so sorry." She'd freaking kissed him! Less than a day after swearing off men, she'd let that swirl of emotion and desire and hope sweep her up into its kingdom of seduction. Her skin tingled. The sunlight seemed too bright. "I didn't mean to...I shouldn't have..." *Kissed* him. On the lips. Like they'd been transported into some sappy chick flick. They were supposed to be searching for Luis! Holy baldheaded cats, what the hell was the matter with her? She couldn't even go one day without swooning. She needed help. Romantics Anonymous. *Hello, my name is Jessa and I'm addicted to love...*

Might as well face it.

Lance simply stood there, saying nothing, an unreadable expression frozen on his face.

Not surprising. He was clearly in a state of shock. Or disbelief? Repulsion? It was impossible to tell. That fight or flight survival instinct kicked her hard under the ribs. "We should find your dad," she said quickly, turning so he wouldn't see the fierce blush that had brought her about two inches from passing out. "Let's go this way."

With desperation in her steps, she tromped toward the boulder field before she could screw up anything else.

Chapter Five

Two seconds ago, he could've sworn Jessa's lips were pressed to his, warm and wet and the slightest bit naughty. If it hadn't been for the smear of some honey-flavored lip gloss on his bottom lip, he would've thought he'd imagined the whole thing because she was gone. As in out of sight. And he was still standing in the same position he'd assumed when she knocked his world off its axis and kissed him.

Shit. He'd screwed that up. Royally. Who could blame him, though? He'd never expected *Jessa* to press herself against him and kiss him. Never expected the rush it brought in him, either. She'd caught him off guard, knocked him off balance. And yes, he could see how stiffening and stepping back may have sent her a certain message, but it was a reflex. Either regain balance or land on his ass. His body had reacted and made the choice for him.

He squinted in the direction that Jessa had stormed off.

The boulder field was sloped and she'd already disappeared on the other side of the rise. "Jessa!" he yelled, not exactly sure how to find her. But he had to. Had to find her, somehow undo the awkwardness he must've made her feel. And they still had to find his dad, too. So he stepped off the way she'd gone, trying to follow her path. He skirted around a hunk of granite as tall as him. Went over a smaller boulder, then hoisted himself up and gazed around. *There.* She was weaving her way through the rocks about thirty yards up.

"Hey!" he called again. "Wait up." He climbed down, trying to formulate an explanation in his head. Except he didn't have one. Usually when women started crying in front of him, his forehead would crank itself tight and he'd slowly back away, scanning for a fast escape. But he kind of hadn't minded comforting Jessa. He certainly hadn't minded the feel of her soft breasts against his chest and her silky lips locked on his...

In fact, he didn't mind this whole excursion as much as he'd thought he would.

Though Jessa slowed her pace, she didn't stop to wait for him. Her chin had lifted with determination, her eyes focused ahead and her arms swooshing at her sides.

The sight drew out a smile. Sure, he felt bad that she seemed embarrassed, but God she was captivating with that fortitude. Continuing on like the whole thing hadn't bothered her at all. He'd met women before who would've whined about his reaction, who would've gone for the guilt trip. Not Jessa. She'd simply hauled off and left him standing there like she didn't need him anyway.

By the time he'd closed in on her, he was out of breath. "Are you okay?" He tried to hide the wheeze in his lungs through a hearty throat clearing.

"Spectacular," she muttered, stomping on.

His hand snagged her shoulder and forced her to stop. "Come on. It's not a big deal." At least it shouldn't have been. Hell, he'd been kissed by his fair share of women. A couple had even caught him off guard before. None had rendered him unable to walk, however. Or to think straight. His eyes searched hers.

They were dark, but the sunlight made the flecks of bronze in them glisten. There was a force in her gaze. She didn't shy away or narrow her eyes angrily at him. She simply stared back, open and unfazed.

"I was surprised," he admitted, leaving out the whole truth. Surprised and thrown off balance by his body's fast response to her. "And I—"

"Can we forget it?" she interrupted. "Please? I'm just emotional. Maybe even a little hormonal this week. You know how it goes."

"Uh." No. He didn't. He *really* didn't.

"And let's face it," she went on. "You're PDF, so it's not my fault, exactly."

"PDF?" he repeated. He sucked at acronyms. Had to use Google to decode most of Levi's Facebook posts. He'd never been good with words. *PDF . . . PDF . . .* "Poor dumb fool?"

Those glistening baby browns rolled. "Pretty. Damn. Fine. Don't you get out?"

"Not as much as you would think," he admitted. Lately he hadn't gotten out at all. He was supposed to be training his ass off.

"So you can see how something like that would've happened," she said, lifting her chin again. "The emotions. The whole smoldering cowboy thing you've got going on. But I'd really appreciate it if we could forget it. Like, completely erase it from our memories. Because, Lance, I've sworn off men. Romance. All of it, really. Gotta shift my focus, you know? Don't need it messing up my life anymore. So please. This never happened."

He'd never enjoyed a woman babbling. Ever. Until today. "Okay. I guess. But—"

"Nope. See, 'but' is a segue back into the same topic we just agreed to forget. As in never mention it; never even *remember* it. We entered into a verbal agreement, which can be legally binding in the state of Colorado," she finished, looking quite proud of herself.

"Can it now?" He didn't even try to hide his amusement. He'd known Jessa for years. Or at least he'd known about her. To him, she'd always been Buzz Love's daughter, the gangly girl with the glasses. He thought her to be nice though somewhat shy, maybe even awkward. But they'd never had a real conversation before this morning. She was actually fun to talk to.

"Yes," she uttered with a definitive nod. "As a matter of fact it can."

"What if I said go ahead and sue me?" He pressed his gaze into hers again. "Because I'm not sure I'll be able to forget. I didn't *mind* you kissing me."

She laughed. "Right. You didn't mind." The words mocked him. "Your shoulders felt like concrete. And the way you stepped back...I actually thought you were gonna bolt." But she waved a hand through the air as if it didn't matter. "Listen, I get it. You're Lance Cortez. Sort of famous. Rugged. Hot. I'm just Jessa. Normal girl who smells like animals half the time."

Not right now she didn't. Right now she smelled like the vanilla beans Naomi sometimes set around his father's kitchen. And what was wrong with normal? Kind of refreshing to have a woman say things like they were instead of what she thought he wanted to hear for once.

"Besides all of that, I've sworn off kissing." She turned away and started to hike again, giving him no choice but to follow.

"That seems a little extreme." He kept his eyes focused on the ground so he wouldn't trip over a rock and look like a dumb ass. "Isn't there something else you could swear off? Sugar? Chocolate? Alcohol? Seems to me kissing is one of those things that's actually good for you." Especially when it led to sex. Weren't there a bunch of health benefits associated with sex? Sure seemed like it. Not that kissing Jessa would lead to sex. Because how weird would that be? Having sex with this woman who hung out with his father? Who wanted marriage and kids and the whole bit so badly she'd been engaged multiple times? His body didn't seem to think it would be weird, though. The quick flash of a conjured image was enough to activate the launch sequence. Steam seemed to radiate off his face and cloud the brisk mountain air.

"Actually, I happen to think alcohol and chocolate are much healthier than kissing. At least in my experience," Jessa insisted, scrambling to climb over a tall boulder that blocked their path. She moved effortlessly. Her feet and hands knew exactly where to go. While she finessed it, he awkwardly scaled the thing with sheer strength.

When they'd gotten past the obstacle he slipped in front of her. Wouldn't be as easy for her to get around *him*.

"So that's it then," he challenged.

"That's it." Her gaze didn't waver and he didn't doubt that she meant it.

"Oh, wait. Actually, one more thing. I'd really appreciate it if you didn't say anything to anyone else. The girls would *kill* me if they knew I'd already slipped up and—"

A shrill whistle cut her off. For a second he thought he'd imagined it, but then it rang out again.

"Luis," she whispered, gripping Lance's coat. "That's your dad."

* * *

"How do you know it's him?" Lance jogged alongside her, seeming to be hardly out of breath while she hiccupped and gagged on the thin mountain air.

"He told me if I ever needed help out here, I should whistle exactly like that," she sputtered, clutching at the pains needling her chest. And then Luis had said he'd find her. He'd told her if he ever heard that whistle, he'd rescue her. A second wind lifted her head and churned her legs faster. "We have to find him." Her eyes drank in the endless blue-gray peaks spread all around them. He could be anywhere. Who knew where that whistle had echoed from...

The shrill sound pierced the air again. They were getting closer. Jessa skidded down a steep section of loose talus, losing her balance and flailing to catch herself.

Lance held on to her arm. "Take it easy. Don't need to do two rescues."

She ignored him, ripping out of his grip. "He's in trouble," she wheezed, her heartbeat throbbing in her temples. Luis was in trouble and he was alone.

Another whistle veered her to the left. She slowed to pick her way down a boulder-strewn slope. So close. It sounded so close...

"There!" Lance darted in front of her and pointed toward a huge rounded boulder.

She strained to see.

Luis stood near it, still and alert.

"Are you okay?" blared from her mouth with surprising force, given how she could hardly breathe.

The man spun and relief whooshed in, filling her lungs, calming that surge of adrenaline. He looked like the same Luis, nothing broken, nothing bleeding. His white hair was bedraggled, but other than that, he seemed fine.

Lance made it to his father before her. "What the hell, Dad?" Now he did seem to run out of breath. And he looked pale, too. Rattled. Like maybe he'd been as worried as her on their little sprint down here.

Jessa doubled over to catch her breath.

"What's the problem, son?" the man asked, clearly clueless as to how worried they'd been.

"What's the *problem*?" Lance's tone inched toward a yell.

"We thought something terrible happened to you," Jessa broke in, before Lance could jump all over him. "You were gone all night. And no one knew where you went." She wasn't yelling, but a bit of a whimper snuck through. If anything had happened to him—

"Course I was gone all night," he said, as ornery and gruff as ever. "I have every right to go out and camp on my land whenever the hell I want."

Jessa cut a glance at Lance. His face had gone red. Molten.

"The hell you do," he ground out. "It's not safe for you to come out here alone."

Now that she agreed with. What if her father had been out here alone when he'd had the heart attack? They never would've known what had happened to him. They may have never found his body. She pressed the back of her hand against her lips before a sob snuck out.

Luis seemed to assess her with those watery gray eyes. "I didn't mean to worry anyone," he said more gently. "I'm fine. Everything's fine."

"Then why were you whistling?" she whispered, still battling how the memories of her dad and her relief at seeing Luis swirled her in a fog of emotion.

"Can't find the damn ATV," Luis said, gazing around. "Woke up at sunrise and been lookin' for it ever since. Left it parked right here. I know I did. Someone must've taken it."

"No," Lance snapped, his body rigid. "Actually you didn't leave it right here."

The worry that had just started to dissipate clouded Jessa's heart again. "You parked it where we always park," she said, studying him, searching his eyes for a sign that he remembered. "Over on the east side of the mountain."

Luis simply blinked at her. He looked...confused. Disoriented. And she'd never seen him that way out here. He always knew where things were, which direction was which, how to get from one point to another. On all of their hikes, he'd been the one to lead her.

"This *is* the east side," he insisted, with a stubborn lift to his stubbled jaw. "I ought to know. This is my land."

She glanced at Lance, but he simply shrugged it off. His head tilted to the right. "Topaz Mountain is right there, which means that way is east. You must've gotten turned around." Whirling, he pointed toward the ridge. "The ATVs are this way. Let's go."

Luis stepped off, too, hiking up the backpack that held all of his gear and passing his son as though he had something to prove. Jessa followed behind, watching him, and something was definitely off. His feet seemed to be stumbling more than usual. Was his balance unsteady?

When Luis had gotten far enough ahead of them that he couldn't hear, she jogged to Lance. "Something's not right," she said.

"Tell me about it." He shook his head. "He can never admit when he's wrong about anything."

She tugged on his arm until he stopped and faced her. "That's not what I mean."

"So what do you mean?" he asked, inching into her space. He was so broad she couldn't see around him. His thick callused hands came to rest on his hips.

Her heart fluttered like a caged butterfly searching for a way out. "I just... I've never seen him get turned around out here."

Once again, Lance's shoulders lifted in that laid-back-cowboy shrug. "It could happen to anyone. Especially if he didn't sleep all that great. He's probably tired."

No. It'd happened to her multiple times but it didn't happen to Luis. She glanced at the older man, still stalking toward the east side of the mountain in a huff. "What if something's wrong? Health-wise or something?"

Sympathy softened Lance's eyes. "It's not like what happened to your dad. Nothing's wrong. I see the man every day. Trust me. He's healthy as a horse."

A sigh sank in her chest. Maybe Lance saw only what he wanted to see. "What if we hadn't come looking for him? How long would it have taken him to find his way?" Or would he have wandered off and gotten lost? If he couldn't even find the ATV, what else would he forget?

"He would've found his way eventually," Lance insisted, as though he was unwilling to consider the alternative.

Well, it was easy to see where he'd gotten his stubbornness. Jessa raised her head and stared him down. "I don't think he should go out alone anymore."

"I couldn't agree more," he said, checking behind his shoulder as though he wanted to make sure his father was out of earshot. "Which is why I'd like you to stay with him for a while."

Her mouth fell open. "Excuse me?" She must not have heard him right.

"I can't babysit him every second. Not for the next few weeks. I'm training for Worlds."

Right. The biggest competition on the bull-riding stage. A laugh tumbled out. "So you want *me* to babysit him." Did he even realize how ridiculous that sounded?

Lance took a step closer, and it wasn't fair how those large silvery eyes of his could look so pleading. "He already spends most of his free time at your rescue thing anyway."

Rescue thing? Heat swathed her forehead. "I'm pretty sure you meant to say my father's animal rescue organization, which happens to be his legacy." *You hot jackass.*

"Right." His lips twitched as though he was trying to hold back a smile. "That's what I meant. You already spend a lot of time with him. We can tell him your house is being fumigated or something and you can move in with him for a few weeks. The upper story of his house is furnished and everything."

"Oh, well in that case." She let the sarcasm in her tone speak for her. "Are you crazy? The man is sixty-seven years old. He's not going to let me babysit him." If he realized what was really going on, Luis would have a conniption.

"He likes you," Lance countered, his eyes melting into some kind of irresistible plea. The same one she often saw on wounded animals. Good God. Sometimes life just wasn't fair.

"In fact, I think he might like you better than he likes me," he said, going for the kill shot with a delicious little smirk. "I can't keep my eye on him when I'm out training. And I don't trust him to be alone. Can't have him wandering off anymore."

Under the power of his gaze, her will had started to cave, but she shook her head, desperately holding on to the shard of pride she had left. "No. I'm sorry. I *do* have a life, you know. I can't drop everything and babysit your—"

"I'll give you half of my winnings," he interrupted.

Jessa staggered back a step. This was absurd. "I won't take your money."

"Fine, then. I'll donate it to your shelter. Half of everything I win at Worlds."

Half of everything? She didn't know much about bull riding, but she knew those purses were worth a lot of money. "That's ... wow ... a chunk of change ..."

He stepped in closer, lowered his head to hers. "I'm gonna win this year. I just need the time to train."

Determination had steeled his face, his voice, and she didn't doubt he'd win. He'd won a World title before, though it had been years back. But he was the real thing—the rider who persevered through every injury, through every disappointment. And given how disappointing she'd heard the past year had been for him in the arena, he'd do whatever it took to get one more title. "I don't want to take your winnings." But she kind of did, too. Not for herself, but for the shelter. That'd give her plenty to make the repairs and improvements they needed, to buy supplies and upgrade their facility until she could establish a good donor base.

"I'm not doing it for the money," Lance uttered, his voice full of conviction.

No. It clearly went much deeper for him. She could read it in his eyes. He had something to prove to the world. She'd seen the articles in the town newspaper. She'd heard what everyone was saying. While Luis had somehow managed to continue competing as a living legend until the age of thirty-eight, they thought Lance had lost his spark. Some people in town said he should've quit a long time ago. How would that feel? To always be stuck in the shadow of your great father? To have the world thinking you're done before you're ready to be?

"Please, Jessa," he said laying a hand on her forearm and effectively wiping out her last scrap of dignified resolve. "I need your help." Judging from the twitch in his jaw, those might've been the most difficult words he'd ever managed to say.

Yeah, who was she kidding? She couldn't say no to the man. Couldn't turn down a large donation to the shelter.

"Fine. I'll do it," she said, starting to walk past him.

On one condition, she should have added. That he'd steer clear of her so she wouldn't lose her heart again.

Chapter Six

Topaz Falls didn't exactly offer much in the way of nightlife. Not that Jessa had ever minded. Since she'd moved here full time last year, her idea of nightlife had been snuggling up with whatever animals she was caring for at the time and enjoying a rom com movie marathon from the comfort of her couch. But one Friday evening last winter, as she was getting settled in for one of her favorites, she realized she was out of chocolate truffles and she simply couldn't watch the fabulous *Chocolat* without any chocolate. So she'd thrown on a hat and a coat and braved a blizzard to walk eight blocks to The Chocolate Therapist, the town's only confectionery and wine bar.

Normally the town was dead at nine o'clock on a snowy Friday night in December, and sure enough The Chocolate Therapist had been closed. Her heart had sunk until she'd noticed a light on somewhere near the back of the store. In a move of desperation, she'd knocked on the door.

The owner, Darla Michelson, had answered. She had one of those friendly inviting faces, with dancing blue eyes and smile lines instead of crow's-feet, all framed by an unruly but adorable nest of curly black hair with hip red streaks. In a halo of light, Darla had hurried to unlock the door and when Jessa explained the situation, the woman had invited her in and had not only filled up a takeout box with the creamiest, loveliest truffles she'd ever seen, Darla also invited her to stay for the book club meeting she was hosting in the back room.

She might not have if she hadn't been freezing, if her pinky toes hadn't been numb. The prospect of staying somewhere warm and cheerful, with that rich chocolate scent billowing all around her, far outweighed the cold, lonely walk home. Darla had taken her coat and poured her a glass of mulled wine that tasted like Heaven. Then she'd taken her into a small back room, which happened to be set up like the coziest living room Jessa had ever seen. There were an overstuffed couch and two lopsided recliners clustered around an antique coffee table. Happy pink and green pillows freshened up the worn sofa while polka-dotted lampshades brightened the whole space.

Cassidy Greer, who was a local EMT, and Naomi had popped off the couch enthusiastically to greet her. They were so warm and friendly, bright rays of sunshine in the winter of her lingering grief. That night, for the first time since her father had passed away, the feeling of loneliness that had shrouded Jessa fell away and the first signs of spring started to bud in her heart.

After that, every week, she headed to The Chocolate Therapist, and it really had become her healing. The chocolate and wine, yes of course, but even more so these women who'd become like her sisters. Maybe it was their shared grief. Darla had lost her husband to cancer two years before, which made her a young widow at thirty-four. Sweet young Cassidy had lost her brother Cash in a bull-riding accident five years previously. And Naomi had been left behind by a husband who wanted nothing to do with her or their amazing daughter. That first night, they'd bonded. Pain has a funny way of bringing people together, and they'd spent the whole night sharing their life stories over countless mugs of mulled wine and God only knew how many boxes of truffles. They were all so different—on the book side of things Darla preferred straight-up smut, Naomi was addicted to self-help books, Cassidy read only suspense and thrillers, and Jessa, of course, was all about sweet character-driven romance novels that told idyllic stories with happy endings. Their vast differences didn't matter, though. They hardly ever discussed the books they were reading, anyway. Every discussion somehow diverged into talking about life, their problems, and the joys or hurts or triumphs they were facing.

Jessa had never had a group of friends like that before, with whom she could say anything she wanted without guarding herself or considering how silly or ignorant or pathetic she might sound. With them she could just be.

So when Darla called an extra meeting, Jessa had hurried right over, expecting to discuss their latest selection. But instead of their normal discussion, it had started to feel like an interrogation. Like always, they were gathered around the coffee table. Red sangria had replaced the mulled wine once the snow had started to melt. Tonight, Darla had made the most addictive chocolate-covered strawberries—white, dark, and cinnamon flavored. Everything had been going wonderfully, until Jessa mentioned Lance's proposition. That's when the gasps and questions had started.

"Lance asked you to move in with him?" Naomi demanded, dabbing a smear of chocolate from the corner of her lips.

"Isn't that a little fast?" Darla chimed in, leaning over to refill her sangria for the fourth time in an hour. Owning a wine bar means you build up quite the tolerance.

"Yeah, you've been on only one date," Cassidy added. Though she had the most somber blue eyes Jessa had ever seen, Cassidy's grin revealed her dimples. She was the quietest in the group, but also could win the award for the wittiest. Not to mention the most reliable. She covered weekends at the shelter so Jessa could have some time off.

They were teasing, she knew that, but she wished she could fan the blush away from her face. The truth was, she knew it was a bad idea, moving to the ranch, babysitting Lance's father for the next couple of weeks. Especially with the way Lance affected her. She'd kissed the man after being in his presence for all of an hour. Not that she could let these women ever find out. She'd never hear the end of it. They were already teasing her enough. And that had to stop before she crumbled and told them everything.

Trying to maintain an air of indifference, she leaned back into the couch cushion as if their chatter didn't faze her. "First of all, he didn't ask me to move in with *him*," she said for at least the fifth time. "He asked me to move in with his *father*."

"That's not weird or anything," Cassidy quipped, sharing a look with Darla.

Jessa gave the women a look of her own. "Second, we have *not* been on any dates. This is strictly a business arrangement." And she intended to keep it that way. All she'd have to do is recall the repulsed stiffening of his upper body when she'd gone to kiss him. That should make it easier.

"He's already seen you naked," Naomi pointed out before popping another strawberry into her mouth.

"Bet he wouldn't mind seeing that again," Cassidy teased. "Like tonight. In his bedroom."

Jessa squirmed. Could not let herself go there. Lance was off-limits. So was romance. And sex. Definitely sex because, in her opinion, those two things went together.

She picked up her glass and took a sip to cool herself down. When was the last time she'd broken out in a sweat simply sitting still?

"I've always wondered how Lance would be in bed," Darla said, licking the chocolate covering off a strawberry. She tended to wonder that about everyone. Did a lot of experimenting, too, though she claimed she'd never fall in love again. "I bet he's rowdy." She bit into the strawberry with a gleam in her eyes.

"That's something I hope I never have to hear about," Naomi answered sternly. Though she was close to Lance, Naomi had been Lucas Cortez's high school sweetheart until he'd gone and gotten himself sent off to prison for arson. She still talked about him sometimes, though. Seemed to wonder what could've been, like everyone does once in a while. Or more than once in a while if you were Jessa. Which is exactly why she'd sworn off men for now. "You can tease me all you want, but nothing is going to happen between Lance and me." He'd made it perfectly clear. "He promised to donate money to the rescue. That's the only reason I agreed." That and Lance's ridiculously convincing wounded puppy eyes.

"Maybe he wanted you around more," Naomi suggested.

Jessa only laughed.

"I'm serious," her friend insisted. "I never dreamed he'd ask someone to move to the ranch. He usually avoids people at all costs." She tilted her head and studied Jessa in a way that made her want to hide. Naomi had one of those intense gazes that made you wonder if she could read your mind. "But he obviously doesn't mind having you around. Which is a little suspicious. He could've asked *me* to keep a better eye on Luis. I already live there."

"You've got enough to do," Jessa shot back, refusing to let hope root itself in her heart. "He knows Luis and I are friends. That's all it is." He knew the man wouldn't put up a fight if Jessa moved in. Luis would do anything for her and his son knew it. "Couldn't be better timing, actually," she said in her best businesslike tone. "Because I'm not interested anyway." Or at least she shouldn't be. Therefore, she'd simply avoid Lance, keep an eye on Luis, and start making plans to upgrade the shelter. That would keep her busy, and before she knew it, the time would be up.

"If your face gets this red when you're not interested, I'd hate to see what happens when you *are* interested," Darla said sweetly.

"It's warm in here," she lied. Actually, there was a wonderful cool breeze floating through the open window.

"I have a feeling it's about to get hotter," Naomi said, elbowing Darla. The three of them laughed in that happy tipsy way.

Jessa fought off another blush with a sip of sangria. She held an ice cube in her mouth and simply rolled her eyes at them, denying that thoughts of Lance generated any heat within her. Which only made her skin burn hotter.

She had only one more night to fix that problem.

* * *

His father had gotten older, no doubt about that. Lance eyed him from across the kitchen table. Wisdom pooled in the grayness of the man's eyes, but they sagged, too. Jagged lines that had started as crow's-feet at the corners now fissured down into his cheeks, which were wrinkled and spotted with age. Most times he didn't look at his father's face for too long, but now he forced his gaze to be still, to note the details, the changes.

If it were up to him, he'd still see Luis Cortez the same way he had when he was a boy. He used to stand on the corral fence whooping while his dad rode, his spirit and strength a force Lance had dreamed of one day harnessing himself. Didn't matter how many times he was thrown, his father always got up, shook off the dust, and shoved his foot right back in that stirrup. Nothing could break the man, nothing inside the corral and nothing outside the corral, either. Even after his mother had left and Lance had worried it might break them both, Luis had simply soldiered on. But no one was indestructible. Not even the toughest cowboy. Life wears on you, little by little, not shattering you all at once, but chipping away from the inside where the damage isn't always visible. Lance had lived enough to know that.

"What're you still doin' here?" Luis asked, scraping the last of the eggs and crumbled bits of bacon off his plate and shoveling them into his mouth. "I thought you'd be training on Ball Buster this mornin'."

"I'm waiting until Jessa gets here." And trying to figure out how time had gone so fast, how his father had gone from an unbreakable wrangler to an old man who lost ATVs. He shook the thought away. It was age, that's all. Old people forgot stuff. It was bound to happen to Luis sometime. Lance reached for the coffeepot and poured himself a refill. "You're okay if she stays here for a while?" he asked, cupping his hands around the mug. The robust scent sparked the memory of drinking coffee with Jessa yesterday, which conjured up the images of her lying almost naked on the floor again.

"Why's Jessa coming?" his father asked from behind a blank stare.

Worry dulled his body's sudden arousal. "We talked about this last night." Maybe the man's hearing was going out...

"Right," Luis said gruffly, eyes cast down at the table as though he was trying to remember.

"Her place is being fumigated," Lance reminded him. "She's got an insect problem."

Luis grunted his disapproval. "She shouldn't have to pay for something like that. What's she got? I could take care of it for free."

A grin broke through Lance's concern. His dad might be aging, but he'd never quit striving to be the hero. Age couldn't take away something like that. "She wanted to leave it to the professionals this time," he said before Luis could ask more questions. "So can she stay here or not?"

"Course she can. Got that whole upstairs that don't get used anyway."

"Great. She should be here by eight." At least he hoped she'd be there. She'd sure left in a hurry after they'd gotten Luis back down the mountain. He'd hoped they'd have time to go over the plan, but next thing he knew, Jessa was gone.

"Well, I'd best get moving." His father stood and carted his dishes to the sink. "I was gonna head up for a hike before I mend the corral fences later on."

Shit. Lance had meant to have a little talk with him about the whole hiking alone thing last night, but hadn't gotten around to it. Okay. He'd completely avoided it. But it looked as though it might be time to force the issue. He stood, too. "I don't think it's a good idea for you to go up the mountain on your own anymore."

Right on cue, his father's shoulders straightened. "Pardon?"

"You forgot where you parked the ATV," Lance said, trying to be careful.

"I didn't forget," Luis shot back. "I was this close to finding it." He held an inch of space between his thumb and pointer finger. "Another ten minutes and I would've been on my way down. You didn't need to come find me."

Of course not. Luis Cortez didn't need anything from anyone. Lance tried to quiet the fight rising in his father's eyes. "All I'm saying is, I'd like you to take somebody with you. What if something *did* happen? I don't want you out there alone."

"Nothin's gonna happen," his father insisted. "I don't need a babysitter out in my own backyard." He went to walk away but Lance stepped in front of him.

"I'll get you a satellite phone then." With a GPS tracker. That way he'd always be able to find him.

"I'm not bringing a phone into the wilderness. I go to get away from that shit."

"Come on, Dad. I'm just—"

A knock sounded at the front door.

"Good morning," Jessa called through the screen.

Sighing out the disgruntled annoyance, Lance gave his father a look before winding through the living room, then down the hallway to the front door.

Jessa stood on the other side. She was dressed differently—more like the old Jessa, in a faded yellow T-shirt and long hiking shorts. Her feathery blond hair had been loosely pulled back and that easy smile was intact. Lance had an urge to hug her. Somehow the sight of her made his body lighter. She was so...easygoing. And that was a rarity in his life at the moment.

"Hey." He stepped out onto the porch and closed the door so his father wouldn't hear anything.

"Everything all set?" she whispered. Her hand curled over the handle of a small wheeled suitcase.

"Yeah. I told Dad your place has an infestation. He's fine with you staying a few weeks." As long as he never found out the real reason...

"Great." She went to pick up her suitcase, but Lance reached out and snatched the handle before she could grasp it. It was light, as unburdened as she seemed to be. "One other thing you should know. I was trying to talk to him about not going up the mountain alone anymore," he half-whispered.

Jessa laughed and somehow the heartiness of it tempted him to join her.

"Bet that went over well," she said.

"Yeah. Not so much." But just being near her for two minutes had purged the tension from his head. "I told him I'd get him a satellite phone, but he wasn't interested."

"I'll work on it," she promised.

He set down the suitcase. "Thank you."

"I can't make any promises. He might not listen to me, either."

"No." He stepped closer. "Thank you for being here. For doing this."

"Oh." She stumbled back a step as if she'd been caught off guard. "Sure. It's nothing."

That was the biggest understatement he'd ever heard. "Actually, it's a lot. And I really appreciate it." She had no guarantees going into this. She didn't know if he'd win, if she'd get anything out of it. Somehow that made it more generous. "There's no way I could handle all of this on my own with the finals coming up," he admitted. Hell, he'd have to put in twice the training hours as those twenty-something guys he was going up against or he'd be humiliated on the biggest stage in bull riding. And there it was...his greatest fear worming its way to the surface of his life. That he really was washed up and too old like everyone said.

"I'm happy to help," Jessa said, smiling again but still keeping her distance. "I love your dad."

She might love his father, but after the awkward exchange yesterday, she didn't seem to want to be anywhere near *him*. Unfortunately for her, Lance wasn't in a real big hurry to get inside.

"Besides that," she went on, "you promised me enough money to make a difference at the shelter. And I happen to think you'll win."

"Really?" She'd be about the only one in the world.

"Sure." She seemed to look him over, size him up. "You've got more experience than those young guys, which means you probably have more composure. You know what to expect. And it looks to me like you're still in pretty good shape." Her eyes shied away from his. "So yes. I think you'll win this year."

The words left his tongue fumbling for something to say. It's a gift when someone believes in you at a time no one else does. When you've lost some of the belief in yourself. Before he could say anything, the front door opened.

"Jessa." Luis already had on his hiking backpack, the stubborn bastard.

"Morning, Luis," she greeted warmly as she leaned in to hug him.

His dad's face seemed to soften whenever Jessa was around, as if she were the daughter he'd never had. "I was headed up the mountain," Luis said, nowhere near as ornery as he'd been with Lance.

Her eyes lit with genuine excitement. "I'd love to come with you. Maybe we should bring the fishing poles."

"Good idea," Luis agreed, already clomping down the porch steps. "Lance can get your things to your room."

"Oh, perfect. Thank you." She winked at Lance and it said so much, that they were co-conspirators, allies, and maybe even friends.

Clutching her light, carefree suitcase in his hand, he turned and watched the two of them hike up the driveway.

Jessa had come for his father, to watch over him, to take care of him. So why did he want her to be here for him, too?

Chapter Seven

So far so good. Jessa tossed another fence post into the ATV's trailer and clapped her gloves together. Clouds of dust puffed into the air, disappearing against the sky's blue radiance. So far she'd managed to avoid Lance all morning. The hike with Luís had eaten up a good three hours, and it had been nothing short of spectacular—the sky clear and blue, just the right breeze sighing through the pine trees. Luís had been in top form, his pace quick and his footsteps sure. Without even a slight hesitation, he'd led her right to the pond nestled into the swell of land at tree line, and between the two of them they'd caught five rainbow trout. Hers had been the largest, she'd pointed out. Luís had simply smiled in his long-suffering way.

Her concerns about being in such close quarters with Lance had started to dissipate with the morning's chill. This wouldn't be so hard. Luís liked to keep busy and the two of them would spend a good portion of time at the shelter during the week. That would leave little time for running into Lance. This morning when she saw him on that porch, a whole flock of butterflies had migrated into her chest, nesting all around her heart and humming with that tantalizing purr. That's why she couldn't allow herself to be close to him. Not alone, anyway. She didn't trust herself one iota. Something else took over when Lance gazed at her. Some*one* else. Her inner slut.

"You got all those posts loaded up already?" Luis careened around the corner hauling a sledgehammer over his shoulder, and for the life of her she couldn't figure out what she'd been so worried about. Apparently the whole getting lost in the mountains thing was an isolated incident because today, Luis looked strong and determined and completely capable. There was nothing feeble about him.

Jessa glanced into the shed where she'd been searching for the fence posts he'd asked for. "I think that's all of them." When Luis said he had to mend some fences on the property, she'd jumped at the chance to help him, just in case he had any more balance issues. But he seemed fine. Plus, it had given her an excuse to hide in the shed and stay busy so she wouldn't risk a Lance sighting.

"All right, let's head on up to the corral then." Luis slid onto the ATV, but Jessa froze next to it.

The butterflies still hibernating in her chest stirred. "The corral?" As in the place where Lance would be training?

"Yeah. Got a bunch of fences all but fallin' down up there." Luis cranked the handlebar and the ATV roared to life. "Gotta get 'em fixed up 'fore one of the horses gets out," he shouted above the noise.

He released the brake and nodded her over. Jessa moved slowly toward the ATV, like her shoes were made of lead.

She'd promised to help Luis with the fences, so she couldn't back out now. Hopefully Lance would be so busy he wouldn't even notice her.

She climbed onto the ATV and buckled her arms around Luis's waist.

Instead of peeling out and tearing up the driveway like he so often did, Luis eased the ATV along. He peered back at her. "Is there somethin' goin' on I don't know about?"

Her shoulders locked. Had he figured out this whole thing was a sham? "What do you mean?" she managed to reply without an echo of fear. Lance would kill her if Luis found out what they were doing.

The ATV stopped. Luis turned his upper body, those wise eyes studying her. "I mean you and my boy seem to have gotten close," he said behind a hint of a smile. "I was surprised when he asked if you could stay with me."

She gulped back a relieved breath. "We're just friends. He's trying to help me out."

The man gave her a nod, then turned around and they puttered along again. "I wouldn't be put out. If it was more than that."

She forced a laugh but it felt like the beef jerky they'd snacked on earlier had gotten stuck in her throat. There *shouldn't* be anything more. He'd backed away when she kissed him, and given the man's reputation, anything more would only lead to heartbreak for her. "Nope. Nothing more." The bat-shit crazy butterflies in her chest called her bluff.

Thankfully, Luis let it go. She'd never been a good liar and had never been good at hiding her emotions, either. They always made their way to her face, out there for the world to see. Which was why she couldn't face Luis. As soon as he parked the ATV, just down the hill from the corral, she slid off and started to unload the fence posts, working with a repetitive precision. She would not look at the corral. She would pretend it wasn't there. She would—

"Come on, Uncle Lance! Hold on!"

Jessa's head snapped up and her eyes honed in on the very scene she'd been trying to avoid. Oh, hell-to-the-no. Across the corral, Gracie stood on the second fence rail, teetering precariously on her sparkly pink cowgirl boots while she gripped the top rail with her hands. Naomi stood next to her, body set as though ready to catch her daughter. Tucker, the Cortez's stable manager, stood next to Naomi, eyes glued to a stopwatch.

Before she could stop herself, Jessa darted her gaze to the right and yes, ladies and gentlemen, there was Lance Cortez in all of his bull-riding glory. Chap-clad legs cinched down over the steer's wide girth, back arched, free arm whipping over his head in a graceful rhythm. Sweat drenched his blue T-shirt, making it cling to every chiseled muscle, and that black cowboy hat on his head made him look downright dangerous.

The maniacal bull snorted and jackknifed his body, but Lance held on, those powerful arms fully engaged, and God they had to be as big around as the fence posts she was loading. Then there were his hands. There was something so seductive about large, rugged hands skilled in the art of holding on. She'd like to bet they were skilled in other arts, too.

A slow heated breath eased out as she thought about all of the places those hands could hold her body.

Lance continued the dance—that's how he made it look, graceful and choreographed—riding that steer like he owned it. In complete control.

Wooooowwww. She couldn't move. Couldn't take her eyes off him.

His body was actually built for this, muscle stacked on muscle, tendons as thick as ropes. The more the bull bucked, the more Lance seemed to come alive.

Awe surged through her, nearly buckling her knees, turning her arms weak.

The fence post dropped from her hands and slammed onto her toes. Pain shredded through her feet.

"Ow!" she screamed as she fell to her knees to push the thing off.

The post rolled down to the ATV.

"Oh no!" she heard Gracie screech. "Hold on, Uncle Lance!"

Jessa looked up. Lance had turned his head in her direction, which threw off his form. The beast below him bucked and kicked its legs in the air.

Jessa scrambled to her knees.

Lance was trying to recover, hands both grasping, but his body was being tossed violently. With a final snorting fury, the bull threw his head back, a horn connecting with Lance, then leaped and sent him flying toward the fence.

"Oh God!" Jessa shot to her feet and hobble-ran the perimeter. It was horrible seeing him sprawled there. He could be dead!

Tucker was already out in the corral, luring the bull away from Lance. Somehow Jessa managed to squeeze herself between the fence posts and sprint to him, but her foot caught a rock. Momentum pitched her forward and launched her right on top of Lance.

His wide eyes stared into hers. They were open. And he was breathing.

"Are you okay?" she choked out. The lingering pain in her toes throbbed with the fast pulse of her heart.

"Of course I'm okay," he said with an amused smile. "That's not the first time I've been tossed, Jessa."

His eyes were so pretty. Grayish blue with heavy thick lashes.

"Are *you* okay?" he asked, lifting his head.

Oh. Right. She was still lying on him. "I'm fine," she said quickly, rolling off to the side, then standing before he could get a glimpse of the humiliation that radiated across her face.

Lance stood, too. His shirt was torn and blood stained the right side beneath his chest plate.

"You're bleeding." She reached out to touch the wound, but he stepped back quickly.

"It's fine. Ball Buster caught me with his horn. Again, not the first time."

So back off, his movements seemed to scream. The same humiliation that heated her face traveled down her throat. She glanced around. Naomi and Gracie were staring. Luis was on the other side of the fence watching the whole spectacle. Tucker had corralled the bull and was now gazing at her and Lance, too. The same question seemed to have stumped all of them: Why had she panicked and run to him when no one else watching—even the ten-year-old—seemed the least bit concerned?

Why indeed.

"I'm sorry," she half-whispered. "I mean, I thought you were hurt . . ."

"I'm fine," he said again, this time with a gruff undertone. "It's part of the job. I'm used to it."

"Right. Good. I'm glad you're fine," she muttered, turning to slink away. "I should get back to the fence, then."

Truth was, she never should've left the damn fence. Never should've glanced at him. Never should've agreed to this in the first place. Her toes scuffed the dirt as she walked away from him. From everyone.

"That was a good one, Uncle Lance," she heard Gracie prattle behind her. "And it was so funny when Jessa fell right on top of you!"

Yeah. Funny. Jessa kept walking. Fast. Head down, arms pumping at her sides, propelling her away from the girl's giggles.

She knew Naomi was behind her, and it didn't matter how fast she walked, somehow her friend matched her stride.

"So wow, you're really not interested in him, huh?" the woman teased.

Jessa stopped. Luis had started digging out a fence post nearby and he didn't need to hear this. "Why would I be interested in him? Every time I get near him his body goes rigid like he's terrified I'll actually touch him. Like he might get cooties if he lets himself get too close." She *shouldn't* be interested. He'd sent plenty of vibes to ward her off. Instead she seemed to want him more. Go figure.

"Come on." Naomi swatted at her. "It's no big deal. I bet no one else could tell. They don't know you like I do." She elbowed her as though trying to make her smile. "They probably just think you're a drama queen."

"Only when Lance is around." She peeked over her shoulder. Tucker was playing chase with Gracie and Lance had disappeared. "I shouldn't be doing this. Staying here."

"Lance would be lucky to have you." Naomi hooked her arm through Jessa's and started towing her toward Luis. "In fact, you're too good for him. The man hasn't had a real relationship with anyone. Ever. And you want it all. Dating. Romance. Marriage. He's completely ignorant. Trust me."

"I know." She sighed. "So what should I do?"

Her friend pulled her in for a half hug. "Stay and help Luis," she whispered. "And see Lance for who he really is. Not for who you want him to become."

* * *

Son of a— That hurt like hell. Lance gritted his teeth and pressed a bandage into the gaping wound Ball Buster had slashed across his ribs. Somehow the bull had managed to get under his chest plate and give him a nasty cut. Not to mention that weight of a serious bruise crushing the air from his lungs.

He latched the first aid kit and hung it back on the nail behind the stable door. When he'd heard Jessa cry out in pain, he'd turned, which gave Ball Buster the perfect opportunity to kick, toss his head back, and catch Lance with his horn. Damn it, he should've stayed focused. Should've tuned out everything else. Usually he could. Except when Jessa was around, evidently.

"You okay?" Tucker stuck his head into the stables. "Didn't realize you took off."

"I'm good." He braced his shoulders so his voice wouldn't wheeze. His whole chest ached like a mother, but no one else needed to know that. He couldn't slow down on his training. Couldn't lose a day. His longest time all morning had been six seconds and that wasn't gonna cut it for Worlds.

"That last one was only four," Tucker informed him. "Not your fault. You got distracted." The man raised his brows and looked him over. "Not like you to get distracted out there."

"Yeah, well, I'm not used to hearing women scream," he grumbled.

"That's surprising, given your revolving bedroom door," Tucker said through a hearty laugh.

Lance shook his head. He'd set himself up for that one. Wasn't worth reminding Tucker that he'd grown up since his early days on the circuit. "I'm not used to hearing *Jessa* scream." That was the plain truth of it. It'd scared him, the pain in her voice. Pulled him right out of the zone.

His friend stepped into the shadows, a funny grin on his face. "I like Jessa. She's good people."

"Yeah." Clumsy, but a good person. She'd pretty much be a saint in his book if she could stick it out with his father for the next couple of weeks.

"So..." Tucker leaned against the wall. "Somethin' goin' on between you two?"

"No." Lance dodged past him and headed out the door and into the sunlight. "Nothing's going on." At least nothing he needed to discuss with Tucker. "She's doing me a favor. Staying with Dad so I can train and not worry about him." Tucker would never give up his secret.

"That all she's doin'?" Tucker called from behind him.

Lance stopped. "Yes." He turned. "Why?"

His friend smirked. "She sure seemed worried about you."

"She's probably not used to seeing stuff like that." Most people were shocked the first time they saw a rider get thrown. Usually it looked worse than it was. Not today, but usually. Thankfully she'd walked away before she could see how much pain he was in. Knowing Jessa, she'd force him to go to the hospital to have his ribs looked at. And he sure as hell couldn't fit that into his schedule today.

"Maybe I'll ask her out," his friend said, poking him in the ribs.

Pain splintered through his bones. *Motherfucker*. Lance sucked in a breath and held it until the stabbing sensation subsided.

"You wouldn't mind, would ya?"

He didn't know if his blood ran hot because of the pain he was in or because of the smug look on his friend's face. He shouldn't mind. Tucker wasn't a bad guy. He was funny, as loyal as they came. The man would do anything for anyone who needed help. But he couldn't stomach the thought of his hands on Jessa. "She's taking a break from dating," Lance informed him. "Said she's sworn off the whole thing so she can focus on the shelter."

"Don't seem right. A woman as good-looking as Jessa not dating anyone."

"Yeah, well, what're you gonna do?" He was fine with it. Her not dating anyone. Didn't bother him none. The thought of her dating someone else? Now that was a different story. One he didn't care to analyze. He straightened his shoulders, battling a wince. "Make sure Ball Buster is ready. I'm going again."

"You sure?" Tucker stared at him like he'd lost it. "Maybe you ought to call it a day. That was a nasty fall. You're movin' kinda slow."

"I'm going again," he repeated. And this time, it didn't matter who screamed. He would hold on for eight seconds.

Chapter Eight

Jessa stood at the kitchen window halfheartedly scrubbing dinner dishes in the sink while she watched the sun slide behind Topaz Mountain. She'd lived in the mountains for almost a year, but the sunsets still stunned her. Darkness had started to spread down the mountain, inviting the sky to come alive with surreal bursts of orange and pink.

She sighed, arms and back weighted with a day of work.

"You don't gotta do the dishes." Luis lumbered over to her. "You're the guest. I can handle it." He eased the lasagna pan off the counter.

"Don't be silly." She turned to smile at him. "I actually like doing the dishes." Strange. At home, she let them pile up in the sink until she *had* to do them. But here, after sharing dinner with someone, it made her happy to stand at the sink, the feel of her hands drenched in the warm, sudsy water. It was nice, not being alone for a meal. It felt more purposeful, somehow.

"Fine, then. But I'm on dish duty tomorrow." Luis set the pan back on the counter. His hands trembled like they had all throughout dinner. Small little tremors she'd pretended not to notice, even when he'd dropped his fork, when he'd knocked over his glass.

Damn arthritis, he'd said, but she'd never noticed tremors before. Stiffness, sure. But not the shaking. She'd casually asked him what his doctor thought about the arthritis, if he was taking anything for it, but he'd quickly changed the subject.

Without turning her head, she stole a quick look at him over her shoulder. While they were eating the lasagna Naomi had brought over, Jessa had noticed the signs of fatigue tugging at his eyes. They'd had polite conversation, but he hadn't said much. The spark he'd had while hiking and working on the fences earlier seemed to have dimmed.

She turned her attention back to the window, to the sunset. "You can go to bed if you want." It was almost seven and they'd had a full day. Back when her father was alive and she'd visit, he'd always fall asleep in his chair after dinner. Until she woke him and sent him off to bed. "I can finish up here."

"You sure you don't mind?" Luis shocked her by saying. She'd expected an argument. "After all that work, I'm done in for the day." Weariness softened his typical gruff tenor.

Jessa shook the water off her hands and turned. "I'm sure. I'll finish up in the kitchen, have a cup of tea, and probably head to bed myself." Well, maybe not bed, but a little book therapy. After the whole debacle with Lance, she'd downloaded a new book on her Kindle. *You Don't Need Him: How to Make Yourself Believe It*. It had gotten three and a half stars...

"All right, then. See you in the morning." Luis plodded out of the kitchen and disappeared down the hallway.

Jessa did her best to sigh out the concern that knotted her stomach. Luis had every right to be tired. He was almost seventy, after all. The man had earned the right to go to bed before eight o'clock at night. She snatched another plate off the pile, plunging it deep into the sink and scouring until the last bits of tomato sauce had been cleaned off.

Outside, the shadows had deepened. Instead of brilliant colors, the sky had muted into a rose-tinted softness, the mountains forming a jagged, dark silhouette. Inhaling the crisp, wood-scented air through the open window, she finished up the last of the dishes and swiped a towel from the stove to start drying.

A click sounded at the back door, interrupting her soft humming. Lance walked into the kitchen, still dusty from his day out in the corral, although it appeared he'd changed into a clean T-shirt.

"Hey." She tried to say it casually, but the quick ascent of her heart made her voice effervescent.

"Hey." He looked around the empty room. "Where's Dad?"

"He seemed tired," she said, focusing hard on drying the dish in her hands so she could avoid the insta-blush that plagued her when she looked directly into his eyes. "Are you hungry? I can reheat some of Naomi's lasagna..."

"Nah. I'm fine, thanks." He walked over and leaned against the counter next to her. "How'd today go?"

His nearness sent her heart spiraling. Damn infatuation. "Things were good," she murmured. "Great actually." Minus the memorable scene of her tackling that man right there. But it was best to make this conversation strictly business.

"We were out on the mountain for a good three hours and there were no problems at all," she reported.

"Good. That's great." Lance stuffed his hands into his pockets and simply stood there gazing at her.

Which made her work extra hard on drying those plates. When she'd finished and stashed them in the cupboard, Lance still stood there. She couldn't take the silence anymore. "So I'm sorry about the whole falling on you thing," she babbled. "I didn't mean to, it just looked like you were hurt—maybe even dead—and I kind of panicked, which I now realize was ridiculous, but at the time I didn't think it through..." *Stop talking. Please stop talking.* But her mouth rarely obeyed her brain. "I didn't *mean* to land on you. I tripped," she said, as though he'd demanded an explanation. "There was a rock and I didn't see it and—"

"It's fine," Lance said through the beginning of a smile. "It didn't bother me."

Mmm-hmmm. Right. She turned to him, not caring that her face was on fire. "The thing is...it kind of seemed like it *did* bother you. Like you got all rigid and glared at me. So I wanted you to know, I didn't mean to make a scene." Though it seemed to be one of her specialties in life.

"You're right." He wore a full-on smile now, the one that quirked his lips and tugged at the corners of his eyes. "I did get all rigid and glare at you."

Well, at least he admitted it. "Don't worry. It won't happen again." Because she would keep her distance. No more humiliating herself in front of Lance. Tomorrow was a new day.

Lance said nothing, but his eyes stayed with hers as he started to roll the edge of his T-shirt, up over the button fly of his jeans, up over a carved, tanned six-pack...

Heat sparked in her chest. She shouldn't be looking. Shouldn't be *ogling*. What was he doing? This was highly unfair...

Finally, he rolled the shirt up his chest...

"Holy mother of God." She gawked at the blood-soaked bandage and the purple and blue splotches that mottled his skin.

"That's why I was so rigid," he said, rolling the shirt back down. "And that's why I glared. It hurt."

Air hissed out of her mouth. "Lance. Geez." How in the world was the man even standing? Breathing?

"It's not as bad as it looks. I've had worse."

Worse? Her ribs ached just thinking about it. She shook her head and tossed the towel aside. "Why do you do that to yourself?" She couldn't imagine it. Couldn't imagine subjecting herself to pain like that day in and day out.

"Why do you rescue wounded and lost animals?" he asked her pointedly.

"Because I love it." She did, but that wasn't the whole reason, and it seemed Lance knew that, because he waited for her to expand.

"And...?" he prompted when she didn't speak.

Damn, he was more perceptive than she'd given him credit for. "Aaannd," she sassed. "Because it's something I can do to carry on my father's legacy." It gave her a connection to him, a way to honor him.

"We have a lot in common," he said as though resting his case.

Maybe so. But dwelling on the things they had in common would not help her put out the flames of infatuation. "You need to redo that bandage," she said, changing the subject. "Did you even clean the wound?"

"No," he admitted, standing straighter. "I was training all afternoon."

Now it was her turn to glare at him. "*Training?* Your ribs might be broken. And not to mention, that cut should probably be stitched. It's definitely going to scar."

"It's not a big deal," he insisted stubbornly.

Not a big deal. Ha! He might be perceptive but he was not as smart as she'd thought. "Have you ever heard of infection? You would not believe the infections I've treated. Wounds fester, Lance. They get full of bacteria and then they get worse and worse until—"

"Fine," he interrupted before she could offer him the gory details. "I'll wash it out."

"Wash it out." She shook her head, already heading for the first aid kit she'd seen in the bathroom earlier. "We can't just wash it out. We're using the strong stuff." She marched back into the kitchen and laid out the kit, seeing what she had to work with.

"Take off your shirt," she ordered.

"Gladly." That naughty smile of his flashed, but she shamed him with a look. This was not a joke. She's seen animals go septic as the result of an infected wound.

He peeled off the shirt gingerly, as if every movement caused him pain, and she forced herself not to examine the muscles, the hard flesh. She had to go into full doctor mode.

Leaning in, she carefully removed the bandage and examined the wound. It had started on one side as a puncture wound, then tore across his flesh with jagged margins. "This is going to hurt," she informed him.

He squeezed his eyes shut. "It already does."

Jessa glanced around. He wouldn't make it through this without something...

There. On top of the fridge sat a small collection of Jack Daniel's bottles. She hurried over and reached for one, then unscrewed the cap. "Here." She held it out to Lance.

He accepted with a grin. "You trying to get me drunk?"

"Yes," she confirmed, digging through drawers until she found a clean rag. "Trust me. You're going to want to be good and drunk for this." Especially if one of his ribs happened to be cracked underneath that gash. The thought brought on a shiver. How had he trained all afternoon with an injury like this?

"All right, then. Bottoms up." Lance raised the bottle to his lips and took a hearty gulp.

Jessa ran the washrag underneath scalding hot water and squirted on some of the antibacterial soap. "Take another shot," she said, inspecting the wound again. A bandage wasn't gonna cut it. They needed something to hold the edges together.

Lance obeyed, albeit wincing. He set down the bottle and swiped his arm across his mouth. "God, that stuff is awful."

The words surprised her. "You don't drink?"

"Sure, a beer once in a while. When I'm not training. But I've never liked the hard stuff."

"Well, you'll like it now. Trust me." She nodded toward the bottle.

Making a disgusted face, Lance downed another shot. "Gah." He pushed it far away. "That's enough. I'll be fine."

"Suit yourself." Jessa approached him with the cloth. "I'll start by cleaning the edges of the wound. We have to clear away the dried blood so we can flush it out." It was best to start prepping him now. This would be the easy part.

Lance straightened his upper body, tensing those carved muscles. "Right. Okay. Go for it."

Doctor mode, she reminded herself, deliberately over-looking the way his upper body flexed. It was just flesh and muscle. *Lots* of muscle…

Ahem. She steadied her hands and carefully pressed the cloth against his skin, lightly running it along the cut's borders.

His chest expanded with a breath, and he let it out slowly.

"Am I hurting you?" she asked, already knowing the answer.

"No worse than I've been hurting," he answered with gritted teeth.

She pulled back a little. "I'm trying to be careful." But that would be difficult as soon as she got into the wound. Hence the use of whiskey. "I have to flush it out a bit." She hurried to the sink and filled a glass with hot water. "This'll sting," she warned. Holding a towel beneath the cut, she poured water over the damaged flesh.

Sure enough, Lance flinched, but she kept her hand and the towel strong against his lower chest.

When the cup had emptied, she blotted the wound with the towel. "You really should have this stitched up," she said again.

"I'm not going to the hospital." His voice had gotten a bit lazy. It appeared the whiskey had done its job.

"Well, I can try to pull it all together with butterfly strips." She riffled through the first aid kit until she found the antibacterial ointment, gauze, and tape.

With the cleaning part over, Lance seemed to relax. "So why did you think I was glaring at *you* earlier?" he asked, searching out her eyes.

Shrugging, she carefully swabbed the ointment thoroughly over the wound. "I guess I thought you were annoyed."

His shoulders flinched, but he seemed focused on her instead of the pain. "Why?"

"Because I made a scene." With a towel, she carefully cleaned off the excess ointment, then cut the gauze. "Because I was worried about you." Using some butterfly strips, she secured the bandage and pulled the edges of his skin together.

"Why would I mind if you were worried about me?" he asked, gazing down at her, his eyes soft and open.

"I don't know." She gently pressed her fingers against the wound, making sure the dressing would hold. "You seemed put off. Just like you were when I accidentally kissed you."

Lance's breathing had gone shallow, but he didn't wince. "I already told you. I didn't mind the kiss. You're the one who said you shouldn't be kissing anyone."

"I shouldn't," she insisted defiantly, peeling the paper off a large bandage, and thanking God she had something to focus on besides his eyes. She plastered the sticky waterproof covering over the dressing and stepped back to admire her work. Yes, her work. Not his pecs...

"Then why did you kiss me?" Lance asked. His voice had deepened, no longer flippant and teasing, but somewhat solemn.

He asked as though he really wanted to know.

Because I couldn't stop myself. Because he'd been so kind and careful and comforting to her that morning. Because his lips were warm and somehow soft, even though the rest of him was so rugged. She cleared her throat. "I already told you. I was extra emotional that day."

His eyes narrowed. "You sure that's all it was?"

"Of course," she lied, straight to his face, locking her jaw for good measure.

"That's a shame. Because I happen to think you're PDF, too." There was a light in his eyes—a heat that made them downright dangerous.

She looked away. "That's the whiskey talking, cowboy," she said through a forced laugh.

His huge hand reached up and cupped her cheek, steering her gaze back to his. "No. It's not."

Air lodged in her lungs, giving her chest that wonderful, tight sensation, like any moment it would burst open and the flood of desire would carry her away.

No. No more getting carried away.

"It's not the whiskey," he murmured, his face lowering to hers. "You're stunning. And funny. And good."

See him as he is... Naomi's words echoed back to her. She did. She saw everything in his eyes. They were so close. So clear. Holding her gaze with a shameless tenderness.

"Kiss me again, Jessa," he tempted. "And I'll prove how much I don't mind."

This time she did laugh. She couldn't hold it back. Pressure had built inside of her, and it had to come out somehow. "You're not attracted to me." Lance Cortez didn't *want* her...

He took her hand and pressed her palm to the crotch of his jeans.

Beneath her fingers a hard bulge made her gasp. *Wow.* Okay, so that was quite impressive...

"That's how much I want you," he uttered. "I haven't kissed you. Haven't even touched you. I'm hard just looking at you. Just being near you." He let go of her hand.

She quickly pulled it to her side. She was not supposed to be doing this. Not now. And yet she couldn't run away. Couldn't even move. Lance still had his shirt off. Oh, why did he have to have his shirt off? He had a body made for touching. So tight and hard, sturdy and strong.

He watched her, saying nothing. Doing nothing. Just watching her.

Naomi had a point. He wasn't marriage material. But should that matter? It wasn't like she was ready to get married tomorrow or anything.

And Lance was still standing there. Shirtless. Watching her with those sexy heavy-lidded eyes.

This was her problem. She overanalyzed things. Thought too much. Tried to plan. A very good-looking man was standing right in front of her. Muscles gleaming in the soft light. Wanting her so badly his groin had to be aching. Asking her to kiss him.

Screw it. No more planning. She might have sworn off relationships, but technically she hadn't sworn off kissing. A surge of adrenaline empowered her. "You're sure?" she asked, desire flooding her throat. Her feet shuffled closer to him, until she stood against his solid body. "You want me to kiss you? Because your life might never be the same after this."

"That's quite the promise." His gaze lowered to her lips.

Jessa swallowed hard. Had she ever kissed a man? Well, besides that awkward moment with Lance on the mountain. She'd never instigated it. Men usually kissed her. Should she just go for it and press her lips into his? Maul him? Ease into it?

"You sure know how to build anticipation," Lance teased.

Her face flamed. "Sorry. I'm...I guess I've never been the one to start it..." And awkward Jessa was back.

"I can start it," he offered. "If it makes you feel better."

"Um, yes please."

His smile grew and his gaze captured hers. They were magnetic, those eyes. The power of his gaze held her still, everything except for her shoulders, which rose and fell with expectant breaths. Nerves seemed to flow through her blood and lodge in her chest, filling it until it pulled tight at the seams again.

Taking his sweet time, Lance slid his fingers underneath her chin and drew her face to his, eyes watching hers—no, conquering hers—overriding the subtle knowledge that this was not the best idea she'd ever had.

"I thought you weren't supposed to be doing this," he murmured, his lips nearly fused to hers.

Talk about building anticipation. That deep, rich coffee scent. The way the stubble on his face grazed her skin. Jessa's head got light. "I talked myself into it," she whispered, bracing her hand securely against the countertop next to him so she didn't collapse.

"I'm glad." His fingers stroked the skin at her jaw as his lips lowered over hers.

Her eyes fell shut and blocked out everything except for the feel of his mouth, the curve of it, the wet warmth, the way his lips melted into hers. They were firm, but tender, too, so skilled and wonderful it broke open her chest.

Heat flowed in until she was dizzy with it, drowning in it, but just as she lost the power to stand on her own, Lance's hands moved to her hips and hitched her closer to his body. She let herself lean into him, sliding her hands up his ripped chest, lightly sweeping her fingers over the bandage. God, he was perfection.

His lips moved to her ear, while his fingers carefully brushed her hair out of the way. "I think you're right," he breathed. "My life might never be the same." His tongue traced the ridge of her ear while his heavy breaths grazed her neck and made her legs falter.

He must've felt her wobble, because he wrapped his arms around her and crushed her body against his. "Damn, Jessa..." He kissed his way down her neck. "You smell good."

"Vanilla sugar shower gel," she gasped, letting her head tilt to the side.

"Mmmm. I like it." He slid his tongue back up her neck and his lips found hers again. This time he kissed her harder, like he wanted more.

Yes. More. There could be so much more...

Lance shifted, guiding her until her back was against the refrigerator. Things were falling, magnets and papers, but none of that mattered because Lance was pressed against her, his tongue stroking hers, his hips grinding against her body. The feel of him hard and desperate against her sent her heart spiraling. A frantic moan escaped, and Lance smiled against her lips. She let her head fall back so she could draw in a breath, but she hit the refrigerator.

A loud crash froze her. Lance pulled away. Those bottles of Jack Daniel's that had been on top of the fridge now lay next to their feet.

"At least they didn't break." Lance started to laugh but she pressed her hand against his mouth. "It's not funny! What if your dad—"

"What in God's name is that racket?" came from down the hall.

"Oh no," she hissed. "Oh God..."

Lance still had a big silly grin on his face. "It's nothing, Dad," he called, but the man came charging around the corner anyway.

Jessa pushed back and pretended to inspect the bandage. "Well, there we go. Everything looks good." She glanced up and forced a smile, but she'd like to bet he could see the vein in her forehead pulsing. "Hey, Luis. Sorry about the noise. I was bandaging Lance up and we accidentally knocked over the bottles." Her bright red face had to be a dead giveaway that the whole sentence was a lie. Not to mention her dilated eyes.

"Uh. Thanks, Jessa," Lance said, reaching past her for his shirt.

"No problem," she intoned, as if answering a complete stranger. "Next time, don't wait so long to get it cleaned up."

A spark smiled in his eyes. "I definitely won't."

Whew. She fought the compulsion to fan her face with a towel.

"Guess I should get going then." Lance clapped his dad's shoulder on his way out the door. "Night, Pops."

Luis didn't respond. He simply watched his son leave, then he turned to Jessa. "So nothing's going on between you two."

She invoked her laser focus to put away the first aid supplies. "Uh-huh. Nope. Nothing."

"From what I could tell that was a whole lot of nothing," Luis muttered as he plodded back down the hall.

That was one way to put it. A whole lot of nothing.

Chapter Nine

The world came back into focus slowly, the way it did when he woke from a dead sleep. Cold air blasted his face. The door slammed shut behind him. Lance stuttered to a stop on the front porch. He should go back in there. Shouldn't end the night with Jessa like that. Should he? Hell. He didn't know. It was still hard to think, but it had nothing to do with the shots of whiskey he'd downed.

He faced the door. What had just happened in there? He'd never planned on kissing her. He'd only wanted to check in, make sure his dad hadn't given her a hard time today. But then she'd ordered his shirt off. And the way she got so close, her delicate fingers pressing against his skin. It should've hurt like hell while she worked on him, but instead it only charged him up, making his body ache with the need for more until it was all he could think about.

She'd taken her time cleaning the cut, applying the bandages so carefully. She'd taken care of him. No one had ever taken care of him...

On the other side of the door, lights glowed. Which meant she hadn't gone to bed yet. Knowing his father, he'd gone back to bed right away. Probably pretended he didn't suspect anything, just like he always had when Lance was growing up. If he pretended he didn't see, they didn't have to talk about it. For once, he was glad Luis didn't like to meddle.

He took a step toward the door, the porch's bright light casting his shadow across the wooden planks.

The ache for a woman's soft touch gripped him. He could still feel her body under his hands, petite but toned. Could still feel her lips burning against his. But he really shouldn't go back in there, because this time he might not be able to stop himself, no matter who walked into the room.

A dog's low bark drifted somewhere behind him. He didn't even have to turn around to figure out who it belonged to. Bogart, Naomi's German shepherd, came trotting regally up the porch steps. Which meant Naomi wouldn't be far behind. He should've anticipated that, seeing as how her house was right across the driveway. She'd probably been spying.

"Well, well, well." Naomi walked into view beneath the porch light, staring up at him like a pissed-off librarian, mouth in a thin line, arms crossed in a stance of unyielding disappointment.

Yeah, there was no way out of this. Lance sauntered down the steps to meet her.

"What're you doing here?" she asked before he could say hello.

He reached down to pat Bogart's perked ears. "Came by to check in with Jessa." The wind picked up, carrying the strong pine scent. He should've been cold without his coat on, but the fire Jessa had lit inside him was still going strong.

"Mmm-hmm. Mmmm-hmmm," Naomi mocked. "You came to check in." Her narrowed eyes invited him to a silent interrogation, which he avoided by glancing down at the dog.

He sucked at lying. "Hey there, Bogart. Out for your nightly stroll?"

"Don't try to change the subject." Naomi's growl was almost as low as the dog's. "Seriously. Your hair is sticking up like someone just ran her fingers through it. What happened in there?"

Actually, he still wasn't exactly sure, but Naomi wouldn't let him off that easy. He leaned a shoulder against the front porch column. "I really did come to check in."

She raised her brows, admonishing him to continue.

"But then she saw the damage Ball Buster inflicted earlier, so she wanted to fix me up." He lifted his shirt to show her the bandage.

The woman rolled her eyes with a hearty shake of her head. "Fix you up?" she snorted. "So let me guess. You took your shirt off to show her the goods and she threw herself at you."

"It was definitely my fault," he admitted. Things had started out innocently enough. She'd seemed genuinely horrified when she saw the wound. Then he had to go and dare her to kiss him again. He shook his head. "She didn't throw herself at me." He'd gone after her. He didn't know what it was about Jessa, but he seemed to lose what little self-control he had when she was around.

"Damn it, Lance." Naomi took a shot at his shoulder.

At least she didn't nail him in the ribs. He backed away before she got any ideas. "We just kissed." Even as the words tumbled out, the argument fell apart. It'd turned into more than a kiss in about two seconds. Two more minutes and he would've had her clothes off. He would've been buried so deep inside her he might never have found his way out.

"Jessa doesn't know how to just kiss," Naomi informed him, one hand placed on her hip in a sassy way that reminded him of Gracie.

He might be losing his touch, too. Used to be a kiss was simply a necessary stepping stone to get a woman where he wanted her, but he couldn't get Jessa out of his head. Hell, he could go for another round of kissing right now. Maybe at his place, so his father wouldn't interrupt this time...

"Oh no you don't." Naomi shook a finger in his face. "You and Jessa is not happening. So stop thinking about it."

He shoved away her finger. "How do you know what I'm thinking?"

"Oh please. Your eyes are all glazed over and you're practically drooling." Her glare could've incinerated him. "Don't do this to her, Lance. She's not like those women who follow you around everywhere."

Actually, that had stopped a long time ago. "They're not there to see me. Not anymore." There were younger guys. Guys who were happy to take them home for a night.

Naomi glared up at him, jutting out her right hip slightly, a signal that she was about to change her approach. "Do you want to get married? Have kids? Has that changed for you?"

"No." Didn't have to think about the answer. He'd never wanted that. Any idealistic views he'd had about love had been obliterated the day his mother looked him in the face, then turned her back on him. He didn't intend to build a life with someone only to watch it fall apart the way it had for his father. The way it had for their family.

"Jessa does," Naomi said. "She wants all of that. A commitment. A family. A man to spend the rest of her life with. She believes in that. We might not, but she does."

"I know." People talked about how many times she'd been engaged. He doubted she'd ever gone on "just a date." She seemed to want something that'd last a lifetime. Everyone in town knew Jessa had that dreamy-eyed view of love. Sometimes he envied that. It wasn't like her parents had some fairy-tale romance, but she still held on to the hope it could happen. What would that be like? He had no clue what it felt like to believe in something.

Naomi stepped closer. She was short, but she sure could look intimidating when she wanted to. "She's been jerked around enough. I can't be responsible for it happening again."

"You? Why would you be responsible?"

"I'm the one who helped her change her look so she could start winning over donors for the shelter. And I told her to use you as a guinea pig. I told her to try to win you over."

That was worth a laugh. "You told her to use me?" Not that he minded...

But Naomi wasn't seeing any humor in the situation. "Come on, Lance." She sighed. "You never even noticed her until she started to dress sexier. Until she wore her contacts. Put on makeup."

Maybe not, but he hadn't had a reason to notice Jessa, either. He didn't exactly get out much. Besides, it wasn't the makeup. He couldn't give a damn about the makeup. That's not what tempted him to kiss her tonight. That's not what drove him to keep kissing her until his mind and body were lost in fantasyland. "She wasn't wearing makeup tonight. And why would you tell her to change her look?" Why did women do that to each other?

"She *wanted* to," Naomi shot back. "And I never thought you'd take advantage of it. I never thought she'd fall for *you*, of all people."

Fall for him. He thought about the way she'd touched him. The way she'd smiled up at him. It all seemed genuine, but… "Maybe she's not falling for me. Maybe it's all part of your little plan."

"No." Naomi's head shook the possibility away. "When she ran over to you today…I knew. She cares about you. And you can't take advantage of that. It's not right."

He blew out a breath. Wow, women sure knew how to use guilt to trip people up. "I didn't mean to take advantage of her." He hadn't meant for anything to happen between them. Maybe if he hadn't seen her naked…

"You and Jessa want two different things. She has a big heart, Lance. And I don't want her to get hurt again." That was the final blow. It didn't matter how much he wanted to kiss her again. Didn't matter how much she turned him on.

"I don't want her to get hurt, either." She deserved to find what she wanted. He couldn't stand in the way of that. "I'll talk to her. Tomorrow. I'll get things straightened out."

But first he had to straighten himself out.

* * *

Morning looked different after sharing a hot kiss with Lance Cortez. Jessa opened her eyes. After last night, everything was different. Sunlight flooded the room, streaming lazily in through the large picture window that framed Topaz Mountain. The cliffs appeared to be so close it seemed she could reach out and brush her fingers along their rugged peaks. She stretched out in the creaky bed and let the rays of light warm her face. She'd never dreamed she'd be so comfortable staying in Luis's house. The room was so simple—a brass queen bed, an old scratched antique dresser, and a wooden rocking chair in the corner. There were no frills, no pops of color, but somehow the simplicity of it put her at ease. You didn't need much when you had that view staring you in the face first thing every morning.

She closed her eyes, letting herself fall back through the hours to last night. A deep vibrato still fluttered her heart. Had Lance really kissed her? Had he really said he wanted her? The images were so soft and hazy, overcast by a thick cloud of desire.

And yet the memories sizzled through her, an assurance that it was real. It had all happened. The kiss, his strong hands on her body, his tongue against her skin. Her body woke with a start, feeling the sensations again.

Noise sounded from downstairs—the creaking of the kitchen's wood floors, running water. Luis must be up.

A shot of embarrassment jolted her out of bed. She rarely slept past seven and it was almost eight. Quickly, she shed her flannel pajamas and pulled on yoga pants and a long-sleeved T-shirt. Stopping in the bathroom, she smoothed her hair and pulled it back into a ponytail. Her eyes looked tired, but happy, too, as though she was still luxuriating in the exhilarating pleasure of being touched and held.

She'd *never* been touched and held exactly the way Lance had done it.

A bounce snuck into her step as she made her way down the narrow wooden staircase. She found Luis in the kitchen.

"Good morning." She greeted the older man with a happy wave. She couldn't help it. Everything felt lighter. It was so freeing not worrying about things with Lance. Not devising a strategy for how to avoid him or overanalyze what last night meant. It had felt so natural and easy. They'd had fun. He'd been good to her. And that was all that mattered. Instead of lying awake agonizing over what might come from it all, she'd slept deeply and restfully. Such a contrast to pretty much every other man she'd ever kissed.

"Morning." Luis nodded with a small smile. He had to have known there was more going on than they cared to admit last night, but she knew him well enough to know he'd never bring it up. He was a *live and let live* type of person.

Jessa sashayed past him and filled a glass of water. She liked to down eight ounces first thing every morning. "Can I make breakfast?" she asked, after she'd finished the glass. Nothing said Sunday morning like her father's sweet potato and egg hash.

"Nah, you don't have to cook for me, Jessa." Luis slipped on a heavy flannel coat. "Besides, Sundays we all go up to Lance's place for breakfast. Me and Naomi and Gracie."

"Oh." Her heart thumped a bit harder. One kiss and she'd been conditioned. She heard the man's name and instantly her lady parts warmed right up.

"Better get your coat," Luis added. "Cold out this morning. The dew's as thick as icing out there."

"Um." She sneaked a quick glance at herself in the microwave's spotted glass. So yeah. She definitely wasn't looking her best. She hadn't showered, hadn't even officially gotten dressed.

She reached up and patted the straggler hairs into place. "You know, I can stay here. I'm sure he doesn't need one more person to feed."

"Unless I miss my guess, he'll want you there." Luis looked her over, those kind eyes crinkled and wise.

And...omniscient. That was the word. Though they were watered down with age, Luis's eyes were so focused and intent they seemed to see everything. "He'll be glad to see you. Trust me. I know my son."

Would he? The thought baited a smile. Would he be as happy to see her as she would be to see him? Already her heart was twirling like she had when her mother would dress her in a frilly skirt.

"Let's get a move on. Luis waved her over to the front door. "We don't want the grub to get cold."

Her hesitation melted away. Luis knew his son. And things didn't have to be awkward. They'd kissed, that's all. Okay, made out. But only for about three minutes. He'd probably made out with a lot of women for much longer than that.

She pulled her coat off the rack and slipped it on, then bent to jam her feet into her shoes. "Should we bring anything?" She'd seen some fruit lying around. She could cut it up and make a salad...

"Nah. Lance cooks for everyone on Sundays." He held open the door for her. "Not sure where he learned. I never could do much in the kitchen."

She paused on her way out to the porch, nerves boiling with the anticipation of seeing him. "You're sure he won't mind if I come?"

Luis looked at her, his face serious and sincere. "You're practically part of the family. I always promised your dad we'd watch out for you if anything ever happened to him. He'd want you to be part of our family."

Unexpected tears pricked at her eyes. Luis had said things like that before, but she'd never felt it hit so close to her heart. In a way, she did feel like she fit. She'd agreed to stay

only to do Lance a favor, but truthfully she loved it at the
ranch—the surrounding peaks, the old creaking floors, the
acres of open space surrounding them. The people. "Thank
you." She squeezed his shoulder and followed him down the
steps to the driveway.

It *was* chilly, but beautiful, too. The early morning sunlight gleamed so bright it almost hurt to look. Thick morning
dew made the ground sparkle. They crunched over the dirt
in a sort of awed silence, taking in the pure air, the warm
sun, the shimmering blue sky. The closer they got to Lance's
house, the more her insides warmed, the more her heart beat
with eagerness. Even though she couldn't wait to see him
again, it wasn't because she wanted something out of him.
For once in her life, she had no expectations. She simply
wanted to be around him. To know him better. To see him
smile like he had last night.

The thought made her smile as she followed Luis up the
porch steps.

She'd heard Lance had built his own house a few years
ago, and it was gorgeous, all log and stone. A wraparound
porch wound around the entire thing, making it cozy and
welcoming. She passed a wicker swing, which looked like
the perfect spot to sit out with a glass of wine on a cool autumn night...

"Here we go." Luis opened the front door, not bothering
to knock.

The inside of Lance's house was as impressive as the outside. Jessa crept across the slate-tiled entryway, trying to take
in everything at once. The comforting smell of black coffee,
the warm tones on the walls, the framed scenes she recognized from around the ranch. The main floor was a completely open concept, a living room with leather furniture

clustered near a large stone fireplace on one wall. Beyond that, the space opened into the masculine gourmet kitchen with dark wood cabinets and grayish concrete countertops.

A large dining table sat in front of a beautiful bay window, and it was already laden with dishes and food—some sort of decadent-looking coffee cake, a pan of eggs, a plate of crisp bacon.

God, it smelled heavenly.

A set of French doors near the kitchen busted open. Gracie came skipping through, followed by Naomi and Lance.

Oh, Lance. A faint humming purred inside her. If it was possible he looked even better than he had last night. Fitted faded Levi's and an unbuttoned flannel with a tattered henley underneath.

Heat flashed the way it had when he'd first pressed his lips into hers.

"We saw some deers!" Gracie cried, skipping over. "A mama and two little ones."

"Wow." Jessa knelt down to her level and folded her into a hug. "I'd love to see them," she said, as though she didn't see deer walking down the street every day in Topaz Falls.

Naomi ruffled her daughter's red curls. "You could've seen them if this little princess hadn't scared them away."

"I was trying to be quiet but they were so cute." Gracie grinned up at her, those jewel-like eyes shining. "One of the babies got this close!" She held her hands about six inches apart while her mother laughed.

Jessa laughed, too. The little girl had some mad skills in the art of exaggeration.

As soon as the laughter faded, an awkward silence settled. Awkward because Lance still stood by the doors, his arms crossed, staring at her.

"Come on, sweet girl," Naomi said, steering her daughter away. "Let's get those grubby hands washed up before breakfast."

As she passed, Naomi gave Jessa a small smile. A tad sympathetic?

Unease spread through her, taming the elation she'd felt since she'd woken up. Why was Naomi looking at her as if she felt sorry for her?

"Grub ready yet?" Luis asked his son, heading for the table without waiting for an answer. "I'm starvin'."

"Uh. Yeah." Lance seemed to shake himself out of whatever held him in a trance. "Just about. You can have a seat if you want."

Luis didn't have to be told twice. He crossed to the far end of the room and sat himself at the head of the dining table.

Lance approached Jessa, but he didn't look at her. Not really. His eyes shifted. "You came." The words weren't happy. They weren't even welcoming. And for someone who'd been so adamant about kissing her last night, he sure was keeping a chilly distance intact.

"Um, yeah." She tried to make eye contact with him, but he looked away. "Luis insisted. I hope that's okay."

"Sure." He seemed to shrug it off like he didn't care either way before he left her standing there and went to the coffeepot in the kitchen.

Gracie skipped back into the great room. "Papa!" Since Naomi's parents had moved to Florida a few years ago, Luis was the closest thing Gracie had to a local grandpa.

He rose from his chair and lifted her into the air while she squealed. Then he set her down in the chair next to his, and their heads bent together as she chattered about the deer.

Jessa watched Lance move stonily in the kitchen, her feet rooted to the floor. Suddenly she felt like she shouldn't be there. Like she didn't belong after all.

Naomi came to stand by her. A little too close. "So how was your night?" she whispered.

"Oh. Fine. Good." She squirmed out of her coat and walked over to hang it on the rack near the front door so they were out of earshot.

"Anything unusual happen?" Naomi asked too innocently. She obviously knew something had happened, and why should that surprise her? The woman lived right across the driveway from Luis.

"How did you know?" Jessa sighed.

"I saw Lance leaving." Naomi glanced toward the other side of the room, where everyone was still otherwise occupied.

"It was nothing," she insisted feebly. Obviously. Lance was completely ignoring her.

"Nothing? Really? Because your face is beet red."

"It's warm in here." She tugged her shirt out a few times to let in some air.

Her friend yanked on her elbow and pulled her closer to the front door. "Have you changed your mind? About banning relationships from your life for a while?"

"No." But she had to admit she could. She could change her mind pretty easily with the right motivation. "We kissed. It's not like I'm hearing wedding bells or anything."

"Good." Naomi let her go. "Because we've already talked about this. He's not commitment material."

"Maybe that's because he hasn't met the right woman." She was just thinking out loud here, but that would make sense. Lance didn't have much time to date. The women she'd heard he'd been with weren't exactly commitment material, either. Besides... "I'm not in a hurry for anything to happen. I liked kissing him." She wouldn't even try to deny it. "But I don't need some big commitment right now anyway."

Naomi rolled her eyes. "Sure, you say that now. But what about in a month when you're more invested? What happens then?"

For once, she didn't know. And she didn't have to. "I'll work that out then."

"And get hurt again," her friend said gently. "Trust me. Lance has baggage. You don't want to be the one to have to deal with his mommy issues. That's exactly why I—"

"Hey, Jessa."

Her head snapped so fast she felt a pull in her neck. Lance was looking at her now. He was even talking to her.

"Can you help me get the drinks ready?" he asked, still hanging out by the coffeepot.

Naomi rolled her eyes, but Jessa simply bumped past her. "Sure. I'd be happy to."

Chapter Ten

Jessa drifted to the other side of the counter and glanced at him as though waiting for instructions. Which was good. Distance would be key for this conversation. When he'd walked in and seen her standing there it hit like a shockwave. He noticed her lips first. The lips that were so smooth and giving against his last night. Then her eyes. Friendly and open, smiling in a way that made him want to smile, too. She had on yoga pants that showcased her tight ass. The tight ass his hands had held just last night. It pretty much looked like she'd rolled right out of bed and come on over. Seeing her disheveled in that sexy carefree way made his brain give out and the little speech he'd rehearsed last night faded into the desire to touch her again.

But he couldn't. So she'd stay over there and he'd stay over here and then maybe he could remember what it was he was supposed to say to her. He checked on the others, who were seated at the table, already piling food onto their plates while Gracie informed them of every fact she knew about deer.

"Sooo... should I pour coffee for everyone?" Jessa asked, stepping into his line of vision.

Their eyes connected and he forced himself not to look away again. "In a second." He shuffled a few steps closer. "Actually, we need to talk first."

Something changed on her face. Her smile fell away, and the bright, wide eyes that kept demanding his attention narrowed. "Okay. So talk." She folded her arms and leaned against the counter, glaring as though she already knew what he was going to say.

Damn it. How had he planned to start this again? "Well..." He cleared his throat. The noise level over at the table rose as Gracie giggled about something his dad had said. Jessa didn't seem to notice. Her glare was relentless.

He blew out a breath. If anyone wondered why he didn't do relationships, this would be a good example. He sucked at having honest, hard conversations. Since there was no easy way to put it, he'd best just get it out there. "I shouldn't have kissed you," he said, quietly enough that the others wouldn't hear.

Jessa's unreadable expression didn't change but her jaw twitched. "And why is that?"

Why was that again? Staring at her made it hard to remember. He glanced down at his plain, uncomplicated boots. "I'm pretty sure we want different things."

When silence thrummed into his ears, he looked up at her.

Her facial expression hadn't budged an inch. "What is it you want, Lance?" The words came out solid and hard. She didn't seem to care much if anyone else heard.

He shoved his hands into his pockets so he wouldn't flip

off Naomi from across the room. What the hell did she know? Talking had been a bad idea. "I want simplicity."

Jessa shocked him with a smirk. Where had all this attitude and sass come from? He'd always heard she was a softie. He must've heard wrong.

"And what is it you think I want?" Her tone came within an inch of mocking him.

"Uh." Was this a trap? He'd learned early in his dating career never to answer a question that could have potentially catastrophic consequences. Truth was, he didn't know what she wanted. Not exactly. He knew what Naomi thought Jessa wanted. But Jessa was waiting.

He blew out the frustration in a hefty sigh. "Look. This isn't about you. I don't do relationships. I'm not interested in that." Life was so much easier without those ties. "I shouldn't have taken those shots last night." Not that he could blame his body's reaction to her on the whiskey. "You're great, but—"

"Did I do something that led you to believe I wanted a relationship with you?" she interrupted in that same bold, *screw you* tone.

"No." *Wow.* This was the last time he'd follow Naomi's advice on anything. Talk about a crash and burn. "But Naomi seemed to think—"

"Did it ever occur to you that maybe *I* wanted a fling?" Jessa marched closer. "That maybe I'm sick of relationships and just want to have fun with no strings attached for once in my life?"

"No." Somehow he managed to get the word out even with his jaw hanging open. That had definitely never occurred to him.

"Would it be so hard to believe that I'm not out searching

for a husband?" she demanded, hands positioned on the rounded curve of her sexy hips.

"Well…" What could he say to that without risking her foot in his balls? She'd built quite the reputation for herself. Wasn't his fault word got around. "Isn't that what you want?"

She laughed. The woman laughed at him. "*You* kissed *me*." Her pointer finger slashed the air between them. "*You* said you were attracted to *me*."

"I am." Damn was he attracted to her. Her shoulders were straight and tight, her perky breasts begging for some attention. And her face had flushed with the same passion he'd seen last night.

"Then what the hell is your problem, Lance, huh?" she demanded.

When she put it that way…he glanced over at the table again.

Gracie and his father were still chatting while they ate, but Naomi was glaring at him. *Oh, right.* That kicked his memory into gear. He was supposed to be putting boundaries between them to save Jessa some heartache. "I don't want you to get hurt." He felt like he was reading a damn script. What he really wanted to tell her was that he'd never been more turned on than he was right now and would she like a tour of his bedroom?

"Maybe I'm the one who'll hurt you." Her head tilted in a flippant gesture. "Did you ever think about that?"

"Noooo," he admitted. But he could be down with some pain…

"Screw you, Lance. I don't need your pity *or* your protection." She marched over to him, and he felt his heart lift at the prospect of her body being against his again.

"You know what I *do* want?" she asked, her voice lowered into an alluring growl.

He could only shake his head. Shock and intrigue surged through him in a way he'd never felt.

"I want some fucking coffee." She bumped past him to the coffeepot. Without a glance back, she filled herself a mug and sashayed over to the table, leaving him staring after her, his body as primed and ready as it'd been last night.

* * *

She was so done. And not just with breakfast, either. Jessa blotted her mouth with a napkin and tossed it onto her empty plate. Lance might be a complete jerk-wad, but he knew how to make breakfast. Normally, she would be a polite guest and offer to help clean up the dishes, but she had to get out of there. Now.

All through breakfast she'd felt Lance's eyes searching her out. But she had studiously avoided him, gushing over Gracie instead. Thank God there was an adorable ten-year-old at the table to distract everyone from the fat-ass purple polka-dotted elephant in the room. Because Naomi had obviously discussed last night's kiss with Lance in great detail, and Luis might be nearing seventy, but he wasn't blind. He had to have witnessed something of what had transpired between her and Lance in the kitchen—an encounter that still had her knees quaking, by the way.

So during the meal the adults in the room had hardly looked at one another, instead enthusiastically indulging Gracie's spirited ideas about how adding pigs to the ranch could be super fun. Because look how much Wilbur livened things up in *Charlotte's Web*. Gracie was always on a mission to bring more animals into the fold. She was a girl after her own heart.

A lull in the conversation presented Jessa with the opportunity she'd been waiting for for at least a half hour. "Well, this has been great," she said, her gaze skimming right over all of them. "But I should check in at the shelter. Make sure Cassidy's holding up okay." It wasn't like Cassidy couldn't handle it, but Jessa couldn't handle *this*. The poor brokenhearted Jessa routine. When she'd realized what Lance was trying to get at in the kitchen, something inside of her had erupted. She was *not* emotionally fragile. And she sure as hell didn't need a man—even Lance Cortez—to be her key to a happy life.

She was done being poor nice Jessa.

The eruption had left behind a force that built inside her, fortifying her. With this newfound courage, she popped right out of her chair. "Thanks for a lovely breakfast," she said to no one in particular. But she did beam a real smile at Gracie. "See you soon, sweet girl."

The girl blew her a kiss, which Jessa returned before she spun and made a break for the door.

"Wait." A chair scraped the plank floors and before she could get too far, Lance slipped in front of her. She forced herself to stare back at him, working her mouth into a line of indifference. "Yes?"

"Don't you need help at the shelter today?" he asked, widening his eyes and glancing in his father's direction.

Right. She was supposed to be on babysitting duty. After everything that had transpired between them, that's what it came down to. That's why she was here. Lance hadn't forgotten and she shouldn't, either. Irritation simmered, but she didn't want to take it out on Luis. It wasn't his fault his son was clueless.

"Actually I could really use some help." Blocking out Lance, she turned to his father. "Do you have time to come today? I might have to do inventory on supplies."

The older man's mustache twitched. "Sure," he said. If he was trying to hide his amusement, he was doing a terrible job. "Gets me outta doin' the dishes." He planted a kiss on the top of Gracie's head and dragged himself out of the chair.

"Great. Thanks." With a prim smile, she sidestepped Lance and led a hearty charge out the front door to the tune of the "Hallelujah" chorus playing in her head. Not surprisingly, Lance didn't try to stop her.

Outside, the day had brightened and the scents of fall permeated the air—dried grass, crisp leaves. Not that she enjoyed it. Her volcanic heart still fumed. As far as she could remember, she hadn't said anything pathetic to Lance. Sure, she'd tried to kiss him, and yes, she'd admired him, but she wasn't Scarlett freaking O'Hara. She hadn't been *pining* after him. She hadn't begged him to kiss her. And maybe she would enjoy a fling. She didn't know for sure, but it was possible. Now she'd never know, since Lance had gone and made it a huge deal.

We want different things. God. How did he know anything about what she wanted? Her feet pounded the dirt harder. He didn't. Mostly because he hadn't bothered to ask her.

Luis tromped along by her side. "You want to talk about it?" he asked in his pleasant way.

"Not especially." There was nothing to talk about. Nothing to think about, except the work she had to do today. Swearing off men had been the right decision all along, but then Lance had come along and screwed it up by kissing her, before doing a complete one-eighty and telling her he wasn't looking for a commitment.

And people thought *she* had issues.

After running into Luis's house to change into some jeans and her *Stay Calm and Help Animals* T-shirt, she led Luis to her truck, which was parked off to the side of his garage. Driving away from the ranch felt freeing. She flicked on the radio and let the country music coax out the tension.

Luis stared ahead, his fingers drumming on his knees to the beat. "Lance took it the hardest when his mom left," he said, his jaw tight. "I never knew what to do. How to talk to him about it. We just tried to survive."

The words caught her off guard. Even though they'd spent a lot of time together, Luis had never mentioned his ex-wife before. She turned down the radio. "Sometimes that's all you can do," she said, her shoulders softening.

"Point is, he didn't learn anything good about relationships. Not from me," the man went on, though he didn't look at her. Luis didn't have to expand. She'd heard the rumors about him after his wife left. He'd had affairs with married women, taking full advantage of his status as a renowned bull rider. For a while, he'd been quite the Casanova. But she didn't hold that against him. She knew how it felt to have a broken heart, to search for something that would soothe away the loneliness, even if it was only temporary.

Luis stared blankly out the windshield. "It's one of the things I regret the most."

Letting silence settle, Jessa turned onto Main Street. The sidewalks were full of people strolling, pausing to window shop at the eclectic mix of boutiques and shops. It was a beautiful day, bright and vivid, yet she couldn't help but feel that a cloud hung over them. Sure, Lance hadn't had it easy after his mom left, but a lot of people hadn't. And Luis had already paid a steep price for his actions. He'd lost a son. After Lucas was sent to prison, the man had cleaned up his act. From what she'd heard, he stayed home with Lance and Levi more, tried to fix things with his boys. People *could* change. But they had to want it.

Stopping at the lone traffic light, she waved at Mrs. Eckles, who owned the bakery across the street. "I didn't exactly learn about healthy relationships from my parents, either," she reminded Luis. But that didn't have to stop her from having a healthy relationship with someone else. "And you know what, Luis? Lance's issues aren't your fault." He had a choice. He could decide what he wanted for his life. It seemed he already had, so there was no point in dwelling on the situation. "Anyway, we don't have to talk about Lance. Like I've said before, there's nothing to talk about." They had a business arrangement and things had gotten too personal. She wouldn't make that mistake again.

On the south end of Main Street, she veered to the right and pulled up in front of the shelter. The building itself wasn't attractive. Before her father had bought it, it had been an old diner, a plain square brick building with a shingled roof. Some people around town called it an eyesore, but it served its purpose. Before Buzz had passed, she'd planned to give it a facelift in hopes that would help donations. Things hadn't exactly worked out that way. Her dad had left behind a couple of debts and after she'd paid them off, she needed what remained to keep things running month-to-month, to pay Cassidy and Xavier, her night shift guy, so she didn't have to be there 24/7.

She parked in the space next to Cassidy's SUV and cut

the engine. It looked like the sign above the door had lost another bolt. It was tilted like it was about to fall to the ground.

Luis noticed her looking at it.

"That's nothin'. I'll get on a ladder and get it all fixed up," he said, unbuckling his seat belt.

She climbed out of the truck, hauling along her bag of paperwork she had to finish up. "Thanks, Luis." Seriously. What would she do without him? Lance might be paying her to stay with the man, but she should be doing it for free, given how much he did to help her out.

"You deserve to be on the payroll," she told him, leading the way inside. The bell chimed a cheerful welcome.

"Nah. I don't need the money," he insisted.

And it was obvious she *did* need some money. Jessa looked around the reception area at the front of the building. Buzz had unearthed the two oak desks from a trash heap in the rubble of a dilapidated building. Sturdy as a rock, he'd claimed, even though they both leaned slightly to the left. And those desks weren't the only monstrosities in the room. The stained gray carpet was pulling up around the edges. It had been snagged from the array of paws that had walked or pranced or scampered or cowered on its surface. Two overstuffed chairs he'd found at a garage sale provided the only seating in the room.

She sighed deeply. It wasn't the neatest place, but it was hard to keep things neat when you had a revolving door of animals coming in and out.

"Hey there." Cassidy walked out from the back room, where they kept the animal pens and supplies.

"Hi," Jessa said brightly, doing her best to cover up her earlier irritation. "How're things going?"

"Good..." Her friend drew out the word as though she

was confused. That would be because technically Jessa wasn't supposed to come in on Sundays. Her friends were always on her about being a workaholic and making sure she took at least one day off during the week. So much so that Cassidy had volunteered to hang out on weekends for a very reasonable wage.

Before Cass could ask her why she'd come in, she got right down to business. "So how's the pig?" The day before Cam had broken up with her, someone had called to report a potbellied pig that was seen wandering around the park. Jessa had found the sweet thing down by the river, and she didn't look healthy. Too thin and very lethargic. She'd brought her in and posted signs around town, but so far no one had claimed her. Which meant she'd likely been abandoned by someone passing through town.

"The poor baby won't eat," Cass said. "I tried everything you recommended, but she just kind of nibbles, then goes back to sleep."

"I figured that might be the case." Which gave her the perfect excuse to come in on a Sunday. She'd already started the pig on antibiotics but might have to up the dosage. "That's why I thought I'd better stop and check in. I'll go take a look." She slipped past the desk and hurried to the back room. Though she'd given the pig the largest crate they had, it had curled up in the farthest corner, snout burrowed into the soft blanket Jessa had used to make a bed. When she unlatched the crate, the pig's head lifted, but it didn't move.

"Come here, sweetie." Carefully, Jessa lifted her out and held her the same way she'd hold a baby. Based on the pig's small size, she'd guess her to be less than a year old. "Why would anyone ever leave you behind?" she cooed, petting her soft head. "You're so pretty, yes you are." Downright irresistible, if you asked her, with that shiny pink snout and those black and white spots. "Such a pretty piggy."

"Think she's gonna make it?" Luis asked from behind her.

"She might have a touch of pneumonia, but we'll take care of her." Jessa scratched the pig's ears and it lifted its snout into the air. "You like that, don't you," she murmured.

The pig gave the cutest little grunt, proving that a little love can help perk up anyone.

"Would you mind if I brought her home?" Jessa turned to Luis. I'd like to keep a closer eye on her."

"Fine by me." Having brought up three boys, Luis seemed to be fazed by nothing. He'd told her plenty of tales of Lance and his brothers bringing home snakes and mice and spiders.

"Not sure Lance'll like the idea, though. He's always sayin' animals belong outside."

She couldn't fight a wicked grin. Even better.

"Got a name for her?" the man asked, scratching under the pig's chin.

Jessa held her up and carefully looked her over. "Ilsa," she said, satisfied. "Because she's fancy." And because she loved *Casablanca*.

Luis grunted out a laugh. "Never met a pig named Ilsa."

"You named her?" Cass asked, walking through the door. "Uh-oh. In my experience naming an animal means it'll be part of your family forever."

"I'd be fine with that." Jessa couldn't take in every animal that came through the shelter's doors, but Ilsa was obviously special.

"So you could've called to check on the pig, you know," her friend said as though she was hurt. "I could've handled it until tomorrow."

Guilt turned Jessa's stomach. "Oh, I know. Of course you could." That wasn't it at all! "It's just..." She paused. There was no way she'd get out of this without telling her the whole story, which she couldn't do in front of Lance's father. She turned to him. "Luis, do you mind getting started on inventory in the storage room?"

"No problem," he said, tipping his cowboy hat in Cassidy's direction as he slipped by.

Once he was gone, Cassidy plopped down at the desk with the aged computer, then rolled another office chair close and pointed at it. "Spill it. What are you doing here? You're supposed to be enjoying a day off."

Jessa sat and settled Ilsa on her lap. She *would've* been enjoying a day off if things hadn't gotten so awkward back at the ranch. In a hushed tone, she shared the whole story in what had to be record time.

Cassidy's eyes grew wider and wider. "Wow. So what're you going to do? You going to stay there?"

"I feel like I have to." She'd made a deal with Lance. Besides, she needed the money. And now she wouldn't feel bad at all taking a cut. She didn't want to give him the satisfaction of bowing out because things had gotten a little uncomfortable.

"I can't believe you kissed Lance Cortez," Cassidy blurted. Her eyes bulged and she covered her mouth. "Sorry. But that's crazy. Was it good?"

"No." *Yes it was*. Her heart sighed. *Sooooo good*.

"I can tell when you're lying, you know."

Jessa simply petted Ilsa's coarse hair and planted a kiss on the pig's head. "I wonder why someone didn't want her," she said, trying to get Cassidy to focus on something besides Lance.

Luis came back, lugging along her father's old metal tool-box. "We're almost out of dog bones," he informed her. "But from what I can tell, everything else looks fine."

Of course it was fine, because she'd done the inventory three days ago. Jessa fanned her face. "Okay," she sang. "Thanks, Luis. I'll add dog bones to the list."

He secured the toolbox under one arm and hooked the other around the ladder they kept behind the counter. "I'm gonna head out and get that sign fixed."

After he'd moseyed through the door, Cassidy looked at Jessa with shiny eyes, a grin brimming. But before the woman could ask more questions, she glanced at the call log on the desk. "Has anything else come in today?"

Cassie snorted. "No. But Hank Green called. Twice in the past half hour, even though I told him you're not in today. I offered to help him out, but it's not me he wants." She wiggled her eyebrows.

Damn it. Not exactly the kind of call she'd hoped for. Give her a fawn tangled in a fence any day over Hank Green. The retired grocery store manager had had a thing for her ever since she'd worked there the summer she'd turned eighteen. He made passes at her every time he saw her.

She sighed. "What's the problem?"

"His cat is stuck in a tree. Again." Cassidy laughed. "He probably *put* him up there so he could call you."

"Oy." Hank did have some delusions about the two of them driving off into the sunset together. Despite the fact that he was a good forty years older than her and she'd tried to tell him repeatedly he wasn't her type.

Cassidy patted her hand sympathetically. "I told him he'd have to check in with you Monday if he wanted to talk with you."

Except that would mean she had nothing to do here today. No reason to keep Luis here, which meant they would have to go back to the ranch. And she dreaded that even more than she dreaded Hank's awkward passes. "Actually, I think I'll go over there." She rose from the chair and started to collect everything she'd need for Ilsa—the crate, the antibiotics, a special bottle so she could help her put on some weight. She could easily drop the pig off at the ranch before heading over to Hank's place.

When she turned around, Cass was gaping at her. "That'll only encourage him, you know."

"The poor cat. It's not his fault his owner is nuts." She crossed to the other desk and pulled out her medical kit from the drawer, just in case Butch the wonder cat was injured during the rescue.

"I'm sure he'll get him down if you don't come," Cassidy muttered.

"I wish I had your faith." But Hank could be quite persistent. She'd been witness to that. "Anyway, this is exactly what I need today. A distraction." A reason to avoid the ranch. Okay, a reason to avoid *Lance*. "I'll bring Luis with me."

"Oh, that'll help." Her friend rolled her eyes. Hank had always had it out for the Cortez boys—called them hoodlums and troublemakers—and now the rivalry between Hank Green and Luis Cortez was legendary. "You might want to bring some rope in case there's a brawl and you have to hogtie the two of them."

"Everything'll be fine," she insisted. Even if it wasn't, it would be a hell of a lot easier than facing Lance again today.

Chapter Eleven

Though she couldn't say much for the man himself, Jessa had always loved Hank Green's house. Located only a few blocks off Main Street, it had that old, small-town curb appeal, with rounded Victorian bay windows and pointed eaves. Pale bricks set off the blue shutters and an intricate white front porch wrapped the length of the house in a charming elegance.

"Hank Green needs your help about as much as Lance needs mine," Luis mumbled as she pulled up to the curb.

"I feel bad for him," Jessa said through a sigh. "He's lonely." So he called her over to help with his animals occasionally. What was the harm in that? Though he was in his late sixties, the man had never been married, never had any family, so she could understand why he'd want some company. "Besides," she continued, withdrawing the keys and unclipping her seat belt, "I can't ignore an animal in distress." The poor cat was probably terrified.

"You sure do have a big heart, Jessa." Luis pulled himself out of her truck, and did she imagine it or was he wincing more than normal?

Before she could make a full assessment, Hank waved from the front porch.

"Jessa. Thank God you're here," he called, teetering down the steps while he clutched the rail. The rim of white hair on his head had been neatly trimmed, and the bald spot on top shone in the sun. "Butch is terrified up there. I can hear him meowing."

Luis snorted and Jessa shoved a gentle elbow into his ribs. "Be nice," she whispered. "At least you have Lance and Naomi and Gracie around."

A small smile fumbled on his lips. "And you," he said. Which made *her* smile. Though she missed her father with heart-aching sorrow, having Luis sure helped.

Hank lumbered down the walkway toward them.

Ah, geez. He'd put on his dress slacks, with a sweater vest and bow tie. If only she could convince him dressing up for her wasn't worth the effort.

"What're you doing here, Cortez?" he asked, as though perturbed that he had some competition.

"Luis is helping at the shelter today," Jessa answered for him. The less these two gentlemen talked, the better off everyone would be. Way back in a previous life, Hank had accused Levi, the youngest Cortez, of shoplifting from his store. Levi, of course, always claimed innocence, and when Luis went down there to straighten things out, it had ended in a brawl that had the town sheriff locking up both men overnight.

Hank still eyed Luis warily. "I've told you, Jessa. *I* can help you at the shelter." He shifted his body as if to block out

Luis and focus solely on her. "I have nothing but time on my hands, and as you know, I *am* an animal lover."

"Lover," Luis scoffed under his breath. Jessa did have to admit that Hank somehow made that word sound rather dirty.

Instead of indulging Hank's offer with an acknowledgment, she brushed past him and continued up the walkway toward the house. "So where is poor Butch?" she asked.

"He's out back. About halfway up that blue spruce." Hank hustled to her side, leaving Luis to walk behind them. "I don't even know how he got out..."

Once again, Luis snorted.

Jessa shot him a look over her shoulder. Hopefully it said, *Let's not make this more painful that it has to be.* Though she had a hard time choking back a laugh. "How high up?" she asked in a businesslike tone. If she could keep them on track, this wouldn't have to take long and she wouldn't risk the two of them getting into another brawl.

"Oh, I don't know..." The man led the way around the side of the house on an intricate stone path that weaved through his prize-winning rose garden. "Maybe twenty feet up."

"Twenty feet?" Was the man trying to kill her? "You could've called the fire department," she reminded him. That was the sort of thing the small-town Topaz Falls Fire and Rescue was famous for. Rescuing kitties, helping little old ladies cross the street, putting out one hell of a scorching calendar every year...

"I did call." Hank escorted her past the large white gazebo in the backyard. It was gorgeous. Flawless and lavish, adorned with hanging baskets of every kind of flower. God, maybe she should just give in and marry the man. He had the best yard in all of Topaz Falls.

"The fire department refused to come."

Yeah, and she was Dolly Parton. The thought brought on a serious cringe. Hank probably *wished* she were Dolly Parton...

This time Luis coughed behind her, but at least he was keeping his mouth shut. She gave him a surreptitious grin before glancing up into the blue spruce that towered over a white picket fence on the back perimeter of the property.

At least twenty feet above the ground, the cat crouched on a wide pluming branch, its face obscured by the pine needles.

Oh, wow. Yeah. That cat was stuck. "Have you tried calling to him? Luring him down with treats?" she asked, shading her eyes from the overpowering sun.

"Of course," Hank assured her emphatically. "I've tried *everything*. I'm so distressed by the whole thing. Butch hates heights."

Again, Jessa called his bluff. Butch did, indeed, look terrified. But there was no way he'd climbed up there by himself. Cassidy was right. Hank had probably hauled over the ladder and stowed the cat up there as a ploy to get her to come over.

"Maybe he'll come down when he sees your beautiful face," Hank murmured, leaning too close for comfort. The smell of Pepto-Bismol wafted around her, stealing the sweet scent of roses from the air.

With a quick sidestep she escaped the assault, drawing closer to Luis.

"The thing is, I can't keep climbing up your tree to get your cat down, Hank." This was the fifth time in less than two months. But this was also the highest she'd ever found Butch.

"I understand," he said through a martyred sigh. "Don't worry. I won't ask for your help anymore."

"There really is a God," Luis muttered, though not nearly soft enough.

Hank whirled. "What the hell does that mean, Cortez? Do you have a problem with me?"

"I think it was you who had a problem with me," Luis shot back.

Jessa stepped between them. "Luis, can you please go get Hank's ladder out of the garage?" she asked in her sweetest-daughter-in-the-world voice. Her father had never been able to resist it, and it appeared Luis couldn't either. He turned away, mumbling some very colorful names for Hank, and hoofed it to the path around the side of the house.

Whew. Crisis averted. Lance would kill her if he knew she'd let his father get into it with Hank Green.

Lance. Right on cue, her stomach dropped and her heart twirled and the warmth of the sun seemed to slip inside her skin.

"So what's the plan?" Hank's low and gritty tone snuffed out the sudden fire burning hot and low in her belly. Well, there it was. Her remedy for shamelessly swooning over Lance. She didn't have to worry about that when Hank was nearby. "Um." She pushed her bangs off her forehead and gazed up again.

Butch was still perched in place, frozen into a fluffy cat statue. She moved closer to the tree. "Here kitty. Come on, Butch, baby. Come down now."

The cat crouched lower and mewed. There was no way in hell he was coming down on his own. Which meant she would have to go up and get him. "We need the ladder." Luis must've found it by now, but he was probably taking his time so he could cool off.

Hank slipped in front of her, gazing down on her with an affectionate look that deepened the creases in the corners of his beady gray eyes. "Jessa... while we wait, I want to thank you. For coming. You're always there for me when I need something."

"Technically I'm always there for Butch—"

Hank didn't seem to hear. "I hope you'll let me take you out to dinner this time. Only to thank you, of course," he said quickly. "Someplace nice. Maybe the Broker?"

"The Broker?" She almost laughed. "But that's in Denver."

"Exactly. We could make it a weekend trip..." Mr. Green rubbed his hand on her shoulder.

She swatted at it like she would a pestering fly. "I'm sorry. That's not going to happen. *Ever.*" And the touching her shoulder thing... that had to stop, too.

"Ever?" he repeated, as though mortally wounded.

A sigh lodged in her throat. The poor man. He wasn't so bad. Hell, at least he had good taste. And at least he didn't look at her like she was some pathetic groupie. "I'm not in a good place for anything like that right now," she said gently.

His lips pursed while his head bobbed in a brave nod. "I understand. I can wait."

Never. She'd told him never. Ain't no way he could wait that long...

"Mew." The cat's soft call commanded her attention. Jessa stood on her tiptoes and tried to see through the pine needles.

"Mew." Butch inched forward on the branch as though ready to jump down to the next one.

"That's it!" Jessa scrambled up the first couple of

branches until she was about five feet off the ground. "Come on, Butchie. Come here." She pulled herself up higher. Somewhere beneath her something cracked.

"Here. I'll give you a boost," Hank offered, raising his hands and cupping them against her ass.

"No thanks," she squawked, darting up to the next branch. The tree was thick and sturdy, shaking only slightly while she climbed higher. After pulling herself up a few more branches, she had to stop. The branches were getting thinner and there was no way they'd support her weight. Butch had climbed down a ways, but he was still a few feet above her. "Here, kitty," she crooned softly. "Come on, now. I'm right here. Jump down and I'll catch you."

The cat crept closer to the edge of the branch, head low, wide, terrified eyes focused on Jessa.

"Okay. It's okay." Hooking one arm around the trunk, she shimmied up one more branch and reached until her fingertips tingled. "There." She grabbed the skin at the back of Butch's neck. The cat hissed and squirmed but she secured him against her chest, gasping and sweating. Carefully, she picked her way back down the tree and dropped to the ground. Heaving from the effort, she handed Butch over to Hank. "Don't let the cat get out again. I can't keep doing this."

The man's chin tipped up defiantly. "If you'd agree to dinner, I wouldn't *have* to keep calling."

Shaking her head, she turned away from him and started toward the path. What could be taking Luis so long?

"Maybe you'd rather have breakfast?" Hank persisted, coming alongside of her.

Wordlessly, she shook her head.

"Coffee?" he tried.

She stopped walking and faced him. "Sorry. It's not going

to work out." This time she patted his shoulder in an effort to ease the dejected look he gave her. "What about Helen Garcia?" she asked. Helen had been the librarian since the turn of the century. "She's so smart. And ... organized." That was about where the list of her attributes stopped.

"Jessa, I know there's a slight age difference, but—"

"Slight?" she interrupted.

"I think you're the loveliest woman in the world," he finished a little desperately.

Okay, so sweet and subtle was not going to work with Hank. She had to give it to him straight. She started walking along the path so she wouldn't have to look into his eyes. "I appreciate that. Really. But it's not going to happen. I don't look at you like that, and—" When they came around the corner of the house she stopped cold.

The ladder lay in the center of the yard, crushing Hank's perfect green grass.

"My grass," he gasped, stalking toward the ladder.

Worry filled her stomach like a cold hard stone. "Where's Luis?" she choked out. The ladder looked like it had been dropped, but he wasn't there.

"I don't know, but this'll ruin my grass." Hank struggled to drag the ladder to the driveway while she scanned the empty street.

Luis wasn't there. He was gone.

Somehow, Jessa faltered to the garage, her eyes searching. It was empty. "Where could he be?" she blurted, frantically looking around.

"Knowing Cortez, he's in the house going through my things," Hank replied tightly. He marched to the garage door and threw it open. "That family is all the same. Thieves, the lot of them."

She reprimanded him with a glare. "None of them are thieves," she said sternly. "But maybe he went in for a drink. Or maybe he had to use the bathroom." Of course that was it. He had to be in the house. Jessa gulped a breath to steady her heart. He hadn't disappeared, for God's sake. She followed Hank inside, inhaling the musty scent of an old closed-in house, searching room by room, not really seeing anything but somehow finding her way. He wasn't in the kitchen or the living room or the dining room or the main floor bathroom. She bolted up the rickety staircase. "Luis?" she screeched, throwing open the upstairs bedroom doors. The house sat in a heavy silence. She broke it again with another shout, half stumbling back down the steps.

Hank met her by the front door. "He's probably gone into town for pie and coffee," he said, his nose scrunched with distaste. "You can't count on the Cortez family for anything except trouble."

"No," Jessa wheezed. Not Luis. He wouldn't leave her when she needed his help. He wouldn't have left the ladder lying in the middle of the front yard. "Oh God." Sidestepping Hank, she broke through the front door and sprinted down the driveway to the sidewalk. Trying to breathe, she looked up and down the deserted street. "Luis?" she yelled.

Nothing. No response. Hands shaking, she dug her keys out of her pocket and flew to her truck.

"Sorry, Hank!" she yelled, fumbling to unlock the doors. "Please call me right away if Luis comes back!" Before he could respond, she thrust herself into the driver's seat and gunned the engine until the truck shot away from the curb.

Chapter Twelve

One more fall like that and he'd be seein' stars. Lance hoisted himself off the ground. Not gonna lie, it was getting harder to get up. That was the third time in an hour Ball Buster had thrown him. Good thing Tucker was a regular master at corralling the mean son of a bitch so he hadn't trampled him.

Shit. He hunched, trying to even out his breathing, which was a hell of a lot harder than it sounded with the laceration and bone bruise sending flames up his rib cage.

"Hey, you okay, man?" Tucker jogged over to where Lance limped near the fence. "You're lookin' tense out there."

Tense. That was one way to put it. "I'm fine," he lied, guarding his right side. Damn bone bruise. Sure wasn't making his training any easier. Every time that pain zinged through him, he also thought back to when Jessa had touched him there. When she'd run her hands over his skin, her fingers light and gentle. That only led to another problem that pretty much made it impossible for him to ride in comfort.

"Maybe you ought to call it a day," Tucker suggested, handing him his water bottle.

Lance removed his hat and took a good long swig. He couldn't call it a day. Not until he'd gotten the better of Ball Buster. There was no way he'd be able to compete at Worlds if he couldn't even stay on that damn bull for more than three fucking seconds.

He shoved the water bottle back into Tucker's hands. "Here. I'm going again. Let's get him ready."

The man shook his head like he wasn't sure if he should pity Lance or argue. But he knew the sport. He knew what it took.

Lance climbed the fence and jumped down on the other side. He removed his gloves to check the tape on his hands. It was already frayed and torn. He'd have to rewrap—

"Lance!"

Naomi raced around the edge of the corral.

Damn. She had that look of drama about her.

"I just got a call from Ginny Eckles," she yelled as he walked to meet her. "It's your dad. She found him in front of the bakery, and something's wrong."

The pain in his ribs intensified with the hitch in his breathing. "What do you mean something's wrong?"

Naomi was wheezing like she'd sprinted all the way from her house. "She said she tried asking him some questions but he wouldn't answer. He wasn't acting like himself."

Oh for chrisssake. "Where the hell is Jessa?" he demanded, as if Naomi were her keeper.

"I don't know," she shot back with just as much attitude.

"I asked Mrs. Eckles if he was alone and she said he was. She said Luis didn't seem to remember where he was supposed to be."

"Of course he remembers," Lance grumbled, already unbuckling his chaps. His dad wouldn't forget where he was supposed to be. He was probably just being ornery. Which Jessa could've prevented had she kept an eye on him like she was supposed to.

Naomi stooped to help him get the chaps off. Always the mother. "She thinks someone should pick him up. I'd go but I have to pick up Gracie at a friend's house on the other side of town in five minutes."

"I'll get him," Lance said, kicking off the leather gear. "Tucker, go ahead and get Ball Buster settled in the stables," he called to his friend. Looked like he was done training for the day after all.

The man tipped his hat and approached the bull while Lance followed Naomi down to the driveway.

"I tried to call Jessa's cell a few times, but she didn't answer," Naomi informed him, almost like she didn't want to get her friend in trouble.

His face steamed. "Don't worry about it." Not like he could blame all of this on Jessa. Knowing his father, he'd probably lost her on purpose.

"Maybe she's really upset," Naomi said. "About your talk this morning."

"She didn't seem upset." The memory of her coy smile tugged at his gut. She seemed fine. Confident. Strong. Like a woman who could hold her own. "You're wrong about her, you know," he told Naomi. "She's stronger than you give her credit for." Strong and sexy. Enticing with that body of hers. Not that he wanted to get slapped...

"Don't you get any ideas," Naomi warned. "I don't know who that woman at breakfast was, but it wasn't Jessa. It was an act. And I don't blame her. You practically humiliated her."

"On your advice," he reminded her.

They parted ways, but before Naomi climbed into her car, she shot him a glare. "You just keep your distance. Take my word for it." Before he could answer that he was done taking her word for anything, she disappeared into her car and peeled out.

Shaking his head, Lance climbed into his truck and drove down to the highway. As far as he could tell, Jessa was a big girl and could take care of herself. He might not go out of his way to pursue her, but if something clicked between them one night, he'd let it happen. Not that he'd be dreaming about that moment. Not dreaming...fantasizing. About those slender fingers grazing his skin again, about the sexy dip in the curve of her upper lip. About the delicate weight of her body against his, all soft curves and creamy flesh...

Shit, he just about missed his turn. He jerked the wheel in a quick left and slowed as he cruised down the strip. Sure enough, a small crowd had gathered in front of Butter Buns Bakery. He slowed and pulled over to parallel park at the curb. This didn't look good.

The people who'd gathered around Luis parted as Lance jogged down the sidewalk.

"Get the hell away from me," his dad was shouting at Mrs. Eckles.

"Whoa." Lance rushed to his father's side. "Dad. What's wrong?"

"He's very agitated," Mrs. Eckles prattled in her know-it-all way. She shook her head, the bifocals strung around her neck clanking. "All I did was ask if he needed something.

He looked so confused. And when I told him I was going to call over to your place, you should've seen him. Cursing and screaming like a lunatic."

"She was badgering me," Luis put in, glaring at Mrs. Eckles like he wanted to pop her in the face.

Damn, this went way beyond ornery. "I'm sorry about this, Mrs. Eckles," Lance said, delivering the words with a polite smile. But chaos raged underneath it. What the hell was his father's problem? Making a scene like this in the middle of town? "I'll get him home." He clamped a hand onto Luis's shoulder and dragged him away before the woman decided to press charges.

His father jerked out of his grip. "I don't need you coming to pick me up. Acting like I'm the one who's crazy."

Lance growled out a sigh. Is that what happened when people got older? They stopped caring what everyone thought and did whatever they wanted? "Where's Jessa, Dad?" he asked, trying to control the venom in his tone.

"How the hell should I know?" his father shot back.

That forced him to a stop. "Because you left the house with her. To go help at the clinic."

A look of understanding dawned in his dad's blank eyes.

Tremors took over Lance's stomach. "Don't you remember?"

"Of course I remember," his father snapped. "I wanted to go for a walk, that's all. I got thirsty and I wanted to go for a walk."

Lance studied him. The man's hands were trembling. Sweat glistened on his forehead. "Are you feeling okay?" he asked.

"I'm fine," his father said, a little softer. "Just so thirsty."

Relief swept through him. He'd probably gotten dehydrated. At some point, he'd have to talk to Jessa about making sure Luis drank plenty of water. "All right, old man," he said lightly, steering his father toward the truck. "I think I've got an extra water bottle in the tr—"

"Luis!"

Lance spun. Jessa sprinted toward them, her arms flailing, long hair sailing behind her.

"Where have you been?" she rasped, pressing one hand against her heaving chest.

Damn...the way she filled out a shirt...

"I went for a walk," Luis muttered, refusing to look at Jessa.

"A walk?" she choked out. "A *walk*?" If it was possible, her face got redder. "How could you do that, Luis? Huh? How could you just walk away without telling me where you were going?"

A couple passing by on the street paused to stare at Jessa.

Yeah, she was a little fired up. "Dad needs some water. He's thirsty." Lance slipped an arm around her waist and tried coaxing her to the truck so they could move this discussion somewhere more private.

"I have the right to go for a walk if I want to," his father insisted.

Jessa halted and squirmed out of Lance's grip. "I asked you to get the ladder out of Hank Green's garage. And you never came back." She turned to Lance, her eyes wild with indignation. "And then I found the ladder lying in the middle of the front yard and Luis had simply disappeared."

What was he supposed to say? He couldn't make excuses for his father's behavior.

"I was thirsty," Luis said again. "I wanted something to drink."

"Then you should've told me that," Jessa whispered, as though she was still having a hard time breathing. "I could've gotten you a drink, Luis." She swayed a little, as if the stress of losing his father had gone to her head. Once again, Lance secured an arm around her, trying not to notice how good she smelled.

This time, she allowed him to lead her to the truck. Luis got into the passenger's seat and Lance handed him a water bottle from a cooler in the back.

Jessa had leaned against the bed of the truck, staring off into space as though trying to collect her wits.

"He didn't mean to scare you," Lance said, coming up beside her and nudging her shoulder with his. "He's always had a mind of his own. But he doesn't do stuff like that on purpose."

"He never does stuff like that to me, Lance," she said quietly. Her face turned to his, and for the first time he noticed the red rims around her eyes. She'd been crying. Some protective instinct ballooned inside him and he wanted to wipe away her tears and make sure she never had another reason to cry.

Yes, Jessa was strong. She had a lot of sass. But she was also compassionate and seemed to feel everything so deeply. Maybe he appreciated that about her even more than he appreciated her sexy legs.

"I'll talk to him. Make sure he doesn't do it again," Lance promised, and God help him, he couldn't keep his hands off her. He trailed his fingers at the base of her jaw, sweeping back the strands of hair that had escaped her ponytail.

"I think..." Her gaze strayed from his. "I think something's wrong."

"What do you mean?"

"With your father. I think something's wrong with him."

"He got thirsty and he's used to doing what he wants when he wants." That was it. The older he got, the more stubborn he got.

"Lance..." Jessa took his hand in hers and it felt so out of place but so right, her soft smooth skin covering his rough callused knuckles. "I think you need to take him to the doctor. To have him checked out."

"What?" He pulled his hands to his sides.

Jessa peered up at him, her face steeled as it had been earlier that morning when they'd had their little chat in the kitchen. "He's had short-term memory loss twice now..."

"That's not memory loss." His hands twitched and he pulled them into fists. Clearly, the man was fine. "He got turned around in the mountains. And today he just wanted a damn drink of water."

"So he left a ladder in the middle of Hank Green's yard and walked ten blocks to Main Street for a drink?" she challenged. "Why didn't he go into the house to get a drink?"

"He hates that man." Everyone knew that. Jessa knew that. Why had she even taken him there? That was probably what started this whole debacle. "He'd never set foot in Hank Green's house willingly."

Jessa stepped up to him. "I think he got disoriented. I think he didn't remember where he was or what he was supposed to be doing." Anger flashed in her eyes. "He wouldn't walk away like that when I asked him to do something. He's never done that."

Lance threw up his hands. What did she want from him? "Cut the man some slack," he said, dismissing her concerns. "He's almost seventy. He probably shouldn't be carrying ladders around anyway."

Jessa glared at him for a silent minute. Then she strode close and got in his face. "I know you don't want to hear this. But something's wrong with him."

She was right about one thing. He didn't want to hear an uneducated diagnosis. "He was at the doctor three months ago and he's healthy as a horse." Those were the doc's exact words. Trying to appease her, he laid his hand on her shoulder. "Now I'm gonna take him home. Let him rest. I'll see you later." He turned and headed for the truck before she could argue.

Chapter Thirteen

There was a reason Darla had named her establishment the Chocolate Therapist. She firmly believed that every problem could be solved with the right wine and chocolate pairing. And in Jessa's experience, she was almost always right.

In need of some serious therapy after that little exchange with Lance, Jessa marched herself down four and a half blocks and charged through the familiar stained-glass door.

A few patrons sat around the tall pub tables, leaf-peeping tourists from the looks of their designer clothing. All of them had flights of wine and an assortment of truffles to match.

Somehow just inhaling that rich, cocoa scent made Jessa feel better already.

Darla was stationed behind the counter, walking a young couple through the menu, so Jessa slunk to the far corner stool at the main bar and plopped herself down, replaying that conversation with Lance again.

He probably shouldn't be carrying ladders around any-way.

As if Luis disappearing was her fault. Her shoulders sank lower. She only wanted to help the man, and yet Lance had completely dismissed her like her opinion didn't matter at all. It wasn't just the situation with the ladder. She'd noticed the tremors, things she'd originally written off as his arthritis acting up, but now she wasn't so sure.

"Wow, who pissed in your coffee today?" Darla appeared before her with a tray of truffles and a flight of reds.

Her angel of mercy.

The woman set the trays on the counter beside Jessa and pulled over a stool. "Looked like you could use something strong, so I brought all darks and a bittersweet."

"Perfect," Jessa, said before popping one of the cocoa-dusted confections into her mouth. Then she sipped on the first glass. Closing her eyes to hold on to the taste, she swallowed. "Better already," she said with a sigh.

"You want to talk about it?" her friend asked in a tone that wouldn't take no for an answer. Who was Jessa kidding? Her face was an open comedic tragedy. She'd never been one to hide her emotions.

"This arrangement is more complicated than I thought it would be," she admitted, going for another truffle. The chocolate melted in her mouth.

"What is? Staying at a ranch with a sexy *single* cowboy while you babysit his aging father?" Sarcasm dripped from her smile. "How could that possibly be complicated?"

Yeah, yeah, yeah. She'd set herself up for this. It had all seemed so simple. Until her body and heart betrayed her and attached themselves to a man who had zero ability to commit.

"All right. This looks bad. What happened?" Darla asked, leaning her chin into her fist as though she knew they'd be there awhile.

"You have customers to take care of." And she felt more like wallowing alone.

"Beth can take care of the customers and I can take care of you." Out of all of them, Darla happened to be the most motherly. Well...if your mother liked to make off-color jokes, flirt with much younger men, and only wear shirts that showed plenty of cleavage.

"Come on," Darla prompted. "You'll feel better if you talk about it."

Not likely. But she relayed the entire story anyway, popping the truffles into her mouth and washing them down with sips of the decadent wine between sentences.

Darla said nothing. She wore the same concentrated expression she did whenever she was testing out a new recipe.

"So that's it, I guess. I think something's wrong with Luis. Lance doesn't care what I think." That about summed it up. He didn't respect her enough to value her opinion.

"Am I missing something here?" Darla leaned in, her dark eyes wide and emphatic. "Isn't *he* the one who asked for your help? For you to stay with his father and keep an eye on him?"

"Yes." Exactly. He wanted her there, but he didn't want to hear what she thought.

"Here's what you're gonna do, honey," Darla said, waiting until Jessa looked her in the eyes. "You're gonna drive back to the ranch. March that cute little ass of yours right up to Lance's front door and ask him if he still wants your help with his father."

Jessa tried to take mental notes. That sounded easy.

"Then, when he says yes—because he *will* say yes—you're going to tell him he doesn't get to ignore you. Since you are doing him a favor, he will listen and consider what you say." A grin broke through her titanium expression. "Then you tell him he's not allowed to kiss you again unless he intends to fully finish the job."

Jessa rolled her eyes. "I'll take everything else and leave out that last part."

"Come on." Darla swatted at her. "What good is taking on a second job if you can't take advantage of some of the perks?" She nibbled on a truffle. "Trust me, honey. Lance Cortez's body is one hell of a perk."

That was one way to describe it...

"Besides, maybe if you two really got it on, all this tension would go away and you'd be able to move on."

Jessa choked on a sip of wine. "I don't think so." If she was going to stick it out at the ranch until Worlds, she couldn't make things more awkward than they already were.

"Here." Darla reached into the pocket of her apron and dug out some wrapped truffles. "Take these with you. A new blend. Pop one in your mouth before you talk to him." Her eyebrows arched. "Trust me."

Jessa held out her palm and carefully examined the dark mounds of goodness. "Isn't chocolate an aphrodisiac?" Because she didn't need any help in that area. Not with Lance.

Darla simply gave her an innocent smile before she stood and waltzed away.

* * *

All the way to Lance's house, Jessa practiced. She practiced saying exactly the words Darla had given her. She practiced in a bitchy voice, an apathetic voice, then decided that was too much and tried to add a note of sympathy. All in all, she must've said the words fifty times and yet as she climbed the stairs to his front porch, her mind blanked.

But there was no turning back now. Before she could overthink it, she knocked on the door. A sudden explosion of nerves blew inside her and she quickly unwrapped the truffle that had been melting in her pocket and popped it into her mouth. Some brand of heavenly merlot leaked through the chocolate, bringing a symphony of fruity notes. *Good, fun-loving lord*, enough of these chocolates and she'd never need sex again.

The door opened and Lance stepped out. He was dressed in a faded gray T-shirt and sinfully tight worn jeans. They should be illegal in all fifty states, those jeans.

Okay. So maybe never needing sex again was a bit strong . . .

"Hi," he said, straightening as though he was surprised to see her. "Everything okay?"

Right. That was her cue. Everything was *not* okay. But she couldn't seem to manage the words. "Um." She cleared her throat so she didn't sound like Lauren Bacall. "We need to talk." Because she had stuff to say. Lots of important stuff . . .

She tried to play back Darla's badass lecture in her mind, but a steady humming drowned it out.

"Okay . . ." Lance stepped aside and made room for her to walk past him. On the way, she caught that alluring scent that seemed to cling to him. Something woodsy and sexy. *Keep going*, she reminded her feet. She couldn't stand too close to him.

"Can I get you something to drink?" he asked politely,

leading her through his family room and into the kitchen, where they'd had their little exchange earlier. Just like that morning, she positioned herself far away, on the opposite side of the kitchen island.

"No." No drinks. She had to get this over with. She braced her hands against the countertop and looked at him directly before she lost the nerve. "You don't get to ignore me," she announced, and wow, Darla would have been so impressed. She sounded *pissed*.

Lance blinked at her.

Courage bloomed. "I mean, I'm only trying to help, and you acted like I'm causing some big problem for your father. Instead of listening to me, you load him up in the car and get out of there like my concerns don't matter. Do you have any idea how worried I was?" She started to pace. Once she got going, it was hard to stop. "I searched everywhere. I ran up and down the block looking in everyone's yard, going up to neighbors' doors and asking if they'd seen him. In case you haven't noticed, Lance," she said glaring at him again, "I care about Luis, too." A silent round of applause broke out in her head. She'd done it! Without letting him get a word in, even.

Lance's eyes were darker, narrow. She braced herself for a defensive tirade like he'd thrown at her earlier, but instead he sighed. "You're right." His hand raked though his hair. "I'm sorry."

"You know what, Lance," she said before she'd had time to process the words. *Hold on.* He hadn't argued with her. He'd...apologized? Just like that? "Huh?"

"You're right." The man's normally broad and powerful shoulders seemed to have bent under some unseen weight. "I shouldn't have brushed you off."

She should be gloating. That was exactly what she'd

wanted him to say. But the clear dejection that pulled at his mouth halted the victory party. "Okay, then. Thank you." The words sounded hollow and awkward. There was no script for this. Darla hadn't told her what to say if Lance started apologizing...

"I should've heard you out. I'm under a lot of pressure right now." His jaw tensed as he studied her, almost like he wanted to say something more, but decided against it.

"Because of Worlds?" she asked, trying to read what he wouldn't say.

Instead of answering, he walked to the table and picked up a magazine, then tossed it on the counter in front of her. "Because of this."

She grabbed the newest copy of *Rodeo World News* and her heart sank at the article's title: "Hometown Letdown."

Her eyes scanned the editorial—written by an anonymous source—which detailed Lance's fall from the highest acclaim in the rodeo world. It outlined his entire career—the early years of his success, the World title years ago. Then it detailed his fall from glory. The disappointing times, the disqualifications, the fact that he'd barely even qualified for Worlds this year. *He has proven that he's not his father, the great Luis Cortez, who at thirty was taking the top score in every competition...*

"They've decided I'm done. Useless. According to the fans, my career should've ended years ago," he said, eyes fixed on the article.

"Unbelievable." The words were cutting. Degrading for a man who'd won so many titles, who'd once been a hero. She read the last sentence: "Lance Cortez was once the greatest rider in the world. Now he's one of the greatest examples of what happens when you don't know when to quit."

A stab of pain lodged itself at the base of her throat. "This is crap," she said, tossing it back on the counter. Her hand shook with the absurdity of it. "Utter and complete crap. You've given your life to this sport." And when he was winning, everyone loved him. They couldn't say enough about him. Hell, there was a whole display about him at the public library...

"Maybe it's not." He raised his head and looked at her but didn't seem to see her. "Do you have any idea what it's like to read that? To hear the world saying you're done before you feel ready?" Those fierce bluish eyes steeled. He snatched the magazine and tossed it into the trash can. "Everything I've given my life to for the past fifteen years is over."

Jessa watched him pace the kitchen, words and anger and passion converging. There was no script for this. No plan for the sympathy that spilled out from inside her. "I can't imagine what that would be like," she said quietly, wishing she had more to offer him.

Lance stopped and turned to face her. "I don't know who I am outside of it. Outside of being my father's son. Outside of the arena. Outside of that world."

She got that. Sometimes when things changed so fast, when all of a sudden life looked different than it had the day before, you had to be reminded of who you were. That's what had happened when her father passed away. She was no longer a daughter and everything in her life was up for grabs.

She closed the distance between them with purposeful steps. "You're a good person, Lance. A good son. You've taken care of your dad. You've worked your ass off and you've accomplished more in fifteen years than most people do in a lifetime." The words were softer than she meant for them to be, more weighted with emotion than the conviction she wanted to offer him. "You can win." She'd seen him out there—that will, the sheer determination that drove him. "I know you can win." She wasn't sure exactly how, but her hand came to rest on his forearm, fingers lightly curled around his skin.

"Don't touch me." He staggered backward. "Not right now." There was a warning in his tone that matched the agony in his eyes.

Her hand froze where his arm had been. "Okay." She studied him, trying to understand what he wasn't saying, but his eyes wouldn't meet hers. What was he thinking? Had she made him angry again? "Did I say something wrong?" she asked quietly. She didn't know what to say, how to ease that tortured expression on his face.

Lance finally looked up, eyes smoldering with a passion she'd seen in him only out in the corral. "You tempt me to forget all of it," he uttered. "You make me think it doesn't matter."

Shock thundered through her. She braced a hand against the countertop and gaped at him. "Wh...what?"

"God, Jessa." He half-laughed while his head shook slowly back and forth. "You don't even know how beautiful you are, do you?"

The words were so unexpected she almost didn't believe them. Lance Cortez was calling her beautiful?

He stepped up to her, and he seemed to be moving so slowly. But maybe it was just the shock of what he was saying...

"When you're here I have a hard time focusing on my training..."

Her lungs locked in anticipation exactly the way they had last night when he'd covered her mouth with his. "D-do you...want me to leave?" she stuttered. She was pretty sure that wasn't what he meant, but sometimes it was best to be a hundred percent certain.

"No." His hands went to her cheeks, his callused fingers stroking them softly. "It wouldn't matter. I'd still see you." He leaned in closer, so that his lips were inches away. "I'd still feel you..."

"What happened to wanting different things?" she sputtered, her throat aching with the desire to lose herself in the feel of his lips over hers, his hands on her body.

"Right now, I only want you," he growled, his shoulders rising and falling with heavy breaths. His hands anchored her face while his lips came for hers—*claimed* hers—ravaging them in a frenzy of desperation and need.

Every fragment of self-protection she'd managed to piece together shattered in the sheer extravagance of his hot mouth, his tongue gliding over hers, his strong hands sliding down her neck, then caressing their way down her chest.

He groaned into her mouth as he brought his hands lower, running his fingers over her breasts.

Greed surged through her, heating the blood in her veins until even her legs tingled. Everything in her core tightened in a hard pull of sensuous tension. Right now, she only wanted him, too. *Needed* him to satisfy this overpowering hunger he'd provoked in her. Taking his bottom lip lightly between her teeth, she bit down and pushed him against the counter, somehow tugging his shirt up and over his head on the way. Stealing a second, she stopped to admire him, the hard muscle of his chest, the sinewed flesh stretched over his abs. His jeans sat low on his carved hips. The bandage she'd dressed him in last night was still intact, purple bruising visible around the edges. She touched it carefully.

"I don't need a nurse right now." His voice ground low in his throat. A sexy grin flashed before he came at her again, this time bypassing her lips and launching a thrilling assault on her neck. It was melting her, his lips, his tongue on her skin. He edged her back against the wall and captured her hands in his, raising them up until her arms were braced above her.

God, her body was so tight, so ready, she needed him to free her, but before she could beg, he pulled off her shirt in one smooth motion. Kissing her lips, then her cheeks, then her jaw, he worked his arms around her, pulling her in tighter and unhooking her bra with one hand. His other hand tore the flimsy satin away from her body but she couldn't see where it ended up because the magic of his mouth and hands teasing at her nipples blurred her vision. He buried his face in the valley of her, sighing, uttering helplessly desperate little noises.

Ragged breaths stole her thoughts. Her hands raked his thick, luxurious hair as he kissed and sucked and nibbled until she quaked with need. *Now.* She wanted him to fill her, to take her. Right. Now. Her hands clawed at his belt buckle until it somehow came unclasped and she could rip open the button fly of his jeans.

His forehead fell to her shoulder as she slid her hands down his hips, pushing down his boxers and jeans, and wrapped both hands around the hard length of him. She started moving her fingers, tightening the pressure, but he grabbed her wrists and brought them back above her head, pinning them against the wall and kissing his way to her ear. "You first."

She kept her hands raised over her head as he kissed her mouth deeply, his fingers undoing her jeans and pushing them down her hips.

His hands cupped her ass, then one of them slid down and hiked up her leg until her knee was at his waist. The other hand snaked around her body, slicing through the swollen flesh between her legs in one long stroke.

"No need for that," she murmured breathlessly. She was so hot, so primed, she only wanted him to break her apart. Now.

The grin flickered on his lips again. He finished removing his jeans, pulling out his wallet and riffling through until he found a condom. Impatiently, he ripped open the package and had that thing on before he'd made it over to where she stood.

Her heart beat against her ribs, pounding blood all through her.

Lance slipped his hands under her and hoisted her up, bracing her back against the wall as he drove into her in one long, hard thrust.

The heated grinding pried a moan from her lips. Her fingers dug into his shoulders as he slid out painstakingly slow, watching her eyes the whole way. By the time he thrust again she was panting, bearing her hips down to meet the rhythm he was using to tease her.

"God, Jessa." He grabbed a fistful of her hair, taking it roughly back from her face, and kissing her harder, deeper. The motion of his hips came faster, all power and strength, surging into her, lifting her higher, grazing the hot wetness. Her legs tightened around his waist, heightening the sensations, until it was all she felt…him. Everywhere. Inside of her and outside of her. With a tortured grunt he thrust again and this time she couldn't hold on. With a cry of exhilaration, she let go, abandoning herself to the release of blinding sensations, floating atop wave after wave of exquisite pleasure.

Lance brought one hand to her face and tipped up her head. A spark seemed to bind their eyes together. He pushed into her faster, harder, until a long groan punched out of his mouth and his body quaked.

Winded, but somehow still holding her up, his shoulders slumped against hers. A lazy grin took over his lips and she leaned her head down to kiss them again. They were so decadent, those lips of his...so wonderfully sensual and giving.

Lance set her feet on the floor and kissed her back, wrapping her in tighter, pulling her naked body snugly against his, and they seemed to fit so perfectly together.

"You're somethin', Jessa Mae," he said, his hungry gaze lowering down her body.

"I could say the same about you." Not once in her life had sex been so spontaneous, so instinctual and free-spirited. So close to the movie sex scenes that she'd always thought were contrived and unbelievable.

One time with Lance and she was a believer.

He took her hands in his, towing her closer. "So that was unexpect—"

The doorbell chimes cut him off.

Jessa snapped her head to stare at the front door on the other side of the great room. "Who's—"

"Uncle Laaa-aance!" The door muffled Gracie's singsongy voice.

"What is she doing here?" Jessa hissed, pushing away from him, breaking their bodies apart.

His eyes squeezed shut. "I'm supposed to give her a riding lesson."

"When?" Not to be dramatic or anything, but one minute ago the girl could've walked in on them having sex in his kitchen!

He glanced at the clock. "In two minutes."

"Holy shit. Good God, Lance." She scrambled around the floor, rummaging through the discarded clothing.

"I'll tell her to go away," he said, his mesmerized eyes locked on her body.

"You can't tell her to go away! Put these on." Jessa hurled his pants and boxers at him. Then his shirt. *Oops.* That was her shirt. *Aha!* His was pooled on the island. She ran over and snatched it, shaking it out so she could pull it over his head.

A knock sounded on the door. "Hello?" It was Naomi! The heavy wood started to creak open.

Jessa hit the floor next to Lance, scooting her knees into her chest and hiding herself behind the island.

He finished buckling his belt with amazing precision, given their current dilemma.

"There you are," she heard Naomi say from across the room, thank the lord.

There was a pause.

"Why didn't you answer the door?" her friend asked, a familiar skepticism creeping in.

Lance cleared his throat. "Um. Sorry. I was...on the phone."

Wow, he was good under pressure. He almost sounded bored. And then there was her...her pulse was racing so fast and hard, it felt like her heart could tear out of her rib cage at any second.

"Oh."

Jessa held her breath. Would Naomi get suspicious and

come over to the island? She edged her back against the cabinets.

"Why is Jessa's truck out there?" the woman asked.

Damn her!

"Dunno." Lance snuck a glance down at her, flashing that grin so fast she almost didn't see it, then he walked away. "Looks like someone's ready to ride, though," he said. And he must've twirled Gracie around because she giggled and squealed.

Slowly, Jessa let out the breath she'd been holding. Footsteps traipsed away from her until they grew faint.

"I wore my pink cowgirl hat," Gracie chirped as the front door opened.

When it closed, Jessa let herself collapse on the floor. Staring up at the ceiling, she tried to grasp what had happened. One minute she was reprimanding him and the next she was practically begging him to ravage her. And it might have been fast but...wow. For some reason that had made it even better. It had never happened that fast for her. Ever.

Trying to breathe like a normal human, she sat up and started dressing herself. She never did this...a quickie in the kitchen with a man she wasn't even *dating*. What the hell had come over her?

Shaking her head at herself, she shimmied on her jeans.

It had to be that damn chocolate.

Chapter Fourteen

Uncle Lance, why aren't you listening to me?" Gracie demanded, waving a hand in his face. Her glittery pink nails caught the sunlight and practically blinded him.

"Oh. Sorry, buckaroo." He shook himself conscious. Normally, he wasn't one to dwell on the past, but he couldn't seem to bring himself back into the present. Not after that mind-blowing rendezvous in his kitchen. It had been so good he might never get himself out of the past. And it wasn't like Gracie needed a ton of supervision. Not on Esmeralda. The mare had been his mother's horse way back when. She was as old as the sun and lumbered along steady and slow no matter what a person did with the reins.

"I asked if I'm holding on right," Gracie said, her bottom lip pouting slightly. She sat up taller on Esmeralda's back. "Because someday, when I'm a beauty queen, I'll need to know how to hold on the right way."

He grinned at her. "You're perfect. Just don't grow up and become a beauty queen too fast."

"Too late for that," Naomi mumbled beside him. "I swear...I don't know where she got her diva tendencies."

He swung his head to give her a proper look of disbelief. "Really?"

"What?" she demanded, just like her daughter.

He gave her a dose of raised eyebrows and braced himself for a fist in his biceps, but she only laughed. "So I like pink. And sparkles."

"And drama," he added, making a silly face so Gracie would laugh.

"Speaking of..." Naomi tugged him back a step while they watched Gracie make another leisurely round along the fence. "You do seem a little checked out. Who were you on the phone with when we came in?" Her expressive green eyes reflected the sunlight. She was already gloating.

Aw hell. He was busted. Naomi knew good and well he avoided the phone like he avoided her drama. "It was a wrong number," he said, heading for the safety of Gracie's presence.

"Where was she hiding?" Naomi asked, following him closely. "And what the hell was she doing in your house in the middle of the afternoon?"

He stopped and faced her. "If only that was your business."

"Oh, it's my business," she fired back. "Jessa is my friend. I thought we were in agreement on this." Her eyes narrowed as though she was calibrating her intuition.

Shit. That wasn't good for him.

"You slept with her didn't you?"

"Technically no." There was no sleeping involved. No lying down, even.

"Damn it, Lance," she said, smacking a hand against her thigh.

"We don't say 'damn it,' Mommy," Gracie called over. "That's a bad word."

Lance busted out laughing.

"You're right, peaches," Naomi muttered through clenched teeth. "What I meant to say is, 'How could you let this happen?'"

He shrugged, waiting until Gracie and Esmeralda had ambled to the other side of the corral. "It just happened. Okay?" He still wasn't sure how. When Jessa had said those things to him, told him she believed in him, something else took over. He couldn't stop himself. Couldn't hold back. Part of him had thought that once it happened, he'd get it out of his system and he'd be able to stop thinking about her. To see her without wanting her so badly it made him ache.

Man, had that backfired. That little tryst had only intensified the thoughts, the physical response to her. Next time it wouldn't be fast and frantic in the kitchen. He'd take his time with her.

"So what does this mean?" Naomi half-whispered. "Is Jessa okay?"

"She sure seemed okay." Way better than okay, actually, given her sexy cries there at the end...

"I mean are you guys together? In a relationship?"

"Not that I'm aware of." Though they hadn't really made time to discuss the details. "This morning, she said that wasn't what she wanted."

"Of course she said that, you idiot."

"We don't say, 'idiot,'" Gracie admonished. "Remember, Mommy? It's not nice to put people down."

Lance laughed again. He loved that girl.

"Right," Naomi said behind a plastic smile. "Thanks for the reminder."

Esmeralda hobbled away from them for another spin around the corral, and Lance took the opportunity to argue his case.

"Why does everything have to be defined right now?" Hell, he and Jessa hadn't even defined anything. He sure wasn't stupid enough to discuss the terms of their relationship with Naomi before he'd talked to Jessa about it. Relationship? Wow...had he ever used that word before? Maybe not, but he didn't exactly mind the sound of it as much as he once had.

"Well, I'm just wondering what you plan to do now," Naomi badgered in her little sister way. "Maybe it's time for you to deal with your commitment issues so you can actually have a healthy functioning relationship with someone."

If a man said that to him, he might haul off and throw a punch. "What the hell is that supposed to mean?"

"'Hell' is a bad word!" Gracie informed him from the other side of the corral.

"Right," he muttered, wondering what would happen if she wasn't around to keep them all in line. "I meant to say heck." He turned to Naomi. "What the *heck* does that mean?"

"You know what it means."

"I've never met anyone worth committing to," he said. That was all. Good women were hard to come by. She couldn't blame that on him.

"No," Naomi argued. "You've never let yourself *trust* anyone. Not since your mom left."

He opened his mouth to object, but she went on. "I know you better than almost anyone, Lance. You have serious trust issues."

Anger rose like a shield. "You're one to talk." She hadn't even dated anyone since Mark took off.

Instead of lashing back at him like he expected her to, Naomi laid a hand on his arm. "Exactly. Which means I can recognize it."

The admission disarmed him. What could he say to that? "Maybe it'll never be possible for me." Maybe his mother's abandonment had jacked him up so bad, he'd never have a relationship. Maybe he didn't even want to try.

"So what're you gonna do?" Naomi asked again.

"I don't know." It wasn't like he'd planned to have wild passionate sex with Jessa. He'd been in a rough place when she walked in. And right when he saw her everything seemed better. The opinion of the rest of the world hadn't mattered so much. She might be the only person in the world who believed he could compete at Worlds. Who believed he could win one more title.

"Oh my God," Naomi gasped. "Did we walk in on you two?"

"Not exactly." The memory of Jessa crouched behind the island next to him baited a smile. That could be their secret, though.

"Is she still at your house?" the woman blurted. "You have to go talk to her! You have to make sure she's all right!"

"She's all right." And yes, he'd talk to her. Later. He wasn't going to stress about it. Wasn't going to force things. And he sure as hell wasn't taking Naomi's advice again. "But after we're done here, I'm gonna call Tucker and have him bring out Wild Willy." The bull should be healed up by now and he needed to get serious.

Two minutes before Jessa had shown up on his doorstep,

he'd been this close to quitting. But she'd given him the determination to train and to fight and to keep going.

And now, he'd do whatever he had to do to get back in that arena for one more dance.

*　*　*

She should probably leave Lance's house, seeing as how *he'd* been gone for a half hour. Jessa had managed to retrieve her clothes—which by divine intervention had been strewn around the floor *behind* the kitchen island, saving them both from a potentially awkward conversation, had Gracie happened to have caught sight of a pair of women's underwear lying out in the open.

After she'd dressed, she'd teetered around the kitchen on her still wobbly legs doing the few dishes that sat in his sink and walking around the living room like it was a museum, noting the beautiful prints hanging on the walls and the detailed woodwork and the titles of the vast array of books he kept on the shelves.

You could tell a lot from a person's book collection and Lance's was extensive. He liked local history and cowboy legends. Political thrillers and classics like Dostoyevsky and Tolstoy. She wouldn't have pegged him for an intellectual, but then again, Lance was too layered to be pegged at all.

She knew she should leave, but she liked being there. She liked learning about him. She liked seeing how he organized his space and life. And yes, she liked *him*. Not just the sex, which had been…wow. But it went deeper than that. His tenderness. His loyalty. His sensitivity. He obviously didn't want people to see those things in him, but she did.

The more time she spent with Lance, the more he revealed his true heart to her—the one that had been wounded and left him wandering, much like her own. And the more she saw of his heart, the more she realized she could love this man. If she let herself. She could. That was a dangerous prospect. Because she already knew he didn't let himself love anyone.

So she had to leave. Walk out his door and not look over her shoulder. Accept the fact that things wouldn't be the same when they saw each other again. He'd be distant like he had been earlier. And she'd be unsure.

Steeling herself, she made her way across the sitting room and peeked out one of the front windows to make sure she wouldn't be caught. If she was honest, part of her hoped Lance would come back and find her there, that they could hold on to the connection that had rooted them together when he was looking into her eyes, holding her body, kissing her. It would be like a scene from a movie. She'd swing open his front door and he'd be standing there, just about to walk in because he'd realized he couldn't live without her. Then he'd kiss her and while he was kissing her, he'd sweep her into his arms and close the front door—locking it this time—and maybe he'd take her on the soft leather couch...

But Lance didn't come. No one was outside, and while disappointment weighted her chest, that was perfect because at least she wouldn't get caught sneaking out of his house. Quickly, she opened the door and slipped outside, eyeing the horizon for any glimpse of Naomi or Gracie. Once on the front porch, she ran, stumbling down the steps before racing to her truck. She climbed inside and sped down the road to Luis's house, taking an extra few seconds behind the wheel to collect herself so she didn't seem harried and panicked.

Carefully she straightened her hair, glancing in the

rearview mirror. God, she *looked* like she'd just had passionate sex. Her face was even still flushed.

Shaking her head at herself, she climbed out of the truck. Hopefully Luis wouldn't notice...

"Hey there." The man himself greeted her from the rocker on his porch as if he'd been sitting there waiting for her. He'd even brought out little Ilsa. The pig was curled up on his lap.

"Hi," she said brightly, going to sit by him. She loved his rocking chairs. He'd made them himself from the thick aspen branches he'd found on the property.

She settled in and stared out at the view. If Luis had noticed her sitting in the truck trying to primp herself back to normal he didn't let on. And he didn't ask why she'd just driven down from Lance's place.

He probably didn't have to.

"So how's our patient?" she asked, reaching over to ruffle Ilsa's ears.

"Seems fine." He handed over the pig and Jessa nuzzled her against her cheek. Ilsa still smelled like the scented shampoo she'd used when she'd bathed her.

The rocking chairs creaked for a few minutes before Luis turned to her. "Sorry I left Green's house like that," he said gruffly.

"No." She patted his hand. "It's okay. I probably overreacted." That morning already felt so long ago. So much had happened between then and now.

"Nah. It was a fool-headed thing to do," he mumbled as though angry at himself. "There's no excuse."

That was what bothered her. Luis never did fool-headed things. He'd always been careful and deliberate. Not rash. He thought things through.

She glanced at him, trying to interpret the disheartened expression on his face. A glimmer of intuition flared inside her and she drew in a breath of courage. "Are you sure you're okay, Luis?" Because he'd left the ladder in the middle of the yard. And even if he *had* been angry at Hank or even if he'd really been thirsty, he would've propped up the ladder near the house or left it in the garage...

"There's nothin' for you to worry about," he said, clearly not answering her question. He could've simply said no, but he hadn't.

Worry weaved itself into the threads of her fears. "If there was something, you could talk to me about it, you know." Though she hadn't meant for it to, emotion laced the words. "I could help you figure it out." She would do her best. In so many ways, this man was all she had left of her father. They'd shared years together. He'd known her dad even better than she had.

Luis rocked in his chair, his old hands gripping the armrests. "It's tough getting old," he finally said. "Feeling your body give out on you."

Give out on you how? she wanted to ask. What wasn't he telling her?

"Makes you think about all the things you'd do differently." He was gazing off to the mountains in the distance as though seeing a whole lifetime of regrets play before him.

The sad pull to his lips clawed at her heart. "What would you do differently?"

"Too many things to list," he said with a humorless laugh. Then he turned to her, those eyes watery and sure. "But you know what I regret the most?"

"No," she said, her eyes locked on his.

"I regret not making things right with Lucas." He looked

away from her again, but not before she saw tears brighten his eyes. "I was hard on him when they came for him after he set that fire. Said a lot of things I can't take back."

For the life of her, she could never imagine Luis saying a mean or hateful thing to anyone. But he'd likely been different back then.

"I'm sure he knew you were just angry," she offered. The fire had tarnished the Cortez family name. It divided the town, hurt Luis's own legacy...

"I told him I never wanted to see his face again." The old man's hands trembled and his grip on the armrests seemed to tighten. "But I didn't mean it. Didn't mean one word of it."

"Of course you didn't," she whispered, hidden tears thickening her throat. This poor man. Living with that grief all these years. "Have you ever tried to contact him?"

"I've kept up on him." His gaze lowered to the ground. "Through other people. He works for the McGowen Ranch down in Pueblo. Tried to send him a letter years back, but didn't ever get a response." Another garbled laugh sputtered out. "Can't say I blame him. He's built a good life for himself. Even after all he went through. No thanks to me."

"You're the one who gave him a foundation," she pointed out.

"But I should've been there for him," he said sternly. "I should've helped him through it."

"You did your best." In her estimation, every parent screwed up in some way or another. But Luis loved his boys. That was obvious. "I mean, look at Lance. And Levi. You have a great relationship with them."

"Not with Levi. He don't ever want to come home. Stays out on the circuit, away for his training." The man looked at her with that hollow gaze again. "Truth is, Jessa, my boys deserved better than me. All of 'em."

That wasn't the truth. Not at all, but she knew nothing she could say would take away his regrets. The only peace he'd find was through rebuilding what he'd lost with Lucas.

"I sure wish I knew 'em now." She barely heard the words above the rocking chair's creaking. "The way I know Lance."

"I'm sure they wish they knew you, too." God, she'd give anything to have her father. He wasn't perfect, but he was still her dad. Surely Lucas felt the same way. "I wish they knew you the way I know you. I wouldn't have survived this past year without you, Luis."

That earned a small smile. "I could say the same," he said, patting her hand. "Buzz would be proud of you."

"Thanks," she whispered. So much of who she was had come from her father. And that had to be true for Lucas and Levi, too. No matter what had happened in the past, Luis was still part of who they were. No one knew that better than her. Her dad's death had left a gaping hole in her life, but Lucas and Levi still had their father. And what if something was wrong with him? Then they might not have him much longer. She studied the tremors in Luis's hands. What would Lucas and Levi think of the symptoms Luis was obviously battling? Would they say it was nothing like Lance had?

Apprehension built inside her. They should at least know what was going on with their father. If Lance wouldn't tell them, someone else should.

She stood abruptly, cradling Ilsa against her chest. "I should go inside. I have some work to do." For starters, she had to contact the McGowen Ranch and talk Lucas into coming home.

Chapter Fifteen

Lance slung his dirty chaps over the stable's gate and brushed the dust off his jeans. He'd had a stellar training day, no doubt thanks to Jessa's pep talk and the extracurricular activities that had taken place in his kitchen. God, had it been almost a week ago? Ever since, he'd been out in the corral at the first light of dawn until well after sunset, occasionally breaking to eat or drink something. All in all, he'd managed to bring up his time consistently to eight seconds. His ribs and back might be aching now, but it was a good ache, familiar and dull. The kind of ache that told just how hard his muscles had been working.

Every day, Jessa's words had driven him. Along with thoughts of seeing her, being with her again. He fantasized about her all the time, but instead of distracting him, those thoughts now drove him. She drove him. But between his training and her and his dad's long hours at the shelter, he hadn't seen much of her. A wave here. A quick hello there.

It was not enough for him. Anticipation had built all week, and he couldn't hold it off anymore. Soon, he'd leave for Worlds. He couldn't miss out on spending some time with her before then.

So, desperate or not, he'd decided to show up at Luis's for dinner tonight. Then maybe the two of them could get out for a walk. Or a drink back at his place.

He hauled his gear onto the shelf and stepped out of the barn into the dusky evening. The sun was already sinking behind Topaz Mountain, giving the world that surreal pinkish glow. *Perfect mood lighting*, he thought as he trekked down the driveway to his dad's place. He really should stop at home and clean himself up, but if he did, he'd risk missing dinner. Besides, maybe after dinner, he could convince Jessa to soak in the hot tub with him. Just the two of them. Under the stars...

He almost broke into a jog as he veered to the left and over the small rise to Luis's house. Jessa's truck sat out front, but there was another truck, too. One he didn't recognize. Wouldn't be right of him to barge in on dinner if they had company, but he couldn't turn around, either. Not knowing Jessa was there. Not when the thought of seeing her made him ache like this.

So he hurried up the porch steps and pushed through the door without knocking. "Hello?" he called inside the entryway, where he stopped to stomp the dirt off his boots.

"Lance?" Jessa careened around the corner and hurried down the hallway.

"Hey." He let his eyes drink her in, the soft hair that framed her face, the smooth skin that had felt so soft against his lips. She wore tight tapered jeans and a long white shirt, casual, but seductive in his eyes. She could be wearing a snowsuit right now and she'd look seductive. God, he could come apart just looking at her.

But then he noticed the thing at her feet. He blinked. A small black-and-white pig. On a harness and leash? "Uh. What's that?"

Jessa looked down as though just remembering she was taking a pig for a walk. *In* the house. "Her name's Ilsa."

"*Ilsa?*" He laughed.

"Yeah," she shot back. "What's wrong with that?"

"Just seems like there's something more suitable. Like Ham Bone. Or Pork Chop. Or Bacon," he said, eyeing the critter like he was hungry.

"Don't even think about it." Jessa scooped the thing up into her arms. "I didn't know you were coming," she said, glancing nervously over her shoulder.

"I wanted to see you." More like *had* to see her. Had to touch her again. Had to kiss her. He closed the distance between them and skimmed his hand along her lower back, nudging her—and the pig—closer.

A pink glow lit up her face just like the sunset outside.

Voices drifted from the kitchen but he tuned them out. He didn't care who was in there. He needed a minute alone with Jessa. Now if he could just figure out how to ditch the pig . . .

"Lance . . ." Jessa's breathing had quickened, and her eyes seemed as hungry as he felt. But then she glanced back over her shoulder again. So distracted. He'd have to take care of that right now. First, he gently took the pig out of her hands. The thing squealed and squirmed as he set it on the floor, then it took off down the hall. Which was fine with him. They could discuss the pig later.

"I missed you," he said, sliding his hand up her back and pressing her against him, meeting her lips in the middle. The need for more of her swelled, threatening to rip him apart. He kissed her harder and her mouth opened to his, a small moan stirring the lust he felt into a fervor.

"Wait," Jessa gasped against his lips. She pushed back. "Just hold on. We have to talk."

Right. Talk. He suppressed the urge to take her hand and tow her back to him. They probably should discuss what happened between them. He still hadn't apologized for abandoning her in the kitchen. "Sorry I had to run out on you," he said. "I didn't want to. Believe me." If she needed proof, he'd be happy to offer it. All she had to do was feel him against her to know how much he wanted her.

"It's fine," she said brushing him off with another glance toward the kitchen.

Right. The company. The voices. They'd go. In a minute. But first he had more to say. He had to tell her what her words meant to him. How they'd given him a second wind. "I wanted to thank you for—"

"You don't have to thank me," she interrupted quickly. "But I think we should talk about—"

"We can talk about it later. Right now, there's something you need to know."

"Jessa!" The call came from the kitchen and knocked the air out of Lance. That voice. He hadn't noticed when it was subdued and murmuring, but now ...

No. No way. That couldn't be Lucas.

But his brother appeared in the hallway. No longer a kid, instead a man with familiar blue-gray eyes. His hair was shorter and neater than he used to keep it, and he looked clean-cut for a rancher.

Shock bolted Lance's heart to his ribs. What the fuck was he doing here?

He said nothing as his brother walked toward them. It'd been so long since he'd seen him. Since they'd agreed it would be best if he cut ties and never came home...

"This is what I was trying to tell you," Jessa whispered. Or maybe she didn't whisper. Maybe Lance just couldn't hear past the blood pounding in his ears.

"Surprise," Lucas said with a healthy apprehension weighting his eyes. They'd agreed he wouldn't come back. It was best for Luis that way. Best for Levi. For the family.

The shock of seeing him started to thaw. "What're you doing here?" he asked, carefully controlling his tone. He didn't want to startle Jessa, but what the hell? No warning or anything. He'd just decided to show up after years of being away?

Lucas and Jessa shared a look. They *shared* a look. And suddenly, he had a bad feeling.

"I called him," Jessa said firmly. "And Levi. I asked them to come home."

He didn't look at her. Couldn't. His eyes were locked on Lucas. "You should've told me." He wasn't sure if he was saying it to his brother or to the woman he'd slept with.

Lucas stepped up to him. "I didn't have time. Jessa told me she's worried about Dad and I wanted to come as soon as possible."

His head turned slowly, like someone was cranking it click by click, until he was staring at Jessa's worried expression.

"Luis and I had a talk," she said, wringing her delicate hands. "And he said how much he missed Lucas and Levi. Given the incidents he's had lately, I thought it would be nice for them to come."

Nice. She'd thought it'd be nice. Well, she didn't know a damn thing about his family. About what they'd been through. Anger prickled his neck. What the hell had she been thinking? She should've talked to him first.

He faced his brother. "Can you give us a minute?"

Lucas slipped in front of Jessa. It'd been years, but obviously his brother could still recognize when he was pissed.

"Don't blame her. She's trying to help." Lucas seemed unfazed by all of it. But then he'd always been the mellow one. The one who didn't worry, who didn't carry the weight of the damn world on his shoulders. That's why they'd decided it should be him who went away. By the time he was fourteen, Levi had already gotten caught stealing twice. He'd thrown a rock through the ice cream shop's storefront and shattered the whole damn thing. He'd been so angry at Luis, who was always out with a different woman, and he'd taken it out on the town, targeting the places where the women worked.

That's why Levi had gone to the stables that night. He'd seen Luis messing around with the commissioner's wife. So he found some gasoline and a lighter. He hadn't meant to hurt anyone, he'd said later. He was just so angry.

Lance didn't have anger issues, but he was stressed all the time. So he drank. Had two underage tickets under his belt by then. But Lucas...he was too serious for stuff like that. Serious about school. Serious about following the rules. Serious about Naomi.

So they were sure he'd get a slap on the hand. Community service. Maybe house arrest. But they hadn't counted on the judge being the commissioner's golf buddy. It seemed he wanted to punish all of them. When Lance heard they were charging him as an adult he'd tried to beg the judge to reconsider. But the man had dismissed him like he was a stray dog, threatening to have him arrested if he came back.

"It was time for me to come home, anyway," Lucas said quietly, as though he'd resigned himself to whatever consequences this little reunion would bring. "Don't you think? Dad's getting older. I want to be around."

Maybe it *was* time. But he should've had a say in it. They should've discussed this, planned out how it would go. Jessa had taken that away from him. As if she had some right to play the healer for his family. His jaw pulled tight as he stared back at Lucas. "Give. Us. A. Minute."

His brother looked at Jessa.

"It's fine," she said, glaring back at Lance and crossing her arms in a fighter's stance. She wasn't afraid of him and it was a damn good thing because they were going to have a serious chat about her butting into his family's business.

Lucas anchored a hand on Jessa's shoulder and gave it a squeeze before walking away. Seeing him touch her like they had some kind of bond didn't do much to douse the anger.

As soon as his brother disappeared Lance faced her. "You had no right to do this."

"What do you mean I had no right?" she fired back. "This isn't about you, Lance. This is about your father."

Exactly. It was about his father and Luis already carried enough guilt. How'd she think he'd feel when he learned Levi had started that fire because he'd caught him in the stables with someone else's wife?

"Do you know what Luis told me?" Jessa asked.

It must've been a rhetorical question because she hardly paused.

"He told me that his biggest regret in life is not making things right with Lucas. Did you know that? Do you know how much it tears him apart?"

He almost laughed, it was so absurd. That was nothing compared to what he'd regret if he found out the truth. "You don't understand." The anger had drained away, but he tried to hold on to it. Anger was easier than the other emotions he was going to have to deal with now that the past stared him in the face. "You have no idea what you've done."

"What *I've* done?" she repeated, her face hardened with indignation. "What I've done is brought your brothers home. And you know what? When your father saw Lucas walk through that door, he was so overjoyed he cried. He *cried*."

That revelation freed the guilt. It flowed out, overpowering everything else. He'd done what he thought was best at the time. They all had. Hell, they were only kids. The day they'd hauled Lucas away, they'd all changed, each trying to atone for it in their own way. Luis stuck around the ranch more, cooked dinner, helped with homework, all the stuff he'd been too distracted to do before. And Lance and Levi trained, taking out the anguish in the arena as if that could bring back their brother.

But it was too late.

"Lance…" Jessa moved closer, studying him carefully. "Why are you so upset? Don't you want your brothers around? Tell me how this could possibly be a bad thing."

"I can't." They'd never told anyone. They'd tried to protect their father. But there'd be no way to keep the secret now. It would come out. Everything would come out.

"What's up, bro?" Levi bounded down the hall and captured him in a bear hug, lifting him off his feet. Typical. They'd always protected him from ever having to deal with reality. He was the party boy, the fun one. Which was ironic, considering he had more to lose right now than any of them.

"Let's head out to the old watering hole and celebrate the

fam getting back together." Levi slung an arm around him. "What do ya say? Drinks are on me."

Jessa still stared at Lance, her eyes focused and intent, demanding an explanation, but he turned away and clapped his long-lost brother on the back. "As long as you're buying, I'm in."

God knew, he could use a drink right now.

Chapter Sixteen

*W*ell, this is awkward. Jessa sat in the back seat of Lance's extended cab, wedged between Levi and Lucas. No one had said a word since they'd gotten in the truck, the jovial tone of the reunion between Luis and his two sons deadened by the eldest son's stony-faced silence.

For the life of her, Jessa couldn't figure out what she'd done wrong. Lucas and Levi had obviously simply needed an invitation to come home. When she'd called them, both of them had been concerned about their father. Both had said how much they'd missed him. *And* Lance, for that matter. Levi had gotten away from Oklahoma as soon as he could and Lucas had picked him up at the airport in Denver. Now all three Cortez boys were together with their father and no one was saying a damn word.

She drummed her fingers on her thigh. She'd had a feeling Lance would be surprised to see his brothers, but this is not how she'd pictured things going. Lucky for them, she'd always been good at breaking the ice.

Scooting forward, she peered between the seats at Lance and Luis. "So how was your training today?" she asked politely.

"Fine," he muttered.

"Training?" Levi, who was sitting behind his oldest brother, ruffled Lance's hair. "Decided not to hang up the spurs yet, eh, old man?"

"Nope." Jessa watched Lance's grip tighten on the steering wheel.

"So, Lucas," she turned to him, hoping to steer the conversation away from Lance's retirement status, which had definitely been a sore subject lately. Having Levi poke fun at him would not end well. "How are things at the McGowen Ranch?" she asked, as if she had some sort of clue as to who the McGowens were and what they did on their ranch.

"Good," he answered dutifully, but he was eyeing Lance as though watching for an impending explosion.

Another silence fell like a heavy blanket, smothering her visions of a happy reunion for a father and his sons. Yes, okay, she was a bit idealistic, but she'd imagined chatter and laughter, not a wary distance. Even Levi, who was always the life of the party, seemed subdued, staring out the window like he wanted to avoid eye contact with everyone else.

Caving under the weight of their solemnity, she remained silent, pulled out her phone, and dashed off a text to Cassidy, Naomi, and Darla.

Meet me at the Tumble Inn ASAP. In case they didn't feel the urgency, she added a *911.* Those girls had known the Cortez family longer than she had, *better* than she did, considering Naomi had seriously dated Lucas before the fire. And Levi had been like a brother to Cassidy before her brother Cash had passed away. Maybe they could help her figure out what was going on, because she was not making progress.

Good thing the Tumble Inn was only an eight-minute drive from the ranch or she might have had to start singing to break up the silence. *No one* would want to hear that.

When they arrived at the bar Lance took his sweet time parking, she couldn't help but notice.

They all piled out of the truck like they were about to head into a funeral instead of the lone country western bar in town.

She hadn't been to the Tumble Inn since the whole Cam fiasco, and now she remembered why. A huge banner hung below the sign.

Two-step Night.

Fabulous. Since she was young, Jessa had absolutely no rhythm. Her mother had attempted to put her in ballet, but after she'd knocked into another girl and caused a domino effect of toppling ballerinas during her first recital, she'd walked away from dancing and never looked back. In college, she'd tried to take a ballroom dancing class and had somehow managed to break her partner's foot during the fox-trot, so nowadays she pretty much avoided any establishment that centered around dancing.

The Cortez brothers followed their father to the entrance, but she hung back.

"I let some friends know we were coming," she called. "I'll wait for them out here."

"Sounds good." Levi was the only one who acknowledged she'd said something. "Make sure you save me a dance when you get in there," he called, working his magic charm with a wink and dimpled grin.

The man had no idea what he was asking. "Sure, I'll do that," she lied. Once she got inside, she planned to order a nice, easygoing glass of chardonnay and park it at the bar for the evening. No breaking her friends' feet tonight.

The men disappeared into the bar right as Darla and Cassidy pulled up in Darla's BMW. Naomi was a few minutes behind, probably because she had to find a sitter.

They all congregated in the middle of the parking lot.

"You told us you'd never step foot in this place again," Darla accused. Though she'd had only a few minutes' warning, the woman had somehow managed to primp and change into a low-cut shirt that displayed her cleavage.

"I didn't exactly have a choice," Jessa said, gathering them in closer. "Lucas and Levi came home and—"

"What?" Naomi interrupted, suddenly appearing pale. "What do you mean Lucas came home?"

Jessa took in the shocked—no, make that horrified— look on her friend's face. Guilt churned her stomach. She should've warned them, but she'd gotten so caught up in the plans, not to mention a crazy week at the shelter. "I called them because of the issues Luis has been having," she half-whispered, watching the doors. "He told me he missed them, so I got in touch and asked them to come home."

"I'm shocked Levi actually listened to you." Cassidy's normally sweet tone had turned bitter.

Oh boy. She really should've thought all of this through. Darla was the only one who didn't seem disturbed by the Cortez family reunion.

The woman elbowed Jessa. "Way to go, girl. About time we got a few hot men back in this town."

Naomi whirled and made a move toward her car. "I'm not going in there."

"You have to!" Jessa caught her arm before she could escape. "It's been horrible since they got home. I thought I was helping but ever since Lance saw his brothers, they're hardly speaking to each other. I don't understand."

"They went through a lot," Naomi informed her, wrenching out of her grasp. "We all went through a lot when Lucas got sent away." Emotion trembled through the words.

But that was a long time ago. It wasn't too late to work things out, even for Naomi and Lucas. Once she got over the shock of it, surely she'd be glad he was back. "I need some support in there, girls." She had no idea what to do. How to make everything better. She needed backup.

"I'm in." Cassidy sighed. "As long as there are margaritas involved." She patted Naomi's arm sympathetically. "It's not like we'll have to talk to them. In an hour this place'll be packed."

"Yeah. We can hang out on the dance floor," Darla offered with a wicked gleam in her eyes. "Or on the mechanical bull."

"I'm not going near that thing." Jessa would leave bull riding to the professionals. "Besides, we'll be too busy to dance. We have to figure out how to get these guys talking so they can get past their issues for Luis's sake." All the man wanted was for his family to be together, and thanks to Lance's rude entrance, they couldn't even give him that.

Before anyone else tried to bail, she swung one arm around Cassidy and the other around Naomi.

"I don't know how I'll face Lucas," Naomi said through a steady exhale. "I mean, I haven't seen him since he was arrested..."

"Can't blame him for not coming back." Darla followed them across the parking lot. "The whole town wanted to hang him."

Maybe back then, but things were different now. Jessa held open the door for everyone. "I never knew him that well, but he seems like a great guy." He'd been so polite to her on the phone, kind even. A little soft-spoken. Thoughtful with words.

"He was always a great guy," Naomi said, pausing before the open door as though gathering courage. "That's why I never believed he'd set the fire."

"It was years ago." Cassidy took Naomi's arm and led her inside. "And things were bad before the fire. They all fell apart after their mom left."

Was that all it was? Were they all still dealing with the resentment of their abandonment? Jessa stepped in behind her friends and let her eyes adjust to the dim lighting. Most of the tables were empty, as it was still early for the party crowd. Thankfully, no one was out on the dance floor, though music played in the background.

The Cortez men had all claimed stools at the bar, sipping their beers while seeming to avoid eye contact.

"Look at them," Jessa grumbled. "After years apart, they have nothing to say to each other?"

"Sure they do," Darla said, sashaying her way to the bar. "Men just need a little help getting the conversation going, that's all."

Cassidy followed Darla, but Jessa had to practically push Naomi. When they finally made it to the bar, her friend slipped behind her as though searching for protection and stared at the floor.

"Well, well, well," Darla said, her voice shattering the

icy silence. "It sure is good to see you boys back in town." She pulled up a stool next to Levi and plopped down. "My friends and I would like a round of margaritas, Rico," she called to the bartender.

"You got it, *mi bombon*."

Ah yes. Every male in town thought of Darla as their chocolate sweetheart. She charmed them all, just like she was doing now, chatting easily with Levi and Lance about the ale they were drinking.

Not everyone was listening, though. Lucas had turned around and was staring steadily over Jessa's shoulder.

"Naomi?" He rose slowly and bypassed Jessa.

Offering Naomi courage with a smile, she stepped aside to retrieve her margarita from the bar and to give them a minute, but stayed close enough that she overheard the nerves in her friend's tone.

"Hi, Lucas," Naomi almost whimpered.

"Hi," he murmured with this sort of awed expression on his face. It was the sweetest thing Jessa had seen since Lance had told her she was beautiful. Since he'd looked at her the way Lucas was looking at Naomi now, like he wanted to take in all the details and remember them. Like he was powerless to look away.

That lost-in-the-moment look only proved that the Cortez men might be made of steel but underneath that, they had this raw passion that ran much deeper than their brooding stares. She should know. She'd felt that passion seep into her skin and set her whole body ablaze...

Levi appeared in front of her. "How about that dance?" he asked, holding out a hand like a true Southern gentleman.

"Oh. Um." Her cheeks pulsed. "Actually, no one's even out on the dance floor."

"So?" She remembered that grin from her high school summers. The grin no girl could deny...

Jessa glanced at Lance. He'd set down his beer and was watching her, his jaw set in a hard, angry line.

And wasn't that just typical? He seemed to be pissed off at her. Again. It'd become a pattern with him. One minute he was ravaging her up against a wall and the next he was glaring at her in a pout. Well, screw that. She faced his younger brother. "You know what? I'd love to dance with you." He was fun, after all. And wearing boots, which would hopefully protect his feet from any significant damage.

"You're not gonna regret this," he promised, leading her to the dance floor.

She laughed. "Let's hope *you* don't regret it." She probably should've had him sign a waiver or something.

"Not possible," he insisted, taking her hand in his and guiding her in front of him. He wrapped one arm around her waist and drew her close, but thankfully left a respectable distance intact.

The song was slow and twangy. Surprisingly, Levi made it very easy to follow his moves.

"You're a good dancer," she said, grinning up at him as he swayed her around the floor.

"I find that dancing only helps my chance at winning a woman's heart," he replied good-naturedly.

"I find that dancing only increases *my* potential for a lawsuit," she confided.

He laughed. "Not when you're dancing with the right person." In perfect rhythm with the music, he twirled her, then reeled her back in and dipped her low. With her head upside down, she caught a view of Lance, who still sat at the bar, but he'd turned around and made it no secret that he was watching her. The dangerous look on his face dried up her mouth.

Levi pulled her back up and resumed their graceful two-step.

Not even the look on Lance's face could deter her from finishing this dance. It actually gave her the perfect opportunity to figure out what was going on between the brothers. She smiled at Levi. "Things seem a little tense between you guys."

"Do they?" he asked, spinning her again.

"Yeah. Did you all have some big fight or something?" she asked innocently. They must've had some kind of falling out. If she could figure out what happened, maybe she could help them get past it.

His charming grin dimmed. "Let's just say some of us have moved on from the past and others are stuck in it."

"You mean—"

"Mind if I cut in?" Lance had left his post at the bar and somehow sneaked up behind her.

"Course not," Levi said, opening his arms to let her go. "She's all yours."

There was never a truer statement spoken in the English language. Seeing Lance, hearing him ask to dance with her, kindled that familiar music in her heart, and yes, right now she did belong to him.

He stepped against her, resting that large skilled hand on the very small of her back, pressing her close to him, not leaving any of the respectable space intact. His other hand swallowed hers, but instead of holding it loosely the way Levi had, Lance threaded his fingers through hers and fused their palms together.

The heat from his body seemed to flow into hers as he

moved against her, sparking her lower half until she wasn't sure she could keep her feet from stumbling.

The song was something sweet and light. Lance moved with the music effortlessly, not carefree and entertaining like Levi had been but deliberate and precise.

There were a few other couples on the floor, but now they seemed so far away under the power of Lance holding her.

"I can't stand seeing you dance with my brother," he said against her hair, as though he was too afraid to look into her eyes.

Jessa could hardly find her voice. "Your brother was the only one talking to me." Somehow the words managed to hold a good amount of attitude, which was impressive, seeing as how all she wanted to do was melt into him.

"I was surprised," he said, pulling back to look at her. His eyes were serious but they held glimmers of light. "Shocked. And I wasn't the only one." He turned to gaze across the room to the table where Lucas and Naomi sat.

"I didn't think about that," she murmured. "I was only thinking about your dad. About how much he seemed to regret what happened with Lucas. I wanted to help."

He smiled, and that smile had the power to change the world. Or at least her world.

"I know," he said, sliding his hand up her back, caressing in a way that made her want to arch into him. "And things'll be fine." He said it like he might be trying to convince himself.

"Why aren't things fine now?" she asked.

His hand slipped low to her waist again, guiding her as they swayed to the music. "It's complicated."

"Families usually are." Or at least, that's how she imagined a family would be. "But even with the complications,

I'd give anything to have a family." She'd always longed for that, a place where she fit. And he might not be willing to tell her any secrets, but she'd give up all of hers if it helped him smooth things over with his family.

Lance stopped moving and gazed down at her. "Don't you have your mom?"

"She's all I have." Not that she could complain, but..."I always wanted brothers and sisters." She used to beg her mother to have another baby. Or adopt.

He pulled her close again, and now his gaze strayed. "Yeah, well, having siblings isn't always easy. Trust me."

"I do trust you." But he didn't trust her. Lance was good at kissing her, touching her, and, let's face it, giving her more pleasure than she'd experienced with any man, ever. But when it came to trusting...that wasn't exactly his strength. "No matter what it is, you guys can work through—"

"Jessa?" Cassidy tapped her on the shoulder. "Can I have a word with you real quick?"

"Oh." She hesitated. They were finally getting somewhere with a real conversation. "Right now?" she asked, hoping her friend would give her a minute.

"Yeah," Cassidy said apologetically. She leaned closer. "We have a situation."

The gravity in her tone forced Jessa to pry herself away from the luxurious warmth of Lance's body. "Be right back?"

He nodded and reluctantly let go of her hand.

Cassidy pulled her away, in the direction of the ladies' room.

She almost had to jog to keep up. "What's wrong?"

"Naomi. We need to get her out of here."

"Why—"

As they neared the ladies' room, the sound of sobbing echoed.

Jessa turned the jog into a sprint. "Good God, what happened?"

"Not exactly sure," Cassidy said as they pushed through the door.

Jessa ran to the open stall and found Naomi sitting on a vacant stool with her face buried in her hands. "I can't do this," she wailed. "I'm sorry. I wasn't prepared to see him."

Lucas. Jessa sank to her knees in front of her friend. "Oh, honey. I'm the one who's sorry. I should've told you he was coming." She knew how much Naomi still thought about him. She should've prepared her for this.

"I loved him so much," Naomi sniffled. "We never had any closure. And he's the same. Kind and thoughtful." She swiped at the tears on her face. "God, I could've married him. We would've been happy. Instead I made a mess of my life with Mark."

"You didn't make a mess of anything," Cassidy insisted, squeezing into the stall with them. "You have a beautiful daughter."

"Exactly," Jessa agreed, squeezing Naomi's hand. This had obviously been a bit too much for her. "Don't worry. We'll take you home. You don't have to stay."

They could stop by Darla's place and calm her down with some wine and chocolate. That always seemed to do the trick when one of them was upset about something.

"Okay," Naomi said, tearing off a piece of toilet paper to dry her eyes. "Just give me a minute to get myself together."

"Take your time, honey." Jessa sighed, her heart aching. Looked like a conversation with Lance would have to wait.

Chapter Seventeen

Lance moseyed over to where Lucas sat at a table. Last he saw, Naomi had been sitting with him, but she seemed to have disappeared. "Hey." He pulled out the chair across from his brother. He'd seen him only a few times since he'd left town. They'd met in Denver, just for a quick lunch or dinner if one of them was going through, but they'd always tried to avoid the subject they now had to discuss. And after they'd avoided it so long, he almost didn't know how to bring it up. "Where'd Naomi go?" he asked. Wouldn't hurt to keep avoiding it a little longer.

"Not sure." Lucas stared blankly at the full beer bottle that sat in front of him. "Didn't realize how much I'd missed her until I saw her."

"Yeah, I wondered about that." Couldn't have been easy for Naomi, either. Back in high school the two of them were pretty hot and heavy, and then one day Lucas was just gone. From all of their lives.

"She looks good," his brother said, taking a drink.

"You never ended up with anyone else." And Lucas could've found someone by now. He didn't seem to carry the baggage Lance did, even after prison. He wasn't bitter about any of it. Their mother leaving, the heavy-handed sentence he'd received...

"I've gone out with plenty of women," Lucas said, staring at his hands.

Guilt bore down on Lance once again. If they hadn't thought up that plan to protect Levi, he had no doubt Naomi and Lucas would be together right now.

"Wasn't in the cards," his brother said with a shrug.

"Because we wrote the cards." He'd never regretted it more than he did right now. When Lucas was gone, he didn't have to think about it, didn't have to face the consequences of covering for Levi. "I'm glad you're back." That surprised him. The shock had worn off and now, sitting across from him, he could see having Lucas around again. Once they waded through the shitstorm that would surely hit.

"Nice try." His brother took another sip.

"I wasn't expecting to see you. But Jessa's right. Maybe it's time." Maybe he wouldn't be able to move forward until he'd dealt with some things from his past. Something about dancing with Jessa, kissing Jessa, making love to Jessa, made him want to move forward.

"I'm not staying long."

That might be his fault. "You can stay. We'll figure out how to tell Dad everything. We'll fix it." Or at least they could try.

Lucas stared past him. "It's not worth going back. Not now."

One hour ago, Lance'd thought the same thing. But Jessa had changed his mind. "He should know the truth."

"And what would that mean for Levi?"

Lance glared over at their younger brother, who now had yet another woman out on the dance floor. What did that make? Four in the span of a half hour? Their little secret obviously didn't weigh on him. Likely because they'd always protected him. He'd never dealt with the consequences for anything.

"What would the truth mean for you?" Lance asked, looking at Lucas directly. It'd mean he'd be exonerated. At least in the eyes of the people who still despised him, who still held the fire against him. Hell, he'd noticed the whispering when people had started to trickle into the bar. The pointing. They'd all taken tables far away from Lucas—the hellion who'd burned down the stables and managed to kill the town's dreams of ever hosting another rodeo.

People in small towns like this held grudges. They wouldn't forget.

"We should keep things the way they are." Lucas had never been one to stir up trouble. "I'll stay for a while, spend some time with Dad, and lay low. Then I'll go back to work."

Except Lance couldn't get Jessa's words out of his head. She'd give anything to have a family—to have siblings—and his were right here, but he couldn't stay connected with them. "We have plenty of work around the ranch. Been leaning toward starting our own stock contracting operation." Once he retired, it would be a natural next step. "There'd be a place for you, too." Given that Lucas had gotten the McGowens' operation out of financial ruin and made it one of the most lucrative in the region, his brother could probably run things a hell of a lot better than he could.

Lucas smirked at him. "No one in this town wants me back. You know it as well as I do."

"That would change if everyone knew the truth."

"Then they'd go after Levi. That's why we protected him. And Dad." He leaned forward, his eyes never looking so much like their father's. "I knew what I was doing, Lance. And I'd do it again, too."

Of course he would. But if he had it to do over again, Lance wouldn't let him. He wouldn't let someone take the fall for something he didn't do. For something he never would've done. "I think we should tell Dad at least. Even if no one else ever knows."

"Not now. Not this trip." His brother looked over at their father, who was arguing with Gil about something. "Maybe I'll pop back in before winter for a few days." He shifted his gaze to Lance. "Jessa seems to think something's not right with him."

"He's fine." Lance brushed aside his concerns. "Just getting ornerier in his old age, that's all. He seemed happy to see you—".

"Look at you guys." Levi bounded over and grabbed a chair, turning it backward, then straddling it. "Why aren't you dancing? Plenty of women to go around."

"Not really in the mood to dance," Lance shot back. Unless it was with Jessa, but she'd been gone a while now.

"So…" Levi eyed him. "You and Jessa, huh? Should've picked up on that earlier. I wouldn't have asked her to dance if I'd known."

Nope. Not going there with Levi. He'd been gone all these years, had hardly called at all, and now he thought they could talk about Lance's personal life. They had a hell of a lot to work through before they got there. "There's nothing to know," he said with a look that would hopefully shut him down.

"Right," Levi mocked. "I saw how you were dancing with her. It was a lot different from the way I danced with her."

"Maybe you suck at dancing." He attempted to slip a warning into his tone.

"I definitely don't suck." Confidence had never been one of Levi's weaknesses.

"Are you two together?" he pressed.

"No." Technically they were not together. Not that they'd had any time to discuss their status . . .

"Do you want to be together?"

None of your damn business. But he went with the easier answer. "No."

"Sure seems like there's something there to me," Levi taunted. His brother had never known when to quit.

"We hooked up once. It was nothing." Classic code for *I'm not discussing this with you.* Especially when he hadn't even discussed it with her.

"So you wouldn't mind if I asked her out?" Levi clearly knew the answer to that question, judging from the smart-ass grin on his face. "'Cause she was into me once. We made out behind the barn the summer of our sophomore year, you know."

"Actually, Levi, it was behind your garage."

Shit. Lance checked over his shoulder and sure enough, Jessa stood behind them, no longer looking soft and sweet. Nice of Lucas to alert him to the fact that the woman they were talking about stood a mere four feet away. How long had she been there?

She stayed where she was, keeping her distance from the table. "I just came to tell you I have to go." The words

sounded hollow. "See you later," she said to no one in particular, then spun and met Naomi, Cassidy, and Darla near the
doors.

"You might want to follow her," Levi said, clapping
Lance on the shoulder. "She seems pretty pissed."

Thanks to him. Instead of indulging his brother's arro-
gance, he leaned back into the chair. "She's fine." He hoped.
Not much he could do about it after he'd told them he
wasn't interested. He'd talk to her later. Right now . . . "We
have to figure out how we're gonna tell Dad the truth about
the fire."

That got Levi's attention. His back went straight as a
fence post. "What do you mean?" Yeah, now he wasn't playing the funny, spoiled-boy role. He looked worried.

"We're not telling anyone anything," Lucas said, as if that
was the end of the discussion.

But it wasn't. Not if Lance had anything to say about it.

* * *

She really should've seen that coming.

Jessa tuned out her friends' chatter and sipped her wine,
fighting to keep her expression neutral. Difficult, considering the humiliation still burned inside. Of course Lance
wasn't interested in her. She'd known that in her head. To be
fair, her judgment had been severely compromised by that
heated passion they'd shared in the kitchen, but still. This
was Lance Cortez. Self-professed commitment-a-phobe. So
it was silly that a tiny seed of hope had embedded itself so
deeply in the overly fertile lands of her heart. Silly and not
a mistake she would make again. Lance seemed to excel in
sending mixed signals, but she wasn't up for games any-

more. And she would not wait around for a man to figure out what he wanted.

"How was it seeing Levi again?" Darla asked Cassidy. They'd all gotten settled back at the Chocolate Therapist, Naomi squished between Jessa and Cassidy on the comfy couch.

"He hardly said two words to me." Cassidy laughed. "I think he's afraid of me."

"He hasn't changed at all," Naomi chimed in. "He was always the party boy. Always the center of attention. Never wanted to deal with anything real."

Though Cassidy was a few years younger than them, Jessa had always wondered about her and Levi. At one time, he'd been so close to her family. "You two never dated?" she asked. Out of everyone here, she had the least background information, seeing as how she'd been around only in the summer.

"God, no." Cassidy's nose wrinkled with disgust. "I thought Levi was hot. Like every other girl in town. But Cash wouldn't let me near him. He was over at our place all the time. Especially after his mom took off. But after the accident..." The words trailed off.

"You want my opinion, I think he took Cash's death hard." Darla leaned over and topped off all of their glasses. "It seemed like he blamed himself."

Cassidy's expression darkened. "It wasn't his fault. It's the sport. It shouldn't even be legal." Since her brother had been killed during a competition, Cassidy despised bull riding, though on a normal night—a sober night—she rarely talked about it.

"You okay, Jessa?" Naomi asked her. "You're awfully quiet." Her sweet friend happened to be doing smashingly well after a potent elixir that consisted of prosecco and lavender liqueur.

"I'm great," she fibbed. She didn't need a chorus of *I told you so*'s ringing out all around her.

"Sure looked like you and Lance were having a *wonderful* time," Darla mentioned with a probing arch of her eyebrows.

"Yeah," Cassidy agreed. "Things were looking pretty hot between you two on the dance floor."

She evaded all of their curious stares with a long, savoring sip of wine.

"Of course they were hot," Naomi said with a giggle. "Once you have sex with someone, you tend to dance a little differently." Her eyes went wide and she slapped a hand across her mouth.

"Sex?" Darla repeated.

"Sex?" Cassidy echoed.

Well. Apparently it was harder to keep secrets at the Cortez Ranch than she'd thought. Calmly, Jessa set down her wineglass. "He told you?" she asked Naomi, wishing her voice didn't sound so strange. It was one thing for her to be humiliated in private, but now his rejection was about to go public.

"No." Rounding her eyes apologetically, Naomi rested a hand on her leg. "He didn't tell me. I figured it out and he didn't deny it."

That was *so* much better.

"Oh my God!" Darla wailed. "I can't believe you've been holding out on us!" She scooted to the edge of her seat as though the suspense was killing her. "When? Where? How?"

"How?" Jessa rolled her eyes. "*You* of all people know how it works, Darla."

Her friend laughed. "Truer words."

"But we *do* need details," Cassidy urged impatiently.

"Fine." They'd never let her get out of there until she spilled her guts. Might as well get it over with. "We were in his kitchen. *Talking.* And..." The images of him holding her body flashed. She couldn't stop them. They took her over...

"And?" Darla prompted.

Jessa sighed. "And it just happened. One minute we were talking. The next kissing. Then..." She let them fill in the blank.

"In the kitchen?" Darla mock-whined. "I love kitchen sex!"

"Pretty hot," Naomi agreed. "Not that I would remember. It's been years for me, ladies," she said a bit sloppily. "I mean *years.*"

"Okay, honey. Maybe we should take a little break from this." Cassidy slipped Naomi's drink out of her hand and set it on the coffee table. "So are you two together, then?" she asked Jessa. "Because it sure looked like it."

"No." She steadied the tremble out of her voice. "We are *definitely* not together. He doesn't have feelings for me." She'd simply walked in on him at a vulnerable moment and they'd both let down their guards.

"How do you know he doesn't have feelings for you?" Naomi asked too loudly. "Because I've known him forever and I have to say...he looks different when he talks about you."

"No. Trust me." Jessa tried to laugh, but it felt more like a gag. "I overheard him tell his brothers he doesn't have feelings for me. So..."

"Are you serious?" Cassidy nearly spilled her drink.

"What an ass," Darla said, looking truly pissed on her behalf.

"I doubt he would tell his brothers if he *did* have feelings for you." Naomi reached for her glass again, her glare warning Jessa not to take it away. "It's not like they're close or anything. You saw how they were acting tonight."

"Maybe not, but we all know how Lance is." Hell, he'd told her himself how much he loathed the prospect of committed relationships. "You're the one who told me to avoid this in the first place." Then she'd thought maybe she really did simply want a one-night stand. Something easy, uncommitted. But that hadn't worked for her. Because now she knew what it could be like with Lance, how he could touch her and satisfy her and how his gaze could pierce her heart. She knew, but she couldn't have him. Lesson learned.

"Wow." Cassidy shook her head slowly back and forth. Being as busy as she was, working two jobs and going to nursing school, she didn't have a lot of her own drama. But she always confessed to loving other people's drama. "So now what're you going to do?"

"Nothing." Jessa shrugged, as though it would really be that easy to move on. "It's fine. It was fun and everything, but I'm not looking for someone like Lance, anyway." Besides, he'd gotten what he wanted. Now he'd probably leave her alone.

"Well you can't *stay* there," Darla scoffed. "For God's sake, here you are doing him a favor and he totally takes advantage of the situation."

"It's not his fault." She wasn't some naïve teenager. She'd wanted it. She'd wanted him. And the sad truth was, she still did. Even hearing those words play back in her head. That's why she had to leave the ranch. She couldn't see him every day. Not the way her soul seemed to crackle to life whenever he was near.

No. She had to walk away. Ever since she'd gone to stay

with Luis, she'd felt like she was part of a family, but it wasn't real. "You're right." She took in a breath of courage. "I need to move back home. Lucas and Levi can help out now, keep an eye on Luis."

"Exactly." Darla refilled her wineglass. "If Lance can't see what a treasure you are, he doesn't deserve you anyway. If you ask me, the best one out of that bunch is Lucas."

She had a point. While Lance seemed suspicious and closed off and Levi was capricious, Lucas was serious and quiet, but also tender, given what she'd seen when he'd been with Naomi earlier. "He really seems like a good man," she said to Naomi. "Maybe you two could reconnect..." Someone had to find a happy ending in this whole thing. And no one deserved it more than Naomi. Not after what she'd been through with her ex.

"No." Her expressive green eyes teared up again. "He's only here for a short time. Then he said he's headed back to the McGowens' place." She blotted her eyes with the sleeve of her shirt. "He seems happy. Like he's built a good life for himself down there."

A good life, but maybe not the best life. From the way he'd looked at Naomi, Jessa could swear he'd give up everything to be with her. "He wouldn't want to come back?" she asked. "Even to be with Luis?"

"He's convinced no one in town would want him back here." Naomi sighed. "Not after everything that happened."

"But that was years ago," Cassidy said. "Surely everyone's over it by now."

"Ha." Darla rolled her eyes. "Not around here. They wouldn't trust him. They'd be watching his every move. Sorry, honey. But I don't blame him for not wanting to come home."

"It's okay." Naomi finished off her drink. "It's not like we even know each other anymore."

"Except you still feel a connection to him." Jessa didn't usually resort to stating the obvious, but how could Naomi give up that easily?

A smile brought life to Naomi's eyes. "He was my first love. So I'll probably always feel connected to him."

"That's exactly why you should give it a chance," Jessa argued.

"You watch too many Hallmark movies," Darla said in her dry way.

"Maybe I do." But those stories kept her heart searching for something real and true. And not just for herself, either. "I think if you have a chance at finding true love, you should take it." No matter what. While the rest of them rolled their eyes and laughed in their *Oh, Jessa* way, she studied Naomi. She had no doubt the woman was scared. She'd been burned in the worst way possible, and now she didn't want to even consider the possibility that the man she loved might still be in love with her, too.

That was okay, though, because Jessa wasn't afraid. She had no problem launching her own secret investigation into the possibility. She had plenty of experience with these things. All she had to do was talk to Lucas.

While she might be surrounded by cynics, she still believed. No matter what happens in her own life, a true romantic never gives up on love.

Chapter Eighteen

Jessa zipped up her duffel and did a quick sweep around the room. She'd managed to shower, get dressed, and pack her things all within twenty minutes. The voices and breakfast noises from downstairs had lit quite the fire under her.

From the sound of things, all three brothers were downstairs with their father.

Levi had crashed in the other main floor bedroom of Luis's house and Lucas had stayed at Lance's place, she found out after she finally made it home around one o'clock in the morning.

Not home.

This was not her home. Luis was not her father. And Lance, while a good lover, was not boyfriend material. So, yes. It was time to go. She had to do this fast. Like ripping off a piece of medical tape that had gotten tangled in her hair while she was attempting to bandage a wounded squirrel with a major attitude problem. It'd happened to her only three times, but it hurt every time. She'd learned from experience, the faster you ripped, the faster you got through the pain.

Bravely, she stepped into her flip-flops before kneeling down to clip Ilsa into her harness. "Time to go home, lil' sweetie." She patted the pig's head affectionately. At least she wasn't going home alone. "We'll have so much fun. We can make popcorn and watch movies. You'll love it." Holding the leash in one hand, she hoisted her bag onto her shoulder. Eventually she'd have to come back for Ilsa's crate, but she wasn't about to ask for help loading her car.

Keeping her spine straight under the guise of confidence, she walked regally down the narrow staircase with her adorable little piggy and halted in the kitchen.

The men were all there together, and they were four peas in a pod. It wasn't their looks so much as their mannerisms, the way they ate, the way they sat hunched slightly, laid back and comfortable. She was glad to see they weren't silent strangers anymore, but talking easily about the ranch.

"I can help get things started," Lucas was saying. "At least from a distance. If you need me to consult on any purchases or—"

"Oh, hey, Jessa." Levi was the first one to notice her.

Lance straightened and turned around.

She looked through him. "So, the fumigator people let me know that my house is done." She gripped the suitcase strap tightly in a fist. "Which means Ilsa and I can move back home and you guys can have the place to yourselves again."

Lance's chin dipped forward slightly as he studied her from across the room. She didn't let her gaze settle in his.

"Thanks for letting me stay, Luis." She quickly led Ilsa over and planted a kiss on the man's cheek.

"Not a word about it." He reached up and pulled her into a half hug that dangerously weakened her resolve. "It's great having you here, Jessa," the man said, cutting a stern look at his firstborn. "Don't be a stranger, now."

"Why don't you stay for breakfast?" Lucas offered, rising to pull out another chair for her.

She swallowed hard. The threatening tears heated her throat. "Actually, I should get going so I can drop off my things at home before I head to the shelter." She turned before they could read any trace of sadness on her face. "But I'm sure I'll see everyone soon." Without a more formal goodbye, she stooped to pick up the pig and walked out, keeping her head low as she made her way down the porch steps. "Here we go." She opened the driver's-side door and settled a snorting, grunting Ilsa on the passenger seat. As she loaded her bag into the back, the screen door banged open behind her.

She didn't turn around. Didn't have to. She could feel Lance behind her, feel him looking at her. Unable to face him, she climbed into the truck next to Ilsa and slammed the door shut. But the damn window was open, and before she could peel out he leaned in to gaze at her with those perceptive silvery eyes. "I'm sorry," he said, slanting his head convincingly. "For what I said last night. I didn't mean...well...it wasn't what it sounded like."

Jessa kept her gaze centered on the windshield. She couldn't look at him or he'd see everything. "It's fine," she insisted, shoving the key into the ignition. "You don't owe me an apology." Technically, he didn't owe her anything. That one morning in the kitchen, she'd told him she wasn't interested in a relationship, either. She'd pretended to be just as detached as he could be.

"Come on, Jessa." His hand rested on her thigh and sent sparks shooting up her chest. "Levi was being an ass. Okay? I was just trying to shut him up."

"Sure. I get it." She moved her leg so his hand fell away, so he couldn't influence her with his touch. "The kitchen thing was..." Incredible. Impressive. Ravishingly hot. Not that she'd admit it right now. "...Fun. But you don't owe me anything. It just happened. Not like I'm expecting you to change your whole philosophy on relationships or anything." A humorless laugh slipped out. "I mean, I knew what I was signing up for. It was only a one-time thing and you—"

He pressed a finger against her lips to quiet her. "Let me take you out."

"What?"

"On a date." He paused as though the words had surprised him, too, but then he nodded. "Yeah. I want to take you on a date."

"A date?" she repeated through a laugh.

"Yes. Is that so hard to believe? Isn't that what people do when they like someone?"

"People, yes. But you?" As far as she knew, Lance had never *dated* a woman. He'd met women at bars. He'd met women out on the circuit. He'd for sure had women in his hotel rooms. But he didn't date.

"Why not me?" he demanded with that sexy half grin that had gotten her into so much trouble in his kitchen.

"Listen..." She raised a hand to stop him right there. "I know what you're trying to do here."

"Do you?"

"Yes."

He leaned in through the window, moving his face dangerously close to hers. "What am I trying to do, Jessa?"

Seduce her again. He was so damn good at it. Those eyes. They could practically undress her. "Um." She attempted to focus. "You're trying to make me feel better about things. Because let's be honest. I don't do one-night stands. Or one-afternoon stands. I've never done that. So maybe you feel bad and now you think you're obligated to take me on a date, but—"

This time he lowered his lips to hers.

A sharp breath sliced through her lungs, cutting them open. God, it was the best kind of pain...

He pulled back. "Or maybe I just want to take you on a date." His eyes held her in a daze. "Maybe I don't want you to go home. Because that means I won't see you every day. And maybe I *want* to see you. Maybe I was just trying to get my asshole brother off my back. And maybe I really do like you, Jessa. Did you ever think of that?"

One kiss and her lungs were nearly out of air. "That possibility hadn't occurred to me," she whispered, which brought back his grin.

"Please go on a date with me, Jessa. I'll beg if I have to. I'll get down on my knees right outside your truck."

He was teasing her again and damn it, she couldn't *not* smile at the man. "Um..."

He draped his arms over the open window and leaned close again. "Pretty please?" Tenderness crinkled the corners of his eyes. "You have to know I'd never tell Levi anything about how I really feel. We don't have that sort of relationship."

That was true. From what she'd seen, the eldest and youngest Cortez brothers had some competition between them.

"Let me take you out. I'll make it worth the trouble." The

promise in the words matched the one beaming suggestively in his eyes.

"Okay." She relented through a put-out sigh, hopefully covering the sudden rush that had her body humming. "Sure. Why not? I *guess* I'll go on a date with you."

His eyes brightened. "When?"

Yeah, like she had any ability to think through her schedule with her heart racing this way. Let's see...he was leaving on Friday for Vegas, so..."Thursday?" she tried.

His lips quirked with exaggerated disappointment. "That's a long time to wait."

Okay, so it didn't matter what she had going on. Based on her kitchen experience with the man, she'd cancel everything. "Wednesday?"

"Much better," he murmured, giving her lips a long, sexy glance. "I'll pick you up. Six o'clock." He glanced at Ilsa. "Leave Pork Chop at home and wear jeans."

Before she could ask him why, he walked back into the house.

*　*　*

He could get used to this. Having his brother home. Lance tossed his gloves onto the stable's shelf. He'd been out training this morning, and somehow with Lucas out there, things had gone smoother than they had in a long time. Not that Lance didn't appreciate Tucker, but Lucas had a way with animals. Somehow he'd calmed Wild Willy at the right moments and gotten his engine going when necessary. "Thanks for helping out today," he said, hanging the halter on a nail.

"You've still got it, you know." Lucas paced the length of the bull run, seeming to inspect it. "Same thing that made

Dad great." He ran his hand along the rotted fence railing. "Even with this shitty setup, you've got the perseverance. You can get the win this year."

"Hope so." Lance joined him near the fence, noticing for the first time how shitty it was. "Haven't had much time for keeping things up around here lately." That wasn't his thing. The equipment. The facilities. He wanted to ride. He wanted to raise bulls. "We're gonna need help getting our operation off the ground. Can't do it myself."

"I can make some notes while I'm here. Look around and give you suggestions." Lucas stuffed his hands into the pockets of his Wranglers and strode out of the stables and into the sunlight.

Lance followed. It was a hot day for the elevation. Had to be at least eighty. He slipped off his hat and swiped at the sweat that ran down his temples. "I'd sure appreciate it." He'd appreciate it even more if his brother would stay on at the ranch. He could use the expertise. But he knew when to push and now was not the time.

After latching the stable door, he followed his brother down to the driveway.

"Where's Levi anyway?" Lucas asked. "He could get his lazy ass out here and work on some of the fences for Dad."

"Think he finally went to bed." After Jessa had left the Tumble Inn last night, Lance hadn't seen much of a point in hanging out, so he'd brought Luis and Lucas home. Levi, of course, had wanted to stay. Hadn't come home until dawn, when they were getting breakfast on. Always the life of the party. Some things never changed. Lucas knew that as well as he did. When it came to the ranch, they wouldn't be able to count on Levi for much other than scoring them free booze.

"Things okay with Jessa?" Lucas asked as they neared Lance's place.

Other than the fact that he had no fucking clue what he was doing? "Think so. I'm taking her out on Wednesday." That was a real shocker, even to him. When he'd seen her loading up her bag in her truck, desperation had washed over him. He'd felt like he was losing her. Which was insane considering he'd never had her in the first place. At least not officially.

"You're taking her on a *date*?" his brother repeated with a low whistle. "Wow. So it's serious then."

The mocking tone hoisted Lance's defenses. "It's a date. Not a marriage proposal."

Lucas stopped walking and faced him. "Have you ever met a woman you *wanted* to take on a date?"

Sure. Of course he had. He scrolled through recent history. Okay. So it'd been a while. "Haven't had much time to date," he pointed out. He'd been too busy building a career.

"You don't have much time now," his brother countered. "But you're making time for this date."

Damn Lucas's insightful, philosophical nature. He never could be just another ordinary guy who stuck to safe topics like sports and rodeo gossip. He had a point, though. Lance had never bothered much with real dates. "Jessa's different." Than any other women he'd ever met. Or slept with. She didn't try too hard. Didn't fake it. She was genuine and empathetic. Honest. Real... Damn, he was whipped.

"Seems to me like she's worth a date," Lucas said, grinning as though he'd read all of Lance's thoughts. "Dad already loves her, you can tell that much. She's like the daughter he never had."

"She loves him, too." Took care of him exactly the way a daughter would...

"She worries about him," his brother said pointedly.

That knot of tension pulled in his neck. "And I keep telling her he's fine." If there was something to worry about, Luis would tell him.

Lucas rubbed at his forehead. Something he used to do when he was nervous.

"What?" Lance asked.

His brother gazed past him, out to the mountains. "He has tremors. I noticed during breakfast. His hands shake. Sometimes his head, too."

"He's gotten old." Not to be a dick, but his brother hadn't been around. He didn't know. "His arthritis flares up sometimes. That's all it is." He'd seen the tremors, too. Asked his dad about them, even. "He's almost seventy."

"You sure it's not more than that?"

Before he could answer, Naomi's car bounced up the driveway and parked in front of her house across the way.

The door opened and Gracie jumped out. "Uncle Lance! Uncle Lance!" She sprinted over and launched herself into his arms.

He swung her up into the air and twirled her around before setting her feet back on the ground. "Hey there, Gracie. Where've you been?"

"I was at my art class!" She held out a paper in her hands. "Look! I drew a picture of you riding Wild Willy."

Lance bent to study the paper, gawking at the fatheaded stick figure as though it were a work of art. "Wow." As he stood, he happened to catch a glimpse of Lucas.

His brother stared at Naomi as she walked toward them.

"Who are you?" Gracie asked, pointing a finger at Lucas.

Naomi approached looking downright spooked, so Lance answered for her. "This is my brother. Lucas."

The girl sized him up with a long glare, her lips puckered as though deep in thought. "So you're sort of like my uncle, too?"

That brought a smile to Lucas's face. He knelt in front of her. "Sure. I'd be happy to be your uncle." He stuck out his hand. "It's very nice to meet you, Gracie. Your mom is an old friend of mine."

The girl's eyes went wide. "Did you know my dad, too?"

"Oh no, honey. He didn't." Naomi lied. Mark had been Lucas's best friend in high school. Naomi's face flushed and Lance had never seen her look so flustered. "Why don't you go and get your backpack out of the car. Okay?" She sent the girl off with a light pat. "I'll be over in a minute and we can have a snack."

"Okay!" Gracie shot away from them, bounding over the ground like a happy golden retriever.

Naomi faced them, but she wouldn't look at either one of them. "Sorry about that. She's never met a stranger."

Lance stayed quiet. She definitely wasn't apologizing to him.

His brother stepped closer to her, still looking at her like she was some sort of goddess. Lance almost shook his head. And Lucas thought *he* was pathetic with Jessa.

"It's okay," Lucas said. "I'm glad I got to meet her. She's beautiful. She looks so much like you."

The compliment was met with a cold shoulder. Naomi turned. "I should get going. Gracie is always starving in the afternoon." She started to walk away, but Lance couldn't let her.

"Wait." He hooked a hand onto her shoulder and steered

her back to them. "I was thinking maybe you could sit down with Lucas and show him the books."

Her normally rosy face looked colorless. "Oh."

"He'll be consulting on our stock contracting operation," he went on before she could say no. "Might be good for him to get an idea of how our budget is allocated."

"Sure." It came out in a nervous whoosh of air. "Uh." She stared at the ground. "Yeah. Maybe this afternoon. Just...just stop by whenever." She turned and hurried away.

She hadn't even made it to her door when Lucas punched him in the arm. "Why the hell did you do that?"

Seemed Lucas didn't like people interfering in his love life, either. "It won't kill you two to spend a little time together."

Lucas glanced over at Naomi's house. "Spending time with me might kill *her*, from the looks of things."

Naomi had definitely been rattled. But not because she hated Lucas. "And why do you think that is?" Lance asked in the same mocking tone Lucas had used on him earlier.

"Same reason no one else wants me around here," his brother muttered. The moron.

Lucas turned and started for Lance's house.

Lance followed him up the porch steps. His brother had lost everything because of a decision they'd made when they were kids. He'd lived through the hell of prison time. Of being blackballed by his hometown. If anyone deserved something good, it was Lucas. "She might be worth coming back for."

His brother's back went stiff the way it used to before they'd start throwing punches. "I can't live here under a label. I'm not like you. I don't want to put myself out there for the judgment. Down at the McGowens' place, I have my freedom. I am who I am. Not the kid who screwed up." A small smile reminded Lance of Luis. "And I'm not one of the Cortez brothers. Not the son of Luis Cortez. No offense."

"None taken." Lance got that. Not wanting the labels. Hell, he'd been labeled his whole career. First as a superstar who was following in his great father's footsteps, now as a has-been.

It sounded good, having that freedom. Setting your own expectations instead of trying to live up to everyone else's. For years, the risk of failure had stalked him, driving him to become what the world needed him to be.

And now, it almost felt like it was too late to become anything else.

Chapter Nineteen

So…she was going on a date. Lance was taking her on a *date*. With Ilsa trailing behind her, Jessa pushed through the door of the shelter in a starry-eyed sort of wonder that made everything seem lovely and clean. She hardly noticed the dingy floors or the peeling drywall. The smell of dog food and animals.

She was going on a date!

"Wow, someone's chipper for a Monday morning." Xavier, her night shift guy, was hunched at the computer with his hand plastered to the mouse like he'd been in that exact position all night. Probably playing Dungeons & Dragons or something. Not that she cared. As long as someone was here to answer phones and take care of any animals that came in, he could do whatever he wanted.

Jessa floated over to the desk gracefully—probably looking like Grace Kelly in *High Society*. Well…minus the glamorous dresses, makeup, and heels. But those things weren't practical for taking care of animals and cleaning out kennels. Giving up the fantasy, she plopped down in the chair next to Xavier and pulled Ilsa into her lap. "Can I help it if it's a beautiful morning?" She swept an arm toward the streaked, grimy window. "I mean look at it. The sun is shining. The sky is so blue and perfect." That was how the world had looked ever since Lance had officially asked her out earlier this morning.

He eyed her travel mug suspiciously. "What'd you put in your coffee this morning?"

"Oh, Xavier." She sighed happily. "I don't need anything in my coffee. I'm just reveling in the beauty of the day." It wouldn't hurt him to get out and enjoy the sunshine. That long black hair of his made his skin look so pale...

"I'm headed out." He shut down the computer and shoved some books into his camo messenger bag. "No calls last night."

"Okay," she sang, scratching behind Ilsa's ears. "Enjoy the day! Maybe you should go for a hike or something. Get a little exercise."

He looked at her like she was suggesting he jump naked into a frigid mountain lake. "Why would *anyone* want to hike?" he asked in his bored monotone. "The only way I would ever hike is if the zombie apocalypse happened and I had to escape."

"That's a cheerful thought," she said, humming the sweet melody that seemed to radiate from her heart.

With a pronounced roll of the eyes, he grunted a wretched goodbye and trudged out the door, ducking his head as though anticipating the sunlight with horror.

Poor man. All he needed was a lovely goth-leaning Dungeons & Dragons princess to brighten up his world. Maybe she should start an online dating profile for him...

Instead, she logged on to the computer and checked her email, then updated the shelter's Facebook page with an adorable picture she'd snapped of Ilsa. Which gave her an idea...

Now that she'd left Luis's house, she couldn't possibly take Lance's money if he happened to win the competition. Even if she did, that wouldn't help her build a long-term donor base. It would only offer a quick, temporary fix, which was all her father could ever seem to find. *But*... if she could launch some type of brilliant social media campaign, maybe she could reach out to donors all over the country. She could have her old MBA study group help her out. Back in school, they'd worked on that kind of thing all the time together. Marketing had been her weakest area, but maybe the rest of the group would offer some pro bono work to beef up their own PR.

Her fingers tapped the keyboard excitedly as she typed out an email. Maybe they'd even know a developer who could build her an online donation page...

The door swung open, sending in a lovely autumn-scented breeze. Jessa pressed send and inhaled deeply, waving at Evie Starlington, who should have been a glamorous actress with that name, but she wasn't. She was a stained-glass artist. A recent transplant from Denver. Jessa had gone to her art show at Darla's place a couple of months ago and she'd hit it off with the woman right away. She was in her mid-sixties, but as hip as a teenager with her pink-streaked hair and bohemian clothing. Today, she wore a gauzy skirt and a peasant blouse with rainbow-colored tassels.

"Good morning," Jessa called, rising from the desk. She set Ilsa on the floor and the pig scurried quickly underneath the desk to hide. She was still working on socializing her.

"It is a good morning, isn't it?" Evie replied, snuggling a ball of fur tightly against her chest. "It got even better when I found this little charmer hanging out on my couch this morning." She held out a familiar cat. The very cat Jessa had rescued from a tree the other day.

"Oh, Butch." She took the cat out of the woman's hands.

"I have no idea how he got into my house," Evie said. "I did leave a window open last night..."

"Well, for being an inside cat, Butch here likes to go on adventures. Don't you, boy?" She held up the cat and he licked her nose as though he remembered her as his savior. "I know the owner. Hank Green. I can call him and have him pick him up." And in the process of returning the cat, shoot down every pass he made at her...

"If you wouldn't mind, that would be appreciated." The woman reached over to scratch behind the cat's ears. "Though I have to say, I did enjoy my short time with him. It was nice sharing coffee with someone. Even if it was someone else's cat."

A pang of sympathy dimmed her own happiness. Poor Evie. She seemed lonely. Her husband had passed away last year. That's why she'd moved away from Denver. She needed a new start, she'd said.

"Here." Jessa held out the cat. "Why don't you hold him while I call Hank?" And actually, the woman could stick around and meet him. He definitely wasn't Jessa's cup of tea, but he wasn't much older than Evie and they were both single.

While Evie sat in a chair gushing over Butch, Jessa hurried to the phone.

"Y-ello," Hank answered.

"Hey, it's Jessa. Butch is here at the shelter."

"What?" The word hurled through a dramatic gasp. "Why, I didn't even know he was gone!"

Uh-huh. Sure. He'd probably sent Butch out again and was getting ready to call her. Despite that, she smiled. Hank was lonely, too. And she knew how that felt. "Miss Starlington brought him in. Do you know her?"

"No. I can't say that I do."

"She's a wonderful woman. New to town." She battled the urge to start listing off all her best qualities. Shouldn't work too hard to sell her. "Somehow Butch managed to climb in her window."

Movement scratched on the other side of the line. "Well, thank her for bringing him in, will you?" he said dismissively. "I'll be right over. Then maybe we can grab a cup of coffee together..."

"Actually, you can thank Miss Starlington yourself," Jessa said before he could finish asking her out. "I'll ask her to stay until you get here."

"But—"

"See you soon!" With an extra flourish, she clicked the off button, then tossed the phone on her desk. "Hank will be over in a few minutes," she called to Evie. "Can I get you a cup of—?"

The door swung open again. *Wow*, busy morning. Jessa turned, expecting an animal situation, but instead Luis ambled in.

She popped up from her desk. "Hey, Luis. I wasn't expecting you today. Not with Lucas and Levi home."

His eyes didn't meet hers. In fact, his head stayed low enough that she could hardly get a look at his face. "I need to talk to you," he said quietly, too seriously.

The happiness that had been floating inside her all morning turned to stone. "Oh. Sure. Of course," she sputtered. She picked up Ilsa's leash and started walking toward the back room, but then noticed Evie watching them. She paused. "Have you met Evie?" she asked him. "She's new around here. An artist from Denver."

"Pleased to meet you," he said in his gentlemanly way. He crossed the room and held out his hand. The two of them shook.

Jessa tried to smile past the panic bells clanging in her heart. "Luis Cortez is..."

"I know who he is," Evie said with quite the blush. "I followed your career for a long time. It's so wonderful to meet you in person." The warm smile the woman offered him was rewarded with a humble grin.

"My career ended years ago," he said, his tone brushing away all of those famous belt buckles he'd earned.

"Maybe so, but you'll always be a legend," Evie said kindly, and suddenly Jessa regretted inviting Hank Green over.

Luis was still smiling when he shoved his hands into his pockets and strode toward the employee lounge.

Jessa followed, tugging Ilsa along behind. Whatever he wanted to say, he didn't want to wait. "Evie, Luis and I are going to have a chat in the back. Can you wait for Hank to come and pick up Butch?"

"Of course." She settled back into the chair. "I'm happy to."

They'd hardly cleared the door before Jessa turned to Luis. "Is everything okay?"

He faced her directly, steeling his hunched shoulders. "Truth is, something's not right. It hasn't been for months." His old hands folded in on themselves, fingers weaving together.

"Wh-what?" Her legs trembled, forcing her to sink to the beat-up leather couch. She swept Ilsa into her arms, holding her close for comfort. The pig nuzzled her snout into Jessa's neck.

Luis sat in the chair across from her, his expression resolute. "I get dizzy sometimes. Lose my balance. Other times I'm confused..."

The bottom dropped out of her lovely happy morning. "Oh, Luis..." *No. Please.* She couldn't do this. She couldn't face the thought of losing him, too.

He shifted, but his gaze still held hers like he was forcing himself not to look away. "When I dropped the ladder in Green's yard...I got disoriented. Couldn't remember what I was supposed to be doing. Don't even know how I ended up down on Main Street."

Don't cry. No crying. She touched a finger to the corner of each eye to catch the tears before they fell. "Have you been to the doctor?" she asked, holding her voice together with a thread of denial. Maybe he wasn't sick. Maybe he really had just been dehydrated that day...

"Yes," he said, abolishing her hope. "A couple times. The doc's done some tests. But he wants me to see a specialist in Denver. A neurologist. On Thursday."

A neurologist? This time there was no stopping the tears. They slipped down her cheeks one by one. She could be strong for him, but she couldn't promise not to show emotion. "Do you need me to come?" she half-whispered, trying to get a handle on her squeaky tone. "I can talk to Lance—"

"No." The firm denial cut her off. "I want you to come. No one else. I'm not telling Lance."

She shot to her feet, holding tightly to Ilsa, her pulse racing. "But Lance should know. He'd *want* to know."

"Not yet," Luis said stubbornly. "Not until I get a diagnosis. He's training. I can't distract him from what he needs to do."

"But..." She sank back to the couch, the gravity of what he was asking too much weight to bear. How could she not tell him? How could she go on a date with him and not tell him his father might be sick? "It's only a competition," she breathed. This was his father's life...

"It's more than that to him," Luis said sternly. "It's what he lives for. And I won't be the reason he fails."

Anger tore through the sadness. "That's ridiculous—"

"Please." The one word held enough sadness to smother her indignation. "I need to know you won't tell him. Not until I'm ready. I don't ask you for much. But I need this."

She pressed her hand against her mouth to hold in a sob and nodded. "Fine," she murmured when she could speak. "I won't tell him. But you'll have to. Eventually."

He nodded. "After the competition."

"And what about Lucas and Levi?" They'd only just reconnected with him...

"I'm not gonna saddle them with this now," he said, looking away from her as if he knew exactly what she thought about that plan.

Because she hated it. The thought of him going to a specialist—maybe hearing a grim diagnosis—without his boys there made her nauseated. "They're your family." She tried to say it gently, but conviction hurtled out.

Luis gave her a sad look as he reached across and patted her hand. "And I'll tell them when the time is right."

* * *

Lance fumbled with the buttons on his shirt. Been a damn long time since he'd worn a dress shirt. But he figured Jessa was worth the trouble, even if the collar did pinch at his neck. He tucked the shirt into his jeans and cinched his belt buckle. A fancy shirt was one thing, but he'd stick with jeans, thank you very much. Besides, what he had planned for their date tonight would require jeans. And with that thought...

He strode out into the living room. He never got nervous around women, but something in his gut churned. Which could mean only one thing. He had it bad.

"Whoa." Lucas stood in the kitchen helping himself to a beer. He whistled. "Someone must have big plans tonight."

Lance positioned himself on the other side of the counter, doing his best to appear casual. "How do you figure?"

His brother eyed him as though racking up a list of reasons. "For starters, you tucked your shirt in."

Lance looked down. *Yeah, okay.* That was a dead giveaway. "So?" he challenged, just like he used to when they were kids. That usually ended in a scuffle around the floor until one of them had the other pinned. But tonight he didn't feel like messing up his hair.

"Where are you headed?" Lucas asked, the smirk on his face making him look thirteen again.

Lance evaded his brother's amused eyes. "Gonna pick up Jessa. Take her up to the lake." A romantic evening picnic. Not that he could take credit. He'd Googled romantic dates in the mountains...

"A picnic?" His brother's jaw hung open.

Yeah, it kind of shocked him, too. But what could he say? "I like her."

"So I see." Lucas took a swig of beer and set the bottle on

the counter. "I'm happy for you. She seems close to perfect for you." The smirk reappeared. "Nice. Kind. Compassionate. Someone to balance you out."

"What the hell is that supposed to—"

The door pounded open and Levi hustled in. "Got any beer around this place? Dad's out."

Probably because Levi had downed it all. Didn't take that kid long to put back a case of beer.

"Plenty in the fridge," Lucas said, moving out of the way so Levi could open it.

He snatched a lager and popped the top like he'd been waiting for a year.

"Ahh..." He swiped his arm across his mouth and looked at Lance as though noticing him for the first time. "Why the hell are you dressed like you're doing a photo shoot for *Rodeo News*?"

"He has a date," Lucas answered for him. "With Jessa."

Damn. If only he could sucker punch him like he used to.

"Knew it." Levi's palm smacked the countertop. "It was so obvious. You were all over her at the bar."

"Noticed you avoided Cassidy," Lance said. He still knew how to put Levi in his place when the situation demanded.

Sure enough, his brother's gaze dropped to the floor.

"Did you even say a word to her?" After being her brother's best friend and practically growing up as part of the family, a hello wouldn't have killed him.

"Cassidy hates me." He took a long pull on the beer and when he set it down the spark was gone from his eyes. "She hates everyone who has anything to do with riding."

Lance doubted that. Cassidy didn't hate Levi. His brother simply felt guilty for being there when Cash died. For not being able to prevent his accident, as if he were God or something.

"Come on, you two." Lucas shook his head at the two of them. "How about we stop trying to push one another's buttons and get along? I'm only gonna be here a few more days, then I gotta head back to the McGowens'."

"A few more days?" That was it? All these years Luis had been waiting for Lucas's return, and now he was staying only a few days.

"I've got stuff to take care of down there. They rely on me."

"I gotta head back to training soon, too," Levi said, finishing off his beer. "Not everyone qualifies for Worlds with just their name." He gave Lance a pointed look. "Some of us gotta work for it."

Lance's temper flared. He *had* worked for it. His whole life. He'd given everything to it. But Levi knew that. Once again, his younger brother was just trying to poke the dragon. Besides, they had other things to discuss. If they were both leaving soon, they didn't have much time. He glanced at the clock. He had to leave in ten minutes, but they had to do this now. He walked to the counter and pulled out a stool, sitting down across from his brothers. "Since you're both here, there's something I want to say." He didn't give them a chance to respond. "I think we should tell Dad. Everything."

Lucas braced his hands against the countertop. "We've been over this."

Maybe so, but their last go-round hadn't convinced him of anything. "I think he deserves to know the truth." If he stood in the man's shoes, he'd want to know.

"There's no point," Lucas growled, more riled up than he should've been. "Not right now. What's done is done. Let's leave it be."

He couldn't. Not anymore. Not for Lucas and not for Levi. Not for their father. "No one else has to know. But he should."

Levi looked back and forth between him and Lucas, his expression unreadable. "Lance is right," he finally said.

"What?" Come again? Had those three words really just come out of his younger brother's mouth?

"You're right," Levi said again, with more conviction this time. "He should know the truth."

Wow. Lance could only stand there blinking like a fool. He'd never thought Levi would be the one to agree on this. Maybe his brother *had* grown up some out there in Oklahoma…

"You don't know what the hell you're talking about," Lucas argued. "You don't want him to know the truth."

Their youngest brother slammed his beer onto the countertop so hard Lance couldn't believe the bottle didn't shatter.

"How do you think I felt knowing you were in prison because of something I did?" he demanded. "I ruined your life."

"We didn't exactly give you a choice," Lance reminded him. He'd never thought about what it had done to Levi. It'd never seemed to bother him. He'd obviously hidden it well.

"Exactly. You didn't give me a choice." His brother's eyes had darkened. "But I could've spoken up. I could've said something. If I had it to do over, I never would let you take the fall for me."

Lucas sighed as though he was more tired than angry. "You were a kid. Hell, we were all kids. We didn't know anything."

That was the truth. For the most part they'd been on their own to make life's big decisions. And there'd been plenty of times they'd screwed up. They could always right those wrongs, though. It wasn't too late. "We can make it right now."

Lucas studied Levi. "But you have your whole career ahead of you..."

"I don't need you to protect me anymore," their younger brother said with more conviction than Lance had thought he was capable of.

Lucas still looked as surprised as he felt. "No. I guess you don't."

Levi walked over and tossed his beer bottle into the re-cycling bin. "They couldn't prosecute me anyway. You've already served the sentence. So yeah, it might suck if every-one else found out. They might hate me. But I won't go to prison."

Lucas still looked undecided, but Lance wasn't. "We can tell him tomorrow. At dinner," he said. "But right now I have to run." Wouldn't do to be late for Jessa. She'd already for-given him for being an ass once. Or twice. Didn't need to add poor punctuality to the list.

"Have fun," his brothers said in unison as he trotted out the door.

Didn't need to tell him twice. It'd been only a few days since he'd spent time with her, but it felt more like months.

Outside, the early evening sun backlit the mountains with a vibrant haze. He climbed into the truck, appreciating the view as he drove toward town. Normally, he didn't consider himself an optimistic sort of fella, but it seemed things were falling into place. His brothers were back home, which meant the family was back together. After all these years, they'd put the past to rest. Worlds were coming up fast, and he'd never felt more ready for a competition in his life.

And all of it was thanks to Jessa.

Chapter Twenty

It was becoming apparent that perhaps Darla hadn't been the best choice in reinforcements to call when Jessa had started to freak out about her date with Lance. The woman had come right over and talked her into wearing her brand-new flowy, low-cut sundress that clearly said, *Make love to me in a flower-dappled meadow.*

And yes, she had to admit, it was the perfect outfit for a first date with a man who'd already convinced her he was worth the effort. But there was a slight complication. She shouldn't go on a date with him. Not when she was leaving for Denver at six thirty in the morning with his father for a secret doctor's appointment. "He told me to wear jeans," she said, glancing at herself in the mirror.

Darla only laughed. "He doesn't want you to wear jeans. When he sees this dress, he'll forget all about jeans," she promised.

"I shouldn't go. I could tell him I have the chickenpox,"

Jessa squeaked, fisting her friend's shirt desperately in her hands. "Or measles. Or a bad case of the stomach flu..." A rising panic crowded into her chest, jamming up her throat. She glanced at the clock. Lance would be there in ten minutes!

"No." Darla plucked Jessa's hands from her clothing and backed away, straightening the wrinkles out of her shirt. "You are going on this date," she said sternly. "I mean, come on! Lance never asks anyone out." Her hands flew up. "Think of what this means. This is like a record. Maybe you'll end up in the Guinness World Records or something."

Jessa deflated to the couch, suddenly exhausted from the weight of carrying such a heavy secret. "I can't go. I can't." How could she look into that man's perceptive eyes and pretend everything was all right?

Darla plopped next to her. "You *have* to go," she argued. "You look gorgeous. And you don't want to discourage his interest in you, right?"

Jessa stared at her hands, trying to even out her breathing. "Well. No. I guess not." She liked Lance. Okay. She more than liked him. But that was the problem. She'd learned enough about him to realize that keeping any sort of secret about his father would be considered an unpardonable sin in his book.

"Come on." Darla gave her shoulders a quick massage, like a coach pumping up a boxer for a big match. "Just forget about everything else and have fun tonight. Let it all go."

"I want to." She wanted to waltz out that door with him and let him sweep her off her feet like they'd been caught up in one of those wonderful Humphrey Bogart movies. Not like it would be all that hard for him to sweep her off her feet. He'd already laid a serious claim on her heart. She wanted to hold his hand and kiss him and, well, depending on where things went, maybe more than kiss him. But. "I feel like I'm lying to him." In a moment of desperation on the phone, she'd given up Luis's secret to Darla. Not that she had to worry. The woman was a vault.

"Pshaw." Darla waved away her concerns. "You're not lying. You're withholding. Totally different," she said, as though she'd suddenly become a relationship expert. "You have to respect Luis's wishes on this, Jess. This is his decision. Not yours."

And that was the sad truth of it. "I know."

"Luis is right. This would completely throw Lance off right before the biggest competition of his life. Is that what you want?"

"No." He needed this win. He needed to go out on top. Surely he'd understand. She was just trying to do what was best for him.

"Now, I'm gonna take off before he gets here and sees me giving you a pep talk." Darla pushed off the couch and walked across the room to the dog bed Jessa had brought home for Ilsa. The pig squealed when she picked her up, but Darla carefully calmed her with a smooch on the head. She'd agreed to watch Ilsa tonight. Just in case things went late.

But Jessa couldn't let things go late. She couldn't sleep with Lance! Not when she was keeping something from him...

"Call me the second you get home," Darla said for the hundredth time. "Got it? I want details. I want to know *everything*."

She followed her friend to the door and opened it for her, then leaned down to kiss Ilsa's snout. "I'm not sure there'll be anything to tell." How could she say one word to him without everything coming out? Let alone kiss the man? It would feel so wrong...

"Oh, there'll be something to tell," Darla insisted on her way down the porch. "Trust me. That dress won't let you down." With a suggestive lift of her eyebrows, she traipsed down the porch, wiggling her fingers in a wave.

Jessa didn't wave back. Her arms felt too weak to move. She tapped the door closed with her toes and paced the living room. Usually the anticipation of seeing Lance brought on the butterflies, but now it had unleashed something far more intense. What if Lance could read the secret on her face? What if she accidentally mentioned something about their trip to Denver? What if—

The doorbell chimed.

Her head whipped around. Lance's sturdy build crowded the window.

"Okay," she breathed. "Okay." Too late to cancel. Too late to make up some sort of illness. Darla was right. She wasn't lying. After it all came out, she'd simply explain to Lance how important the secret had been to Luis. He would understand. He had to understand.

Slowly, she shuffled to the door, her insides quivering the whole way. She reached for the knob and suddenly the damn thing felt like it was solid steel. Somehow she managed to get the door open, even with her failing muscles. And that image of him standing there... that burned into her brain. He was dreamy... a rugged cowboy fantasy. Dark tight jeans. Black button-down shirt tucked in so as not to hide any of his goods. His hair had been somewhat tamed but not to the point of looking like he cared all that much, and God, that made him sexy.

"Hi, there," she said as casually as she could, considering the pulse in her throat.

"Hey." His gaze lazily trailed down her body and back up to her eyes, and the desire she saw there rendered her speechless.

"I know I told you to wear jeans, but that's one hell of a dress, Jessa Love," he uttered in a rather provocative, scraping tone that tempted her to do away with the dress altogether.

Instead of disrobing, she turned away to snatch her purse off the sofa table. And to talk her cheeks out of a blush. "Thanks," she muttered as soon as she could speak.

When she turned around, he stood closer, almost right against her, and even though he hadn't touched her yet, she felt him, inhaled that dangerous scent that made her think of the powerful trees lining the mountains outside.

"I thought we'd go for a picnic." His gaze lowered to her cleavage as though he wanted her to know how much he appreciated it. "That sound okay with you?"

A picnic. It sounded perfect. In the great outdoors, maybe she could think about something besides leading him right into her bedroom. Skip the small talk. Skip the food. Who needed a date when Lance was so good at seducing her? *Ahem.* Yes. A picnic would be much safer. "I love picnics," she told him, going to the closet to pick out a sweater. Delicate and white to match the dress.

"Can't say I've ever been on a picnic," he said, holding open the front door for her. "But I figure it'll be a nice evening up at the lake."

"Mmm-hmmm," she squeaked, hightailing it down the sidewalk to his old pickup. She'd already climbed in and gotten belted before he could open the door for her.

Lance hoisted himself into the driver's seat and started the engine. As he pulled away from the curb, he glanced over at her. "You okay?" he asked, more unsure than she'd ever seen him.

"Yes." A fake laugh tumbled out. "Of course I'm okay." Oh God. She might as well have said, *No, Lance. I'm not okay. I'm taking your father to Denver in the morning.* She was terrible at pretending.

Sure enough, he gave her a skeptical look.

"Um." She scraped at a piece of nail polish on the tip of her finger. *Think. Think, damn it.* Maybe sex would've been a better idea. Then she wouldn't actually have to talk to him. "It's just... it's been a stressful week."

His eyes watched the windshield now as he navigated the town streets. "Things at the shelter okay?"

"Yes." As far as she could tell. Though she'd been a bit distracted lately, courtesy of that man sitting right there. "Just a lot to do."

The truck lurched to a stop as he waited to turn onto the highway. "My offer's still good, you know." His hand swept down her arm and brought on a rush of longing. "Even though you're not staying with Dad anymore, I'll still donate half my winnings to the shelter."

Her shoulders went stiff. "You don't have to do that," she choked out. He shouldn't do that.

"I want to." He sped onto the highway, sneaking glances at her as they headed toward the ranch. "You've done a lot for us, Jessa. Bringing my brothers home... helping out Dad."

Her hands squeezed into fists. She was still trying to help out Luis. She had to remember that. "It's nothing," she insisted, staring out the passenger window, watching the familiar mountains roll by. They'd turned off the highway and onto the ranch's vast acreage and were heading up the same switchback road she and Luis took on the ATVs. The secret seemed to sear against her chest, but she battled back an urge to tell him. "So how are things going with your brothers?" she asked in an attempt to take the focus off her.

"Things are pretty good." He kind of laughed. "Surprisingly."

That drew her gaze to him. "Why is that surprising?"

"Let's just say there've always been some things between us." He focused on the road as though he wanted to evade her eyes. "But we're dealing with them. Finally. After all these years, I think we can be like a family again." There was a gravity in his voice, half hope, half fear. But when his face turned to her she saw only strength. "Thanks to you."

Guilt spilled through her again, forcing her to look away. "I can't take credit for that." After he found out about his father's situation, he likely wouldn't be singing her praises anymore.

Silence ensued as the truck crawled up the steep incline. When the road leveled out, he glanced over at her again. "I didn't think I'd be thankful for them coming back. But I am. And Dad is." His eyes locked on hers. "I haven't seen him this happy in a long time."

She felt the color drain from her face. His father was not a safe subject right now. Not at all. "How's training coming?" she rasped, hoping to divert the conversation away from Luis. She couldn't talk about him at all or she might burst into tears. She'd nearly driven herself crazy looking up his symptoms on the Internet, fearing everything from a brain tumor to dementia to Alzheimer's.

"I feel ready," Lance said, parking the truck near the short path that led down to the lake. "I don't think I've ever felt this ready for a competition."

"I'm glad." It was the most genuine thing she'd said since he rang her doorbell. She was glad for him. After the hell everyone was giving him, he deserved to win.

Which is why she wouldn't tell him. As soon as he came back from Worlds, he'd find out everything. Right now, she had to give him space to concentrate. Comforted by the thought, she climbed out of the truck, thankful for the fresh air, the expanse of space between them. Maybe out here in the openness things wouldn't feel as intimate. Maybe she could keep her distance.

While Lance unloaded a huge basket from the bed of his truck, she wandered to the path. Evening was just starting to settle, hushing the world, making everything glow. God, it was romantic. The lighting, the soft breeze, the faraway rush of a stream. The peace of it made reality seem a little farther away, like they really had entered some dream world where happiness could never come to a screeching halt with one diagnosis, with one little lie. Her body let go of some of the tension it had been carrying as she inhaled the scent of honeysuckle and pine. So lovely, these mountains. So far away from everything else.

"Hope you like cheese. And wine," Lance said, coming up behind her.

She turned, letting herself take him in, letting her eyes linger on his. "I like both." She smiled at him. And it felt real. Not forced. "That's quite the basket. I'm so impressed," she teased, eyeing the huge woven work of art he carried.

"Borrowed it from Naomi," he admitted with a grin. "I was just gonna pack it all in a good old saddle bag. But I figured we might not want hay in our food."

She laughed, and somehow it made a surge of tingling anticipation slip through her hesitations. Lance had gone to a lot of trouble planning this date. A picnic. Something intimate and sweet. He could've taken her to a restaurant, but instead he'd brought her out here. The effort he'd put in warmed her.

They walked in an easy silence down to the lake. She'd been there a couple of times, fishing with Luis, mostly, but she'd never seen it at dusk. When the trees opened into a clearing, she stopped suddenly. It almost looked fake. The glassy surface, smooth and turquoise, fed from the glacier nestled between two cliffs above. The setting sun streaked the sky with colors, reflecting off the water. "This is incredible," she breathed.

"Yeah. Sometimes I come up here at sunset. It's probably the most peaceful spot on the entire ranch." Lance led her down to the water, where a big flat rock sat mere feet away from the shoreline.

"This is where I usually sit." He lowered the basket to the ground and took out a red-and-white-checkered tablecloth, shaking it slightly before he spread it out.

"It's perfect." She sat, letting her legs stretch out in front of her, crossing them at the ankles as her skin soaked in the gentle evening sun.

Lance sat beside her, pulling things out of the basket, one by one. A plastic-wrapped plate of some yummy-looking cheeses, a container of grapes, a platter of what looked to be prosciutto and salami. Then, two wineglasses and a bottle of merlot. He uncorked the wine and poured a glass for each of them. Then he held his out to her, a sparkle of mystery in his eyes. "To great views," he said, eyeing her dress again, and this time she let herself blush.

"To great views," she repeated, clanking her glass against his.

He pulled out two plates and served her. It was all perfectly thought out. The saltiness of the cheese with the bitterness of the wine and the sweetness of the grapes. The two of them ate leisurely while the pink hues deepened in the sky.

Jessa set down her wineglass, still mesmerized by how the lake's surface mirrored the sky. "So what do you think about when you come up here?"

Lance gazed up at the peaks above them. "Life. Competitions. Sometimes my mom." That last sentence seemed garbled with an emotion she couldn't quite peg. Anger? Resentment? Sadness?

She munched on the amazing Brie he'd selected and sipped her wine. "Did you stay in touch with her? Ever hear from her?"

Instead of answering, he shook his head. Then he popped some grapes into his mouth, chewing thoughtfully before he swallowed. "For a while I thought she'd come back. That she'd realize her mistake and make things right."

By the sound of things, he'd given up on that dream a long time ago. But she'd never been one to lose hope easily. "Maybe she still will," Jessa said, her tone treading carefully.

"Nah. She would've already. If she wanted to." He set his plate on the ground next to the rock and hunched, resting his elbows on his knees. "I've looked for her more than once. Didn't find anything. She obviously doesn't want to be found."

The pain on his face ground itself into her heart. What would that be like? To have this important piece of your life missing? Did he feel incomplete because of it? "You boys deserved better," she said, covering his hand with hers. His was warm and rough. Battered by the constant tug-of-war with leather. She loved the feel of it. Of him. His hands were so distinct, the lines and ridges and scars...

Lance scooted closer to her. "You didn't have it so easy with your family, either, huh? Always going back and forth the way you did." His arm settled around her.

"No." She let herself lean into him. "That's true. But both of my parents were always there for me." They may not have been in love, but they both loved her. She'd never had to doubt that. "I consider myself very blessed to have had that."

Lance peered down at her, his eyes searching hers. "How do you do that?"

She turned to face him. "What?"

"See the best in every situation. In everyone?"

Maybe because she'd overdosed on romance her entire life and now she thought only in terms of happily-ever-afters? That didn't sound very intelligent. "I guess I like to focus on what I have instead of what I think I need. I only see the things I'm grateful for."

His face lowered to hers. "Want to know what I'm grateful for?" he murmured, nearly against her lips.

"What?" she breathed, her heart pounding its way out of her chest.

"That dress." The grin that accompanied the words was downright naughty. And close. *So* close.

She laughed as his lips nudged hers, and he laughed, too, but only for a second before he pulled her closer, teasing her with a scrap of his extravagant mouth against hers. The heat on their lips thawed the fears and the hesitations that had chilled her heart before. Because she loved kissing him. Loved how his firm lips moved against hers, slow and sensual. Savoring. She loved the feel of his hard chest under her palms, the way his hands held her, the way his stubble scraped her skin.

"You really know how to plan a date," she whispered against his neck.

Carefully he lowered her back to the rock, then hovered over her while he traced her collarbone with his finger. "It'll only get better," he promised,

"Can't wait," she whispered, bringing her lips to his again. Losing herself in the rhythm of his kiss and the peaceful breeze and the glowing sunset, she took Darla's advice.

She let the secret between them go.

Chapter Twenty-One

This evening wasn't supposed to be about sex, but God almighty was it hard to convince his body of that. Especially with Jessa underneath him, making those hot little noises while he kissed the soft warm flesh of her neck. He wanted sex. No. He should rephrase that. He wanted sex with Jessa again. Slow this time. Deliberate. So he could touch every inch of her skin. Taste it with his tongue. So he could revel in the sensation of burying himself inside her again, taking her to that place where her control shattered and she clung to him as she rode out the pleasure he gave her...

His hands fisted and he pulled back, eased himself onto his side next to her. He wanted her more than he'd ever wanted a woman, but he wanted more than her body. Tonight was not about sex. It was about taking her on a date. When he'd picked her up, she'd been distant, and who the hell could blame her? They'd already had a quickie in the kitchen but since then, they'd hardly talked. Had hardly spent any time alone, getting to know each other the way a woman like Jessa would want to. She might say she was fine with a fling, but he knew better. She'd never given herself away to just anyone. Hell, that's what made her special. He knew she wanted more. And she deserved it, too.

"Everything okay?" she asked quietly, touching her fingers to her lips. Even in the dusky light, he could see the rosiness of her cheeks, heated and alive, the same way his body felt.

He gazed down at her, playing with the strands of hair around her face, breathing in her sweet honey scent. "Everything's more than okay." Because he had her here, alone. Because right now in this moment, she belonged to him. He couldn't say what would happen tomorrow, where tonight would lead them, but right now he had everything he wanted. "Are *you* okay?"

She smiled up at the stars that were starting to prick the sky with their twinkling light. "Yes, Lance. I am definitely okay." Her gaze met his, and he had to hold his breath and count backward from ten so he wouldn't say screw getting to know her and maul her instead. He could do this. Talk to a woman he was interested in. Talk without expecting anything else. They had a lot of things to discuss. He knew a lot about her but he didn't know *her*.

She turned on her side, so that her perfect breasts pressed against his chest. Instead of caressing them the way he'd been fantasizing about, he rested his hand on her hip. "I figured we should talk some. Get to know each other."

Jessa busted out laughing.

"What?" he demanded, though her laughter lured out a grin. She had a great laugh. Happy and buoyant. A laugh that could make even the biggest miser smile. He needed more of that laugh in his life.

"Sorry," she managed to say through a lingering giggle. "I'm sorry." She made a face as though she was struggling to put on a more serious expression. "So what do you want to know about me? Favorite color? Favorite food?" Judging from the glimmer in her eyes she was teasing him.

And he liked it. "Bra size," he shot back, though he'd had enough experience to guess she was safely within the C category.

"Why don't you take a look?" she said, temptingly.

He could. He could take the thing off with his teeth right now. But he'd already decided. Next time he made love to Jessa, it wouldn't be on an uncomfortable rock in the great outdoors. It would be in his king-size bed, where they could spend the entire night exploring each other, where he could take his time figuring out how she liked it best. Where he could send her over the edge as many times as she'd let him and then they could fall asleep with their naked bodies tangled together.

He eased out a breath. "When's your birthday?" he asked, jaw tensed with restraint.

Jessa propped herself up on her elbow and gave him that soft smile that made him want to trace her lips with his tongue. "September. The sixteenth."

He nodded as though checking her answer off the list. He tried to think of another stupid question, something insignificant, but the truth was he didn't care what her favorite color was. He didn't care what she liked to eat. That would all be learned in time. What fascinated him most about Jessa was her heart. The woman had been hurt. Engaged a couple of times, rumor had it. She'd been cast aside. Abandoned just like him.

But she had this resilience he envied. Only one person had rejected him in his whole life and yet in that one moment he'd shut himself off to the very connection he was starting to feel with Jessa. He'd ridden bulls, been bucked around, thrown. He'd broken too many bones to count. But this...this terrified him. The risk seemed so much greater than just his own life. Yet he didn't want to turn back. He didn't want to run scared this time. Jessa had managed to do what no other woman could all these years. She'd earned his trust.

He braved a look into her stunning eyes. "What do you want most in life?" he asked her, wondering if maybe he could offer it to her.

Her expression sobered. She rolled onto her back and stared up at the sky again.

Figuring it might make it easier for her to answer, he did the same.

Wind rustled the pine needles and made the water quietly lap at the shoreline. He said nothing, though Jessa's silence tempted him to let her off the hook.

Finally, she sighed, as though she'd resigned herself to honesty. "Love," she murmured as though somewhat ashamed. "That's what I want most in life. To love someone wholly and truly. And to have them love me back."

The words struck him with their simplicity. Wasn't that what most people wanted but were too afraid to admit? He leaned over, kissing her tenderly yet firmly. When he pulled back, his heart pounded. "I don't know how to do that," he admitted. To love someone. Even more than that, to let someone love *him*. "But maybe I can learn."

Jessa turned her body to his again, placing her palm at the curve of his jaw. "You're far better at it than you think you are," she whispered. "You love your father." Was it tears that made her eyes brighter? Or just the deepening darkness? He didn't know why that filled her with so much emotion, but he loved that in her. Loved how she let herself feel. He stroked her cheek, steering her lips back to his, and this time the kiss felt deeper, more meaningful. It was even harder to pull back, harder to keep his hands from wandering all of the places they wanted to go. Instead, he drew her into a tight embrace, trying to convince himself he was satisfied simply holding her. "Come with us. To Worlds." The words surprised him as much as they seemed to surprise Jessa. He hadn't planned on saying them, on inviting her. But he wanted her with him.

She pushed back and sat up. "What?"

"Come to Vegas." He sat up, too, gazing into her eyes to convince her. "We'll get you your own suite. Dad would love it."

Her head tilted to the side. "You want me to come along for your dad?"

"Yeah." He bit back a smile. She was much smarter than that, but she apparently wanted to make him say it. "And maybe I want you there for me, too." He wanted her light. Her laugh. Her smile. Her happiness. It wouldn't be easy for him to face his critics, the people who were hungrily awaiting his downfall. But something told him he could manage it better if she were with him.

Jessa's whole face lit. "Okay," she said slowly, as though it was sinking in. "Yes. I'd love to go with you."

"Okay," he repeated, already making the arrangements in his head. He'd have his agent set everything up, find her plane reservations, get her the best suite at the hotel. "You'll have a great time," he said, kissing her sweet lips again. "I promise."

She kissed him back, clinging to him, running her hands down his chest. Before they could travel any lower, he pulled back and cut off the kissing. "Right now, though, I should get you home," he growled, breaking apart their bodies before he wasn't able.

"You sure?" she whispered.

No. He was not at all sure. But the cold hardness of the rock was enough to remind him. "This isn't the most comfortable place to make out," he said.

"I noticed." She laughed. "And I really do need to get home," she agreed, scrambling off the rock and to her feet as though her balance had been compromised.

He could relate. He steadied her with a hand against her lower back. "We can go on a date in Vegas." He packed plenty of heat into the suggestive expression. "Then you can spend the night. If you want to."

The slightest hesitation flickered across her face but then she smiled. "Sure. It'll give us something to look forward to."

Hell yes, it would. He'd be counting down the minutes.

* * *

Doctor examination rooms were all the same. Bland white walls. Lights too bright. Inevitably one cheesy framed picture that someone had likely ordered as part of a special offer per dozen. From the chair where she sat next to Luis, Jessa studied the amateurish painting of an eagle perched on the sturdy branch of an evergreen tree. The creature's eyes glowered at her from all the way across the room. Not exactly the most comforting image while waiting to hear your fate.

A clock on the wall ticked off the seconds. Earlier, while she'd killed time in the waiting room, Luis had undergone some tests. Then the nurse had invited her into the exam room while they waited to hear from the doctor. And they'd been waiting ever since.

Luis sat tall and composed, much better off than she was, evidently. The anticipation of waiting for the doctor was slowly killing her. Her knee pumped with the frantic beat of her heart. What was taking so long? Had they found something terrible? Why hadn't the doctor come in yet? She watched the clock, tucking her hands under her thighs so she wouldn't fidget.

"You okay?" Luis asked, without turning his head to face her.

"No. I'm not." She couldn't lie. He'd see right through her, anyway. "This place is terrible. So depressing. I mean, would it hurt to put some color on the walls? And what's this?" she demanded, snatching a magazine off the small countertop next to them. "*Financial Times*? Are you kidding me? Who wants to sit in here and read boring old investment articles?" Indignation rolled off her face in waves, giving release to her misplaced anger. Sometimes anger was easier. Because truth be told, she was downright scared. The *what-if*s had been stirring a potion of fear that boiled in her stomach. She wanted to run from here. Far away. Before they found out the worst.

And God, she couldn't let herself think about last night. How perfect it had been. How truly wonderful Lance had treated her. Even while she'd withheld the knowledge that his father might be dying of some horrible disease . . .

"Everything will be all right, Jess," Luis said with a quiet confidence.

That only got her more riled up. "What if it's not?" Her throat was raw. How could she go through losing another father one year after her own had left her? Yes, that was selfish, but there it was. She loved Luis, and the thought of watching him suffer made her want to double over.

The old man patted her hand with warm affection. "I'm not worried, honey. Don't matter what the doc says. I've got everything I've ever wanted. My boys are all home. Together. Don't matter what's wrong with me." He spoke as though he knew something was wrong, as though he'd already accepted it.

So why couldn't she?

"Saw Lance's truck drive in awful late last night," Luis mentioned casually. "I reckon you two had a good time on your date?"

"A great time." The flashbacks of Lance touching her and kissing her with such tenderness filled her with warmth and longing. It was the best date she'd ever been on...

"You didn't tell him about the appointment?" his father asked carefully.

Her eyes fell shut. "No. I didn't."

"Sorry, Jess. I know that had to be real hard."

"It was." She tried not to glare at him. She loved the man, but she hated this. "I don't want to lie to him."

"I'll tell him when the time is right. I promise. As soon as—"

The door swung open, leaving the promise unfinished. Jessa snapped her spine to full attention as the neurologist—a short man with a neatly trimmed rim of graying hair—walked in.

"Sorry for the wait," he said briskly as he plunked himself on the rolling stool across from them. "I wanted to take a few extra minutes to go over your test results." He fumbled through a manila folder and Jessa glimpsed stacks of pictures. MRI scans, charts, diagrams. She turned to look at Luis, her mouth gaping. He must've been undergoing tests for months...

The doctor focused only on Luis, his expression a mask of polite detachment. "Based on all we've learned over the past months, and my conversations with your primary physician, I believe we have a diagnosis."

Jessa inhaled deeply, trying her hardest to be brave, trying to find strength for Luis. She snuck her hand over to his, holding on tightly, desperate to siphon some of his courage.

"I believe you're battling Parkinson's disease. And it would appear you've had it for some time," the doctor went on in a monotone.

"That's what Dr. Potter thought." Luis's voice didn't even waver. He wasn't surprised. He'd known for months. But Jessa was reeling. In anger, in sadness, in fear of how Lance would handle a blow like this...

"There's no way to know how quickly it will progress or exactly how the symptoms will manifest. Parkinson's is difficult to define. Each patient is different." The man handed Luis a large envelope. "Here are some resources. Potential treatments. Results from the latest trials. There are definitely methods we can try to slow down the progression. Medications, certain therapies."

"Is it fatal?" Jessa choked out, needing to know the prognosis.

"Not necessarily." For the first time since he'd come in, the doctor acknowledged her with direct eye contact. "But there are complications. It makes life significantly more challenging due to the mental and mobility implications."

"Okay," she whispered, nodding, trying to swallow past the emotion that snagged her throat. "Okay."

"I'd like to set up a meeting in two weeks. To give you time to digest this and read through the literature we've provided." The doctor stood, already on his way to the door. "Then we can formulate the treatment plan you feel is best for you and your situation."

He spoke like this was an everyday occurrence, like he hadn't just upturned Luis's world with one sentence. Fury climbed up to Jessa's face. She stood, too. "That's it? Shouldn't we start treatment now? Shouldn't we discuss all of the options now?" Her voice teetered on the brink of a breakdown, but seriously? They shouldn't waste any time!

The doctor looked at her patiently. "We find it's best in these situations to allow patients some time to process everything before we move forward with a treatment plan."

Her hands fisted tightly, the anger needing release. "But—"

"It's all right, Jess." Luis rested his hand on her shoulder to quiet her. "Thank you, Dr. Ellis." While Jessa wanted to wring the aloof doctor's neck, Luis reached out to shake the man's hand. "I'll see you in a couple weeks."

After the door closed, Jessa turned away from Luis so he wouldn't see her tears, but he wouldn't let her hide. The man took her arms in his hands, turning her to face him. "I'm not afraid. Not stupid enough to think it'll be easy, but I don't fear it, either." He offered her a comforting smile. "I have everything I've ever wanted," he said again. "My boys are home."

"So you'll tell Lance?" she asked, her voice watered down with tears.

"After the competition," he promised, pulling her into a reassuring hug. "After the competition, I'll tell them everything."

Chapter Twenty-Two

Hell yes. Lance swung himself up into the driver's seat of his pickup. He'd just finished kicking Wild Willy's ass. Clocked his best time yet. As in ever. Right after he'd hung it up for the day, he'd rushed through a quick shower and even slapped on some cologne. He may have told Jessa he'd take her out in Vegas, but he couldn't wait that long. Besides, they were supposed to leave tomorrow night for Worlds, and he wanted to bring her up to speed on the details. They'd already added her to the plane reservations and the suite had been booked. One of their suites wouldn't get much use, but it was best to keep up appearances.

Lance sped down the drive, kicking up a trail of dust behind his wheels. He could've called her first, but where was the fun in that? Since he'd dropped her off and kissed her on her doorstep last night, he'd been aching to see her, to feel that soft body of hers against his. It'd taken him ten minutes of sitting in his truck to actually pull away from her house.

He would've gone in, if she'd invited him, but she hadn't. After they shared a rather hot kiss that could've been considered a warm-up for other stuff, she'd said she had an early morning and should get inside. And he'd had to talk himself down the whole way home.

Figuring she'd still be at the shelter, he headed in that direction, tapping his hands to the rhythms playing on the country station. During his jaunt down Main Street, he waved to Kat Temple, the lone female deputy within a hundred-mile radius, and even at Hank Green, who was walking his cat on a leash. Because why the hell not?

Outside the shelter, he didn't see Jessa's car, but he parked anyway. He could wait until she got back if need be. Once he approached the windows, though, he saw that the lights were on, so he tried the door. It was open.

Cassidy sat at the front desk, working on the computer. She sat straighter as he came in.

"Hey," he said. "Didn't expect to see you here today." Far as he knew, she covered only on the weekends or when the boss was away. "Is Jessa around?"

"Oh." Her blue eyes grew round and her gaze wandered. "Um. No. Actually. She's not here." There was no evidence of her typical friendly smile. Why did she look so worried?

"What about my father?" he asked, his stomach coming unsettled. Something wasn't right. According to Levi, Jessa had picked up Luis early that morning. He'd told him they had a lot to do at the shelter today . . .

"Um. Your dad's not here, either."

"Where are they?"

"They're out," she said, staring hard at the computer screen. To avoid his probing gaze, if he wasn't mistaken.

"Out where?" He hadn't meant for it to sound so harsh, but this was starting to feel like a game.

"On a call."

"Oh." Why hadn't she said that in the first place? From the intensity of her worried expression, it had to be something bad. "Where are they? Maybe I can help out."

"I'm not sure," she mumbled, but Cassidy was a very bad liar. Her eyes shifted too much. And her voice carried the hoarseness of a bald-faced lie.

"What do you mean you're not sure?" He pinned her with his eyes, trying to read what she wouldn't tell him. "If she called you in to cover for her, she must've told you where she was going."

A sigh broke through her tight lips. "I think it's best if you talk to Jessa. Okay?" Without waiting for an answer, she went back to typing.

He reached over her and shut off the damn monitor. "What the hell is going on?" Something big, judging from the way she was putting him off. And he didn't like being the only one in the dark. "She wouldn't have called you in for an hour or two..." He knew that much. And Jessa rarely went out on calls outside the county limits.

"I'm not telling you anything," Cassidy said stubbornly. "It's not my place or my business. Understand?"

No. He didn't understand. Didn't understand how worry could boil up in his gut this way when he'd felt fine only five minutes ago. Was Jessa all right? Had something happened to her? "Is she with Dad?" He let his eyes beg. "Please. You at least have to tell me that." So he'd know whatever she was off dealing with she wasn't alone.

"Yes." Cassidy sighed. "She's with your father. He asked her to go to Denver with him today."

That stood him up straighter. "What?"

"That's all I'm gonna say." She walked to the door and held it open for him, gesturing for him to leave. "If you want to know more you'll have to talk to them. Okay? I'm guessing she'll have him home within the hour."

He lumbered out the door in a stunned fog. Last night, Jessa had said nothing about taking his father to Denver, but she must've been planning on it. Why would she keep something like that from him?

He wasn't sure he wanted to find out.

* * *

Jessa couldn't remember the last time she'd been silent for more than an hour. Even when she was home alone, she had a tendency to talk to herself. But most of the ride home from Denver, Luis had been quiet and introspective, as if processing what he'd learned. And she knew he had to process it alone. He wasn't like her. He didn't verbally analyze everything, so she'd let him be while she listened to the sad country songs playing on the radio.

Now that they'd almost made it back to the ranch, the urge to burst into tears intensified again. It wasn't like Luis would die in three months; she knew it could be worse. But she couldn't help wondering how long it would be before he'd have to give up the hikes he loved so much, the time wandering in the wilderness that seemed to keep him sane. *That* would slowly kill him.

"I sure appreciate you coming," he said, turning his head in her direction for the first time since they'd gotten in her truck.

"I'll do anything I can to help." She'd research until they

found the best doctors, the latest treatments. "As soon as we get home from the competition, we need to sit down with Lance and go over everything the doctor gave you." Then they could come up with a plan...

"We?" Luis asked, as though he hadn't heard right.

With all her apprehension, she'd forgotten to mention that she was tagging along to Vegas. "Lance asked me to come." Even with the sadness weighting her heart, she smiled. "I hope that's okay."

"It's more than okay," he said, smiling, too. "I couldn't be happier."

She knew he wasn't talking only about Vegas. As she veered onto the country road that led to the ranch, hope swelled inside her, seeming to stretch her ribs, to give her more room to breathe. They would get Luis through this. All of them. Together. "It won't be easy to keep it from him." Even for one more week.

"I know," he agreed. "But it's best."

She turned into Luis's driveway. "We might have to agree to disagree on—"

Her mouth froze open, the rest of the sentence disintegrating in an explosion of panic. Lance sat on Luis's front porch. As the truck rolled toward him, he looked up. Even though she couldn't see his face, she knew. He'd found out where they'd been.

"Oh God." She slowed and parked, but let the car idle. Her heart idled right along with it.

"You go on home, Jess," Luis murmured, unbuckling his seat belt. "I'll handle this."

It was tempting to take him up on that, to avoid the impending confrontation, but she couldn't. "No. I'll stay." How could she turn around and leave when Lance's expression had twisted with suspicion and anger? She had to make him understand. There'd be no way to protect him from the truth now.

Grasping at courage, she cut the engine and slowly withdrew the keys.

Luis got out first. While she struggled to find her balance, he approached the porch. "Hey, son. You've got some questions, I reckon."

Jessa hung back, bracing one hand against the truck's fender to steady herself.

Without looking in her direction, Lance walked down the steps to meet his father. "What were you doing in Denver, Dad?" he asked, and Jessa didn't recognize that voice. She'd never heard it before.

"That's my business," Luis said, not unkindly. "I'm allowed to have my own life. Don't have to answer to you."

Ignoring him, Lance turned to her. The indifference on his face sent a blow to her heart.

"Why did you go to Denver?" He repeated the question, but this time directed it at her.

Jessa eased in a steady breath, trading a look with Luis. She couldn't lie to Lance. Not right to his face. And he wasn't about to let this go. He knew something was wrong.

"I had an appointment," Luis told his son before she could speak. "And I asked Jessa to take me."

"What kind of appointment?" Lance asked impatiently.

Jessa crept closer to him. They had to tell the truth. Didn't Luis see that? The longer he stalled, the angrier Lance would be.

"I had to see a doctor. A specialist."

"A specialist." He seemed to carefully control his voice, but Jessa recognized the fury rising in his eyes, and she couldn't take it, couldn't force him to keep guessing.

"Luis saw a neurologist today," she blurted. "They diagnosed him with Parkinson's."

"What?" Lance staggered back a step, his eyes widening with a sudden wrenching pain. "Jesus, Dad." The words were breathless. "How could you keep that from me?" He shook his head as though he couldn't believe it, then set his sights on her. "And how the fuck could you pretend everything was fine? Last night. You knew. And you let me think everything was dandy." His hand raked through his hair as he paced away from them. "Jesus."

"Don't blame Jessa," Luis said, matching his son's furious tone. "It wasn't her fault. I told her to keep it quiet. I wasn't ready to tell you."

"You weren't *ready*?" Lance yelled. "Well, shit, Dad. By all means, take your time."

Jessa flinched.

"Easy, son," his father reprimanded. "Why don't we all go inside? We can tell you what the doc said. Get everything sorted out."

But Lance didn't seem to be in the place to sort anything out at the moment. He still paced in front of Jessa's truck, back and forth, staring at the ground.

She glanced at Luis. "Can you give us a minute?"

Luis hesitated, as though worried what Lance might do or say. But she could handle it. She could handle him. If they were alone, she could remind him of the connection they'd built. Just last night he'd said maybe he could learn to love, learn to let someone love him. He was still that man. He might be angry, but he was still the same Lance who'd taken her on a picnic in the mountains. "It'll be fine," she assured Luis, shooing him toward the front door. "We'll be in soon. Then we can all talk through this together."

The man nodded silently, but the look he gave his son sent a clear message. *Be careful.* Then he walked up the steps and disappeared into the house.

The hard slam of the screen door seemed to shake Lance out of his daze. He spun to face her, his face still flushed with anger, his eyes hard and distant. And who could blame him? She'd just unloaded this horrible news on him, without warning. He had to be in shock. Had to be reeling the same way she had in the doctor's office.

She approached him slowly. "I wanted to tell you," she said, reaching for his hand so she could thread their fingers together. "But I had to respect Luis's decision. He didn't want to distract you before Worlds. And it was his news to tell you. Not mine."

Lance yanked his arm away. "I didn't spend last night with him," he snapped. The ice in his tone sent her back a step. Her arms fell to her sides. She was losing him. Or... she'd already lost him. "I'm sorry. Maybe we should go inside—"

"We don't need you here for this discussion," he said, turning his back on her.

"Lance." She followed him up the steps. "Please. I was only doing what he asked me to do. I want to stay. I want to *help*." She touched his arm, tried to bring him back to her. "We can get him through this. The doctor said there are treatment options. Things that will slow the progression."

Shrugging away from her touch, he assessed her from behind a curtain of apathy. "Go home, Jessa. You're not a part of this family."

The words drove into her, sharp and cutting. And he knew. He knew exactly what kind of damage he'd just inflicted. Because she'd told him. What she wanted most in the world, what mattered to her more than anything in life. Loving and being loved. Those family connections she'd longed for to anchor her but had never managed to build.

Tears stung, but she would not give him the satisfaction of seeing them fall. "You're right. I'm not part of this family." Instead of shying away like he obviously wanted her to, she marched right to him, piercing his eyes with hers. "But I could've been." Her own anger hummed through her, building into a pressure that made her unbreakable. "And you know something, Lance? You would've been damn lucky to have me." She started to walk away, but whirled back to him. "You can think about that while you're alone in Vegas," she snapped. Then she hurried to her truck and drove away before her strength crumbled.

Chapter Twenty-Three

Instead of following Jessa like he knew he ought to, Lance hunched over and leaned his elbows on the porch railing, letting his forehead fall to his hands. All this time, he'd thought the forgetfulness, the shaking, the weakening physicality in his father was simply old age. But he'd been wrong. He'd ignored the signs, the symptoms. His own hand trembled some as he kneaded his forehead, trying to force it all to sink in. His father had Parkinson's. A label. A disease that would slowly eat away at him until there was nothing left...

Pain shot through his chest, then traveled down his arms, forcing his hands into fists. He was half-tempted to put one of those fists through the wall.

Before he could, the door banged open and Luis poked out his head.

"Where's Jessa?" he asked, glancing toward the empty spot where her truck had been parked before Lance'd gone and run her off.

He straightened, but his shoulders bore the weight of a new burden. "She went home." Because he'd been an asshole. He'd directed the brunt of his anger and shock at her. He turned to his father, trying to block out the image of her wounded eyes.

"You mean you sent her home," his father corrected.

"I was blindsided," he muttered. All afternoon, the fears and possibilities had stewed somewhere deep inside him while he'd sat on the porch waiting for Luis and Jessa to get home. Then when he saw her, without warning, it'd all boiled over, the venom spilling onto Jessa. He'd let the familiar feeling of betrayal get the best of him.

Luis stepped out onto the porch, his thumbs hooked through his belt loops. "She loves you, ya know. I've never been lucky enough to have a woman look at me the way Jess looks at you."

"I know." But he was completely unworthy of it. This little tantrum only proved he could never give her what she deserved. God, he wanted to try, though.

"I know it was a shock to hear it that way." Luis lumbered over to the old bench he'd made with his own two hands. He sat with a wince. "You don't need all this hoopla right now. I wanted to wait until after Worlds."

Lance sat beside him, letting himself notice the age spots on Luis's hands, the arthritic hunch to his shoulders. Truth is, he didn't want his father to get old. Didn't want him to get sick. He was the only one who'd stuck around, who'd stuck it out with him all these years and he couldn't imagine it. Couldn't let himself picture that day when his dad would take his last breath.

Emotion clogged his throat, but he didn't bother to clear it away. "How long have you known?"

Luis stared out at the mountains. "A while. Doc's been running tests over the past couple months."

"And you kept it to yourself." That hurt more than anything else. The fact that he hadn't trusted Lance with it. Or that he hadn't thought Lance would consider it important enough to put his training on hold. But maybe that was on him. Maybe he'd focused so much on winning that he'd made his father believe he wouldn't care. "You should've told me. I would've helped you. I would've taken you to the appointments." He would've sat by his side today while he heard the news. Instead, Luis had chosen Jessa. Maybe that was it, what had set him off. He'd chosen Jessa and Lance couldn't deny she'd been the better choice.

"I did what I thought was best." Luis turned to him, his expression donning that fatherly disappointment. "And you had no right to take it out on Jessa. She's done nothing but help this family."

"I know." Regret had already pooled in his gut, making him feel full to the gills, even though he hadn't eaten since breakfast. "But maybe it's better we end it now. Jessa deserves more than I can give her." Naomi was right. He was too screwed up to do this. He had one foot in, but kept one foot out, just in case. And when things got hard, he found an excuse to be an asshole to keep distance between them.

"That's a copout," Luis muttered. He'd always been one to call it like it was. "You're a better man than I ever was. You love someone, you gotta make it work. You gotta work hard, face up to the troubles, and get past 'em. Trust me. I wish I would've made the effort."

Before he could ask what Luis meant, Levi's truck rumbled into the driveway.

Right. He'd forgotten he'd called in his brothers. He

turned to his dad. "I should warn you. When I found out you'd gone to Denver with Jessa, I called in backup. Told them to meet me here as soon as they could."

"Swell," his father muttered, rising as though preparing to face the music.

"What's the emergency?" Lucas asked, stomping the mud off his boots as he made his way up the steps.

When Lance had finally gotten ahold of them, he'd learned the two slackers had gone fly-fishing.

"Yeah...who up and died?" Levi asked, obviously annoyed he'd been interrupted before he'd caught the big one.

Lance cringed. "No one died." *Yet.* But his brother was gonna have to grow up for this conversation. It wouldn't be easy for either of them to hear. Especially seeing as how they'd both missed out on the last ten years of their father's life.

Silence ate away at his ears, but he had no idea where to start.

"We ought to go inside, sit down," Luis said, plodding to the door. He held it open, and one by one, they headed to the same kitchen table they'd sat around every night for their meat-and-potatoes dinners growing up. Lance took a chair next to Luis while Levi and Lucas faced off on the other side of the table.

Once they'd all sat, Luis didn't waste any time getting right to it.

"Parkinson's?" Levi's voice had shrunk and he almost sounded like a little kid again.

Lucas said nothing, simply stared at Luis as though he was waiting for him to continue.

But the man was a stubborn old ox. He didn't even want to tell them what the doctor said. So Lance broke the silence.

"What's the treatment?" He steeled himself, but that was all he really wanted to know. *Needed* to know.

"Not sure, yet," Luis said, looking neither worried nor confident. "The doc gave me some information. He wants to have a meeting to discuss treatment options in a couple of weeks."

The color had finally started to come back to Levi's face. "Parkinson's isn't bad, right? It's not fatal."

"Nah." Their father dug into the wood with his fingernail. "Might make it harder for me to get around. Harder to think clear, to remember things." He shot them an ornery grin. "Hell, that's been happening for years."

Not funny. None of this was funny. There was plenty Luis wasn't saying. Lance could tell. He knew a few things about Parkinson's. One of his old high school teachers had been diagnosed a few years after Lance'd graduated. Far as he remembered, the man had suffered complication after complication until he'd passed away.

"What can we do?" Lucas finally spoke. The terrified look in his eyes reminded Lance of the day they'd sentenced him to prison.

"Nothin'. Not right now, anyway." Luis took a minute to look at each one of them. "I'm sorry I kept it from you. But I wanted to be sure. Before I went and got everyone all riled up."

"It's okay, Dad." Levi's eyes steeled with determination. "Truth is, we've been keeping something from you, too."

Tension gripped Lance's neck. This was it. The conversation he'd dreaded for years. But he nodded at his brother. It was time. Long past time. "A lot longer than a couple of months," he added.

Lucas seemed bent on fading into the background, but they had to do this. And now was as good a time as any.

Luis sat straighter, his posture apprehensive. "I don't understand."

"Lucas didn't set the fire that night. I did," Levi said directly.

Their father's head shook. He clearly didn't believe them. "But you were only fourteen. And Lucas confessed."

"Because we worked out a plan," Lance cut in. He was so ready to be done with this. To put the past behind them so they could be family for whatever time they had left. "Levi'd already been in enough trouble. We were afraid of what juvie would do to him. So Lucas said he'd take the blame instead. He had the cleanest record." It had made so much sense at the time.

"Why?" Their father was raking his hand through the tufts of white hair that were already sticking straight up on his head.

Levi's jaw tightened. "You were meeting Maureen Dobbins there. And I was so pissed off." He cut a glance to Lance. They'd all been pissed off. Levi was the one who'd caught Luis kissing Maureen in the stables, but they'd all been angry about his frequent indiscretions. They'd heard the rumors around town. And Maureen was married. To the rodeo commissioner.

Levi wouldn't look at any of them. "I thought Mom would come back. So I wanted to destroy it. The place you met up with Maureen. To make you stop."

Their father stared at the table, hands flat and motionless against the wood. "I'm sorry." His voice cracked, nearly breaking the words. "I'm so sorry, boys." An expression of stunned anguish drew Lance's hand to his father's shoulder.

"I didn't know how to be what you needed," Luis uttered.

"I didn't know how to be what she needed. I couldn't hold it all together."

"Doesn't matter now," Lucas insisted. "Things are different. You're different."

"We're all different," Lance threw in. And maybe that meant things could change now.

Luis seemed to shut everything else out as he gazed at his middle son. "All these years..." It was barely over a whisper. "I was so hard on you..."

Lucas slipped out of his chair and knelt in front of their father. "It's okay. You didn't know. I don't want you to think about it now."

The old man couldn't seem to lift his head.

"You did your best." Lance waited until Luis looked at him. "Things might not've been perfect, but we knew you wanted us. We knew you loved us. We never had to question that." Didn't matter what happened, Luis wouldn't have left them. He never would've walked out on them. And in Lance's book, that made him a saint.

"None of us care about the past." Lucas went back to his chair. "Time to move on, focus on you. Figure out how we can get you the best treatment available."

A breath lifted Lance's chest. Hope. He breathed it in. Six months ago, he would've been on his own with this. But now his brothers were home. They could navigate it together.

"I don't deserve you boys." Luis's eyes were all watery. "But I sure am glad to have you."

"I know a couple of doctors back in Oklahoma," Levi said, pushing back from the table. "I'm gonna call them and see if they have any recommendations for a good neurologist. We need the best."

"And I'm gonna call the McGowens. Let them know I'll

be delayed for a while," Lucas said, already pulling out his cell.

After they'd stepped out, Luis faced Lance. "Why'd you keep the truth from me all these years?"

That was a no brainer. "To protect you."

"Some secrets are meant to protect, son," Luis said with a resolute quietness. "Sometimes that's all you can do for the people you love. Try to protect them. Even if it backfires on you."

Ouch. Nothing like tasting the truth of your own words. He slumped against the chair back. "I had no right to get so angry at her." Jessa had the best intentions. Always. She'd already proven that more than once. "Shit." He rested his forehead on the table, trying to formulate some kind of plan for how to take those words back, how to convince her he wanted her around. To be a part of this family.

A hell of a lot of time passed, but nothing came to him.

"Got a lead," Levi said, coming back to the table.

Lucas joined them, too. "They said to take all the time I need," he said, brushing a hand over Luis's shoulder. "We'll do whatever we have to do. You're not gonna go through this alone."

A long-forgotten sting pricked Lance's eyes.

"I made a lot of mistakes," Luis said, looking around at his sons. "But you boys...you're the only thing I did right."

"Come on." Levi rose from the table. "Let's head downtown. Beer's on me."

They all stood, but Lance hung back. "Actually, I have somewhere else I've gotta be."

A knowing look bounced between the others.

"Good luck, man." Lucas whacked him on the back.

Luis only shook his head. "Trust me. He's gonna need it."

Chapter Twenty-Four

*W*e'll always have Paris.

God, was there a more tragic phrase in the English language?

Jessa blubbered into the wad of Kleenex she'd fisted in her hands. "Isn't this the best movie ever?" she asked, reaching over to pat Ilsa's head.

On the couch next to her, the pig was too busy rooting her mouth around a bowl of fresh salad to actually watch the movie. A few days on antibiotics and the pig couldn't stop eating.

Jessa turned her attention back to the television. On a normal night, *Casablanca* drew a sort of dreamy-eyed teary sadness, but tonight it *moved* her. Lance's words had embedded themselves in her heart. She heard them play over and over. Even one of her favorite movies of all time hadn't drowned them out. And maybe it wasn't so much the words as what hid behind them. He'd wounded her on purpose, and she didn't understand, couldn't fathom, ever doing that to someone.

She wrapped her father's old wool blanket tighter around her shoulders, needing to feel that connection with him. With someone. The past few weeks of her life had been so wonderfully sweet. She'd actually felt like a part of the Cortez family. But that was her fault. She'd let herself read too much into it, let herself hope for something she knew she'd likely never have.

Headlights cut across the windows outside. She paused the movie and popped to her knees on the couch, stomach quaking with that familiar hunger Lance teased out in her. All it took was one thought of seeing him and suddenly her stomach groaned as though she hadn't eaten for two weeks.

Sure enough, his truck parked along the curb in front of her house.

Damn it! She slouched down trying to hide herself from those windows. "Quiet, Ilsa, baby," she hissed. She couldn't face him right now! Her eyes had nearly swollen shut from the tears. How pathetic was that?

The dreaded knock came at the door and Jessa scrunched herself down farther into the couch.

"Jessa?" Lance called.

She didn't move. Didn't even breathe. Maybe he'd take the hint that she didn't want to talk to him. Except she did want to talk to him. She really did. Her heart thrummed and her palms grew warm. But that was why she had to ignore him. If she let things go any further with him, he'd break her. He'd hurt her and she'd never recover.

"Come on," Lance said. "I can see you sitting there. Don't make me break in again," he added.

As if he'd earned the right to be cute.

"Fine." But when he saw her ugly, makeup-smeared eyes, he'd regret the threat. She'd always known makeup was a bad idea. What was the point anyway? A girl had to be able to cry without worrying she'd scare people away.

Keeping the blanket snug around her shoulders, she stood and plodded to the door, sneaking in a fortifying breath as she unlocked the deadbolt and opened it a crack. Just a crack.

"I'm sorry," he blurted. "I shouldn't have said that. I was upset. Surely you can understand that. He's all I have..."

She shuffled out onto the porch so he couldn't step foot in her house. If that happened she wouldn't have the strength to make him leave. And she had to. She deserved more than this. The cycle of him losing his shit and apologizing to her. "I get that," she said, forcing herself to look at him. "I know you love him." Luis may be the only person in the world Lance loved. "But he doesn't have to be all you have. That's what you've chosen." He chose that an hour ago when he took the one shot at her he knew would destroy her.

A look of desperation widened his eyes. "I won't give up. I'm gonna make you forgive me."

"That's the thing, Lance," she murmured through a sigh that admitted defeat. "I've already forgiven you." She'd forgiven him the moment he'd said those words. Because she loved him. Once again she loved someone as hard as her heart knew how, but he didn't love her back. And she couldn't do that to herself. After Cam had walked out on her, she'd thought she needed to give up on men, dating, relationships...but that wasn't true. She didn't have to give up on every man. On every relationship. But she had to choose the ones that built her up. She had to be strong enough to hold out for someone who would love her the way she craved. And let's face it...Lance didn't love her. He loved that she made him feel better about himself. That she believed he could win this competition. But what would happen when there were no more competitions? When he no longer needed her to boost his confidence?

He stepped closer, gazing down into her eyes with so much emotion she had to look away. "Let me come in. Please," he begged, brushing his hand across her arm as though he knew how much weight his touch held.

It did. One light touch from him ignited her. That's why he couldn't come in. She had no self-control when it came to Lance. If she let him in, he'd have her naked and in bed within five minutes, which would only make her love him and want him more. At some point she had to stop doing this to herself. She edged toward the door, gripping it for stability. "Here's the thing," she said, scrubbing the emotion from her voice. "I can't keep loving someone more than they love me. It hurts too much." There was no other way to say it. This whole thing with Lance had been more intense, more powerful, than any relationship she'd ever had. She felt it deeper and she had to protect herself.

He held her shoulders in her hands and forced her to face him. "I *want* to love you."

"But you don't."

He sighed and let his arms fall to his sides. "I'm not sure how to yet."

The admission purged her anger and gave sympathy room to grow. "It's not something I can teach you," she told him softly. "I always thought it was. Every relationship I've ever been in. I've tried." But that wasn't the way it worked. "Turns out, it's not so easy. Turns out that it ends up only hurting me. I don't have the energy for it anymore. I'm tired." Of getting hurt, but maybe even more than that, she was tired of trying so hard.

"You don't have to be the one to teach me," he insisted. "I'll learn it on my own. I'll figure it out."

She stepped backward, underneath the open door. Half inside her house and half outside. "It's not something you figure out like some kind of puzzle." It didn't have to be so complicated. It wasn't like passing a test or forcing yourself to work hard. "Love is something you choose. Every day. In the happy moments. But in the terrible moments, too. In the moments you're so angry you want to hurt someone. You still choose love." And he hadn't.

"God." The word came out through a tortured sigh. He lifted his hand to her face and drew her lips closer to his. "I want you so much it makes me hurt." His lips brushed hers and held on, locking her in a passionate kiss.

A sigh gave her away and she wilted against him, letting him bring her arms around him and pull her close. Just once more.

"Jessa, I will make this up to you," he uttered, kissing her mouth as though desperate to prove his words.

But a kiss wasn't enough. Mind-blowing sex wasn't enough. Him running to her when he needed comfort or confidence was not enough. Not for her.

She pushed him away and held him at arm's length. "You need to go now." Before it got any harder for her. Before she wasn't able to do what she knew was best. "Good night, Lance," she whispered.

Then she turned away and escaped into the house.

* * *

It wasn't like Jessa didn't have *anyone*. Surrounded by the light of her friends, the night didn't seem so dark. Darla, Cassidy, and Naomi all sat around her in the living room, forming what had become their sacred circle. They each still wore expressions that ranged from outrage to shock to indignation based on her explanation of what had transpired with Lance.

She hadn't held anything back—nope, the whole ugly truth was out there in the safest place possible. These women would guard it with their lives. When she'd put out the SOS text, they hadn't asked why, they'd simply come over right away, toting along chocolate and wine and ice cream, even thought it was almost midnight.

Naomi hadn't even bothered to change out of her pajamas. She'd simply gone over and asked Luis to sit at the house with Gracie while she ran an errand. Jessa imagined his eyebrows had gone up, but Naomi said he hadn't asked any questions. Of course he hadn't. That was Luis. He strictly minded his own business.

So they were here. All her best girls. And her amazing little piggy was perched comfortably on her lap. And you know what? That was enough. Who needed boys anyway?

"I can't believe he said something so stupid," Naomi fumed around a mouthful of intense dark.

"Oh, I can," Darla cut in. "Lance has no clue when it comes to women. Or love."

"Seems to run in the Cortez family blood," Cassidy grumbled. Jessa didn't know all of the history between her and Levi, but the woman didn't exactly sing his praises.

"I don't know," Naomi murmured, looking down. "I always felt like Lucas understood me just fine."

Jessa reached over Ilsa's head and patted her friend's hand. Seemed she wasn't the only one hurting. Ever since Lucas had come back, Naomi had been subdued and sullen.

"I hope you told him where he could stuff his sorry-ass apology," Darla muttered, pouring Jessa another glass of the good cab.

"I stayed pretty strong." Much stronger than she'd ever imagined she could be. Of course, the confrontation had been pretty short. One more minute alone with him and she would've totally caved. "But I don't trust myself to *stay* strong."

"Of course you can," Cassidy insisted valiantly. "You kept him out of your house. That was smart."

"You got this," Darla agreed.

Jessa withheld the story about getting in the car twice to go throw herself into his arms before they'd arrived. "The thing is, I don't think I can stay away from him. So Ilsa and I are heading to Denver first thing in the morning. To spend the weekend with Mom."

"You sure that's a good idea?" Naomi asked, wide-eyed.

"Yes." She'd thought it over and she didn't have a choice. "She might say I told you so, but she'll also take me out to dinner, and we can go shopping. Maybe even for a pedi and massage." Her mother still loved to take care of her, no matter how pathetic she was. "She'll love Ilsa," she said, giving her girl a squeeze. "Besides, I don't trust myself." She had to get out of there for a while. At least until Lance left for Worlds. Then she wouldn't have to see him, or accidentally run into him at the grocery store or the bar. She glanced at Cassidy. "Can you cover for me at the shelter tomorrow?"

"Of course. I can take more shifts, too. If you want to stay longer."

"That's okay. I don't want to be gone too long." She didn't plan to put her life on hold this time.

If her many breakups had taught her anything, it was that she couldn't sit and wallow.

Chapter Twenty-Five

He sure wished talking to a woman was as uncomplicated as talking to a bull. Wild Willy didn't care what the hell you said to him as long as you fed him. Lance walked away from the corral. Last day of training before he left tonight and he didn't even feel like being out there.

As he neared the fence, he noticed Levi hanging out waiting for him. Knots of tension pulled tight in his shoulders.

"So how'd things go with Jessa last night?" his brother asked, though he had to have some clue, given the fact that Lance couldn't seem to focus.

Damn. He whipped out his bandanna and mopped his face. Levi would love this, knowing he'd struck out. "She told me to take a hike." Not like he could deny it. Levi would find out soon enough anyway.

"Seriously?" he asked through a laugh. "What the hell did you say to her?"

"I don't know." Wasn't like he'd scripted out anything eloquent. He sucked at talking. "I said sorry."

"That's it?"

Thinking back, his words did seem inadequate. He'd been so desperate, but he had no clue what to say to undo the damage. That was the worst part, that he'd hurt her. He'd caused her pain. It definitely sucked that she'd rejected him, but he could take it. What he couldn't take was the deep sadness in her eyes. "I get why she wouldn't hear me out. It's fine. I just wish I knew how to make her feel better. Even if she never wants to see my face again..."

Levi whistled low. "Good thing I came back when I did." Head shaking, he nailed Lance's shoulder with his fist. "Come on." Without an explanation, he trotted away.

"Where're we going?" he called, jogging to keep up.

"To Jessa's house, idiot. I'm gonna help you get her back."

Oh, sure. Like it'd be that easy. "She seemed pretty serious about not wanting me around." All night he'd stewed on the whole mess, trying to think up a way to fix it, and so far he had jack.

"Trust me." Levi swaggered past his front porch. "Women only need to hear the right words. She'll come around."

As they were climbing into the truck, Lucas rode up on his mountain bike. He leaned it against the garage and sauntered over. "What're you two up to?"

"We're going to win Jessa back for Lance," Levi said, turning the key in the ignition. "Wanna come?"

"Hell, yeah." Lucas ripped off his helmet and tossed it into the yard. "I could use some entertainment today."

"Great," Lance muttered, reaching around to unlock the

door for his brother. If he couldn't even beg for her back when they were alone how was he supposed to do it in front of an audience?

Lucas climbed in and belted up, just in time, as Levi gunned the engine and they were skidding down the driveway. He'd always been a shitty driver. Not surprising, given the fact that Lance was the one who'd taught him.

"So what's the plan?" Lance asked, hoping Levi could come up with something better than he had last night.

"The first thing you gotta do is admit you were wrong," his youngest brother instructed, as if he were some kind of expert.

"Did that." And it'd gotten him nowhere.

"But did you justify it?" Levi revved the truck out onto the highway. "Or did you just tell her you fucked up and you were sorry?"

He tried to think back. "I said, 'I'm sorry, but—'"

"*But?*" Levi and Lucas said in unison.

His middle brother shook his head. "Man, even I know you never say 'but' after the word 'sorry.'"

"Why didn't I know that?"

"Because the women you've tended to surround yourself with don't exactly expect apologies," Levi said. "Jessa's different."

"Yeah. I've figured out that much." As painful as it was to let his youngest brother give him advice, that's the only thing that made this worth it. The fact that Jessa was special.

"Don't worry. We'll get her back. It'll take some finesse, but I can help you out with that."

Lance shared an amused, albeit irritated look with Lucas. "And you know this how?"

"I know women," his brother bragged, in full swagger

mode. "Trust me. When you see her, you take her hand, look into her eyes, and tell her you're sorry. And that you love her."

Wait. Love? "What?"

"Tell her you love her," Levi repeated.

"But..." Did he love her? "I shouldn't say it unless it's true."

"It's true. You're definitely in love with Jessa." Levi glanced at Lucas in the rearview mirror as though searching for confirmation.

"Yep," their brother agreed. "Definitely."

He jerked his head to stare at Levi, the cocky prick. "How do you know I'm in love with her?"

"Because you care more about her than what you're missing out on," his brother pointed out. "You said you didn't care that she'd rejected you. You only care about making her happy. That clearly means you're in love."

"Okay, Dr. Phil," he mumbled.

"Lucas? Back me up?"

"I don't know what he's talking about, but I do see the way you look at Jessa." Lucas stared out the window. "I recognize that look."

Of course he would. He still got it every time he saw Naomi. "You ever sit down with Naomi? Go over any of the numbers?" Maybe have the conversation they both seemed too terrified to have?

"That's difficult when she doesn't want to be in the same room with me."

"Yeah, I guess it would be." The woman had definitely been avoiding him. "I'll talk to her."

"Not a lot of good that'll do either one of us. I don't belong in Topaz Falls anymore." He said it like it was a fact.

Lance would have to keep working on that, too.

The truck bounced down Main Street, but instead of heading to the shelter, Levi took a fast left and parked in front of the KaBloom Flower Shop and Boutique.

Despite living here his whole life, Lance had never stepped foot in that store. "What're we doing?"

Levi uttered a long-suffering sigh. "Getting flowers, dumbass. You can't expect to get her back without flowers."

"Really?" He eyed the shop windows.

"Come on." Lucas put a hand on his shoulder and dragged him to the door.

Ten minutes and one bouquet of colorful wildflowers later, they pulled up at the shelter.

Nerves lit him up the same way they did before he got into the arena. "Her car's not here." Maybe he should come back later. Alone. So his brothers didn't hear him sound like a fool.

"Let's go in and see where she is," Levi said, cutting the engine.

Since when was he the boss? Gathering up the bouquet, Lance got out of the truck and led the way inside.

Cassidy was sitting behind the reception desk. She looked up, but then turned to focus on a computer screen as though determined to ignore him.

"Hey," he said, snagging her attention back to him.

"Can I help you with something?" she asked as though she'd never met him before.

Damn. She'd obviously heard what had happened. He tried not to let her glare ruffle him. "I need to talk to Jessa. Do you know where she is?"

She refused to look at him. "Of course I know where she is."

"But you're not going to tell me." That much was obvious. Jessa must've informed her little group what he'd said to her.

"Why would I tell you?" Cassidy asked with a chilly glance.

"Because I care about her?" Love. He loved her. Why did he find it so hard to say out loud?

"Whatever." She rolled her eyes and went back to the computer screen. "Maybe you should call her," she suggested.

"Right. Okay." He retreated to the doors, ready to hightail it out of there, but Levi blocked him.

"Leave this to me," he whispered, then nudged him out of the way and strode to the counter. "Hey there, Cass. How's your mom?"

Her eyes narrowed into dangerous blue slits. "She's not so good. But you wouldn't know that, would you? You don't exactly check in anymore."

Whoa. Lance winced.

"Ouch," Lucas whispered.

"Oh. Uh. Well…" Levi sputtered. "You know how it is out on the road." The fact that Levi didn't have her swooning under the power of his signature smile seemed to throw off his confidence.

Cassidy glared at him, hands stacked on her hips. "Yeah, I know how it is. No time for the people you knew before. So you'd better get going, Levi. Rush on back to that spotlight before it gets too dim."

Lance hid a chuckle behind a hearty throat clearing. He wondered how long she'd been waiting to say that.

"Can you at least tell us when Jessa will be back?" Levi asked meekly.

"No," she shot back without missing a beat. "I can't." Without another glance in his direction, she stood and stalked into the back room.

Levi turned to them, a stunned expression flattening his normally charismatic eyes.

They stepped out the door single file.

"Smooth," Lucas said, giving their youngest brother a cheerful pat on the shoulder. "Real smooth."

Levi sulked his way to the truck while Lance and Lucas laughed behind him.

"We can swing by the Chocolate Therapist," Lucas suggested.

"Maybe Darla won't be so mean to you," Lance badgered as they all climbed into the truck. But Levi didn't grin. It seemed Cassidy had gotten to him.

After a quick stop at Darla's, where she'd flipped them off from behind the locked glass door, they stood on Naomi's porch.

Lance was almost afraid to knock. "Hell hath no fury like a scorned woman's friends."

"No shit," Levi said, shaking his head. He obviously didn't know *everything* about women. In fact, he seemed as clueless as the rest of them.

"Naomi *will* talk," Lucas said, raising his hand to knock. "She'll know how important this is."

It took a while for the door to open. Lance wondered if she'd seen them through the window and had to prepare herself. She said nothing, simply watched them all walk through her front door. Not surprisingly, her gaze lingered on Lucas, but when he came near her, she retreated to the other side of the small entryway.

Man, she wouldn't even stand next to him...

"What're you doing here, Lance?" she asked as if she already knew. Cassidy and Darla had likely warned her.

Guess that meant he had to level with her. "I need to talk to Jessa. Where is she?"

"Does it matter where she went?" Naomi's cheeks looked rosier than normal and she completely avoided Lucas's gaze. "She left. Because of what you said to her."

"It matters." More than she realized. "I'm leaving and I need to see her before I go." He needed to know she was okay. He needed to see her smile and hear her laugh and he needed to tell her he loved her.

"Jessa doesn't want to be found right now," she said, leaving them behind while she walked into the kitchen.

"Wait. Hold on." Lucas followed her.

The woman's eyes instantly went soft, like she saw some warm glow haloed around him. Man, talk about love.

"I know you're trying to protect her," Lucas said gently. "But I'd hate for her to miss out on something because she's too afraid to hear what he has to say," he murmured.

Naomi's tense shoulders collapsed under a sigh. "She's at her mom's. In Denver."

"Thank you," Lucas almost whispered. Their eyes held for a moment before Naomi turned to the counter and snatched a plate out of the dishpan, drying it with frantic motions. "You didn't hear that from me," she said, her voice shaky.

Lucas shoved his hands into his pockets, leading the way to the front door. "See you later, then." His tone was as subdued as hers.

Lance was tempted to drag Naomi over there and force her to talk to Lucas. They were obviously still hung up on each other. Before he had the chance, Lucas slipped out the front door. Guess that confrontation would have to wait. He could only manage one relationship crisis at a time.

On the porch, Levi turned to face him. "What're you gonna do?" Seemed like his younger brother was all out of good ideas.

But Lance had one more. "I guess I'm going to Denver."

* * *

If Jessa had learned one truth in her life, it was that you are never too old to bake cookies with your mom. There was something so comforting about it—being in the kitchen together, measuring out the ingredients, whipping and stirring while a sweet little pig dozed contentedly in a dog bed at her feet.

Jessa's mother had never been much of a domestic diva, but she'd always baked the best cookies, and somehow she did it in heels and a lovely fitted dress, which she'd covered with an apron, of course. Jessa, however, was still in the *I don't feel like showering* phase of wallowing, so she'd opted for sweats. Elastic waistbands always came in handy after a breakup.

She dumped an extra handful of chocolate chips into the dough and went to work folding them in with a spatula.

"Wow." Her mom peered over her shoulder. "That's some serious chocolate therapy."

"I need it." Though they'd already managed to fit in a lovely breakfast at a local café and pedicures, her heart still drooped with sadness. During the last few hours, she'd filled her mother in on the latest romantic debacle. And, surprisingly, her mom hadn't resorted to any lectures. She'd simply listened and asked her questions about Lance. It made it sort of hard to forget about him while talking about how wonderful he was.

"The oven is all preheated. Here." Carla withdrew a cookie sheet from the cupboard and set it on the counter. "Make them as big as you want."

"Don't mind if I do," Jessa said, pulling out a spoon and scooping up a huge blob of dough. These babies were going to be her lunch. Maybe her dinner, too. She was wearing sweats, after all.

"I thought we could go shopping a little later," her mother suggested. "If you—"

The doorbell twinkled a lovely tune. Good lord. Even Carla's doorbell was elegant and refined.

"I'll be right back," she said, untying her apron and pulling it over her head. God forbid anyone see her looking the least bit frumpy. If only Jessa'd inherited *that* gene. The one that cared what people thought about her appearance.

She glanced down at her attire. Nope. She hadn't. "Trust me, sweats are way more comfortable," she informed Ilsa as she continued scooping huge mounds of dough onto the cookie sheet. She'd already bought too many new clothes, but shoe shopping could be fun. At least it would momentarily distract her. And she always loved to people watch at the mall . . .

Her mother rushed back into the kitchen and ripped the spoon out of her had. "Lance is at the door," she whispered. "He'd like to talk to you."

"*Lance?*" She shot to the other side of the kitchen—as far away from the front door as possible. "What is he *doing* here?" How the hell did he find her?

"Maybe you should ask him," Carla said, ushering her toward the hallway.

She dug in her heels and stopped, looking down at her clothes again. They seemed to scream *You broke my heart!* and *I'm too pathetic to even get dressed!* "No." She shook her head. "I can't talk to him. I can't see him." Her heart fell to pieces just thinking about it. "Tell him to leave me alone," she said, her voice wavering.

Her mother smoothed a comforting hand down her hair. "Are you sure?"

It was so tempting. He'd driven all the way down from Topaz Falls. Topaz Falls! But this is what she did. She always gave in. She never stood her ground. "Please. I can't." Yes, she was being a coward, but they'd both already said everything there was to say. "Tell him to go."

"All right," Carla said uncertainly before she walked briskly down the hall.

Jessa held her breath, but she couldn't hear anything. After checking on Ilsa, she crept down the hallway and hid around the corner closest to the front door.

"I'm sorry," Carla was saying. "Jessa's tired and not up for company."

"I won't stay long." The sound of Lance's voice struck her. It was polite, but firm, too. "I just need two minutes."

"Well . . ." Her mother hesitated.

Come on, Mom! Jessa almost yelled. Though she understood how hard it could be to resist Lance Cortez.

"I'm sorry," Carla said again. "She seemed adamant, and—"

The pig chose that moment to come barreling down the hall, squealing like she'd been stuck with a pin, her dainty little hooves skidding on the polished wood floors.

"Ilsa!" Jessa screeched, lunging to catch her as the pig shot by. But she missed and ended up sprawled on the floor in full view of the front door.

Lance bent and somehow captured the pig while holding on to a bouquet of flowers.

Ilsa grunted and thrashed, her little legs trying to run away.

"Simmer down, Pork Chop," Lance said, subduing her in his arms. "Not gonna hurt you."

Jessa lay on the floor looking up at him, and he seemed so broad and powerful that he made the pig look like a stuffed animal.

"Hi," he said, gazing down at her.

"Hello," she managed. Not like she could avoid him now.

"I'll go ahead and take Ilsa," her mother offered, reaching out her hands. "And we'll give you two a minute."

Before Jessa could latch on to her ankle and beg her to stay, Carla hurried down the hall, calmly soothing the poor pig.

"I know you don't want to see me." Lance reached down and took hold of her hand, pulling her up effortlessly.

She glanced at her frumpy attire. "I'm not really dressed to see anyone." Especially Lance. Especially looking like this. God! Why'd she have to eavesdrop?

"You're beautiful," he said, his eyes seeming to take her—and all of her frumpiness—in. He held out the wilted and battered bouquet of wildflowers—daisies and wax flowers and snapdragons.

She took them, focusing on the vivid colors so she didn't have to look into his eyes.

"I just came to tell you I love you," he said quickly, as though afraid she might slam the door in his face. "You might not believe me, and I might not be great at show-ing it, but I do. I know I do." He handed her an envelope that had been tucked in his pocket. "This is everything you need to come to Vegas. If you decide you want to. My flight leaves soon, but if you decide to come, there's a flight and hotel voucher in there. And I put in special passes to the events."

Jessa's hand shook so hard, she could barely grip the flimsy paper. "I can't come." She wouldn't go running back to him. Not this time. She'd be like her mom and guard her-self. She'd be better than the girl who went back for another round of heartache. "Sorry. It's not going to work out." She tried to return the envelope to him, but he backed away.

"Keep it," he said quietly. Hopefully. "Just in case you change your mind." He stared at her a minute more as though storing up the vision of her face, then turned around and left.

Trying to hold it together, Jessa dragged herself back to the kitchen, the flowers and envelope weighting her hands.

Carla smiled brightly. "Is everything better?"

"No." She dumped the gifts he'd given her on the kitchen counter. "He told me he loved me. And I didn't say any-thing."

Her mother's sigh was both disapproving and sympa-thetic. Carla leaned against the counter, arms crossed, eyes so much like Jessa's honed in on her face.

"Why are you looking at me like that?" she demanded. "You of all people should be thrilled that I sent him away." She's the one who always told her she should be more care-ful about who she gave her heart to.

Instead of snapping back, Carla gestured for Jessa to sit on a stool.

"Why do I feel like I'm the one in trouble?" She slumped onto the stool. Wasn't this what Carla wanted for her? To be an independent, strong, unaffected woman?

"I guess I understand where he's coming from," her mother murmured as though the admission embarrassed her.

Where *he* was coming from? "I'm sorry?"

"I loved your father, Jessa."

"What?" She must not have heard that right.

"It took me ten years of therapy to figure it out."

"Therapy?" *Whoa*. Wait a minute. Who was this woman? "You don't do therapy." Or at least she'd never said anything.

"Actually, I do." Her mother's smile appeared almost apologetic. "You never knew your grandparents. That was on purpose. My father...he was the worst kind of bully."

Jessa had suspected as much, but Carla had never been exactly open about her own childhood. "You've never talked about him."

"There weren't many good things to say." She paused as though she had forced herself to say them now. "He wasn't abusive, but he was controlling. And he insulted my mother constantly. He treated her like a child. Wouldn't even let her get her driver's license."

"God. Really?" Well, she was glad she'd never known him, then.

"When I left home, I decided I'd never marry. Never fall in love. I thought it made you weak."

Like her grandmother. Her mom didn't have to say it. Jessa could sense the feelings of resentment.

Carla reached over and gripped her hand firmly. "But you're one of the strongest people I know, Jessa. And your father was, too." Tears glistened in her regal brown eyes, softening them. "He always told me he'd love me forever.

Even if I never loved him back. And he did. He sent me cards and letters and gifts all those years."

The mention of her father sent a wave of grief crashing over her.

"I felt so unworthy," Carla went on. "I pushed him away every chance I had. I told him to move on so many times."

"He never did." Buzz had never gone out on another date. He'd never said why, although Jessa had suspected he hadn't gotten over her mom. The two of them never dragged her into their complicated relationship, though. She'd had no clue he'd sent her mother letters.

"No. He never did move on." She laughed a little. "He was so stubborn, that man."

Jessa smiled, too. Stubborn in the best way possible.

"After you left home, I realized I wasn't healthy," Carla admitted, as though somewhat ashamed. "Emotionally. So I started therapy, and it helped me understand how afraid I'd been." Her lips pursed bravely. "The week before he passed, I wrote him a letter and told him how much I loved him. I was going to go up there to see him as soon as the summer session ended..."

But she hadn't made it in time.

Her mother's obvious pain pinched Jessa's heart. "Why didn't you tell me?"

"I don't know." Her head shook. "I guess I was embarrassed. I wasted all those years. We could've been happy. We could've been a family."

"We were a family." Definitely not conventional, but bonded by love all the same. "And at least he knew. Before. At least you told him you loved him." It changed things, knowing that. Knowing he had everything he'd wanted at the end.

Mom's eyes sought out hers. They were so solemn. "Fear does strange things to people. It makes them lash out." An unmistakable empathy echoed through the words.

"You think Lance is afraid." Yeah, well he wasn't the only one.

Carla held her hands. "I think he loves you and I think it terrifies him."

"I can't help him with that." Not again. Not this time. He'd probably just push her away like he had before.

Her mother lifted Jessa's chin like she had so many times when she was young. But this was different. She understood so much more now. Looking back at Carla, she saw a woman who had been wounded, who had spent her life running from relationships. Kind of like someone else she knew...

"How many times have you almost been attacked by an animal you were trying to rescue?" her mom asked quietly.

"Too many to count."

"Why do they try to attack?"

"Because they're in a vulnerable position. They feel threatened, and..." As she said them, the words struck her with meaning. "Oh."

"What do you usually do when an animal feels vulnerable and frightened?" She already knew, but Carla obviously wanted her to say the words.

"I move slowly," she whispered, tears weakening her throat. "And carefully. I show it I'm not there to hurt it." Sometimes it took a lot of convincing, especially when the animal had been neglected or abused.

"And you never walk away," Carla said through a sad smile.

"No." She'd never given up, even in the most hopeless

of situations. She'd always stuck it out, done whatever it took.

"What are you going to do this time?" Carla asked as though she already knew the answer.

Reaching over, she slid the envelope off the counter. "I guess I'm going to Vegas."

Chapter Twenty-Six

Lance had hardly stepped his spur inside the doorway to the swanky media reception before a curvaceous redhead cornered him. Up against a wall and way too far away from the bar for his comfort.

"Lance Cortez," she said in a flirty tone. "I'm Amber Hart."

He did his best to keep the cringe inside as he returned her dainty handshake. "Nice to meet you," he said politely, sneaking a glance at the media badge that dangled from a lanyard hanging over her fake breasts. He didn't recognize the name of the publication. Probably some small-town newspaper or one of those ad publications. They let just about anyone in here.

"So how are you feeling about the final ride?" she asked, leaning into him slightly.

Shitty. Actually, indifferent would be a better way to describe it. For the first five rounds of competition, he'd tried to maintain his focus, but each day that passed was another day he didn't hear from Jessa. Didn't know how she was doing. Didn't know *what* she was doing. He'd held out hope, and every time he went into the arena, he'd checked the seat number he'd given her. But she hadn't come.

Even with that distraction, he'd managed to maintain a spot as fourth overall in the competition, which meant he'd have to have a damn near perfect ride tomorrow to take the title.

If only he could shake the sinking feeling that maybe he'd really lost Jessa for good…

Not that Red had rights to any of that information. Avoiding eye contact, he shrugged. "Oh, you know. I feel ready."

"You sure look ready," she murmured, stripping him down with her eyes.

Five years ago that little suggestion beaming in her gaze would've invited him to take her arm and lead her to the bar, where he'd buy her drinks and charm her all the way up to his hotel room, but apparently Jessa had ruined him for any uninvolved fun because, despite the slinky dress and the impressive curves, this woman did nothing for him. "Um, will you please excuse me, Miss Hart?" He made a quick sidestep and scanned the restaurant over her shoulder. "I should go find my father." They'd come in together, but in true Luis Cortez form, he seemed to have wandered off. Smart man.

"Oh, sure, okay," she bubbled. "Here's my number." Her hand expertly slipped a card into his jean pocket, patting a little too close to his package. "Maybe we can hang out later."

"Maybe." He gave her a smile even though he had no intention of following up.

After he'd left her behind, he worked his way across the room, saying hello to some of the guys he'd competed against over the years and avoiding eye contact with every woman who seemed to be there to snag herself a stag. Finally, he saw Luis sitting at the end of the bar alone, which was exactly where he wanted to be. Head down, he elbowed his way through the lively crowd and plopped down on the stool next to Luis.

His father looked him over. "You look as miserable as a hog who's had his tail straightened," he said, taking a pull on his beer.

"I am," he admitted, signaling to the bartender to bring him whatever Luis was drinking.

"What're you doing here, son?"

He knew Luis didn't mean at the party. He meant why was he here when things weren't resolved with Jessa. Lance inhaled deeply. "Actually...I have no idea." For months he'd had this clear vision, this laser focus on Worlds. Like the closer he got to losing his career, the tighter he'd held on. Except now he couldn't for the life of him think why. It suddenly seemed a hell of a lot less important.

"This world...it doesn't give back to you." Luis looked at him square in the face, wearing the same expression he had when Lance was a teenage delinquent. "You sacrifice your body—hell, your whole life—and in the end you don't have much to show for it."

"So I guess the joke's on us, huh?" Funny. The only guarantee when you were a professional athlete was that you'd have to retire early. You had to be prepared to walk away and start something new. Walk into a whole new life. No one told you that when you were starting out, though.

"If I hadn't had you boys when I retired, I would've lost

myself." Luis turned the stool to face him. "I did for a while. Took some time to get myself straightened out. I don't want that to happen to you. You're a lot like me. The most like me out of all you boys."

"I'll take that as a compliment." Even though that wasn't how Luis meant it. And he understood. He hid behind his career. Used it as an excuse to block out everything else. He'd learned from watching his old man. He studied his father, still saw that spark of a young cowboy in his eyes, even with all of the lines the years had carved into his skin. "Why couldn't you stop Mom from leaving?" He'd never asked, but now seemed like as good a time as any, seeing as how he was going to have to deal with his issues if he ever wanted to get Jessa back.

Instead of deflecting the question with a gruff shrug of his shoulders like he usually did when Lance brought up something he didn't want to talk about, Luis set down his beer. It clanked against the bar top with the tremor in his hand. "Maybe I could've. Truth is, I didn't try." His solemn eyes lifted and found Lance's. "We got married young, and your mom...she worried an awful lot."

"I know. I remember." She was always fussing over the three of them. Though as they'd gotten older she seemed to detach herself more and more.

"It wasn't normal worry. It consumed her, made her sick." His father's cheeks hollowed. "They'd call it anxiety now. And it was constant."

"I guess I didn't realize it was so bad." But now that he thought about it, she stayed home as often as she could. Didn't have many friends. Tended to keep them home, too. She never hung around the corral, never went to any of their competitions.

"They didn't have medication for it then," Luis said. "No help. And I didn't know what to do for her."

"That's why she left?" Because of anxiety? It seemed like such a simple thing...

"She couldn't handle it. The fact that all you boys were following in my footsteps. Riding bulls. She wasn't sleeping, wasn't eating. She was so afraid something would happen to you."

Something did happen to them. All three of them. The day she left, she broke them. God, just look at them. All around thirty years old and not one healthy positive relationship among them...

"She didn't leave because she didn't love you," Luis said quietly. "I never wanted you to think that."

Remnants of the familiar anger stirred. "She could've chosen to stay." She could've tried to get help. She could've gone to counseling or something.

Luis shook his head. "Anxiety's a hard thing to understand if you've never had it. It's not just in your head. It's physical. I saw it in her. It was killing her." For the first time, Lance noticed a tremor in his father's head. It ticked, making Lance look away. He couldn't stand to see it, the evidence of a disease.

"I should've tried harder. I wish I would've done more. I wish I would've at least taken time off to try and help her before it got so bad."

For the first time, Lance let himself consider the possibility she hadn't wanted to leave. Maybe she didn't feel she had a choice. "You think it would've made a difference?"

"Maybe." Luis sighed. "If I'd fought for her. If she would've had more support." He gave Lance a long, steady glare, the same one he'd used when Lance would mouth off as an angry teen. "I know it cut you deep when she left. But it might be time to stop blaming her, son. As a parent you try to do your best with what you've got. In her way that's what she did. That fear she had...it lied to her. Told her you'd be better off without her. I know it's hard to understand, but that's the truth of it."

"Guess I don't have to understand it." All these years, he'd tried. And even knowing what he knew now, he *couldn't* understand. Luis was right. He hadn't stood where she stood. He had no idea what she struggled with. But he did know one thing. He couldn't let fear rob him of loving someone, of letting her love him. He wanted to do better than his mother had. All these years, he hadn't. When he'd lashed out at Jessa, it wasn't because he was pissed. It was because he was afraid. For his father, sure, but also for himself. "You regret it?" he asked his father. "Sticking with your career instead of walking away to be what she needed?"

A deep inhale seemed to steady Luis's tremors. "More than I can say. I was too busy collecting a whole lot of shiny shit that doesn't mean much." He looked around the party surrounding them. "Thing is, that's not my legacy. That room of buckles and trophies and news clippings. No one here gives a rat's ass who I am now."

"I do," Lance argued. His father had done his best for them. In his imperfect way. But it was enough. He'd earned their loyalty, their love, even if he didn't feel he deserved it.

Hope sparked inside of him, filling that empty coldness that'd hounded him since Jessa had sent him away. Maybe his pathetic, imperfect offering could be enough for her, too.

His father reached over and squeezed his shoulder. "You can leave your mark on this world only in the people you love. Not in the stuff you accomplish. You remember that, son."

If Luis had said that to him six months ago, he would've laughed. But now he was starting to understand.

* * *

"It's gotta be perfect, Cortez," Tucker said, pacing on the outside of the chute. "I mean, one hundred percent flawless. You gotta get your leg off him. You need the extra points."

"You think I don't know that?" Lance tightened the chin-strap on his helmet. He eyed the bull that snorted on the other side of the fence. Loco Motive made Ball Buster and Wild Willy look like kittens. The damn bull had already taken eight riders out of the competition and had sent two to the hospital.

Adrenaline boiled in his gut, shooting his body temperature up about a hundred degrees. Damn all the gear they made 'em wear these days. When he'd started out, he hadn't had to bear half his weight in body armor.

"Stay loose up there," Tucker instructed.

How was that possible when he felt this tense? He glanced around at the television cameras, all starting to swing his way. The announcers were no doubt detailing his story, his last title from six years ago to now, when he'd barely qualified to be here.

Was Jessa watching? Would she be cheering him on? God, he wanted to call her right now, tell her everything he'd wanted to say to her. But she hadn't returned any of his messages. Five days. It had been only five days since he'd seen her and yet it felt like five months.

All week, he'd held on to her words. *You can win*. They'd

kept him going. Jessa thought he could do this, so he'd ride perfect. Not for the cheering fans. Not for Luis or Tucker. Not even for himself. For her. From this moment on, he wanted everything to be about her.

The manager gave him the signal to climb up and get into position.

Here we go. He tried to clear his head the way he'd always been able to do. Took some deep breaths, inhaling that manure-tinged scent of the bull. Took about five guys to hold Loco Motive in place while Lance climbed the fence.

Tucker gave him a final pat on the arm, looking a hell of a lot more nervous than him. He couldn't blame him. Lance hadn't exactly had a stellar ride this week. Solid, but nothing that could put him on top. Not yet at least.

"You're on," the director said.

Lance swung his leg over the fence and slid onto the bull. Instantly agitated, the son of a bitch snorted and bucked.

Lance got his right hand gripped onto the rope and kept his left hand up. Had to keep his left arm raised, no matter what happened. If it came down, if it so much as grazed the bull, he'd lose points.

The chute opened.

Loco Motive shot straight into the corral, bucking and kicking. Pissed off as all hell.

But Lance kept his form. Left arm waving, right hand fisting that rope so damn hard it felt like his knuckles would break. The arena flashed around him, fragmented glimpses of the crowd, the judges, the scoreboard.

One...

The bull's body jackknifed, but he saw it coming. His body whipped forward and he clenched his legs tight around the bull's wide girth, waving his left arm over his head.

Two...

The loud roar of the crowd muted Loco Motive's angry snorts. The bull reared up again launching them both.

Three...

Fuck! Could this get any longer? He curved his back, let his upper body jolt freely with the bull's enraged kicks.

Four...

His right hand burned like someone had stuck it in a fire. Another hard jerk sent a shot straight to his back, the muscles threatening to cave in.

Five...

Loco Motive spun in a rage, kicking up the dirt, tossing his head back like he'd had it. Lance's body thrashed, ribs separating, whiplash starting to weaken his neck.

Six...

Every muscle in Lance's body pinched, sending rivers of pain all through him. Not enough. This ride was not enough.

Seven...

He saw lights. Blurred faces. His leg. He had to get his leg up. Straining his back, he raised his left arm higher over his head and shifted his balance. His back spasmed as he lifted his right leg away from the bull, holding his posture, fighting like hell to keep his grip. The crowd's praise droned in his ears.

Eight!

His grip loosened. The right wrist was giving out. He hugged his knees into the bull's sides and flung his left arm high into the air with a whoop. Loco Motive gave one last bucking kick as though he'd taken personal offense to that, and flung Lance toward the corral fence.

A collective gasp hushed the crowd, but elation drowned out the pain in his body. That was the ride of his life. He

knew it, felt it. While the bullfighter lured away Loco Motive, Lance lay flat on his back in the dirt, staring up at
the scoreboard. Two medics rushed over but he waved them
away. He'd be fine. As soon as he saw the score, he'd be fine.
It seemed to take forever while the crowd murmured. He lay
there under the lights, taking it all in, wishing he would see
Jessa's face in the stands.

"Ninety-four point eight," the announcer called with an
excitement that reignited the arena.

He had to blink, had to squint his eyes to make sure that
was right.

Sure enough, the red numbers lit up the screen: 94.8.
There were three riders left, but no one would beat that. No
one *could* beat that. His eyes closed and he breathed out,
now feeling every aching muscle, every sore bone.

He flattened his hands against the ground, ready to get
up, but Tucker catapulted in and landed right on top of him.
"Hell yeah!" his friend yelled. "Hell! Yeah!" He slapped him
square in the chest. "You nailed it!"

Wincing, Lance rolled out from underneath Tucker and
pushed to his feet. The crowd noise deafened him. He waved
and started to limp toward the gate, trying to keep a rowdy
smile intact for the cameras. But it wasn't real.

There were thousands of people here. The one person he
wanted, though, the one who mattered, wasn't. He looked
around, at the crowd, all watching the replay on the Jumbotron
in an awed silence. And he felt no different. No better than he
had twenty minutes ago. He'd just taken the world title he'd
been striving for, and he didn't even feel like celebrating.

The crowd, the fanfare, the cheering...none of it even
came close to giving him the same rush he got when he made
Jessa smile.

Tucker launched himself into another man hug. "I can't believe it, you son of a bitch! You did it."

Lance pushed him off and backed away. He couldn't stay. All he could think about was pulling Jessa into his arms. He didn't care what she said, she belonged with him. And he belonged with her. "I have to get out of here. Now."

"You can't go!" Tucker tried to block him. "You just won the world title, jackass! They're not gonna let you cut out. You've gotta stay for the hoopla!"

He couldn't. Not without Jessa here. He never would've been able to do this if it hadn't been for her.

And she was all he needed.

Chapter Twenty-Seven

"OhmyGod, ohmyGod, ohmyGod!" Jessa sprinted down some steps in the dark arena, trying to find her way out so she could get to him. That image of him flying toward the fence replayed again and again, sending her stomach into a downward spiral. When he'd hit the ground, Lance hadn't moved. And before she knew what she was doing, she'd jumped up in a panic, stepping on toes and purses and drinks until she'd made her way to the end of the row. But where was she now? And where was Lance?

Was he *dead*?

Finally, she saw a door and charged it, jogging out into the concessions area. But the place was so big—so many stairs and food stands and doors...

"How can I get down there?" she asked some poor older man pushing a trash can. "I have to find Lance Cortez! I have to get to him."

He looked down as though embarrassed for her.

"I'm not a groupie!" she shrieked. "He gave me this pass!" She tugged at the lanyard hanging around her neck. "Where's the staging area? Where do they take injured riders?"

He pointed at an escalator and got the hell out of there.

Gripping the handrail, she stumble-jogged down the escalator to the main floor and tore down a corridor, searching for a door that would get her back there.

There! Official-looking steel double doors. She bolted for them, but before she got there, they flew open.

Lance ran out. Ran! He was running!

"What're you doing?" she yelled, floating to him in a stupefied jog. "Oh my God, Lance! I thought you were hurt!"

He caught her in his arms, looking her over, touching her like he had to make sure she was really standing there. "What are *you* doing?" he asked breathlessly. "I thought you didn't come..."

Seeing him whole, strong and upright, brought a fast rush of relief that made her dizzy. "I came." She cupped her hand on his uninjured cheek. "Of course I came." A happy sigh pushed her closer to him and she felt his heartbeat against her chest. "I couldn't get a flight out until this morning. Everything was booked." And she'd had to get coverage at the shelter, and find someone to watch Ilsa, and then Naomi and Darla and Cassidy had all wanted to come, so they'd had to find flights, too...

"But you weren't in your seat," he said, smoothing his hand down her hair. "I looked for you..."

"I got here late, so I just sat in an empty seat." Who knew how long it would've taken her to find the right section?

She ran her hands down his arms, searching for damage.

"And when the bull threw you, I got up and ran." She peered up at him, all teary and pathetic. "I couldn't stand it. I thought—"

"I'm fine. Hardly felt it." He hugged her close, kissing her forehead, her cheek, her lips. "When I won, all I could think about was you. You weren't there..."

"You won?" She gasped. She'd been so panicked she hadn't even realized. She pushed him away. "If you won you have to go back in there!" What the hell was he doing standing out here talking to her?

He gazed down at her and his eyes had the power to kill her and revive her all at once.

"I had to find you so I just...ran out."

"You shouldn't have." She never would've asked him to do that. "This was your dream. You should enjoy all of it. Everything the experience will offer you."

"I guess you could say I have a new dream." He lifted his hand to her face, trailing his fingers down her cheek. "One that matters more."

Jessa pressed her hand against her chest, tears welling. His nearness stirred a craving, a tingling rush that covered her skin and while the rest of her felt weak, her heart beat strongly.

"Fact is, I'm pretty messed up," he said, pressing his hand against hers, stroking her fingers. "What I said about you not being part of the family..." His head shook. "It wasn't you I was mad at. I've blamed my mom for everything. Every bad thing that's happened since she left, I put it on her."

"I can understand that," Jessa whispered.

"But I'm ready to let it go. Get past it. I have to or I'll never have anything that matters." His fingertips brushed hers but he didn't hold on. "You didn't betray me. You've only been good to me. And to my family. I'm sorry I hurt you."

She peered up at him, and with that one simple apology, it seemed he'd let her see so much more of his heart. "Thank you."

"This whole week, all I could think about was how you weren't here." He inched closer, and she closed her eyes, feeling his presence up against her. "Without you, I didn't care anymore. I've won competitions. And it's never made me feel as good as I feel when I'm with you."

"Lance..." There were so many things she wanted to say, but he took her hand, stealing the words along with her breath.

"I want you," he said through an utterly helpless sigh. "I don't have much to offer. But I want to be there for you. I want to make you happy. I want to hold you in my arms and feel you against me. Nothing in my life has ever felt as good as holding you. Nothing."

The quiet conviction in his voice filled her eyes. "I want you, too."

He said nothing more, only pulled her against him and sealed her lips with his, right there in the brightly lit corridor with people walking past them, his mouth devouring hers, hungry and passionate, as if he'd been saving up his whole life to offer her this one kiss.

It carried her away, the feel of his chest heaving against hers, the strength of his hands as they held her. "Lance," she murmured, letting her purse drop to the ground. "My God, Lance."

"Let's get out of here," he groaned.

And she couldn't have said no if she tried.

* * *

"My room is closer." She wrapped her arms around his sturdy back, holding on as he urged her into the elevator.

"Floor ten," she said, against his mouth. As the elevator zoomed up, his tongue teased its way into her mouth, weakening her knees, which made her cling to him tighter. The doors rolled open and they stumbled out, moving clumsily down the hall, unable to let go of each other.

"Key's in my pocket," she breathed, already undoing the buttons on his shirt.

He groped a hand into the pocket of her jeans until he found it.

As he unlocked the door, he caught her waist and pulled her against him again, bringing his lips to hers as he somehow pushed into the hotel room.

Her feet faltered along with his and before they'd made it to the bed, she kicked off her tennis shoes while he stepped out of his boots.

"I don't know how I lived without you so long," he murmured in her ear while his hands tugged up the hem of her shirt. "I don't think I was ever really alive."

She opened her mouth to answer, to tell him that she must've never really been in love before because this all felt new. Her heart pounded her ribs so hard they threatened to fracture. And it was so good. So good it almost hurt.

He pulled her shirt over her head and slipped his fingers into her bra and *ohhhhhh*. What was she going to say again? Nothing. She couldn't speak. She slumped against him while he touched her, teasing her nipples in long strokes while she clumsily undid the rest of the buttons on his shirt until she could push it off his shoulders and run her hands over the hard muscled plane of his abs.

H-ello. Just the sight of him was foreplay...

But looking wasn't enough. She wanted to feel him, to taste him. Threading her fingers between his, she ducked her head and kissed her way down his neck to his chest, sucking and licking and breathing hotly against his skin. When she reached the waist of his pants, she let his hands go and started to work at that rather impressive belt buckle, but before she could get it undone, he hauled her back up to him. "Not yet."

Tearing back the comforter and sheets, he laid her down on the bed, hovering over her, those eyes seeming to note every detail.

"I can't get enough of you," he breathed over her. "I'll never get enough of you." With that, he lowered his lips to her neck, sneaking his hands underneath her back so he could pop the clasp of her bra. Rising, he slowly slid the straps down her shoulders as though he enjoyed the torture.

"Too slow," she breathed, pushing up to her elbows. She tore the bra away and drew his face to her breasts.

His warm tongue traced every inch of her skin, forcing her head to fall back to the pillows. Without taking his lips away from her, his hands hitched up her hips and he took down her pants and sensible cotton underwear in one fluid motion.

"Should've worn my pretty underwear," she said with a gasp.

"I like you better without any." He pulled his body over hers, kissing her lips with a sensual rhythm that charged every part of her. God, no one had ever made her ache like this...

His lips moved down her neck again, covering her chest with warm, wet kisses, then moving lower to her stomach.

Sparks flashed low in her belly, sending flares of heat between her legs. She pressed her lips together so she wouldn't moan. She shouldn't be this close this fast...

He paused and glanced up at her. "You can be as loud as you want," he teased. "No one'll walk in on us this time."

Before she could respond, he took her hips in his hands, kissing and nibbling his way down to the inside of her thigh.

Her legs fell open. She did make noise then—a long groan flowed out of her lungs, deflating them completely.

"I love turning you on," Lance said, all low and hot as his fingers parted her.

She felt his sultry breath against her most sensitive parts first, then the slick wetness of his tongue. Her hands grasped for something to hold on to, finding only fistfuls of the sheets. Cries stammered from her lips as his mouth sucked and nibbled while his fingers slid in and out. A powerful tightening in her abdomen intensified until she broke apart, and it came so fast and so forcefully she may have cried out.

Lance's face appeared in front of hers, sly grin firmly in place. "You might've disturbed the neighbors," he said, playfully kissing her forehead.

"That would be a first," she admitted, her breathing still ragged. She'd never had a reason to be so loud before. She'd never been so overtaken that she lost control that way...

"I liked it." His eyebrows danced enticingly. "Let's do it again."

"Nope." Because it wasn't nearly as fun when she was the only one being so noisy. She squirmed out from underneath him, rising to her knees, which might never stop wobbling. "This belt is coming off now, cowboy." Her hands fumbled with the brass buckle until it released. Locking her eyes on his, she gave him a small smile while she ripped open the button fly on his jeans and shoved them down, taking the boxer briefs with them. "I can turn you on, too, you know." She climbed onto him, wrapping her legs around him and grinding her hips into his.

"I'm turned on just looking at you," he uttered, pulling her so tightly against his body that nothing stood between them. His eyes locked hers in an intimate stare and he brushed some hair away from her forehead. "Seriously, Jessa. I want to give you everything. I want to be the person who loves you."

She cupped his cheeks in her hands and drew his lips to hers. "That's enough." She didn't need him to be perfect. She wasn't looking for the perfect relationship. Only someone who was willing to try every day. That was enough.

Still kissing his mouth, she straddled him and adjusted her hips until she slid onto him, pausing there, feeling him quake beneath her. He filled her so perfectly, so deeply, that her body started that delicious throb again.

His fingers dug into her shoulders, urging her chest lower until he took her breast in his mouth and swirled his tongue around the nipple. Urgency pulsed inside of her, forcing her to move. She lifted her hips and thrust down onto him hard but smooth, again and again until his head fell back to the pillow. "Hell yes, Jessa," he panted. "God, I'm so fucking lost in you."

"I have some tricks, too," she murmured, hoping she could hold on long enough. Before it was too late, she squeezed her thighs together, rocking her hips against his, cradling him as tightly into her as she could.

A cross between a growl and a groan purred against

her skin. Lance's hands went to her backside, bringing her against him faster and harder until she was completely lost in the breathless anticipation of what was coming. She tightened her legs around him even more and his body bucked beneath hers, sending a final thrust so deep into her that she came apart again, shuddering and crying out and delighting in the sound of her name on his lips as he convulsed beneath her.

A happy exhaustion took her over as she draped her body over his. He held her, nestling her head into the crook of his arm while his lips sought hers. She kissed him back somewhat lazily, given the fact that her body was sedated.

"I'll love you the best I can, Jessa Mae Love," he whispered in her ear.

And she knew it was true.

* * *

He'd never woken up with a woman in his arms. Not once in his life. And damn, it seemed he'd been missing out. Jessa lay against him, her silky back against his chest, her soft hair spilling over his arm. He didn't want to move, didn't want to disturb her and end this moment. But he also wanted to see her face.

Slowly, he eased up his head to peek over her shoulder.

Her eyes were wide open in a look of fear.

The feeling of contentment snapped and he sat up straight. "What's wrong?" How long had she been awake? Why didn't she look as calm and content as he felt?

She shifted onto her back, her captivating eyes staring at the ceiling. "I just...things moved so fast last night. We may have gotten a little carried away."

Hell yes, they'd gotten carried away and he hoped they'd do it again. As soon as possible.

"Do you regret it?" she whispered. "Walking away from the celebration? I mean, has anyone ever done that? Will you be disqualified? What'll happen?"

"Everything'll be fine." Easing out a breath of relief, he lay back down, gathering her into his arms to coax out her concerns. He didn't care what happened. "The only regret I have is that I didn't discover you sooner." The rest of his life seemed like such a waste compared to this. Compared to being connected so deeply with someone as good and bright and beautiful as Jessa.

"What about Ilsa?" she asked, suddenly looking worried again.

"The pig?" He laughed. He didn't mean to, but Pork Chop was the last thing on his mind right now.

"Yes." She searched his face. "I know you're not that crazy about her, but I love her. She's such a little sweetheart, and if we ever end up...you know...together someday..." She seemed too embarrassed to finish.

He brought her hand to his lips, kissing her fingers. "Actually, she's growing on me."

"Really?" She didn't look convinced.

"If it weren't for Pork—I mean Ilsa—you might never have talked to me again," he said, stroking her arm. "That makes her a saint in my book."

Smiling happily, Jessa propped herself up, gazing down at him, beauty spilling from her bottomless brown eyes. "I don't want the money, you know."

"You deserve the money." And she needed it for the shelter. "I always keep my word."

Her head shook. "I won't take it. You might need it. For

your dad. For his treatments." A smile plumped her lips. "Besides, some of my old grad school friends are helping me create a social media campaign to build a donor base. I guilted them into doing it for free."

He doubted she had to guilt them. Everyone who knew Jessa seemed to love her. And she would always be one of those people who gave more than she took. "We'll see," he said, not willing to argue about it now. If she refused to take the money he'd promised her, he'd simply find another way to give it to her.

"What did it feel like to win?" she asked, trailing her fingertips over his biceps.

And God she was so sexy, her blond hair trailing over her shoulder, her eyes glistening as if he could tell her anything and it would stay safely locked away in the vault of her heart.

"It felt like the end." He hadn't considered that until he said it, but the truth was, it felt like a relief.

"You're okay with that?"

"I'm ready to start the next phase." A whole new life waited for him. One he'd never thought he'd have. "I don't want to be anywhere but here right now. With you," he murmured, running his fingers over her shoulders, down her breasts. He couldn't resist the temptation of touching her. "Doing what we did last night. As many times as you'll let me."

"Mmmm-hmmm," she hummed, her eyes closing as she shimmied her hand underneath the sheets. "I can see you're up to the task." Her hand clasped the solid length of him.

Yeah, there was that. He'd woken up hard. With her in his bed, that'd most likely be the norm. He slipped his hand under the sheets, too, letting it wander down her hip...

Turning, she wrapped her legs around his waist and

brought his body against hers. "No need to bother with all the foreplay."

"I like the foreplay," he said as he sank into her. The power of it stole his breath. He had plenty of ways to draw it out as long as possible, to tease her. "It'll be worth it—"

A knock pounded on the door. "Jessa!" a woman's voice screeched from the hallway.

She froze underneath him, her eyes wide.

"Are you in there?" came from another woman.

Lance lifted his head. "Who the hell—?"

She pushed him off her and started to scramble. "It's Cassidy. And Darla!"

"What're they doing here?" he demanded, trying to pull her back to him.

"They wanted to come to Vegas." She gave him a sheepish smile. "They're staying at the Bellagio. Sorry. I forgot to mention that."

He captured her in a hug, settling her back to the mattress. "It's okay. We don't have to answer the door."

"But I was supposed to meet them for breakfast this morning..." She snatched her phone off the bedside table. "Twenty-three missed calls."

Shit. "Will we ever be able to make love without being interrupted?" he wondered aloud.

"Jessa!" Now that was Naomi. He'd heard her worked up enough times to recognize it.

"What's got them all riled?" he whispered. Maybe if they were real quiet the crazies would go away and let him finish what he'd started.

"I should've called them," she whispered back. "They get worried." Squirming out of his grip, Jessa threw on a bathrobe and unclicked the deadbolt.

"Where've you been?" The door burst open and Cassidy, Naomi, and Darla all charged in, then halted, gaping at the two of them like they'd caught them doing jumping jacks naked.

"We thought you'd been kidnapped!" Naomi squealed.

"Vegas is a huge hub for human trafficking," Cassidy added knowingly.

"Then you wouldn't return our calls!" Darla finished as if the whole thing had been scripted.

"Nope. Not kidnapped." Jessa glanced at Lance, biting her lip as though trying not to laugh. "Sorry. I kind of lost track of time."

Despite the fact that there were three high-drama women staring at him naked in bed, Lance grinned back. They'd lost track of a lot of stuff. Shoes. Clothes...

"Obviously." Darla eyed Lance like he was a big juicy cut of meat.

He pulled the covers up to his chin.

Naomi stared at him, too, but it was more of a glare. And judging from the way her hands sat rigidly on her hips, she didn't like this at all. "So you two figured things out?" she asked suspiciously.

You could say that. He still had some work to do, but he'd do whatever it took. "I realized nothing I did seemed to matter without Jessa," he said, even though there would've been a more appropriate time for this conversation. Later. After he'd had his way with Jessa and was fully clothed.

Beaming a happy, teary smile, Jessa sat on the bed next to him and took his hand.

"Awww," Darla and Cassidy said collectively.

But Naomi simply narrowed her eyes protectively. "What does that mean?"

He turned his face to Jessa's and couldn't help but pull himself up to kiss her lightly on the lips. From the sound of the sniffles in the room, that was a good move. "It means I love her. It means I'm dealing with my shit so I can be with her."

"It means that you three need to get out of my room," Jessa added. "If you couldn't tell, we were kind of in the middle of something."

"Oh! Right! Sorry!" Darla clamped her hands onto Cassidy's and Naomi's shoulders, dragging them backward to the door. "You can give us all the details later."

Lance shot Jessa a look.

"Not *all* of them," she promised.

"OhmyGod, I'm so happy for you two!" Cassidy sighed before she disappeared.

Naomi wriggled free from Darla's grasp.

Lance half-expected another angry glare, seeing as how she didn't exactly think he was worthy of Jessa. But instead, she smiled. "I'm happy for you, too. Really."

"Thanks," Jessa called, shooing her away impatiently with a hand. "Okay. Bye, now. We'll talk later."

When the door *finally* slammed, he gathered Jessa into his arms and rolled her onto his body.

She laughed. "Wow, someone's got energy."

"The pressure's on," he said, showering her shoulders with hot little kisses. "I'd better give you some incredible details to tell your friends."

Epilogue

ot once in the history of Topaz Falls had the Cortez fam-

Not once in the history of Topaz Falls had the Cortez family ever hosted a party. Until Lance started dating Jessa, that was.

Jessa stood on the front porch of Lance's home, admiring how the ranch came to life in the spring. All the aspens had their baby green leaves back. Wildflowers were starting to dot the meadows. Though they'd still likely get a few more snowstorms, the land looked like it was finally emerging from winter, so bright and fresh and new. *Every*thing at the ranch felt new and exciting and hopeful. It didn't hurt that half the town had turned out for the first shindig of the season. The laughter and murmur of gossip seemed to give the place a new life.

All winter she'd drifted in and out of this house, laughing and living and loving with this family while she and Lance got to know each other. Lucas and Levi had both stayed on for the holiday months, helping cart Luis to doctor appointments and therapy treatments. They'd all spent the evenings out by the fire pit, surrounded by drifts of crisp white snow while they roasted marshmallows and laughed as the three brothers relived their childhood antics. When the fire burned low, they'd pour the wine and listen to Lucas play his guitar. That was her favorite, snuggling with Lance and his wandering hands underneath a blanket while the soft notes of strings floated around them.

These days if anyone dared tell her she wasn't a part of this family, she wouldn't believe them. The proof was all around her. The Cortez men had actually let her plan a party at their ranch, and even though they'd grumbled about it, they sure seemed to be having a great time.

She gazed out over the white party tents they'd rented, then over to the prefab stage, where a local bluegrass band played. Okay, so it was possible that she'd gone a bit overboard. She couldn't help herself. A while back, they'd received word that Lance was being inducted into the Pro Rodeo Hall of Fame, just like his father, and right away she'd started planning the celebration of the century.

It had turned out perfectly, if she did say so herself. "Come on, Ilsa," she said, tugging gently on her not-so-little piggy's leash. They ambled down the steps and into the crowds. She almost couldn't believe how many people had turned out to honor him. She smiled at each one as she passed, saying hello, even to Hank Green, though she didn't dare get too close to him.

On the outskirts of the tent, she spotted Evie Starlington standing alone, sipping a glass of Darla's special white sangria. Still being considered a newbie in town, the poor woman wouldn't know many people, so Jessa hurried toward her.

Ilsa grunted. She didn't like hurrying. Over the winter, the pig had fully recovered and was quite a bit wider than she'd been when Jessa had found her. Wider and happier, especially when there was a party and there were plenty of scraps on the ground. "Come on, girl," she prompted. "A little exercise will do you some good." Even with Ilsa's protests, they finally made it to the tent.

"Evie! I'm so happy you could make it. Come with me." She took her hand warmly before the woman could answer, and guided her to the tables she'd happened to see Luis sitting at earlier.

Sure enough, the man was still there, chatting with Deputy Dev Jenkins about the unusually warm weather. She hated to interrupt but this was important.

"Hey there, Luis," she said, pulling out the chair next to him. Ilsa plopped down at her feet and started munching on a stray carrot that had rolled off someone's plate.

Evie took a seat across the table. "You remember Evie, right?" Jessa said, presenting the woman grandly.

"Of course." He tipped his hat to her. "Nice to see you again."

"Evie is an artist," Jessa informed him. "You should see her stained-glass work."

"That so?" The man looked at her with interest. "How'd you get into that?"

It seemed her work here was done. "Oh!" Jessa jumped out of her chair. "I completely forgot. I need to check in with Darla. Make sure she has everything she needs."

Luis squinted at her with a small smile as though he knew exactly what she was doing. But that wouldn't stop her. She waved and tugged Ilsa away to give them some time alone. To keep up appearances, she headed straight for the catering tent, even though Darla clearly had everything under control.

"This is all amazing," Jessa said to her friend as she approached what had become the food and drink control command center.

Her friend straightened her apron proudly. "Everyone seems happy and properly drunk, which means I've done my job."

"Everyone definitely seems happy." Even Cassidy was out on the dance floor letting Levi twirl her around. "She must be *really* tipsy if she's dancing with him."

"I think she lost a bet," Darla answered drily. She looked toward the corral. "Naomi's the only one who doesn't seem exactly thrilled to be here."

Jessa peeked over to where Darla was staring. Both Naomi and Lucas were mingling with a group of their old high school friends. Lucas knelt on the ground and said something that made Gracie laugh, but Naomi simply turned and wandered away alone.

"Is he still leaving tomorrow?" Darla asked, fiddling with the chocolate fountain, then dipping in a plastic spoon.

"Yes." Jessa sighed. She'd done her best to convince him to stay. "He says he has to get back to the McGowen Ranch, that they've given him long enough." He also said he'd be back and forth as much as possible, but who knew how often they'd see him.

Her friend licked the melted chocolate off her spoon and dipped in another one, handing it to Jessa. "Naomi sure avoided him the last couple of months, huh?"

"Avoided him? She pretended he didn't exist." She taste-tested the sample Darla had given her. Their friend had taken Gracie to Florida for a month to visit her parents. When she *had* been at the ranch, she'd kept herself busy with running her daughter to camps and volunteering at the school. The only time Naomi and Lucas seemed to politely chat was when they all had dinner together, but the woman always begged out early. Before they built a fire. Before Lucas played his guitar. As far as Jessa knew, they hadn't spent one second alone all winter.

A wave of panic washed over her, making her feel the heat of the evening more intensely. "I wish I could make him stay."

"Guess it's not up to us," Darla said, turning back to the chocolate fountain to refill the plates of strawberries.

"I know, it's just—"

An arm slid around her waist. "I need you," her sexy cowboy breathed into her ear. "Alone."

Those words were all it took to restart her heart. She swore it beat only for him these days.

"You can have me whenever and wherever you want me." She turned to him, and he pulled her into a scandalous hug.

Behind them, Darla made gagging noises. "Not near the food, you two!" she scolded. "And don't get any ideas about the melted chocolate."

"I already *have* ideas," Lance said, eyeing the fountain.

"He does," Jessa agreed. "He has *a lot* of good ideas."

"Okay. That's it." Her friend shooed them away. "Get out. Out of my tent."

"Fine." Jessa held out Ilsa's leash. "But would you mind holding on to her for a while? And don't give her any chocolate. I have her on a diet."

"Of course. I'd love to babysit your pig while you go off and get some." Darla rolled her eyes, but she smiled as she took the leash.

Laughing, Lance swept Jessa up the hill toward the corral. "I have a surprise for you," he murmured, drawing her close to his side.

"Ohhhh. A surprise for me? But this is supposed to be *your* special day."

Just outside the old barn, he stopped and faced her. "The surprise is for you. But I'm hoping it'll benefit me, too."

"Huh?" That didn't make any sense...

Wearing a mysterious grin, he urged her to the barn's entrance, which as far as she knew, stored their old tractor parts and animal feed.

As they stepped inside, he covered her eyes with his hand. She saw nothing but darkness, but that was okay because she'd blindly follow this man anywhere.

After a couple of steps he stopped, pulling his hand away.

Bright lights lit up the space, and this was no barn. It had been transformed into something else. Something sophisticated and clean. The walls had been dry-walled and were painted a lovely soft green. Ceramic tiles covered the once dusty floor. A long counter and desk sat at the front of the room and kennels lined the back.

Jessa gaped at him.

"Welcome to the new Helping Paws Animal Shelter," he said, spreading out his arms in grand presentation. "And don't worry. We'll get the outside fixed up as nice as the inside."

"What?" She gasped, turning herself in a slow circle, trying to take it in, but the blinding tears made it difficult. He'd thought of everything. *Everything*. From the brand-new computer sitting on the desk to the framed animal posters dressing up the walls. There were kennels and examining tables and supplies...

A happy sob squeaked out.

She turned back to him, ready to throw herself at him in a hug, but he'd taken a knee. And he was holding up a small black velvet box.

"Yes!" she blurted before he'd even said anything. Her whole body trembled with a yes. He didn't have to ask.

His exaggerated expression of shock teased her. "I haven't said anything yet."

"Oh. Right." She did her best to rein in her excitement so she didn't steal this moment from him. Knowing Lance, he'd planned out exactly what he wanted to say down to the syllable.

He took her hand in his. "You taught me how to love, Jessa," he began. "Showed me it was possible."

Tears snuck into her eyes. The man definitely knew how to write a speech...

"I know we haven't been together long," he went on. "But I've never been as sure of anything as I am of us. You brought me to life and now I want a life with you. Always. I hate it when you go home. I want the ranch to be our home now. Together. You and me and a whole bunch of kids."

The words warmed her through. Kids. A family...

"Marry me, beautiful," he uttered, tears filling his eyes, too. "Please marry me." He opened the box, revealing the most delicate ring she'd ever seen. It was a solitaire diamond, inset into a wide band, rose gold to match the necklace her father had given her. The last gift he'd given her before he passed away.

"I can answer now?" she whispered, crying softly.

He grinned and rolled his eyes up to the ceiling as though thinking about it. "Sure," he said. "I'm done."

"In that case..." She tugged him to his feet. "I can't wait to marry you. *Obviously*."

He slipped the ring onto her finger and pulled her close. "I'll make you the happiest woman in the world. I promise you." A wicked gleam lit his eyes. "And not just in bed, either."

"You already make me happy. In bed and in everything else." She embraced him as tightly as she could, holding happiness in her arms. "Oh my God, I'm getting married!" she sang, letting it soak into the deepest parts of her. She gazed up into Lance's tender eyes. Tom Hanks and Meg Ryan had nothing on them.

"I can't believe you did all of this." She looked around the room again, at all of the details, the months and months of work he'd kept secret from her. "It's perfect. The most beautiful thing I've ever seen."

"I'm gonna give you everything." He leaned down to kiss her, and she savored it, the feeling of belonging to someone again. She'd always miss her father, but for the first time since he'd passed away, her heart felt whole.

He danced her to the window and together they peered out. "Look at that. It's all ours. Yours and mine." His palms cradled her stomach. "And someday it'll belong to all of our little buckaroos, too."

She stared out at the snowcapped mountains that sheltered the houses all lined up in a row farther down the hill. "I love this place." It would be their place—a haven for their family and friends, a place where they gathered and celebrated and built a life together. All of them.

Lance drew closer behind her, wrapping her up in his arms. "Let's go out and share the news," he murmured against her neck. "Then we'll kick everyone outta here so I can try to get you pregnant."

Eyeing him seductively, she slipped out of his embrace,

backed to the main door, and clicked the lock into place. "We don't have to kick anyone out. No one'll miss us."

"In that case, come here." Her fiancé made his way to her, those breathtaking bluish eyes focused and intent. He slid his hands down her body, and she loved those big manly hands, loved how they made her feel so petite. "I love you," she whispered, kissing him again and again.

"I love you, too," he said, easing his arms around her. "And I love that you're going to be my wife."

His wife! A burst of happiness could've carried her straight to the clouds.

She'd finally found it, what her heart had so desperately craved. Love. And it was braver and bigger and deeper than she ever knew it could be.

About the Author

Sara Richardson grew up chasing adventure in Colorado's rugged mountains. She's climbed to the top of a 14,000-foot peak at midnight, swum through Class IV rapids, completed her wilderness first-aid certification, and spent seven days at a time tromping through the wilderness with a thirty-pound backpack strapped to her shoulders.

Eventually Sara did the responsible thing and got an education in writing and journalism. After a brief stint in the corporate writing world, she stopped ignoring the voices in her head and started writing fiction. Now she uses her experience as a mountain adventure guide to write stories that incorporate adventure with romance. Still indulging her adventurous spirit, Sara lives and plays in Colorado with her saint of a husband and two young sons.

You can learn more at:

SaraRichardson.net

Twitter @SaraR_Books

Facebook.com/SaraRichardsonBooks

Looking for more hot cowboys?
Forever has you covered!

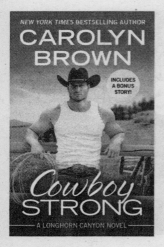

COWBOY STRONG
by Carolyn Brown

Alana Carey can out-rope and out-ride the toughest Texas cowboys. But she does have one soft spot—Paxton Callahan. So when her father falls ill, Alana presents Pax with a crazy proposal: to pretend to be her fiancé so her father can die in peace. But as the faux-wedding day draws near, Alana and Paxton must decide whether to come clean about their charade or finally admit their love is the real deal. Includes the bonus story *Sunrise Ranch*!

COWBOY COURAGE
by Carolyn Brown

Heading back to Texas to hold down the fort at her aunt's bed-and-breakfast will give Rose O'Malley just the break she needs from the military. But while she may speak seven languages, she can't repair a leaky sink to save her life. When Hudson Baker strides in like a hero and effortlessly figures out the fix, Rose can't help wondering if the boy she once crushed on as a kid could now be her saving grace. Includes the bonus story *Wildflower Ranch*!

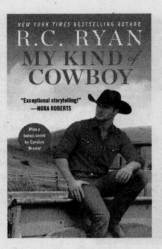

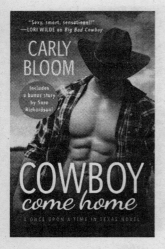
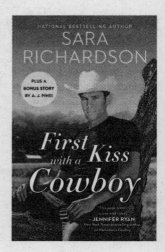

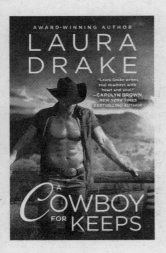
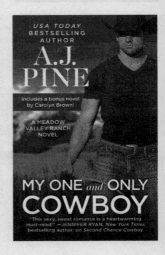